Taledisa Fiction imprint of Black Crow Press LLC

Black Crow Press LLC
P.O. Box 185626
2514 Whitney Avenue
Hamden, CT 06518

FIRST EDITION
Author's full text edition
10 9 8 7 6 5 4 3 2 1

Editor Judy Roth
Cover illustration Beth Janelle Stone
Cover design The Killion Group
Interior design The Killion Group

Published in the United States of America

PUBLISHER'S NOTE
This is a work of fiction. All characters, names, places, business
establishments, agencies, situations, dialogue and incidents are
the products of the author's creative imagination or are used in
a fictitious way. Any resemblance to persons living or dead is
entirely coincidental.
ISBN   978-1-7321685-0-3
eISBN 978-1-7321685-1-0

MYSTERY
AT THE
SPRING HOUSE

SPRING HOUSE MYSTERIES · BOOK ONE

K. M. UMBRICHT

TABLE OF CONTENTS

1

LAWYERS, LAWYERS, LAWYERS

FREEZING RAIN SLASHED ACROSS THE leaded glass panes of the Law Offices of Fliegel, Simon & O'Neill. The historic two story brick withstood the gale as it squalled against the slate roof and tore down through the old lead gutters. A March nor'easter drove in, drenching the city, flooding the streets and swirling down the drains back to Long Island Sound. In the conference room, tucked under the eaves on the second floor, another kind of storm brewed. Even the air seemed to have a tang to it.

"You can't afford to divorce me." Over the sounds of the storm, Harley Travis Huber's voice rang with satisfaction, edged with contempt for the quiet woman who stood composed and skeptical. A wide old polished oak conference table stood like a bulwark between them, and it was a good thing, too. On guard, a younger woman attorney edged beside her client, Mrs. Miranda Huber, documents in hand. Huber's eyes narrowed. Not a head taller, he made an effort to look down at his wife, waiting for a response.

Miranda Elice Huber, nicknamed Em in childhood, intently regarded her soon to be ex, letting him feel her scrutiny. She took a calming breath and thought, *I can do this, so many other women have. The children will just have to accept it. They are old enough. I can make it on my own.*

It had been six months since she last saw him. Looking for the sexy, scruffy graduate student fresh off the Texas ranch, the one who captivated and won her easily, she found barely a trace. Fuller of face, chestnut hair going grey around the edges, beginning a gentleman's paunch, Huber had forsaken a university professor's classic blue blazer and khakis. A tailor-made suit of fine dead-charcoal wool seemed befitting for an oil company executive. Her chin came up, she shook her near grey curls until her crystal earrings glittered in the light, and spoke softly. Just loud enough for him to hear her over the wind and sleet pelting the windows in waves of buckshot, she said, "Like hell."

Shooting his cuffs, Huber paced before the windows, backlit only by the streetlights on early in the midst of the storm. His high-ticket lawyer had left him alone with these two women to take an urgent call.

Unmoving, his wife watched him. Prepared for this meeting, rehearsing, anticipating the need to brave his displeasure, and making a power dress of gold tussah silk to wear, she watched and waited. The silk dress shimmered even in the waning light. His exasperated huff directed towards the conference room door told Em the lawyer would meet with Huber's displeasure, later on.

"Why do you have to do this now, Em? You're not working. The house is being sold, you won't have any place to live."

"So you have said. It won't make me stay. First, it was that administrative assistant. Now, I'm here in New Haven, and you are in Texas with that kinky blonde, Brigitte...."

The blood receded quickly from under Huber's Gulf Coast tan. Mentioning Brigitte gave him a shock. Clearly, he was unaware of the extent of their knowledge.

Em's lawyer gave her client a small, discreet smile. Mireille's long wavy black hair surrounded a slender face with shrewd dark eyes and an elegant French nose. A dry sense of humor showed on her face. She was a truly a worthy courtroom adversary.

"What are you going to do for money? You lost your corporate job. No one's going to hire a woman of your age. You're done professionally. Some occupation for a faculty wife. What were you? A corporate spy? You should have stayed with Art History, you would be a Curator by now." He was not going to go down easily or reasonably.

"It's Competitive Intelligence. We don't use the 'S' word. Legal research and business analysis. Dull stuff and numbers." Em heard a chuckle. To the amusement of her lawyer, Em had crossed her fingers behind her back.

"Yes, sure, that's why you came home at night and said, 'You'll never guess what I did to today and I can't tell you.' Who needs that stuff anyway?" Huber challenged and continued to pace the rug in front of the windows.

"Businesses here used to think they only had to watch out for each other. Now out of country entities will steal our eyeteeth if we let them. Don't you get the news in Texas?" Thinking on her feet she continued. "It should be a growth industry. I'll go into business for myself, 'M.E. Huber & Associates, Competitive Intelligence Consultants' for hire. My business plan is all ready." Em was bluffing about the plan, it was only the start of a new idea.

Huber stopped pacing to face her. "Don't you dare involve my daughters. The three of them follow you wherever you go! You know that."

"Three daughters?" the young lawyer asked, clasping her documents to her chest with a puzzled look on her face.

Turning towards her, in a stage whisper Em said, "He pays little attention to them. Sandy has been our guest so long, he's forgotten she's not his daughter, too."

"I heard that," Huber barked. "Don't think I don't know about all that volunteer stuff you do. Why can't you just pick one charity and write a check? Figure out how much you need for tax purposes, and then just send it? Why do you have to get *involved*? That can get dangerous. I know where they take those Bibles you collect...."

"Silence!" Fire in her eyes, Em's voice was low-pitched and full of force. "How dangerous can it be? It's research." She was to remember his outburst and reflect, a good dose of premonition would have been useful. "One more word on the subject, and you will never see that precious little rock of yours again. Weren't you supposed to turn it in to the geology department when you left? Huh, weren't you?"

"My meteorite! You found it?" Stunned, Huber's tone was conspiratorial, his look furtive.

"You left your damned rock collection in the garage," she accused, crossing her arms over the simple, elegant dress she'd fabricated from a Donna Karan pattern.

"It's not there, I looked." Huber grabbed the high back of the bucket chair and thrust his body forward as if to come across the breadth of the table towards her.

She stood her ground before him, locking her knees together to stand straight. "But not hard enough. You never think, where was I when I saw it last? What was I doing? You need to pick things up and look behind them. If that doesn't work, think, it's sort of round, like a golf ball, where could it have rolled away?" She paused a minute too long for emphasis to watch his eyes pop and his cheeks redden. The sharp almost bitter smell of sweat reached Em and her lawyer. "It was under the workbench in the corner, covered in dust and grit. And now it's in my custody. You were supposed to have taken all your stuff."

"It's mine, give it back. I don't want this to be in the court papers." Huber cast a glance at the door to make sure his lawyer wasn't coming back.

"Silence. Or it will end up in the nice muddy backwater of Lake Whitney where only I can find it again. I mean it." She lowered her chin in determination.

"You can't do that."

"You know me. What do you think?" Mischief in her

eye, she let him see that she would enjoy throwing his prized bit of cosmic metal into the lake. "We can negotiate its return *privately*. Privileged lawyer-client conversation, right Mireille?"

"Many things can be negotiated, shall we say, informally. Among other things, I believe Mrs. Huber is requesting airfare for your children to visit you and the elderly aunt at the family ranch in Texas. This is a good thing for everyone, yes?" The lawyer directed her remarks towards the man across the table who appeared to shutter at the mention of his aunt. "Is it she who owns the oil?"

"Alright, yes, but I get the meteorite back." Red in the face, he added with bluster, loud, to intimidate. "You'll get nothing more out of me."

The conference room door opened quietly, admitting Huber's lawyer.

With a French woman's asperity, Mireille replied, "*Ah non*, we do not anticipate that will be all. We have the newspaper clippings and this woman Brigitte's Facebook status changes. She has been most forthcoming. And the pictures. Artistic, yes. She was, after all, a model of the highest class. All that is in the *past*, of course." Mireille, ever the lawyer, smiled apparently conscious of a larger audience.

As if electrified by the tension in the room, Em's curly hair sprang out of control as she turned her head sharply to her lawyer. "I thought we were going to wait to mention that. Don't forget those passionate emails." Turning to Huber she said with humor and reproach, "You put Prince Charles to shame with those. Such elegant phrasing, 'in your britches.' Not an original thought between the two of you, the prince or the cowboy."

"I don't have to be original, it's how I felt. How did you get those?" Huber froze, a look of fear flashed across his face and came to rest in his eyes.

"And you with a Ph.D. Britches and all? Did you expect me to put up with all of that? Just because I didn't explode in front of the children? You went off on sabbatical, left me with the kids, and didn't come back. You didn't even think to change the password to the email account. That I am still paying for, so I am the owner."

Huber reached out over the table towards Em. The sleek grey haired, distinguished member of the firm also proved to be nimble on his feet. The lawyer made it around the conference table in time to restrain his client's arm.

"Calm, now, Professor Huber, we should address these matters calmly. In private first."

Huber turned on his lawyer. "I'm not paying you to calm me down, I'm paying you to get her to…"

Taking his client by the arm, speaking in muffled undertones, the lawyer attempted to usher Huber from the room and succeeded in a forced march out the door.

"Ladies, we will rejoin you shortly. Please make yourselves comfortable. My assistant will be in with coffee." The lawyer's smooth oyster grey head disappeared, and the door shut firmly behind the two men.

"Well, Em, such anger towards you. And you have done nothing to merit it. You have told me that he was given to the little fits of temper. The blood pressure, surely it is high. Tell me, why is he so reluctant to give you the divorce?"

"Maybe he doesn't wish to marry Brigitte. Aunt Marlene must be seriously displeased, and he works for her now. He might prefer to have wife and children in Connecticut, and live-in mistress in Texas. I did a little research. Poor Brigitte hasn't two nickels to rub together, or perhaps I should say two francs. It seems she backed a two timing race car driver, and between the expensive car crash and his hospital bills, she lost everything. Bet she wants marriage now. On the surface, he looks like a good catch, I have to admit."

"Ah, but we know better, don't we now? Nice dress, by the way." Mireille stifled a discreet little laugh.

"Get me out of this, please. Negotiate as much for the

children as you can. I'll work on that imaginary business plan, and I'll need to find a new house."

This time, Mireille took the liberty of laughing out loud. "Say, rather visionary business plan. I believe Philippe and I can help you along with the house hunt. A neighbor wishes to sell the Spring House, *une charmante maison.*"

A muted knock on the conference room door announced a very organized assistant pushing a cart with a carafe of coffee, mugs and a plate of Danish butter cookies.

"It's so chilly and wet outside, we thought you might like something hot while you wait." The young man smiled nervously. The old horsehair plaster walls were thin, and Huber's voice carried over the accompanying wind and freezing rain.

"Indeed, we would," said Em. "Thank you so much."

2

PROFESSOR OLIVER SELLS THE
SPRING HOUSE TO EM

———◆———

NOT TOO LONG AFTER EM Huber's divorce from
Harley Travis Huber became final, she found herself
in the unenviable position of having to vacate the family
home and find another house for her and the girls. Em
reasoned that if so many other people had found themselves
in this quandary and survived, she might too. And so she
pursued the path that had been successful for her, she
resorted to her network of friends.

Mireille shook her long wavy black hair vigorously as
she stood in the kitchen of the farmhouse. Philippe was
on the phone with her friend and sometime legal client
Em Huber.

Philippe kicked into sales mode. "Mireille suggested it,
you know. The Spring House is for sale. Everyone along
the road can see the sign. It is a little different. People walk
in, and some walk right out again. The professor told her
that the right person will come along. He's turned down
generous offers from developers over the years and finally
sold the development rights to the State. Now, there's no
new construction anyway. He's trying to sell the house to
move back into town. He says he's waiting. It's a special

place and we'd love to have you as a neighbor," Philippe finished. Mireille nodded encouragement to her significant other. She'd coached him on this speech.

Seen from the winding country road, the Spring House property looked like a charming New England farm with old sugar maples lining up along the approach. Surely, the house appeared in the nightmares of its last real estate agent. The fieldstone cellar featured a free running spring with a documented history of overflowing during heavy seasonal rain and becoming a raging torrent during the occasional hurricane. White asbestos wrapped heating pipes, once top of the line insulation, ran the full length of the long narrow building. Since proper asbestos removal cost would be predicated on the linear footage of the covered old pipes and require hazmat suited professionals with outdoor showers, the pipes would likely stay intact for another generation of owners.

On its conversion to a residence, the upper shingled stories were painted white several times with lead-based paint. Another renovation was done as well. There was that little cellar once used to winter over fruits and vegetables, repurposed in the 1960's as a fallout shelter, given a cinder block baffle wall and a small spider hole exiting to the garden above. How to explain the cots, blankets, the Bible, ancient crossword puzzle books and the bright yellow Geiger counter the size of a small shoebox that graced the peculiar underground room? The elderly owner, a bit eccentric, had been adamant that all supplies and equipment be left for the new owner as they might be needed in the future. Could it be described as a coal bin? Surely not.

Em finished her coffee, luscious French Vanilla from a local coffee house, a luxury for her. Money was tight. The process of finding a new home for herself and her children was daunting. She faced her van north on the country road, passing Mireille and Philippe's white clapboard farmhouse with its side yard garden of vegetables and grapevines. The winding road, an old cow path, followed the contours of the valley with a long curve that led over the ridge. The agricultural pond and the strawberry fields were to her right. Em spotted the sign under the brow of the hill. "For Sale Inquire Within" was painted in brown on a peeling white barn board in a style of lettering not used in fifty years.

A small courtyard paved with smooth river stones lay in front of the house, which looked like a long narrow barn with a carved wooden door. The foundation and ground floor were built of fieldstones. In this area of the state, the stones were basalt chunks tumbled smooth by rivers and glaciers and gathered from the surrounding land. The second story under the eaves was wood shingle, now painted barn red.

After a moment's hesitation, Em pulled her car on to the cobblestone pavement. As she made up her mind to "inquire within" a small sprightly man with a shock of pure white hair appeared to spring up from the right side of the house.

"Oh, you mustn't park there! I'm expecting a delivery. Do park across the road in front of the wagon barn."

Em obediently reversed the car and backed across the narrow road onto the cobblestones in front of a weathered barn. She parked under the maple trees, next to an aging blue Cadillac. It was the oldest Cadillac she had ever seen and badly in need of a polish.

"Come in, come in. Our friends Mireille and Philippe called. Welcome to Wintergreen Springs, Ms. Huber. I'm Oliver Martin." The elderly man took off his work gloves, wiped his hands on his khakis to extend a hand for a greeting. His white eyebrows were beyond bushy, over bright blue eyes, a long straight nose, and well shaped lips. He was

clean shaven with the precision of a straight razor, except
for a small patch of curly hair under his jawline, which Em
guessed he habitually missed.

She couldn't help smiling at her cheerful host. *Unless I
miss my guess, he's a Connecticut Yankee, whose folks have been
here since the 1700's or even earlier. One doesn't find them often.*

"Do come in. Let's have tea and I'll show you the house.
I understand you need something quickly. By coincidence,
I've been anxious to move along to other endeavors as
well." He ushered her through the stout wooden front
door, into a cool hallway paved with flag stones. Pegs for
coats and hats lined the narrow paneled hall.

"Here is the kitchen to the right. We'll put the kettle
on." The professor lit the gas under the large enamel kettle.
"The water for washing, flushing and watering the garden
comes from an artesian well. For drinking and cooking,
we use the spring water, of course. The oven, stove and hot
water are all propane gas. The heat was originally, wood,
then coal and now is oil. The lights are all electric, and
there is a generator in the barn for emergencies. We'll leave
the conversion to solar power to the next owner."

Em surveyed the kitchen. The ceiling was at least nine
feet high, and the cabinets were of an aged dark wood,
stopping well below the ceiling. A few antique kitchen
implements were scattered at random along the length of
the cabinet tops as if some had been removed.

Professor Martin followed her gaze. "My children have
taken some of the large china pieces and jugs already."

The countertops were inlaid with Mexican ceramic tiles
in earthen colors, dark browns, golds and greens. A variety of ceramic mugs hung from hooks under the cabinets.
Double casement windows looked out down the wooded
hillside to the stream in the valley below. Em simply stood
and looked, taking in the sense of the place. The old refrigerator hummed an uneven tune of its own composition.

"Well?" asked Oliver. "The kitchen is the heart of the

home, you know."

"Yes," replied Em.

The professor smiled, and his eyes crinkled. "Yes, indeed," he speculated as he watched her.

"The living room and dining room are this way." He led her out of the kitchen into the long main room that spanned the width of the house. The post and beam construction of exposed beams placed at regular intervals on the ceiling gave her the feeling of shelter as if the house was alive with warmth, and its best bones were showing. To the left, a dining room table and chairs were placed along the wall. The east wall contained a fieldstone fireplace flanked by windows and a door. Through the windows she could see that the ridge moved back from the building creating an open space for a patio surrounded by a garden on the curved side of the hill. A door on the far wall led through to the sunroom with windows on all three sides.

A Craftsman style couch built of wide fumed quarter sawn oak slats showed mortise and tenon joinery. It sat in the center of the room in front of the fireplace. She admired the pottery glazed in matte blues and greens on the bookshelves and on the wooden mantel. Temptation to reach out for a beautiful melon shaped bowl stirred her hand, but good manners intervened, and she sighed. Small tables supported lamps with hammered brass bases. Double windows faced the west with a window seat below them. She could imagine her daughters curled up there reading in the sunlight.

"My children don't like the furniture, too old, too heavy and too dark." Oliver watched his guest closely.

"Oh, are you taking it?" Em asked cautiously.

"That depends."

Em advanced into the room. She ran her hand over the dark oak back of the couch. "It's beautiful. Is it Stickley, Professor?" Em recognized the solid construction and craftsmanship of the Stickley workshop from upstate New

York.

"I expect so, yes. It came with the house when we bought it. I'm glad you appreciate it. There are three bedrooms upstairs, and a full bathroom with a ball and claw footed tub. The shower stall is newer. And there's a mural. Let's save that." The professor smiled, and Em wondered why. "You might like to see the spring.

"This house was originally part of an extensive family farm. You can still see the farmhouse up on the ridge. This was built to enclose Wintergreen Spring and to serve as the ice house to store ice cut from the lakes. They stored ice in the cellar packed in straw or sawdust. It was never a barn for animals. The spring provides good tasting water, but the flow varies by season. That's why we have the deeper well now.

"It's this way." The spritely senior led Em back towards the front hall. He removed a large metal ring with a variety of keys from a peg to unlock the door to the cellar. He led her down stone stairs, worn down smooth in the center by many years of foot traffic. "This is the oldest part of the house." A bare bulb lit the cellar stairs. At the base, the professor unlocked another door.

Inside the dimly lit spring room, a bare wall of cement and stone surrounded the east wall — a grotto of bare rock that dripped with rivulets of crystal clear water. A bowl had been hollowed out of the living rock to form a catch basin at waist height. A metal pipe led out of the basin, pouring the free running water into a large oblong metal holding tank. The overflow ran through a large pipe in the floor. Ceramic jugs of various ages and shapes lined shelves on the walls. Sizable glass containers were placed on the floor beneath the shelves. Some of these were labeled with a floral design and the name Blackmun's Wintergreen Spring. More plastic gallon jugs were still in boxes on the floor, ready for use.

"This is Blackmun's Wintergreen Spring, known and

used by the Native American people and the European colonists. Taste it, here's a mug." The professor rinsed a chipped blue enamel cup under the stream from the pipe. He filled a mug for himself and one for Em directly from the stone basin. Em took the proffered cup from the professor's thin hand and sipped the cool water. He watched her skeptical expression light up with surprise as she sipped. She finished her cup.

"That's great! What makes it taste that way?"

"It does have its own distinctive taste, a snap to it. Could be from the iron and basalt in the ridge. You see Ms. Huber, may I call you Em? This is why the Spring House needs a very special owner, to tend the spring. The owner can't spend only six months of the year here and retreat to Florida for the winter."

"Is that what you're planning to do, Professor?"

"Who me? No, I'm hoping to travel to Greece for a visit and some research." He smiled with characteristic charm. Em wasn't sure what kind of research an Emeritus Professor of Physics would pursue in Greece, outside of ancient concepts of physics.

A sensitive woman, she was attuned to her surroundings, and the people in it. Moving closer to the spring, she cocked her head, listening to a curious sound that seemed to be coming from the rock face. Not quite a hissing, not exactly the sound of a reed instrument, the spring seemed to have a background accompaniment that varied against the dripping sound of the water. "Professor, what's that sound? Like piping?"

"Ah, you hear it! Not everyone does. My wife did. It's as if the spring water is under pressure and vibrates in its natural channels through the rocks. It's louder after a heavy rain. Native Americans called it a singing spring and treated it with reverence. Springs in Europe were also held in special awe." He paused to see the effect of his words. Em merely nodded. "Ancient Greeks especially."

"Singing? I hear something more like pipes, little reedy things."

"I think everyone who can hear them may hear their frequencies differently. Shall we go up and have tea?"

As they turned to go, Em paused, fascinated by her surroundings. In the corner of the room up against the fieldstone wall stood a large jug that looked very much like an ancient amphora. It showed a long crack as if it had been pieced back together. What caught her attention though, was a perfectly constructed funnel shaped spider web that graced the neck of the jug and extended to the back wall. A spider, with a leg span close to two inches, crept around the neck of the jar to observe them.

"Professor, watch out! There's an enormous spider!"

"A spider, certainly, but hardly enormous. Good afternoon, Ariadne. She's made quite a beautiful web, hasn't she?" Oliver addressed the spider in a kindly voice.

"Friend of yours?"

"Oh my, yes. She and all her ancestors. They have a special place in the ecology of the spring. Spiders capture the other insects and help to keep the spring clean for us. They seem to prefer that corner though. We are quite careful and apologize nicely if we have to move anything over here. Do you know your Charlemagne?" Oliver asked, always the professor.

"No, Professor."

"Well, at least you do remember *Indiana Jones and the Last Crusade*? 'Let my armies be the beasts of the fields and the birds of the air.' Ah, I see that you do. We've become a very video culture. Ariadne is a guardian of Wintergreen Spring." Em noticed the spider's legs twitch.

"Does she understand you?" she asked inquisitively.

"Who knows what they understand. She is always attentive when I speak to her. I can't say the same for all of my students. She appreciates my occasional gift of a fly. Preferably alive."

"You mean you feed her flies?"

"Do you have pets, Ms. Huber? You would feed a dog or a cat. Ariadne doesn't scratch. We are all creatures of equal merit, even the least of these has their own special niche. As I said, mind if you have to move anything over there.

"After you, my dear. I should show you the rest of the cellar," the professor said with some reluctance. He locked the door of the spring room behind them and guided her into the cellar.

The center space was clear, right down past the workbench, to the lawn mower and garden tools. The slant of the floor towards the sump pump in the center saved the cellar from water damage. For very high water the swinging wooden cellar doors on the valley side could be opened to let the water flow out onto the garden path and straight down the hill in a waterfall to the glen below.

At the time of sale the professor was not one not to be gainsaid. He insisted on leaving the contents of the entire cellar intact, including a nearly antique laundry facilities purchased in Sears's heyday. Sporting equipment spanning at least three generations, possibly four, hung from the rafters and were stored on shelves, all above anticipated high water levels. Figure skates, carved wooden blade skates, hockey skates and sticks, heavy wooden snow shoes, a variety of skis, boats and poles, baseball bats, tennis rackets, oars, paddles, all ranged around the cellar. Two canoes, one dented aluminum and a newer shorter green canoe, hung from the rafters. Several pairs of homemade stilts leaned against the wall among the ski poles and carved hiking sticks.

Em imagined the multiple listing service description of the Spring House: Extra features, free flowing natural spring, family fallout shelter, Knowledge of lead, yes, Knowledge of asbestos, yes, Mold, not often, Radon, no knowledge, cellar too porous to trap radon gas. UFFI, too old to contain.

"You still haven't seen the gardens and the bathroom upstairs. My wife and daughter painted the walls of the bath. Let's go upstairs first."

They climbed the stairs to the second floor, with only a few creaking stair treads. The hallway floor was bare, although there was an outline of a runner down the center. The wallpaper was a faded pattern of floral sprigs on cream. Em recognized it as a classic English print, perhaps from Liberty of London. One of the small bedrooms was currently in use, all needed fresh paint. The floors were worn, but in good condition with few scrapes. A tolerant woman could surely live without the added expense of refinishing the floor. They paused in their tour at the back bedroom window so Em might look out at the raised bed vegetable and flower gardens and a small out building and the woods beyond. Charmed, she felt a deep longing to call the place her home.

Professor Martin slyly saved the best for last. He took Em back to the front of the house to show her the bathroom, not usually the beauty spot of any old house. He waited in the hall as Em first stuck her nose in. It surprised her, it was the size of a bedroom, and sited directly over the kitchen. Sun streamed in through the small high west facing windows. The old fashioned white and black subway tile floors and walls surrounded a ball and claw footed tub of a reasonable, though not large size. A new marble tiled shower stall stood in one corner next to an antique white ceramic pedestal sink.

A colorful mural of undersea life painted around the room at shoulder height above the tile caught and held Em's eyes. The marine animals, waving seaweed and sea floor life were obviously of Mediterranean origin. A cheerful little octopus winked from over the toilet. It looked very much like one Em had seen painted on an early piece of pottery from Crete. There were amphorae, large jugs used to store food, wine or oil scattered on the seafloor, along with coins and other pieces from an ancient shipwreck.

"Step in, Em, then turn back towards me," the professor urged. He could see the light in her eyes.

Em did as the professor suggested and turned towards him. When she did so, she burst out laughing. Painted over the doorway was a generously depicted mermaid with a mischievous smile on her face. Her scaly tail wrapped around one side of the doorframe, and her long dark tresses flowed down the other side of the door.

"My wife and daughter painted the bathroom. I hope you like it. Her name is either Minerva or Calliope, depending on who you ask. They couldn't agree."

"I do like it, Professor. I love it!"

"Let's have tea and talk about the house," he said.

Once seated at the breakfast table in the kitchen, Em faced the professor over a plate of fresh shortbread cookies and a barrel shaped blue and white teapot. The cobalt blue of the glaze was so intensely deep and flown together that the design was barely distinguishable like the most valuable antique Flow Blue china.

For a moment, the elderly man stared into his teacup as if he expected something to arise from it.

"Reading your tea leaves, Professor? It's good tea, is it Oolong?" Em asked as she savored the smoky green tea. The sun warmed the kitchen, the light mottled by leaves of an overhanging tree, an ancient being that reminded Em of Tolkien's Ents.

"Lapsang Souchong made with spring water, my dear. It's my afternoon tea." The elderly man paused for a moment, then continued as if he had come to a decision.

"My first wife died rather young, leaving me with two children. I met my second wife, Elena, on a summer trip to Greece. She taught at the university and gave special historical tours for visiting academic types. We married and she came back here with me. She wanted to live in the countryside, not the city. We found this place, it reminded her of her childhood home. My older children grew up mostly in town. My younger daughter is also named Elena, she's married to a diplomat and lives in Europe now. My Elena passed away two years ago this summer. It feels like time for me to travel and to pursue some interests that I've put aside for quite awhile."

"It's a wonderful house, Professor. We haven't discussed what you are asking for it."

"We can come to that. Tell me about your family. I see scratches on your arm, do you have pets? Do you like gardens?" Oliver took another shortbread while watching Em with his sharp eyes.

"The scratches are from my rose bushes. We have a stray cat that lives with us. He's a classic black, but he's also half Siamese, so he talks constantly." *And being a male, it's mostly complaints.* "His name is Ash, my youngest daughter Deanna wanted to call him Ashurnasirpal. She had finished an Archeology course in college. It's a family interest.

"Depending on how you count them, I have five children. My son and daughter-in-law who currently live in Boston. And with me, middle daughter Celina who is in graduate school studying pharmacological weeds." *Who is out to change the world one herb at a time.* "There's Dee, Deeanna, and her high school friend Sandy who live with me when they're not at school. The two girls will be seniors in college next fall. Sandy's family lost their home here and went back to Tennessee to live with grandparents, but their house is too small for all the kids." *I wish the story was that simple.*

"I'm divorced, as you may know. We have to sell the house, I can't afford to buy the other half, and the oil bills last winter about killed me."

The professor nodded with understanding as he finished his tea.

"I want to grow grapes. The girls want a fire pit. We like to cook outdoors. Celina wants to grow whatever she's studying.

"I am a little desperate. Our house is sold. The closing is in four weeks. We will have to put everything in storage unless we can find something soon. I honestly don't think I can give you what this property must be worth." Her voice was low, and although she didn't mean to, she realized that she might sound dispirited.

Professor Martin sighed. "Well, perhaps we can negotiate that. The land is not all useable. The woods are full of till from the ridge down, glacial boulders. The soil is shallow. The cellar is damp and can be a good deal more with spring rains. I could be negotiable about the price if you will let me leave things for you. Cleaning out the cellar, all those things, and the garden tools, might be useful. Tell me how much you would offer."

Em made a quick calculation, leaving money for moving expenses, she mentioned a figure at the top of her price range.

Martin cocked his head to one side. "Good. I have an apartment in a nice old building in New Haven already. I'll have my lawyer call you to set up an appointment to discuss the property deed rights and restrictions. You might want to be aware of them before buying the Spring House. Did I mention that the house comes with the business called Blackmun's Wintergreen Springs and Ice House?"

Surprised by the professor's apparent willingness to sell the Spring House without further negotiation of price, Em came within a hair of dropping her teacup, which would not have been a good thing at all. The teacup came from an antique English Flow Blue set.

"Do be careful with the cup, it's Amoy, my dear. I think you and your girls might do quite well here. I understand that we have several mutual friends in the area."

"May I bring my children to see the house?"

"Why of course, call anytime. I do need to be ready for that delivery now though." With cordial wishes the elderly man ushered Em out to her car, waving to her as she drove off. In her rearview mirror she caught a glimpse of the professor as he stood by the front door rubbing his hands together in satisfaction.

———— • ————

Professor Martin received Em Huber's offer for the Spring House, check attached, and did two things — packed his bags and called his very distinguished elderly colleague and neighbor down the road. "It's done. I'm leaving, Gertie. You watch out for her, she may need you if what we think is true."

Early next morning, he summoned his buyer to the Spring House. All brushed and neatly dressed, he greeted Em warmly, although hurriedly, and led her into the living room where several large pieces of furniture and a faded Turkish carpet remained. He placed three fat rings of labeled keys into her hands.

"I expect you'll want to clean before you move in. My lawyer has the signed papers, close whenever you are ready. What you see stays, I've taken or given away whatever I wanted. My best wishes, the house is all yours, my dear."

"You're leaving all the Stickley, Professor? It's…" Em was truly stunned.

"All listed in the bill of sale. My children didn't want it. I feel it should stay with the house. Too big to get out the doors anyway. I have no idea how they got it in, in the first place." He shook his white head with pleasure.

"Oh, one thing I almost forgot. They turned the root cellar into a fallout shelter in the '60s. I've kept it fully stocked, although you might want to test the Geiger counter and the dosimeter. They haven't been used since Three Mile Island. Now, forgive me, but I have a meeting in town. Here's my new address, contact me with any questions." He picked up a scuffed leather satchel and well used brief case. "I'll leave you to it." And he left Em Huber standing in her new living room.

I have a home. We have a home. Alone, Em let the house encompass her senses, the telltale scent of wood fires, ashes still on the hearth, dust and the leather of the valuable old couch, birdsong and feathered arguments from the garden and the play of morning sunlight across soft hues in the intricate pattern of the carpet. Her eyes teared up and her throat grew tight with gratitude and relief, and sadness, too, *A new house, a new life for us. Now, I just have to pay for it, and move in. Two weeks to closing. OMG!*

Her eyes strayed to the windows, which badly needed washing. This inheritance from a widowed bachelor needed a thorough scrubbing and buckets of fresh paint. Not one to stand on ceremony or shilly-shally when she could act, Em dropped her new keys and her bag on the couch, pushed up her sleeves and made for the kitchen to assess the condition.

Every day for the next two weeks, sometimes late into the night, Em, her children and every friend or relative she could persuade to help, cleaned, painted and moved unwanted furniture and boxes of belongings to the attic. The cellar was a source of despair, so they left it as is was. Their cat, Ash, was made anxious about abandonment by the packing to move and had to be brought to the new house each day. Once out of the carrier, he scented the air, three species of mice were present for the discriminating feline. Field mice had winkled their way into the field-stone basement and it was his delight to give chase. Traps were set to help his determined efforts. They left the cellar to the cat. On moving day, the two budget-priced movers swore they would never come back, the family moved with too many boxes of books.

———◆———

And so, Em and her girls settled in. It took two years to acclimate to the house, and for the house to further decimate Em's finances. *Can it be possible?* she wondered. *Can an old experienced house judge the balances in both checking and savings accounts so nicely?* Whenever there was any bit to spare, something else would go wrong, break, leak or need fixing that she couldn't do herself. Sump pump, well pump, dehumidifier, electrical fixtures, outlets and clogged gutters and the awful dishwasher that should be packed and shipped to the Smithsonian with a note "Do Not Return," joined the litany.

But there was freedom and peace, too. Without the restraining and toxic influence of her ex-husband's moods, and his need to control every decision of family life, the family rediscovered laughter. Life could be good, though money was short. Always a volunteer, without Huber to hinder her, Em found even more challenging activities, which might have an element of risk. Life was even becoming pleasantly routine with seasons changing as they did in Southern New England.

So, after two years of repairing and patching and replacing, Em sat at her kitchen table, cradling a stout mug of Earl Grey in her hands, and reviewed her prospects. *How the merry hell am I going to pay the taxes in July? We can economize on the utilities and the small stuff, but the taxes won't go away. Hum, what are my assets? Working retail is out, not enough money to buy groceries, not fast enough. Corporations don't hire anyone over fifty, especially not women and I've been there, done that, worn the tee shirt and took the buyout. I must have been cray-cray to buy this place.*

The view from the kitchen window looked out at the softly swishing young maple leaves, fresh in spring green. Down the hill almost hidden, Em could see the roofline of Mireille and Philippe's farmhouse, and she did what any enterprising woman might do, she called her lawyer.

"*Ma chere amie,* so good to hear your voice. I am sitting here fighting the boredom with my feet up. The doctor, he forbids me to go out. Too many *Times* crossword puzzles, and too much John Grisham, *mon Dieu*. The baby is so active, I must lie down and play opera to quiet him. He likes the high notes. Such kicks, my diaphragm, it feels like it is up to my teeth." Mireille gave a long sigh and rubbed her belly fondly. "I cannot wait!"

"I'm sure it will be soon. Listen, before you go, I need some advice. I need to go back to work." Em sucked in a deep breath and took the plunge. "There have got to be people who could use my research skills, I wouldn't have to say competitive intelligence. No one knows what that is anyway."

"What will you tell them, *cherie*? Corporate spy for hire? All reasonable offers accepted?" Mireille laughed softly, careful not to wake the baby napping quietly inside.

"Sorta, yes, I know it sounds unusual," Em replied.

"You have the high skills, I understand this. If you are ready to go back to work, we can talk. But you have the accountant from the divorce. He can help you set up your business." Mireille yawned. "Now I, too, need the nap. I will help as I can, you know that. I encourage you to proceed." With good wishes on both sides, they closed their call. Mireille, however, made a call of her own, to the distinguished elderly Gertrude down the road to enlist her help on Em Huber's behalf.

———◆———

Much paperwork and well placed local ads later, Em launched her new business, M.E. Huber & Associates. The first two clients were a disappointment topped off by a lugubriously detailed research project that garnered Em more than she ever wanted to know about competition in the funeral industry. Then, with a little help from her friends, new clients found her.

3

THE THIRD CLIENT

———◆———

TWO DISTINGUISHED TENURED PROFESSORS STOOD at opposite ends of their Research and Development lab shouting at each other.

"That's outrageous! How could someone steal the plans for Version 3? Then they have the consummate balls to manufacture it three different ways? Do they think we're stupid, that we wouldn't find out?" Professor Frank Kirbee bellowed across the lab at his longtime friend and business partner Professor Ali Hussein.

They were alone in their secure lab, hidden discretely in a business incubator park developed from a former munitions factory. Solar panels of various designs, both invented by the lab and produced by competitors, were concealed on the roof. Their ability to absorb the sun's energy was carefully monitored and analyzed by a computer within the lab. A storage device of their own innovative design received the electricity from the solar panels testing its capacity and durability.

Advanced fire suppression (recently updated), security, temperature and air quality sensor panels lined the wall by the door. These were above code and were specified by the professors who were careful men. There were no windows. Light was provided by retractable frosted skylights that were carefully angled away from view of any other structure and could be closed at night to secure the lab.

A long workbench with many measuring and fabricating devices of the professors' own design ran down the center. Long black flexible tubes with yellow vacuum hoods hung at intervals from the exposed steel rafters above the bench. Respirators were scattered within easy reach along the bench. An eye washing station for industrial accidents stood by the door looking like a high school water fountain. An open shower stood next to it.

Three D printing machines lined the short wall of the lab, their bases full of liquid resin. Thin blue lines of industrial lasers beamed down to trace patterns in the resin forming thin layer after layer to build the inventors' intricate model parts.

The two professors in white lab coats stood at each end of the high tech workbench. They had seen each other through Kirbee's two divorces and the death of Hussein's beloved wife. Shouting matches were their way of settling the differences between them. Kirbee moved around the bench to see the other man more clearly over the scientific gear on the bench. Hussein was sorting and labeling what looked like a heap of small metal parts.

"I assure you, it is the truth. We have been robbed!" Professor Hussein yelled back. Pointing to the array of miniature solar collector parts on the bench, he said, "You see the proof there in front of you." All of the parts were carefully labeled. "I have taken apart all of the three products. The technology is ours without question. I can even tell when it was stolen using our lab notebooks."

"How is this possible, Al? We are so careful." Kirbee's usually jovial round face grew red under his short white hair.

"That is exactly right. And that is how we can prove the theft. Based on the flaws in the manufacture and design of these products, that we later fixed, I might add, I can tell you to the week when the theft took place. It was before Version 3 was finished to our liking."

"Is there any sign they have access to any other version?"

"None. These products are barely viable. I cannot understand why anyone would wish to market them as they are. Frank, this is serious enough without having to worry that they may try to steal Version 5. I don't even like to think about that." Professor Hussein rubbed his forehead as if it ached. He was of a more moderate and reserved temperament than the outgoing Kirbee.

"So we need to finish Version 5 and get it to the government before it can be compromised. If we lose this, we may never get another government contract."

The two business partners glared at each other across the lab.

"It is much worse than that my friend, and we both know it." Ali Hussein dropped his voice. "Version 3 of SunSprite is only just a commercial application. Version 5 is a strategic advantage, worth millions to another government. We should prepare to prosecute this theft."

"I agree, and I thought about what you said yesterday. I'll make the call. We need to investigate this on our own before we turn it over to them." Kirbee laughed under his breath. "An old friend of mine recommended someone with expertise in corporate intelligence. If we can present them with a strong case and deliver Version 5 safely, we can do damage control. We can argue it's safe to do the development here in our lab and don't need to be in a secure government facility."

"Damage control, yes, I see. We are supposed to be running a secure lab here. Who could have done this to us?" Hussein seemed mystified and outraged at the same time.

"You've got me there, Al. We handpick our graduate student assistants. They never have access to any more than the bits and pieces that they need. Never enough to steal a whole version. Besides, after Sondra, they know what is at stake here. I'd bet my job on it!"

"The students are our job," Professor Hussein reminded him.

Professor Francis Xavier Kirbee, a rather roundish man with a full head of short white hair and fiercely friendly blue eyes gave a loud sigh that sounded like the huff of an angry wild boar.

Although the lab was stark white, several colorful mobiles of small test parts hung from wire frames. These were Professor Kirbee's whimsies in homage to the mobiles of Alexander Calder. As he turned to stalk out of the lab to their office, Kirbee reached up with his hand and gently batted at one of his mobiles, setting it into a gentle twirl.

Professor Hussein, a man of similar age, grey hair and inquisitive dark eyes returned to his work disassembling the solar collector parts on the workbench. He knew he had won his point.

Kirbee secured the lab door behind him. His nickname was Prof FX, or simply called FX by his students because all teachers of renown or infamy needed a nickname. He could be exasperating to work for, a notoriously hard grader, and he could also be the life of the party when success was to be celebrated. A career reference from Kirbee was the aspiration of his students, an accolade to be coveted, pursued and fought over. A likeable man, he had many connections, academic, scientific, personal and even some he never mentioned to anyone.

He took a seat at the long desk in their office that faced the reinforced glass wall spanning the length of the lab. Using the phone with the secure line and unlisted number, he dialed.

"Hullo?" The young woman answered in an intentionally casual voice.

"This is Frank Kirbee, I need to talk to him immediately."

"He's not in his office right now."

"I know he's not. He's working on his damned shoot 'em up program. He's waiting for me." Professor Kirbee tried to control his agitation.

The young woman duty officer couldn't deny this, so she wisely kept silent.

"It's an emergency. I can't come in today."

"I'll call downstairs, Professor. Hold one moment please."

Kirbee fumed and drummed his fingers on the desk.

"Oh shit," the duty officer said. "Garvey, the boss is down in the firing range, right? I've got a hysterical Professor on the line."

"Yes, I saw him go about half an hour ago. He left instructions to escort Professor Kirbee down as soon as he arrived."

"Doesn't sound like he's going to make it. Sounds like trouble."

"Trouble is our first, last and middle name," Garvey replied in his rich baritone without looking up. He dressed in his fatigues that day and sat at the security console simultaneously monitoring their computer network and the facility's cameras.

In the basement firing range, their director, a tall man named Michael Halloran, shirt sleeves rolled up, stood stork-like on his left leg with his right leg bent at the knee. His cane was propped up on the wall next to him. Shooting deliberately, he paused every few shots to check the display on the tablet on the shelf in front of him. He was not shooting at the customary target of a man's outline with a bullseye on his chest. Using the tablet he changed the display projected over his head and down the range at the blank piece of graph paper. The moving image projected on the graph paper showed small bull's eyes that appeared at random on the arms, legs, shoulders and hands of a full-sized silhouette of a man.

The shooter could control the pace of the bullseyes as

they appeared on the figure, and he could also set the silhouette in motion at a run. In a more complex program, the silhouette could bob and weave before him as well, but the scoring for that sequence of motions proved to be problematic. Not satisfied with the standard nail them in the chest target for his agents, Halloran decided to design his own more challenging target practice with the help of one of their contractors, the inventor, Frank Kirbee.

An agent in plain clothes who looked like a scrawny high school dropout with an attitude came in from the field to do his mandatory requalification. Agent Steve Rankel took one look at the man in the firing range and turned tail. He retreated to the range attendant's booth where he spoke to the agent doing his rotation as attendant and firing instructor.

"Hey Vargas, has the boss been at this long? I am not going in there with him. The last time I did he made me test that damned new program of his. When I blew it, he did it himself and made it look easy."

"The man's a menace, no doubt about it. He says it's harder to take them alive and walk away yourself," Vargas replied with barely concealed admiration for their director.

"He's got that right. I'm going for coffee. Call me if he's done before quitting time."

"As if we have one," Vargas muttered at the departing back of Steve Rankel, his partner. He returned his attention to inputting his cursed case notes and arrest reports until the phone rang. Generally speaking, nobody called the range so he was primed when he answered. Through the speaker Vargas said, "Sir, Professor Kirbee on the line for you. He says it's an emergency."

"Bloody hell, has he set fire to the lab again?" Halloran holstered his weapon, picked up the cane and walked carefully into the booth to pick up the phone.

"Michael, is that you?" Kirbee's voice boomed over the phone.

"No, it's my maiden Aunt Mary. What's wrong Frank? You were due here half an hour ago."

"I'm not coming. Al's onto something. He thinks that plans for Version 3 have been compromised. He's found products that match our early designs, piece by piece."

"When? How did it happen?" Halloran asked as he relaxed into the chair and reflected, *At least it's not the lab this time.*

"Almost two years ago, and we can't figure out how."

"You're just telling me now?" Halloran motioned for Vargas to go change the graph paper on the target as it was now riddled with bullet holes. His friends Kirbee and Hussein could be a truly trying pair, certainly near genius level in everything but common sense. To him Version 3 was not a great loss, a patent application had been made. The real prize was the software and hardware combination in Version 5.

"Al figured it out *now*. We're going to double check his results. I'm going to hire a consultant to go over patent filings for infringement." The professor determined to get ahead of trouble.

"Is Version 5 compromised?" the director unconsciously held his breath waiting for the answer and let it out slowly when he heard the negative response. He was charged with providing the security necessary for their sensitive research project.

"No, not so far as we can tell. In fact, even some of the design and fabrication improvements that we made to Version 3 aren't present in the copies."

"You know you can't give anyone access...."

"I know, I know. The consultant won't have access to the lab. And I'll get all your damned paperwork filled out and signed."

"You said that Ali found this. Can I talk to him?" Halloran asked.

"Not right now, he's observant, you know that." Kirbee

was not anxious to have his partner share his concerns quite yet.

"Of course, have him call me when he's available. Keep me updated."

Kirbee hung up with a promise to do that promptly. *That went well*, Kirbee said to himself.

Back in the firing range, Halloran reloaded his gun, walked around to face off against a conventional target, and emptied his gun into it in rapid fire. "I think I re-qualified, Vargas," he said. "I'm done for the day. Tell your friend Rankel he can come back now."

4

M.E. HUBER MEETS
PROFESSOR F.X. KIRBEE

———◆———

EARLY THAT QUIET MONDAY MORNING in June, Em sat in the living room of the Spring House at the table she used for a desk. She gazed up at the cross-stitch motto that served as a sign and a warning. Her spirits were low. She paid her bills from a stack sorted by date and priority. The mists and sporadic light rain suited her mood. The trees outside the window dripped chilly rain. Fog cloaked the ground and reached up into the treetops like a huge cool damp cloud descending on them off the North Atlantic.

Temptation arrived via the Internet, as it so frequently did now. A lucrative offer to work for her former competitors appeared in her email once again. Her intuition told her that the job might only last two years at most, or until they were convinced they had learned all they could from her. Still, two years of respite from managing on a fixed income and a tight budget had its attractions. The Spring House was a source of enjoyment and satisfaction and a financial challenge to maintain.

Surely she would need to find some sort of gainful employment, not a part time job. With no alimony, temptation reared its lively head. She stared at the cross-stitch design above her head, so close she could reach out to touch it. To the casual observer, it would seem to be a cute idea, an update on the maxim by Gandhi. Three little monkeys faced front pantomiming, "Hear no evil, see no evil, speak no evil." The fourth seated little monkey appeared in profile, typing away on a laptop. The words under his picture read, "Type no evil." Em created the needlework piece as both penance and a constant reminder.

During her corporate career Em resisted pressure to do research that shouldn't be done. Early on, she figured out no one could justifiably order her to violate the company code of ethics. But handling information could be powerfully seductive, the temptation to pass along insights, to figure out how to get that elusive piece of data were ever present. Em enjoyed free associating, matching wits with a data base until the wanted information could be coaxed to appear on her screen. For some who understood and could manipulate digital information, the idea that if it could be done, it was really okay to do it, seemed to pervade their lives. The ability to stop short, to hold back, to respect the confidentiality of others' information, was not an easy discipline to maintain.

That morning Em ruminated on her decision to follow the narrow path. An ingenious, creative, skillful and persistent researcher, she was often able to find that which otherwise wouldn't be found. She felt the responsibility of that and also the temptation.

Summer stretched before them. In the living room on the Stickley couch sat Deanna. Home from college, she was in the crucial process of catching up on her TV shows. Sandy Waitely, their resident guest, studied. She was joining the family in the Spring House for an internship in the area. Em turned from her budget spreadsheet to the cup of Earl Grey. In *Pride and Prejudice*, Mr. Bennet, father of the heroines, finished his own barely balancing accounts and turned to an expensive glass of Port wine in consolation. Em reflected she couldn't even afford the Port.

It was a good thing for temptation that the phone beside her rang, jarring her back from her thoughts.

"Is this M.E. Huber and Associates?" said a man whom Em judged to be well-spoken and of middle age.

"Uh, yes of course." Em, flustered at first said, "This is Em Huber speaking."

"Very good. We have need of your specialized services, my partner and I. You come highly recommended. You can do patent and trademark searching?"

"Yes. I'm not a paralegal, but I've been told I can turn up more potential conflicts. If you are planning to file, it may be less expensive for me to prescreen a trademark for you."

"That's right. That's what I've heard from a mutual friend. My name is Kirbee, Frank Kirbee, professor in the physics department."

"May I ask who…?"

"Not important. Can you meet with us this afternoon?"

Em hesitated. She turned to her laptop and typed. First she double checked the phone number displayed on her Caller ID. Then she made a quick check on the university website for a faculty listing in the physics department where she found Francis Xavier Kirbee. She followed that with a search in a database of U.S. university professors for a brief biography.

"Say yes that you will come. It's quite urgent. We're developing a new product, and we've run into a snag, so to speak."

"Well, in that case, I'll be happy…"

"This afternoon, Ms. Huber. My house. It's not far, 164 Bacon Avenue in New Haven."

Em already knew his address. She stared at it on her screen.

"Two thirty. We'll pay whatever your going rate."

That clinched it for Em. She had not yet finished reading his rather impressive biography, but even for a faculty member at a major American university, Kirbee looked like an overachiever with a long career.

"I'll be there, Professor," she said and resisted the impulse to add aloud, "with bells on my twinkling little toes." In her experience, inventors were the most secretive and illusive of clients with the most unpredictable potential for payment. This call was at least a potential for a job, and she quickly recalculated her fee schedule upward.

"Good, we'll see you then," replied the professor and the line went dead.

Em looked down at the address and time that she'd scribbled on the notepad as well as the phone number from the Caller ID displayed on her handset. Being it was only mid-morning, she had plenty of time to find out who Professor Kirbee might be and what product he referred to that provoked his concern. A well-placed phone call or two might turn up a reference, but in this she was disappointed. None of her former coworkers in corporate had any knowledge of Kirbee. That left her with the less likely source of academic contacts through her ex-husband, and she was not about to make those calls.

Deanna lounged on the living room couch, her long thin legs none too gracefully flung over the back of it. She pulled her earbuds out of her ears long enough to ask, "What's up, Mom?" It amazed her mother that she could hear nothing when called, but had no trouble hearing anything sensitive or confidential going on around her through the earbuds.

"We have a potential client for M.E. Huber and Associates."

"The Associates, that's me and Sandy, right?"

"It sounded better that way, more like an established business," Em admitted to her daughter.

"Great, then when do we start? All I've got so far this summer is twenty hours tops making shakes and scooping ice cream at Marcella's. I don't do table service, that would be a disaster, so there are no tips unless the rest of them are feeling generous."

Deanna had a gift behind the counter. Her mango smoothies were velvet on the tongue, and her custom ice cream sodas and shakes were much sought after. The previous summer several people developed the habit of calling Marcella's to see if Deanna was behind the counter before they came in. She could make a latte that satisfied even her mother.

Em laughed out loud. "The idea of either one of us as a waitress, truly disastrous. I would never remember who ordered what. It's hard work."

"And I'd trip and drop cold stuff on some big ol' guy's crotch...."

"Deanna!"

"Alright, lap. Well, I did. They tried me at it once, and they said it would have to be a national emergency to have me do it again. No, I'm better off behind the counter. I don't have to talk to people either that way."

"If you want to help, find out everything you can in half an hour about a Professor Frank Kirbee, physics department. I'm going to make a few phone calls."

"That long, Mom?" Deanna had a notoriously short attention span when it came to work.

At lunch Deanna presented her mother with her profile of Professor Francis X. Kirbee, a biographical note from the university website, a meaty entry from *Who's Who in Colleges and Universities*, a short bibliography of his recent publications, several articles by and about him and his work, and a humorous photo of Kirbee and fellow alumni at their last Class Reunion.

"So how much do I get paid an hour for research? Time and a half for O.T.?"

"Honey, when you own your own business, there is no such thing as Over Time pay. You do more than you bill out. It's just that way," Em explained. If Deanna worked for her she was going to need to earn her pay.

"Mom, this is highly skilled work, you've said so yourself. Three times the minimum wage."

"That's outrageous, Deanna," Em replied with good humor.

"How much are you going to bill the client?"

"Well, that's different, a girl has to make a profit." Em was not about to let Deanna get the best of her.

"On the work of the laborer. Capitalist!"

"Oh, yeah, right. A little more capital would go a long way around here right now. Tuition is due in July, remember?"

Deanna tried hard not to roll her eyes at her mother. She did understand the change in their fortunes as a result of the divorce and Em's layoff.

Her mother continued. "I guess the best capital we have now are our brains, skills and our willingness to be in business for ourselves." Em tried to sound confident and cheerful. "And it's about the only free capital that we'll get."

Deanna sighed.

They haggled over Deanna's hourly rate for several minutes more for the fun of it. Em thought Deanna optimistic, and Deanna felt her mother cheap. A tentative agreement was in place by the time Em needed to prep and dress for the appointment with her new client.

———•———

Em's closet contained business wear in two different sizes, all several years old. Choosing a grey pinstripe pantsuit was not a problem. Wedging herself into the pants proved more of a challenge requiring the fast removal and replacement of the button at the waist to gain that extra inch. Since Em had not considered it necessary to remove the pants to sew the button back on, she managed to prick her finger on the needle and to get a splotch of blood on her white blouse, fortunately below the waist line. Em swore under her breath. She hoped it was not a bad omen for her meeting. Peaceful retirement pushed Em once again into the boundary between size 14 and size 16. She was not a happy woman when she came downstairs, muttering to herself, to take her slimmest courier bag to go out to meet her client.

"Break a leg, Mom," Deanna called from the living room couch.

Em's face fell. Deanna saw her mother's response and launched herself off the couch to give her mother an impulsive hug.

"It means good luck in theater, you know."

"I know, Dee. It's just that I have a feeling about this client. It feels real, like I've finally got one. And I hope it goes well!"

———◆———

At precisely forty-five minutes before the time agreed on with Kirbee, Em drove her aging van down the country road that led from the Spring House towards the city of New Haven. It rained steadily.

Through a neighbor's farmhouse window a pair of shrewd eyes watched her pass through the gathering storm. A smile of satisfaction rested on the face of the watcher. Action had been set in motion. The sound of rapid typing on the wireless keyboard resumed. She had much to do that day to reach the self-defined quota of words. Although long retired, Gertrude found the imperative to publish or perish was difficult to lose. Her career in intelligence long over, her time as a professor of American Cold War political history passed, still her contacts remained. It was amusing to use them, and to be useful to them, too.

Bacon Avenue was a well-known street with tall wonderfully unique old houses built in a time of prosperity and optimism. That day the stately trees of great height had branches hanging heavy with the weight of the rain. As Em pulled up in front of Kirbee's residence, the rain took that moment to turn into a squall. Wind driven rain forced Em to cling to her umbrella and clutch her bag close to her body. She heard the sharp crack of a tree limb breaking and the rushing sound of a falling branch that landed on the sidewalk two doors up the street. Em ran up the front walk to the brick steps of the house. About to ring the doorbell, Em reached out her hand to find the elaborately paneled wooden door swing open with alacrity.

"Ms. Huber, welcome! Do come in out of that impossible rain. We say if you don't like the weather here in New England, wait fifteen minutes and it will change, but today it only seems to get worse. I'm Frank Kirbee."

A grey haired man, who exuded the personality of the genial professor, relieved her of her umbrella, and thrust it into a brass umbrella stand. They were standing in an old fashioned vestibule with a tiled floor and a carved wooden hall stand with a mirror surrounded by brass coat hooks. Kirbee hung Em's rain coat on the hall stand, opened the hallway door and ushered her in.

"We have good coffee, my business partner Ali Hussein made it. Would you like some? Al doesn't drink alcohol, but I'm putting whiskey in mine. It's a chilly afternoon." Kirbee rubbed his hands together. The old house did seem to hold a chill.

The rain beat a tattoo on the roof, lashed against the windows and rattled in the gutters. Em wondered if there weren't ice crystals in the rain, or pellets of hail the noise was so loud.

"Sounds like we're in for quite a little storm. Should be over by the time we're through. The seasons are changing and the weather has been so unstable," Kirbee remarked by way of apology for bringing her out.

Kirbee guided Em through a wide hallway, by a long

curving staircase, and into a room that, at first glance, seemed out of place in a house of that age. Formerly a parlor, the room now served as an office. Its walls were stark white and the furniture was distinctly modern and factory made. Actually the chairs, tables and desks looked like illustrations from a book on the International Style of the early and middle twentieth century, chrome, leather, molded plastic and birch wood.

"Let me introduce you to my partner, Professor Ali Hussein." A man of middle age, dark olive skin and black hair showing grey, rose to his feet to greet Em.

"We are grateful that you have come out on such a day, Ms. Huber. We have a project of some importance to put before you. Please sit with us," he motioned to a Barcelona chair with a leather seat and back perched on top of chrome legs. A low pedestal table of smooth white molded plastic held a coffee pot, mugs, sugar, creamer and a bottle of good Irish whiskey.

Kirbee pulled up a sled-based tubular steel chair with a caned seat that glided easily over the Turkish carpet in a deep blue and red pattern. He proceeded to pour coffee and to pass the sugar and creamer to their guest.

After the preliminaries, and the coffee had been passed around, Professor Hussein spoke. "Are you aware of our work? No? Let me tell you briefly that we are working in the field of solar energy and have invented a new technology. We believe that it is capable of generating electricity at a higher rate relative to its size than anything now available in the market, but it is still not perfected. To protect our rights we have filed a patent submission for our third version. We decided not to move to manufacture it yet because we wished to confirm its reliability for a good length of time."

"Al is being diplomatic here. Version 3 still had a ways to go yet to be a commercial product. Getting something to work in the lab is one thing. Getting it manufactured to strict tolerances and to be durable enough to stand up to constant use in the field is quite another."

Professor Hussein indicated his agreement with a nod of his head and a gesture with his mug.

Kirbee added, "We moved on to fix some of the manufacturing problems with Version 4 and are now almost ready with the fifth version that will be…"

"That's all very well, Frank, but tell her what has happened."

Frank Kirbee sat on the edge of his chair and leaned forward towards them. "Al has convinced me that someone, more than one company, is using the technical specifications for Version 3 to manufacture products. They are being used to produce cheap consumer products here in the U.S. that are sold in small regional markets. He believes that the specifications were stolen before Version 3 was even complete. So the products are unreliable."

"Flying under the radar?" Em speculated.

"Yes, but not for long. Al caught on." Kirbee proceeded to tell Em how Professor Hussein discovered the competing products, and how he attempted to buy them in untraceable ways.

Professor Kirbee flexed his fingers as if the joints were stiff and absent mindedly drummed them on the table. Em recognized the distinctive rhythm.

"We need you to trace any patent or trademark filings these companies may have made. Our application is still pending. See if you can tell how these people came to make our least successful version. Also, how did different companies come to have the specifications?"

"They have stolen them, Frank, that's how." Professor Hussein was most definite.

"Is there a chance another research team could have developed something similar?" Em asked in innocence.

"No!" the two partners exclaimed, one in disbelief and the other in frustration. Kirbee took a sheet of paper from a folder on the table and handed it to Em.

Well, that was a misstep, thought Em to herself, *right out of the script for what not to do as the perfect consultant.* She said, "Fine, I can do patent and trademark searching for you. Do you want me to go beyond that in any way?"

"How far do you think you can go?" Kirbee was intrigued.

Em made a quick calculation. "Company ownership would be a good start."

The two men looked at each other, "Go as far as you can without breaking the law," Kirbee said, looking at Em shrewdly. "Or stretching it too far. We have a government contract for our most advanced work."

There it is again, reflected Em, *it is hard to know what's a stretch, and what is an outright violation if caught.*

"I'll make sure I keep it legal for you," she replied firmly.

"You see we want to move to sue in court so it is imperative that we prepare a strong case with documentation," Professor Hussein asserted.

"I think we should nail the bastards, whatever it takes!" Kirbee coughed and added a little more whiskey to his remaining coffee.

"One thing that I will tell you, rapid prototyping using 3-D printing is making it easier to imitate our work. We can tell this, but the manufacturing standards are lower. The mold marks are not removed. The tolerances for the size and shape of the pieces are not exacting. They may have many defective pieces that they must need to throw away. Wasteful. It indicates to me that their factories are operated poorly." Professor Hussein served as the quality control expert in their enterprise.

"Foreign?" Em conjectured.

"No, but it is good that you ask that question. The raw materials used were sourced here in this country. And they cannot be making all of that much money on the products. The poor quality seems to indicate to me that they are not reputable businesses."

"Thieves seldom are, Al," Frank Kirbee concluded.

"Hmm." Em's eyes narrowed. "I'll look for another reason then, gentlemen."

Two men smiled back at her.

"We'll start with a patent search and work from there," Em enthused. She was anxious to get on the case, keyboard in hand. If she'd been invited, she would have started right then and there.

Professor Hussein rose to leave. "Ms. Huber, it is my pleasure to meet you. I wish you the best in your researches. I have a daily commitment to keep. Frank will handle the formalities for us. I have prepared a folder for you with the companies that I have identified. He also has my technical analysis. It may be of use to you, but you may only view it with myself or Frank present. Good afternoon and good luck." Having said his goodbyes, the professor retreated to the front hall, and in a moment the heavy front door slammed solidly.

"Eyes only?" Em sent a searching gaze at Kirbee.

"Exactly right, my dear. We fixed the defects in Version 3 and call it Version 4, but Version 5 is a classified project. Without clearance, you cannot see the material or enter our lab. We must be quite strict on that. Here, fill out and sign these forms, please."

Em raised her eyebrows and looked askance at the sheaf of papers Kirbee handed to her from his folder.

"Oh, the security clearance request for you, and shall we say, standard non-compete, non-disclosure and confidentiality agreements for any of your associates as well."

"What about an agreement for fees and payment? I have one right here." Em reached into her courier bag for the custom fee schedule she created that morning. "Shall we discuss a fee schedule?" She tried for a low key professional approach.

"Anything you think reasonable. Your fee is the least of

our worries right now, my dear Ms. Huber." Kirbee smiled, and his eyes brightened. He felt a sense of relief and pleasure in making a new acquaintance.

"I'm truly glad of that, thank you, Professor." Em worked the numbers on the specially edited brochure and calculated an additional markup of twenty five percent. She wrote the numbers into her agreement for his signature. She did this based on the perception that a project that required more paperwork than a Bell System accident report must be worth more than her proposed fee structure.

Truth be told, Kirbee and Hussein were prepared to pay anything she asked, as they would have for a nationally recognized consultant. Em Huber had been personally recommended as a speedy, discrete, local alternative by a knowledgeable colleague with an interesting past, by a woman who was now quite elderly.

"More coffee? I'll leave you with the forms." Kirbee retreated to his desk.

Em sat by herself at the table, helped herself to another mug of the excellent coffee, added a chunk of Demerara brown sugar and drowned it in the remaining milk from the pitcher. She filled out and signed her way through the stack of forms, conscious Kirbee observed her in between playing with the little parts. By the time Em finished her stack of papers, reserving copies of the non-compete and non-disclosure forms for her associates at home, Kirbee had finished assembling his model. He set it in the patch of light from his high intensity desk lamp. The brightly colored little object had a skinny pyramid for a base topped by what resembled a Plains windmill with a flat horizontal tail to collect light. It whirled slowly at first.

Fascinated by the miniature windmill, Em walked over to the chrome tube and birch wood desk where Kirbee sat admiring his model.

"It's a desk fan. It needs stronger light. I charged the solar cell first, you see." The professor looked up at her with the pleased grin of a little boy with his original creation.

He isn't an unattractive man. Probably single mindedly devoted to whatever catches his attention at the moment and oblivious to anything, or anyone, else, assessed Em. *I've heard he has two ex-wives, would they agree with my analysis?*

"Professor, there's a question I've been wanting to ask you. All the furniture here, is it a collection of twentieth century architect designed and factory made furniture?"

"Oh, yes, do you like it?"

Em looked up at a spiky wire construction with a variety of irregular paddle shapes that hung from the ceiling above her head. It was set in motion by her walk across the room to the desk. "Is that an Alexander Calder mobile over my head?"

"I see we're going to get along very well. Are you done with your paperwork? When can we expect your results? Soon is good, tomorrow is better." The professor swiveled around in his rather large shaped wood and padded desk chair to face Em. He smiled enigmatically without answering her question.

"I'll start with Professor Hussein's company material tonight. We'll pursue the research tomorrow, and I will call as soon as we have it put together for your review. I'm looking forward to working with you and Professor Hussein."

"We'll need your research on disk. I don't trust jump drives. Had a bad experience with one. I dropped it out of my pocket and I nearly flushed it." The distinguished professor grinned at his admission of his own fallibility and the vulnerability of new technology.

After a terribly wet ride home, the worst of the storm was over. Em, anxious to get to work on her new project, never noticed her return to the Spring House was observed. The sound of the wireless keyboard barely slowed as Em drove by the farmhouse on her way up the hill. Gertie, the elderly woman, a retired professor of American History of the cold war period, nodded and smiled. Kirbee's report was favorable.

5

HIRING STAFF

———•———

"THE NEW GUY IS HERE," Garvey announced. Michael Halloran sat behind his desk in the small office he had chosen. It was right across from the duty officer's desk and the cluster of staff desks for the agents. It suited him. Maps were posted on the interior wall. Behind him hung a white board. A tinted window showed a view of the Interstate highway, the harbor, and across the mouth of the New Haven Harbor, Long Island in the distance. The wall opposite the desk was covered by a long Andrew Wyeth print of a sailing ship run aground. The watercolor sketch was painted in deep tones of blue grey.

Halloran had turned the larger director's corner office next door into a conference room with a long table and an assortment of chairs. With high, tinted, thick windows on two sides and a full view of the harbor, it made an excellent lookout post. A flag stood in one corner as a useful reminder of their mission. Several telescopes were lined up pointing at strategic angles.

Halloran prepared to hoist himself up out of his chair to meet the new staff member but stopped abruptly. He heard Anson approach before seeing him round the corner into the office. The man's new wheelchair was black, low to the ground and obviously built for speed. A well-muscled man in his mid-twenties sitting in the chair maneuvered it with precision directly in front of the director's desk. Halloran judged that the first meeting with his new agent would be best conducted if he did not stand over him but sat face to face. Anson presented a pleasant open but determined aspect, clear light brown eyes set in a tanned face, regular features, and a square jaw. Sandy blond hair grew in an unruly crop above a lined brow. He was dressed in a charcoal grey suit and tie. The suit was a little too large for him, and its trouser legs were of uneven lengths.

"Good morning, sir, I'm David Anson."

"Welcome to New Haven. We have all your paperwork. I see that you grew up in Bath, Maine. Near the Iron Works? Handle a boat? Swim?"

"Yes to all three, sir," Anson reacted. Obviously this was not the direction expected for the first interview with the head of the department.

"Fluent in Canadian French, Kurdish and spoken Uzbecki. I see that your middle name is LaRoche. French Canadian?"

"My mother's people, sir. She insisted that we learn the language at home. It wasn't a popular thing to do in Maine, speaking it outside the house."

"Understood. My Gaelic is seriously limited for that reason, useful in bars and at sporting events only.

"I have a few questions for you that are not quite so easy. Think before you answer." The director smiled. "You have an excellent military service record, can you be a successful civilian? Not always an easy adjustment."

"Had enough of Army life. Time to go back to sleeping in a bed at night, bars down the street, and women. Maybe a home and family someday."

"Alright. We're not a paramilitary organization. We're civilians defending civilians. By the laws of the country and the state. On my watch we also observe, without exception, the rules of the Geneva Convention. Read it. On my watch no one abuses suspects, witnesses, aliens or perps. Anything less is a breach of trust with the people of this country. Can you adhere to that? Any abuse is cause for dismissal." Halloran looked sharply at the new recruit.

"Yes, sir, most gladly sir." Anson heaved a sigh of relief and looked away.

Halloran watched the younger man gather himself together again. "Concern?"

"Not with that. It's good to be home." Anson smiled.

"Understand, then, that no one should expect you to follow an order that breaks the laws of this country or the rules of this agency. No matter how high up they are, or how intimidating they can be. At the end of the day, we all have to be able to account for our own actions. To ourselves, to our country, to our families." The older man paused. "Takes some guts sometimes, and may mean taking a fall or two." He shook his head ruefully. "Are we clear?"

"Very. Been there, more than once, too." The two men shook their heads at each other.

"C'est la guerre," commented Halloran in a flat voice.

"May I ask a question? You said 'defending civilians.' Isn't this a law enforcement agency?"

"Good question. The answer is yes and then again no. American law enforcement is for the most part reactive. Break a law and someone will chase you down, if it's reported. Other countries may have a more proactive approach. Like police intelligence and all that." He waved his hand in the air.

"Right now staff and money are tight for local and national agencies. After 9/11 it became clear that the reactive approach failed to fight organized and planned activity with a single event in mind. Information had been collected and reported in various places by various agencies. No one group had the time or information assets to put the data together, to see a pattern and to recommend action.

Or to act, to cut 'em off at the pass, so to speak. That's us now, IIA. All the other alpha organizations, agencies and departments have specific legal mandates and jurisdictions. They have to operate within those.

"We are to connect the dots, fill in the gaps and provide as needed research backup for all the other agencies. We're who they call when there's something unexplained in the neighborhood. Say the Department of Agriculture picks up on something that isn't quite right. Safe food supply is crucial. Or a Congressman or Congresswoman gets repeated phone calls from constituents that cause concern. No laws broken, but their instincts tell them something is up. We get those requests. We investigate, research and analyze. If the pattern that emerges is troubling, we can act or we can recommend action by another agency." Halloran paused for questions.

"I see, sir, I think." Anson was still puzzled.

"Think of it this way, we investigate, we put the pieces together, and we do the triage. Triage can mean we act or we can refer the case to another agency. If it's not clear, don't worry, it changes with each assignment. We have teams in the field now. The people you are meeting today are the Regional headquarters' staff."

"My next question for you, and think about this carefully. You've lost a lot, can you put it all on the line again? We will expect you to go into the field with the rest of the team when it's needed."

"Field work. Damn, that's great." Anson jumped forward in his chair.

"Think about it, take a minute," Halloran cautioned. "You haven't answered my question."

Anson replied in a steady voice, "Yes, sir, give me a chance to show you what I can do." The two men stared at each other intently, and the bond between officers began.

"I've read your record, I think I have a pretty clear idea of what you've been able to do. You need more small arms training. Learn to bring them down if you can, not kill 'em. We need them for questioning. Not as easy as it sounds. Takes marksmanship. Practice. Law enforcement officers are drilled to do the double tap in the center of the chest, to down the subject to limit the possibility of harm to themselves. In intelligence work, we want them alive, breathing and able to talk. Ours is a risky business. Wear the damned vest at all times." He paused.

"Anson, not to make too fine a point of it, but you were issued prostheses. You're not wearing them."

"They're not exactly comfortable yet, and I'm faster in the chair." Anson shook his head.

"Racing wheels?"

"Yeah, good ones."

Halloran realized that accounted for the upper body strength and flexibility that he saw displayed in the younger man's movements. "Alright, I don't care if you use them in the office, but bring your feet with you to work. Get some solid shoes and some field boots if you don't have them already. Monday morning, business casual for the office, bring extra sets of clothing for the field to store in your locker. First few months you will be training to fill in for the day duty officer who will be out on leave soon. You will learn the laws, procedures, study maps, and maintain staff schedules, among other things. Do the weapons training and the self-defense courses. In your boots, please. Duty officer's name is Gladys Rodriquez, pronounced Glah-dees, it's a kind of lily. Don't forget that."

"You mean I'm hired?" the younger man reacted with astonishment.

"Yes, you passed all the tests, your recommendations were fine. Probation is six months. I was out of the office in Washington when you were interviewed by Joel Schwartz. He is second here, Chief of Forensic Accounting. Behind the door there's a cane."

"I don't need a cane, sir."

"Quit calling me 'sir,' so often." Halloran looked at the new recruit with a glare that said, "I know that, hand me that damned cane."

Anson quickly swung his chair around, grabbed the carved wooden cane from its spot behind the door and stuck it over the desk into Halloran's outstretched hand. He watched the tall distinguished man, face yet unlined, black hair greying. Halloran used the cane to assist getting up from his ergonomic armchair that was not exactly standard issue. The older man came carefully around his desk to shake the hand of the younger man.

"Welcome. Tell the people in Portland you got a job as dog catcher, or office manager, something, whatever suits. Use your judgment. If you need housing, ask Gladys for a list of approved, reasonably safe places." Halloran leaned against the wall to take the weight off his right leg.

"Are you a vet, sir?"

"Oh, the leg? Line of duty. Fell off a dock." Halloran pulled a face, everyone asked him that. No one expected a director to have taken a dive in the field. Damn stupid thing to do all together.

"Docks can be slippery."

"I had help. Turn up at 8:30 Monday morning ready for work. See me at 10:00, I'll give you your first assignment. Alright?"

"What would be my first assignment, can I ask if it will be in the field?" Anson looked eagerly across the desk.

"Not quite yet." Halloran shook his head. "Figure out how to get us a fleet car that anyone on the team can drive. Hand controls installed. Used government vehicle is fine. Something heavy, seriously roadworthy. Not black. Urban camouflage. Battleship grey. Get it repainted if it comes in black. Equipped with communications. I didn't have any luck the last time I tried myself."

"I have some buddies, I'll make some phone calls." Anson smiled. "Thank you for the opportunity, I'll see that you won't regret it."

Halloran took one look at Anson's smiling face. Anson's reputation for ingenuity preceded him. *It's a car*, Halloran thought. *How the hell much trouble can he get into in his first week on the job?*

"Good. Monday. I've got to get on a conference call with Washington now. See Gladys. She's back at her desk now. She'll give you the list of preferred housing." The two men shook hands solemnly, and Anson speedily wheeled around towards the duty officer's desk.

6

ANSON'S FIRST DAY —
IF HE SAYS IT HE MEANS IT

———◆———

DAVID ANSON, ALL BRIGHT AND shiny in new business casual attire arrived early for his first day in the office. New job. New clothes. Not quite a new man yet. He found his grey government issue metal desk. Having had one on a remote Army base, he explored it. It took him five minutes to decide he must be missing something. There had to be more to this job than an old docking station and monitor, pencils, no pens, paper clips and a stapler that was jammed. Anson looked around for other assets. Finding none, he wheeled over to the duty officer's desk. Gladys only just arrived.

"Good morning, ma'am. I was wondering what to do until my appointment with Mr. Halloran at 10:00," he said pleasantly.

Gladys could see that keeping Anson busy was to be her own personal challenge, that, and preparing him to fill in for her on her impending leave. *Nice guy. He's another one of Halloran's overactive types, and not an office tamed one in the bunch. I'll kill him with paperwork first,* she decided. She seated herself firmly, swiveled around in her chair to face Anson.

"Okay, let me tell you how it is around here. It's Monday morning. Seems quiet, doesn't it? All hell will break out by 10:00 if it hasn't already. Halloran, we never call him Mister, only sir, if we can get away with it. He was a Naval officer, and they're into rank. He's into respect, not titles. He's here at 7:30 every morning. Orders are to leave him alone until 8:30, start of the business day. Emergencies only before 8:30, and that's a laugh because it's the one time you can catch him alone if you need to."

"I have an appointment with him at 10:00 to get my first assignment." Anson was concerned, how on earth could he survive a whole hour and a half with nothing to do?

"Yes, I see it on his calendar." She glanced at her computer monitor. "Not a good time, he'll miss it, not that he wants to," Gladys assured him. "They're just waking up in Washington now, and they will have him on a conference call by then. If he does miss your appointment, I can give you your assignment and help you to begin it."

"He mentioned getting him a car."

"You can do that and a few dozen other things. We will keep you more than busy, don't worry." Gladys laughed. "He had a problem doing that himself. They said his disability was temporary and wouldn't give him a vehicle to accommodate that. Personally, I think they're set on trying to keep him in the office. Safer that way. Andy, Fernando Vargas, is supposed to watch out for him, be his driver and his bodyguard."

V.J. Agarwal emerged from Halloran's office, notes in hand, waving to Gladys. "Good day, Glahdees, and you must be the new man. Hello and welcome! He is in a rare mood, I say! He is not liking that we have not yet found the group smuggling in the Russian Mafia. Another one has arrived. Best not to go near him for a while yet!" V.J. said this with all good humor in the voice he reserved for friends and relatives, sounding of his native Calcutta, then headed down the hall to his supervisor Joel Schwartz's office to regale him with details of Halloran's reception of their carefully harvested financial data.

"That doesn't sound promising," Anson remarked to Gladys.

"The boss gets over it quickly. We leave him alone for a while. Let's get started. Here's the Personnel Manual, read it and throw it in your desk drawer. Now for the good parts. Whatever you do, don't ever do anything other than work on your computer, or your Sat phone. You have unrestricted access for research only. Everything is tracked. You got something to do, online shopping, chat with the buds in 'Stan, whatever else, forget it. Get your own connection, do it out of the office. Be careful even then. Get paranoid early and stay that way. Remember that once you digitize anything it can be subpoenaed and seized. Think it, don't say it in print. We even have to watch what we say on the phone.

"Don't think that your desk is your own, either. Everything here is government property and subject to search and seizure. We respect each other's privacy, but Garvey, who is the security officer, has keys to everything.

"You got the confidentiality lecture from Joel Schwartz, right? The 'what happens in Vegas stays in Vegas's' type thing. What you see here, everything we do here is confidential, even the location of the building. People are going to ask you what you do, make up a cover story and stick to it. Personally, I lie a little bit, I tell the friends and relatives I'm a bookkeeper for a restaurant." The duty officer laughed. "You might tell people you work for a social service organization, and that you answer phones. Same thing, sorta true, and sorta not. Easy to remember. Got that?"

"I understand mostly. Halloran suggested I tell the folks at home I got a job as a dog catcher," said Anson with a humorous look on his face.

"He would, rat catcher is more like it," Gladys replied. "You'll catch on, sometimes it is as simple as thinking about what you say or do before you screw it up. Takes discipline to work here. He's not negotiable about some things which brings me to this." She passed Anson a copy of a pamphlet, the *Geneva Conventions with Protocols through 2005*.

Anson looked down at it dubiously, "The Geneva Convention?"

"Did he give you the lecture? It must be on the agenda for this morning. Read it. Memorize it. He's not negotiable about the treatment of suspects. Got himself into serious hot water in Washington about it. A previous Administration at one time had a set of different interpretations, and we heard that he gave them the benefit of his. He was a lawyer specializing in international treaties. We think that's what got him sent up here. Like you give a good lecture, you think you're so smart, let's see you practice it. Think you can handle that, Anson?"

"I am aware of the Convention. He did mention the subject, and I told him it would be a relief, and I meant it." Anson looked at Gladys with a sobering gaze.

"Good, because if he says it, he means it. Take notes if you have to.

"Moving right along here. Halloran insists on weapons and self-defense training and such like for all staff. Boss says you have to be in good condition to do any job. Fitness counts around here. We have our own gym on the third floor that doubles as an emergency accommodation for First Responders if necessary. Showers, decontamination, stuff like that. That's why we have the commercial kitchen, too.

"We'll get you your own custom classes, that is as soon as we find another instructor," Gladys paused and sighed. "It takes special qualities to work here. We go through instructors on a regular basis."

"What happened?" Anson asked anticipating a good story.

"It seems that the last instructor arrived late for a session. The group was in the gym waiting for him. Rankel and Andy Vargas took over and were demonstrating some moves. Rankel climbed up the rope to the ceiling. Andy was concealed behind a punching bag. As soon as the instructor came through the door they attacked. Damn near gave him heart failure. He wasn't that old either. We have an AED in the gym."

Anson laughed out loud. His day was looking up. "Thanks for warning me!"

"You'll have to do arms training," Gladys continued. "Even the analysts have to qualify every year. They are a challenge, let me tell you. The analysts are the kind of people who get up out of bed first thing in the morning, trip over their own brains, and think, 'What was that, some time I'll have to stop and figure that out. I'm too busy now.' That's the type of person you want in that job, always thinking. But they have to be able to protect themselves and others, too."

"Do I get to meet them?" Anson had the Cook's tour of the place already without seeing them.

"The analysts mostly stay in their own rooms. They have their own restrooms and everything for security reasons. They spend most of their time on calls, and reading and typing reports, stuff like that. We don't go in there unless invited. The place is all covered with charts and graphs, and maps. All sorts of different kinds of maps. The analysts come in handy when no one can figure out what's going on, especially if it's bad. Good at what they do or they wouldn't be here.

"You can tell who the analysts are because when they get out, all they do is talk and argue with each other. And with the self-defense instructor, we lost one that way too. All that physical activity makes them feisty. Watch yourself if you see one with a gun on the firing range, some of them can't shoot worth a damn."

Anson looked around the office, still unsure where the analysts might be located.

"You will have to qualify every year on small arms," she emphasized.

"How small?" Anson had reservations.

"Hand guns, me amigo, hand guns."

"Oh, that small," Anson stood over six feet and had ample sized hands to match.

"I've called our armorer. Bertha Wilkinson will fix you up with something you will feel comfortable using." Gladys smiled, already her new assistant yearned for guns and ammo. This was after all an armed federal agency.

"Wasn't this supposed to be a desk job?" Anson was still trying to figure out what he had gotten himself into by accepting a job offer from a federal agency about which virtually nothing was publicly known.

"Most days it is, but we need to be prepared for when it isn't. We don't put the real stuff in the job description." Gladys pulled open a drawer in her desk. "I keep my service piece here." She pulled up her maternity blouse, enough to show Anson the smaller gun in a holster at her waist. "This is the one I wear home. Used to wear it on my ankle, but it's getting tough to reach it down there." Gladys was about seven months and growing nicely. "You'll want to be armed most of the time on this job."

"I'm joining your party this morning. And how are we all doing? Good?" Bertha, an African American woman of stature, came up to Gladys's desk. She offered her hand to Anson, who found her handshake a strong one. She dressed in khaki work clothes because she was building a project on the bench in the Armory. "I've read your weapons qualifications. Good stuff. Should be useful."

Anson puzzled, field artillery experience in a war zone seemed a little off target for home country law enforcement.

Seeing his inquiring look, Bertha explained, "No experience is ever a loss. Expect the unpredictable around here. Perps can have military grade weapons, a problem for the locals who are not armed that way. We are not that limited. A person with recent battlefield experience could be a plus. You'll see things that you will recognize in the Armory, old favorites and some new foreign arrivals I find very interesting." She smiled knowingly. Anson was reputed to be a crack shot.

"First, let me ask, what do you have under those pants?" Bertha inquired.

"What?" Anson looked shocked.

"Not the top part. I understand you have prosthetic feet. Show me. Don't be shy. This is a professional consultation between, you, me and your supervisor. Roll up your pants Agent Anson."

The two women looked at him with quiet anticipation. He looked back. *She called me Agent Anson.* He felt an adrenalin rush. He rolled up his pants legs with alacrity, glad he'd worn his feet and his shoes for the first day at work.

"Hmm, standard VA issue." Bertha looked appraisingly at his lower limbs. "We can work with these. Right handed? Like knives?" Anson replied that he did have a favorite Army knife. "You just come right down with me to the Armory. We'll issue you some weapons. Can't hang around though. You'll have to go to the range to try them out. I'm building something special. Got a deadline. Can't buy everything out of a catalog. It's going to be here's your gun, what's your hurry!"

As Gladys predicted, Halloran missed his 10:00 a.m. meeting. Anson cheerfully spent the better part of the morning in the basement firing range and the afternoon calling a buddy strictly on the task of acquiring his idea of a suitable ride for his new commanding officer.

7

FINDING THINGS —
RESEARCH FOR THE BEGINNERS

———◆———

EM RALLIED DEANNA AND SANDY early the next morning, bravely fighting their end of college term lethargy. She needed them to work on her first important new clients' project.

"I need this not to be traced back to our IP address at home. Each device on the Internet has its own distinctive number, an Internet Protocol or IP address. It's structured like a long distance phone number with the first group of numbers indicating the largest network, and the last group of numbers indicating the device number."

"Boring, Mom." Deanna crossed her arms. She, her mother and Sandy were seated around the dining table plotting competitive research for Em's new client, Professor Kirbee.

"I'm going to teach you to research companies online, and you are going to the public library to use their computers. They have a thirty minute limit. Just change computers, go out for snacks, whatever, come back and do more until you finish. Take a notebook and a zippered folder each. Take everything with you every time you leave the computers. Take a handful of change from the jar in the kitchen for the printer.

"It's not boring if you like mind games. You are the hunter, matching wits with our targets. They are trying to hide their evil ways, and you are going to find them out."

Deanna mugged patience.

"How do you know they have evil ways?" Sandy looked puzzled.

"If they were doing legitimate business, they wouldn't be hiding it. I'll teach you the techniques to uncover what they might wish to keep hidden. Whatever you do, do not go into the university library. Too many inquisitive brains sitting in the seats, walking around, looking over your shoulder. Your right to privacy is a little better covered in a public library. Years ago the FBI tried to get librarians to report suspicious activity regarding a theft of patent data, I think. Too hard to do. Librarians fought turning over circulation records. Of course, now we have the Patriot Act, so any type of communication can be searched.

"Here's how we start, with the list of the companies and the product names, Alagash SunShyne, Prairie SunFyre, and Big River SunShyne. You will be looking for the people associated with these and comparing them to find the linkage. What do you see in them?" Em passed out papers to Deanna and Sandy. Neither girl replied. "Always ask yourself a lot of questions. Each name has a 'y' substituted for the 'i' that you would usually find in the word. Why?"

"To make it sound special, like advertising?" Sandy replied.

"Good, but also to make it unique, quick to find if you do a database search if you know it, and more difficult to find if you don't know the exact spelling. Hiding in plain sight. Adding a hyphen to a word also can make it more difficult. Some websites don't like hyphens at all, and you will have to search through an alphabetical list to find the word.

"Okay, so here's the method, type the word exactly, if it's

not found, search again by first letters," Em said.

"When computers first became common outside the government, universities and large organizations, I was not interested. All they did was crunch numbers and turn out bills. When they were used to handle information for the public, I got hooked on database searching during graduate school. It was simply a case of basic algebraic logic meets the Library of Congress card catalog online."

"Mom, cut to the chase." Deanna yawned dramatically.

"This stuff is fabulous, you'll love it. Basically, if you can figure out a library card catalog, an old one, or a library online catalog, you can search any database. They are all built on the same principles. Author, title, subjects and numerical access. Simple. Elegant. The OSS (Office of Strategic Services), the World War II predecessor of the CIA, used a card catalog system to organize intelligence data. So did the British intelligence operation at Bletchley Park. After World War II, the U.S. needed computer databases to organize the information in the massive amount of captured German documents. I even heard a rumor that Tim Gunn's mother started the library at the CIA.

"DARPA (Defense Advanced Research Projects Administration) used its brain trust to develop a high speed data network and designed it to be fault tolerant and fully redundant, able to withstand the destruction of part of its network in case of thermonuclear war. The network used the Internet Protocol, or fast packet switching, and it's now ubiquitous. The survivability causes difficulties when the government tries to close down rogue websites. It's an American homegrown innovation. Our tax dollars at work."

The girls looked at each other and rolled their eyes.

"After that, the government contracted with Lockheed Missiles, Air & Space to design a computer database interface called Dialog that could be used to search many different databases, even if they were created by a variety of organizations. The first two public government databases in Dialog were ERIC, Education Resources Information Center, and NTIS, National Technical Information Service. Originally, Dialog was command driven and required special training for librarians and other professional users."

"Mom, you're lecturing. We need to know this why?"

"What you need to remember is that the people who create the entries in the database can choose to make the information easily accessible or to hide the goodies so that only the people who know where they are already can find them. There are tricks to every trade, and library and information science has some good ones!"

"Librarians wouldn't hide things." Sandy looked doubtful.

"You're thinking of the sweet image of the person behind the Reference Desk or the Circulation Desk in a public library. Ask any serious researcher in a library or in an archives if they think they've been shown everything. The Freedom of Information Act is used to get government repositories to cough up what they've got.

"Librarians, curators, archivists, people charged with caring for information resources are generally smarter than the average bear and can be trickier. If they have something that needs to be protected from casual eyes or even determined eyes, they have a few simple ways to hide it in the database for the next generation of keepers to find. They can create one unique access point for the item, with no additional subject access. You need to know its exact name or its number. Each entry in a database needs at least one entry in the title/name file, or failing that at least one entry in the master numerical/accession file.

"With me so far?" Em paused to look at the girls who were munching bagel chips and looking distinctly bored.

"At least one name, or one number," Deanna said as she dug a chip deep into the cream cheese dip.

"No double dipping," chided Sandy.

Em sighed, she'd learned while working with children that they learned quickly even if you could have sworn they were not listening to you at all.

"Right, Deanna. Now, to make that name more difficult to find they can give the name an unusual form. It can be made into a phrase with words that have little meaning that must be searched as a completely correct phrase to be found, like 'this, that, and, one.' There are twenty five or more of these little words in English that are called 'stop words' that don't return valid search results. Can you imagine how many results you would get if you searched on the word one?"

"Hundreds of thousands." Deanna demolished the bag of bagel chips.

"Yes, and many more. Or, the name can be turned into an acronym that you have to know to find like MVS TSO, TIRKS or UNHCR. Those are all real but are unusual combinations of letters.

"So, back to your list of what we know. Before you go to the library take the list and enlarge it. List all of the variations you can think of, put in hyphens, spaces, abbreviations, initials and common misspellings and typos. How many times have you seen collectible spelled 'collectable?' Be creative. Be thorough. I use free association, sounds like, looks like…that's what I did for the patent and trademark searching I've already done for Professor Kirbee. Check off the ones that you've searched on the list, make notes, and print what you find. Checking off is important because at the end of the day, no one can remember everything that they've searched."

"How do you know all this stuff, Mom?"

"Good training and lots of experience, and a good budget for commercial database use. I go back to before the Internet had color and images, when we had to Telnet and FTP, and the search engines were called Archie and Jughead. A devious mind comes in handy, of course. That's why I picked you to do this. The devious mind, I mean." Em smiled that wide wicked grin of hers.

"Here's a twenty for a snack and cappuccino. Enjoy yourselves. This is a marketable skill you are learning."

The landline phone rang, and Em rose from the table to answer it. She insisted that a secure wireline phone was a mission critical part of any home. The girls couldn't quite see that yet.

"Your mother is scary," Sandy said in an undertone.

"No, really? Try growing up with that. Did she say, 'don't ask me how I know that' every other sentence?"

"No, I don't think so." Sandy was not about to remind her friend she had pretty much grown up with it through her high school and now college years.

"Then she hasn't gotten to the good stuff yet. Let's go before she gets off the phone. Coffee first!"

8

PROFESSOR KIRBEE TAKES A CHANCE

———————

EM WAS PLEASED, AND RELIEVED. It seemed her apprentices had done well. Deanna and Sandy returned from the public library before lunch, each with a stack of printouts for her to review. They stood in front of her looking happy and secretive, ready to surprise her with their business savvy and competitive research results.

"You were right! They are up to it!" Sandy exclaimed. She rarely spoke up to anyone except to Deanna, so Em knew their efforts in the library were fruitful.

"Or into it deep, up to their asses!" Deanna claimed in triumph.

"Deanna!"

"They are hip deep in the ol' muddy. Look what we found!" She shoved a seemingly disorganized sheaf of papers at her mother.

"I'll read everything. But why don't you tell me what you found. Hit the high spots, I'll read the details. Tell me what to look for in this pile of dead trees." Em smiled at them and raised her eyebrows in that way she had. It transformed her from mother into head of the enterprise and a formidable one at that. Em was anxious to make it a quick project for Kirbee and Hussein who desired speedy results.

Her patent and trademark searching had been done on the previous evening, and she finished the credit reports that morning.

"Okay, so we each took a company first, and we banged out the third one together. We looked for all the news articles we could find in the local newspapers and business journals. Not a lot of info there, but two of them got raided. One got raided by OSHA for violations, you know, unsafe working conditions. There were barrels of chemical waste leaking into a storm drain. The neighbors complained of the smell." Deanna paused to catch her breath. "They got fined."

Sandy took up her pile of papers, on top of which Em could see a neatly organized sheet of notes. Sandy read aloud, looking to Em for approval. "I did the Missouri company. They were raided for hiring illegal aliens and housing them on the property in trailers behind the factory with no running water or electricity, only port-a-johns."

"Let me guess, they got fined, too," Em conjectured disapprovingly. "Anybody go to jail over this?"

Sandy shook her head regretfully. "Not that we could find."

"What about the company in Maine?"

"They were a little bit of both. They were operating out of a rented warehouse in town. When they left that one, the next people found drains clogged with this awful polluted sludge stuff. They moved farther out and set up business in another old factory building. When the inspectors caught up with them, the employees ran away, out the back door and into the woods. Unbelievable, right?" Deanna asked.

"No, actually, all too believable. It's consistent with their credit reports, they are a mess as well. They have a decided tendency to step away from their bills."

"Funny, Mom, this company called Transaxia in West Virginia turns up in all three searches somewhere."

"Did you both find that?"

The girls nodded.

"That's good research, that's not easy to pull out. It's only in some of the credit histories. Some credit rating services dig more deeply than others. Transaxia is listed as the corporate parent, which means they own these three little bad guys. I can call the bad guys thieves and pirates, 'cause I don't work for a corporation that has to be careful not to be sued by the competition. It's refreshing, actually. Congratulations!"

The girls could see the grin, Em was pleased with them and their work. Deanna did a little happy jive around the room as Sandy looked on grinning.

"Give me your time and expenses. I'll scan your material, which I hope you have in some sort of order, Deanna, and I'll see if I can get it all pulled together to give to the professors this afternoon after lunch."

Em crossed the living room into the kitchen to pick up a basket to take out with her to the garden. She spotted an upright box partially hidden behind a kitchen chair. "What's that?" she asked.

"Just a little something we bought for the kitchen." Deanna saw the skeptical look on her mother's face. "It's a sort of a mixer. We thought it would be good to have." Deanna's smile showed her orthodontically straight teeth. After so many years in braces hiding her smile, an all-out toothy grin showed Em that something was up.

"Please organize your work. I'm going out to the garden to pick things for lunch."

Deanna and Sandy exchanged glances. They were careful to wait until Em, wicker basket in hand, cleared the living room door and the porch outside.

"Okay, let's do it!" Deanna pulled the box out from its hiding place behind the chair.

———◆———

Em returned from the garden with a selection of greens

and fresh veggies for salad — leaf lettuce, Boston Bibb, Oak Leaf, Butter Crunch, baby carrots and snow peas. She was almost to the kitchen when she heard a loud pop followed immediately by an intense fizzing, hissing sound. Then came gales of laughter from Sandy and guffaws from Deanna.

In the kitchen she was astonished to see Deanna, and Sandy, too, covered in bright yellow orange slime. The slime dripped from the ceiling, splattered the counters, cabinets and the floor. The girls stood in front of a stand, on it stood an almost empty liter plastic soda bottle containing the remaining inch of orange sludge.

Em sucked in her breath and dropped the basket onto the kitchen table.

"I think it got too thick." Deanna wiped some of the goo off her face and licked her fingers. "It tastes good though." She had obviously been standing closest.

"Lord in Heaven, what were you doing?" Em stood there, stunned. This was not a day when she needed an accidental spill of room sized proportions.

Deanna and Sandy turned around quickly, guilt literally plastered all over their faces. Only their eyes were not covered in orange. For once, Deanna was speechless.

Sandy pitched in. "Deanna's trying to make mango pineapple soda with the spring water. It's the bomb!"

"I can see that. It's all over my kitchen." Em fought back the impulse to yell. After all, they had a great uncle who made a successful business of bathtub gin.

Deanna, seeing her opportunity, brought her mother a small glass of the orange drink. Em found it very tasty.

"You may have to strain the mango puree or cook it. I think you probably need essence of mango and not all the pulp. Carbonated soda is usually thin. I'll take a refill on my glass and go read your research while both of you clean up the kitchen before lunch. Em retreated to the living room to digest their research and prepare a presentation for the clients. Sometime later, Em had prepared a summary of their research, a listing of materials, scanned the paper copies and burned it all to disks. Lunch was late.

By the time Deanna called her in, the kitchen floor gleamed, the cabinets shone and the counters were almost dry. However, Em was convinced she would be finding dripping mango pulp inside the cabinets for some time. The sand painted ceiling was another matter, there were still splotches of color. Fortunately, sand paint seemed to have fallen out of style, like wing tips on shoes and fins on cars.

The girls had changed clothes, and Deanna's hair was still damp. But the kitchen smelled delicious, and there were large chunks of mango and pineapple in the salad that the girls proudly presented to Em for lunch.

By midafternoon Em was prepared to call Professor Kirbee. He answered on the first ring and invited Em to meet with him at his home at 4:00. This gave her barely enough time to put together the paper copies and the disk and to change hastily into a dress suitable for a business conference with her client. She chose a favorite tailored dark navy shirtdress with buttons that stopped above the knee and a hem that landed right below it. Now a wee bit tighter than before, the dress would be likely to ride up when she sat down. With limited options, this seemed to be her best choice. Em slipped on low heels and was ready to go.

Her parting words to her daughter and Sandy were, "Make dinner!"

"How's mango chicken sound?" Deanna asked sheepishly.

"How many mangos did you buy?" Seeing the look on her daughter's face she said, "Forget that I even asked. Can you make it hot and spicy? That would be great."

Once in the car, Em tried to relax. Her dress rode up but she ignored it. Her mind was on Professor Kirbee. This would be her second meeting with her first serious client. She liked both Professors and enjoyed their back and forth conversation, the way old friends argued good naturedly with one another. Kirbee himself seemed to be a genial man and had an open and intelligent countenance. His face was roundish with bright blue eyes, and a little red, probably from exposure to sunlight, Em guessed.

Although the weather was fair, Em barely took the time to admire the well-tended lawns and shrubbery of Kirbee's neighborhood or the intricate designs of the terracotta and brickwork of his house. She hiked up the brick walk with determined steps.

Kirbee, of course, anxiously waited for her and stood at the open door to greet her.

"I am so pleased to see you so soon, Ms. Huber. From what you told me on the phone, it sounds as if you've done exactly what we needed." Kirbee placed a friendly hand on her shoulder and invited her into the house before she could even say, "Good afternoon, Professor."

"We can go over it together in the living room. Al can't be with us this afternoon, so I'm making tea. He makes much better coffee that I do. Ah, here's my girl. Here's Cleome."

An elegant Siamese cat with dark chocolate brown markings, alert eyes and graceful long legs approached from the living room. She made a mew of greeting that sounded almost like a word.

"Hello, to you, too. She's beautiful, Professor. Does she talk often? I have a black half Siamese named Ash who has a lot to say, it mostly sounds like he's complaining."

"Cleo is good company, and yes, she does talk. Please sit here on the sofa, and I'll go get the tea." The professor hustled off through the dining room towards the back of the house.

Em found a comfortable spot on the oatmeal colored roll arm upholstered sofa and looked around her. The fireplace on the outside wall was made of red brick, wide and deep, perfect for a good blaze. The wall above the mantel was bare. Telltale nail holes showed that two pictures of different sizes once hung there. Other walls in the room were bare, too, except for a well-known black and white photo of the Flat Iron Building in New York. The building's unusual triangular shape made it a landmark. It was a handsome room, with leather club chairs by the fireplace and lamps on small tables. The woodwork was dark mahogany, as it had been when the house was new. A rich red Bokhara oriental carpet in the Elephant Tracks pattern of large repeating diamond shapes surrounded by a decorative border lay on the floor.

When the professor returned carrying a large silver finish tray with tea things and two unopened bags of good cookies, he found Em staring at the carpet. Her work organized on the coffee table in front of her for a formal presentation to her client, she seemed more intent on surveying Kirbee's floor covering. He set the tray down and watched her.

Em looked up at him, and he saw a smile playing across her lips. "I love patterns, the more intricate the better. This is a wonderful rug."

"Have you found it?" Kirbee asked. "I assume you are looking for the intentional flaw."

"There," she pointed to a discontinuity in the border, in the corner. "Am I right?"

"You could be. Al would say that only Allah can make a perfect thing. The workers who made the carpet created an imperfection in the design."

"Shall I pour?" Em took up the teapot that had been placed before her. Kirbee took his tea and several cookies and sat down in the club chair closest to her.

Em set her tea aside after a few polite minutes. She commenced by showing Kirbee her lists and flow charts with circles and arrows showing the supply chain from Transaxia, the manufacturer of the parts, to the three smaller companies that did the assembly, marketing and sales. She had another chart showing how the officers and directors of Transaxia related to the subsidiaries. During her presentation Kirbee spent much of the time studying Em, and only occasionally glancing down at her carefully prepared charts. She tried the spreadsheets with projected sales and revenue. Finding his eyes more often on her, she stopped.

"So, what do you think, Professor?"

"Al has convinced me we are being swindled, so what you report about these companies doesn't surprise me. Both of you point out they cannot be making much real money on this. SunSprite Version 3, even incomplete when it was stolen, was worth more than these ridiculous little products."

As Em handed Kirbee a refill of his cup of tea, his fingers brushed hers. Kirbee absent mindedly loaded his cup with cream and at least four teaspoons of sugar that Em counted. He stirred it vigorously. Kirbee returned to his club chair, abstracted.

"If you are going to go to all the trouble to steal something like SunSprite, why not go all out?" Kirbee said at last.

"Why not indeed, Professor?" Em was skeptical as well.

"Call me Frank. If we are going to work together, can we be on a first name basis? May I call you, Em?" He smiled at her, blues eyes bright with interest over his very strong, very rich and sweet cup of tea.

"Yes, if you like," replied Em. She looked down at the spreadsheet in her hand and then up again quickly to find Kirbee still smiling at her. The house was still. They were alone except for the Siamese cat who chose that moment to jump up on the couch to sit next to Em.

"She must like you. Cleome's usually quite shy of strangers. She takes a while to be at ease with new people," Kirbee said, looking at the cat fondly.

"Cleome probably smells my cat, Ash," suggested Em.

"Perhaps it's that lovely perfume you are wearing, like delicious fruit," ventured Kirbee.

Em tried to stifle a laugh but couldn't hold it in. "I'm afraid that's not perfume. I raised three very inventive children, and sometimes I didn't think my sanity would survive it. You may appreciate this. My youngest Deanna has a semi-professional interest in beverages. She was trying to make sparkling mango pineapple soda in the kitchen before lunch. Her mixture was either too thick or she used too much carbonation. Her new fizz making gadget must have created too much pressure in the large bottle and it went whoosh!" Em raised her hands in a sweeping gesture to demonstrate the explosion. "And it blew up all over the kitchen." Her hands flew out clipping the cat's nose. "Sorry Cleome! I must have picked some up on my skirt," Em said, mildly embarrassed.

Charmed, Kirbee asked, "What did you do?"

"Well, I was sorely tempted to shriek. Then I remembered that children who take things apart often end up as engineers. Even Snapple had to start somewhere. It tasted very good. I think that I'll suggest she add a little coconut milk and make it into a smoothie. Her mango smoothie is to die for."

Kirbee laughed knowingly. "I set fire to my lab last year. We were at a crucial stage of development of Version 4. We were working on the amplification of sunlight on a very bright day in August. You can guess the rest. It set off all the smoke alarms in the building. Everybody from the other labs evacuated. The street vendors in their trucks did a booming business. We had it out before the fire engine, the hook and ladder, and the fire marshal arrived. We may never live it down. It was a small fire. We made some upgrades to our lab after that. Your daughter has my sympathies." Kirbee looked to Em for her understanding.

"I can only hope her experiments don't get out of hand.

Again." Em sighed. "It really was an awful mess."

"If I remember correctly, Em, your son was gifted. Acoustics, wasn't it?" Kirbee surprised Em with this, and she wondered who he might have been talking to about her and her family.

"Joshua was always a noisy kid, banging pots and pans. His first instrument was the alto saxophone, and then he wanted to learn the drums. The sax was bad enough, but then there was drum practice. We didn't even get a good drum solo, it turned out that he was experimenting with the production of sound. When Deanna first took up the cello, she sounded like a dying cow. He was fascinated, he studied wind, percussion and string instruments. We sent him off to college to get a little peace around the house. I can't think who he takes after."

With humorous disdain Kirbee, the distinguished inventor, said, "You can't? I don't remember that your ex-husband had a particularly original mind."

"No, you have to be able to allow the possibility of being wrong once in a while to be creative. Sometimes things don't work out. Huber is never wrong." Em clanked her teacup back in its saucer. The subject of Harley Travis Huber was closed as far as she was concerned. Frank Kirbee recognized this with some satisfaction.

"Time to get back to the business at hand. We have three disreputable companies linked to one that looks, on first pass to be a more legitimate operation. Transaxia has a better physical plant, and balanced financials, which we have to allow may be the result of illicit enterprises." She paused. "Frank, will you play twenty questions with me?"

Kirbee raised his eyebrows. He looked at her, his smile grew into a grin of anticipation. If the lady wanted to play games, he could easily be persuaded to do that.

Em read his expression accurately. "No, no, it isn't a game like that. It's a way of," she wanted to say eliciting information, but thought better of that, and said instead, "figuring out what we're dealing with. If any of the questions I ask cause you concern over sensitive issues, let me know."

Kirbee was amused. He flirted with Em, "I'll do my best to be…"

"Answer simply. Let's start with the officer list of the four companies. Please look at it and tell me if you know any of them or recognize any of the names. Notice how the names reappear on the various lists."

"No, sorry, Em."

"No one? Not a single one?"

"More cookies? These are quite good. They are from the bakery down on Orange Street." Kirbee pulled a saucer sized cookie out of the bag. He munched happily. Em reached for the bag. The cookies were rapidly disappearing in Kirbee's direction, and she took one to be on the safe side. "I almost bought cupcakes," he said with relish.

"All business meetings should be so well provisioned. Thank you, Frank. The men on the list." Em made an effort to keep Kirbee on task. He was distractible and enjoying her company as much as appreciating her research.

"Should I know them?"

"I was afraid that you wouldn't. One way to extend the research on a company is to gather personal and professional information about its executives, directors and key players. It might be considered profiling. I prefer to think of it as biographical research, it sounds innocuous that way."

"But it is really profiling," Kirbee reached for another cookie.

"Well, yes, and when I did it on this crew there wasn't a genius in the bunch. No offense, Frank. But they are not playing in your league. There's not a single scientist in among them, a couple undergraduate degrees in business for what that's worth, some jail time for fraud, and several DUIs. Not a good sign. We are missing something. The brains are elsewhere. I think that the money is elsewhere, too. I suspect the parent company could be a domestic chop shop for counterfeiting products. No need to get them by Customs that way.

"Have you ever heard mention of Transaxia?" Em moved forward on the couch and tried valiantly to get Kirbee to focus on her questions.

"No, and I haven't been to West Virginia since long before we thought up this project, before we even planned it," Kirbee replied, a slight grin on his lips.

"That was going to be my next question." Em rewarded herself with a bite of chocolate chip cookie. "Do you have any enemies, Frank?"

Kirbee looked at her sharply, the smile dropped from his face. His lips tightened and his eyes narrowed. It was an unusual look for such a seemingly good natured man. He was silent. Em waited for him to speak. What he chose to say, and when he chose to say it, might give her a strong indication of a direction to pursue. She could see Kirbee sorted memories. When he spoke after several minutes, he gave an obviously well edited statement.

He said, "No one who would operate in this way. We know our professional colleagues in academic institutions and our commercial competition. They would exploit the technology themselves, claiming independent development. As a precaution, we use only our own graduate students as lab assistants, and we are obsessive about security. More tea?"

This of course, was not an answer helpful to Em. The length of time that Kirbee took to compose his answer made her suspicious. She accepted his encouragement to have another cup of tea.

"May I say that you don't seem surprised by all of this?" Em looked at Kirbee over her teacup.

"I had found some of it out myself, yes. And I trust Al's judgment. We needed an outsider with qualifications to confirm it for us, as we've said." Kirbee's smile returned.

"Professor Kirbee, Frank, these people have no scruples.

You can see that from the news coverage, especially the way they treat their workers, and their contempt for environmental safety. There is something badly off here." Em sat forward on the edge of the sofa, towards Frank Kirbee who was seated comfortably on the club chair facing her.

"Organizations are like individual people, they have patterns of behavior. We call them business models when we are being diplomatic. This takes in everything the business does from how they treat their employees, suppliers, creditors and customers, to how they handle their trash. With these companies, we have documented abuse of workers and the environment. In this case, I think it's fair to say of their business model that it's based on fraudulent practices." Em paused for effect. "Their websites are only about two years old, and all of them were created by the same Internet developer that doesn't appear to exist. I don't know what they use for funds. They seem to have no established credit relationships. The subsidiaries might even pay their workers in cash.

"One of the easiest ways to tell if a company is not doing good business is its pattern of paying bills. These three either pay their bills late or don't pay them at all, and may change suppliers to avoid payment. When they move, they leave bills behind.

"On top of that, the numbers don't make any sense. There's not enough profit generated to go through all this effort. There has to be something else that we are missing." As she spoke, Em used her hands to emphasize her points as she often did when she warmed to a topic. It caused her to slip further forward on the couch.

Professor Kirbee broke eye contact with her and looked down. She followed his gaze, the lowest buttons on her dress had managed to work themselves free, and her dress had hiked up her thigh. She'd given Kirbee an ample view of her inner thighs and brief flash views of blue with pink polka dots. Em felt her face flush as she pressed her knees together swiftly and tugged the skirt of her dress down.

"Version 5, that has to be it," Kirbee said in a genial voice. With growing amusement, he watched Em wriggle, maneuvering her dress while jouncing a surprised Cleome on the couch next to her.

Em managed to tug the skirt down enough and to secure one of the errant buttons before she decided to move on. *This is certainly not the most embarrassing thing that I've had happen in a business meeting, not by a long stretch,* she reflected.

"We know where the specs went now, to Transaxia. Is it possible that they are being paid to do this, in anticipation of being able to prove first use of the technology?" Em asked as she gave her skirt one last frustrated tug.

Kirbee admired both the scenery and her determination to continue. "We have published some of our early work and have had a patent application pending on Version 3 for some time, so we would be first filers. Patent laws have changed, Em."

"I think we need to find the link between here and West Virginia, between your lab and Transaxia. It almost seems like a subcontract to them." Em gave Cleome a pat, the cat accepted it readily from her.

"It has Al on the verge of closing the lab to anyone besides either one of us. Or moving the project to a… more secure facility, shall we say. He is that concerned." Kirbee shook his head, worry apparent on his face.

"Em, can you keep looking, is there more that you can do?" Kirbee hesitated, and said, "Even if we can't use it in court?"

Em nodded her head in agreement. She had a few more creative ideas to pursue.

"You will have to do it without access to the lab or our logs, unfortunately. Leave that aspect to us." Kirbee focused again, now that the very pleasant distraction had been remedied.

"I'll see what I can dig out for you and be in touch in a

day or two at the most."

"Well, I'll read your material and I'll get Al to read it to see if any of the names mean anything to him. I've enjoyed our meeting. It is getting late, would you care to stay to dinner? I have a nice filet of Mahi Mahi to share, and a good wine to go with it. Cleome's fond of fish, too. We could continue with your game of Twenty Questions, I don't think we got past five." The cat purred emphatically as Kirbee stroked her head.

"Thank you so much, Professor. I appreciate the offer, that's certainly tempting. Another time perhaps. My daughter and her friend are making me a special dinner, with mangos," Em said with a little genuine regret.

Kirbee passed her an envelope. "Here's the first payment towards your fee."

Em, who had not yet given him an invoice, hoped he didn't know she could truly use the money that month. She thanked him for it without opening the envelope. They agreed that M. E. Huber & Associates would continue to work on the project, and that they would meet again that week.

Em rose and with relief smoothed down her dress. Kirbee stood up with her. At the front door, he shook her hand warmly, placing one hand over hers.

As Em walked down to the van, she was pleased to have a check. And, after several lean months in which she had no dates, she'd been asked to stay to dinner. And games. She'd just turned down, at least for the duration of the project, the company of an interesting man of suitable age, who had an appreciation for short skirts. Her practical side couldn't help noticing the substantial house, but also the empty walls. Had he sold the art that once hung there? Curiosity got the better of her, she pulled over a block away from Kirbee's house. When she opened Kirbee's envelope she found a check drawn on his business account signed by both partners for double anything she could conceivably have billed for two days of work. Em was determined to get to work to earn the full amount. She was not in business to give refunds, and she could easily pass her bank branch on the way home to deposit the very nice check.

9

NEW CAR — IS THERE A HUMMER IN YOUR FUTURE?

———

A T THE STROKE OF 8:30 that morning, Anson presented himself in Michael Halloran's office. It was surprising what constituted an emergency for one or another of the staff who saw Halloran as a sitting duck that early. Anson's timing was military precise. Bertha was just leaving.

"Good morning, sir. The new car is coming in this morning by rail. We'll need to go down to the station to pick it up." Anson had a handful of paperwork he attempted to place on the desk in front of Halloran. Andy Vargas and Rankel jostled behind Anson for space in Halloran's small office.

"Good morning, that was fast. Why is the car coming by rail? And what am I signing for?" Halloran made no move to touch the paperwork.

"It's coming by rail because they are sending some replacement equipment north, and it's cheaper. No driver, no gas required." Anson paused, and seeing no response, he continued. "And it still needs some work. It's a used vehicle and has got dings in service and needs some engine work. Nothing serious, sir."

"How serious?"

"It stalls in low gear sometimes. They flushed the lines, and it's better. Probably sand in the fuel line. Leroy says no problem, he can fix it. The new lines were ordered. We can pick them up at the main Post Office on our way back, along with the adaptive controls and commo gear. The boxes have gone through security check, and they're being held for us. That's what you're signing for, sir, the gear," Anson stated and held his breath. He sat in the wheelchair in front of Halloran's desk in anticipation.

Halloran reviewed the requisitions, which seemed to be in order. Without looking up he asked, "Why are you in your boots and fatigues this morning, Lieutenant? Would this have anything to do with the fact that this vehicle is coming from the Army? We won't put that vehicle in our inventory until it's tested and road worthy."

"Uh, everything else was in the wash. You let Garvey wear his," Anson said hopefully.

Having raised three sons alone, Halloran had heard this justification more often than he cared to remember and contented himself with a stern look.

"I'll need some help driving down and back, sir."

"We can go with him," Andy Vargas volunteered instantaneously.

"I figured. Okay, Anson, here's your paperwork, you can go. This better be legit. Rankel and Vargas stay here a minute."

The men changed places in front of the boss's desk, Anson wheeled around them and out into the hallway.

"Come straight back here, no test driving around the state. And keep Anson out of trouble." He paused. "Why do I feel like I have Radar O'Reilly working for me?"

"Probably because you do. We'll take care of him, he's new," replied Andy. The two agents made it out of the office as quickly as they could, almost taking Anson down with them. "We're all good, let's go!"

Anson wedged himself into the back seat of the economy sized black fleet car. "You need a bigger staff car."

"Tell us about it, buddy. Try doing extended surveillance in this. We roll up in one of these, and we look damned silly. Here come the analysts," quipped Rankel riding shotgun.

Anson smiled, this was about to change. "I'll work on that next." They drove around to the back of the railroad yards, to a siding off the main line. A freight train composed of sealed box cars and flatcars with bulky equipment covered by tarp or in full camo stood ready for departure. The three men watched as a crane lifted the vehicle off the flat car. Several soldiers in fatigues pulled the dust cover off the Humvee. It did show the dings Anson mentioned in passing to Halloran. One fender was obviously a replacement, the other dented, and there was a spray of pockmarks all over the front and sides.

A young woman in camo approached the three agents. "Lieutenant Anson, nice to get to meet you. Skip's told us about you. Sign here. What are you going to do with this old thing?"

Anson gave her a winning smile. "We are repurposing it for civilian work. Tell Skip thanks for me."

Anson guided his wheelchair over to the Humvee, placed his hand on the fender and said, "Okay civilians, who wants to take it for a drive?" After some haggling between them, the choice made, Rankel climbed into the driver's seat for his first lesson. Andy Vargas had relevant experience having driven a Humvee in 'Stan, so he let his partner drive, for once. As directed they did a tour of the city, not the state, with a stop to load up gear at the Post Office shipping dock.

"Approach the building from the west. If we go up the street, we'll drive under the boss's window," Anson told Andy who now drove the new "bus."

"Roger that, Lieutenant."

Once alone with his prize in the basement motor pool, Anson reviewed the transmittal paperwork and the manifest of communications gear and new controls for the Hummer.

A shorter man with slicked back black hair and a dark suntan on his well-developed biceps wiped his hands on an oily rag and sauntered over. "So, you got it. Sweet ride."

"Well, not quite yet I'm afraid, Leroy. Skip's report said it stalls at low speed. We experienced that, too, driving it over here. Coughs when it does it. Loudly. Sent some people scurrying out on the street." The two men laughed.

"If it's got wheels and an engine, I can handle it. We won't show it off until it's fixed though." Leroy took the several sheets of paper containing scrawled notes from Anson. "Looks like your friend Skip's thorough. Lots of replacement parts." Opening the back cargo doors, Leroy asked, "What's all this stuff?"

"Most of it is communications. One of my specialties. I'll install it. If I run into problems, I have a buddy who will help out." Anson could claim useful friends in all sorts of places. "You've got to keep it locked up. There's some sensitive stuff here. I had to get the boss to sign for it. Listen, before we put that stuff in, what about your friend in the neighborhood, the one that does the paint work? If I give you a sketch for urban camo with the colors, can he do it?"

"Oh, he can do it alright. The man is an artist. Problem is, can we pay him? Even the boss must have a budget for 'candy.' Some of my man's business is, how shall I say, not quite…"

"Legit?"

"Yeah, maybe, anyway we can't exactly have him submit an invoice for payment. If you want the boss to pay for it, it has to be grey. You know that right?"

"I've heard. Battleship grey. Well, we sure as hell can't drive it out on the street looking like that, it looks like it belongs in a war zone," he said with a laugh. "I'll ask

Gladys if the boss has money for 'candy,' off the record expenses.

"Listen, I've got another one coming. A fast one. Needs some paperwork signed so it can be adopted. It's khaki right now and will need another paint job. I'm thinking something in the silver range." Anson rightly determined that one batch of paperwork at a time was all he could get across Halloran's desk.

"Fair warning. A twofer. I'll tell him." Leroy eyed his new charge, anticipating the challenge of returning it to good running order. "Anson, you could be a valuable addition to the team."

10

FEEDING CLEOME

———◆———

THE SPRING AFTERNOON, MILD AND sunlit, drew Em's gaze away from her computer and out a window of the Spring House. The centenarian sugar maples were spreading their half grown leaves to the sun. With hidden intelligence, the trees reached outward and upward with intent to catch every unobstructed ray of sunlight. On days like this, with a light breeze in their branches, it was almost as if you could hear the trees growing fresh new leaves. Em dressed in her work clothes, a favorite old tee shirt with a worn collar band and a design of whales across the front and old khaki pants. She curled her bare toes into the wool of the Indian Oriental carpet beneath her feet. Gazing out the window, she sipped her tea and absorbed the calm after the emotional tempest of the previous evening. She had an uncanny instinct for TV news, perhaps developed over a lifetime of viewing that included the first moon landing and coverage of the Kennedy assassination. In any case, her instinct for when to tune in had been spot on the previous evening.

———◆———

On her return from her evening out to the concert, Em

flipped through the channels and was startled by a local newsflash. Standing against a darkened background of a usually quiet city park, a local news personality announced that the body of a distinguished science professor had been found there. Witnesses reported hearing raised voices, a woman's screams and shots fired. To Em's horror, the body was identified as Professor Ali Hussein. The time of death given was shortly after 9:30. Whatever might happen in other parts of town, drive by shootings, convenience store holdups, gang violence, or plain interpersonal disputes turned violent, street crime happened less frequently in and around that particular park.

Deanna recognized their client's name and exclaimed, "Didn't you tell me you and your friends from work saw him at the concert in Woolsey Hall tonight?"

"No, no! It was Professor Kirbee who I saw with a group of his faculty friends. They have some of the best subscription seats in the center of the orchestra section. He has a full head of white hair that's pretty unmistakable. We were up in cheaper seats in the balcony. We were on the right side up close enough to see the orchestra very well, so we were almost directly above him."

"Was he there for the *entire* concert?" Deanna asked.

"That's the odd thing. You know the audience for a classical concert is generally dead quiet." Deanna nodded her head ruefully, she'd been dragged to enough of them to know what it was like. "Most of the audience is either older people, or music students. No one whispers, no one gets up, and if you cough too loudly, your seat neighbors give you dirty looks."

"I could never last past the Intermission when I was a kid."

"Too true, Dee. Anyway, it surprised me when I saw a university policewoman come down the aisle to call Professor Kirbee out. He got right up and left with her. Several people had to stand up to let him out quickly. It came towards the end of the concert."

"Probably about the other Professor," Deanna conjectured. "Maybe they needed him to make a statement, or maybe they needed him to identify the body."

"And that's not the only odd thing that happened last night...."

A chime from the laptop startled Em out of her memories. Only the inbox for her new research business chimed with incoming mail. To date there had been few of those emails, from one active client, Professor Frank Kirbee. Em hastened to open the email box, hoping there wasn't more seriously bad news. The death of her client's partner threw the future of her research project into question as well as her plans for the income it might provide. Sure enough, a note arrived from Frank Kirbee, but it was certainly not what she expected.

—◆—

M.E.,

Can't make meeting. Need to be away for a few days. Please feed Cleome. Start today. Key in the base of the small flowerpot. 6R 9L pass1R 12L

Thanks,

Frank

—◆—

"There goes our afternoon appointment," Em announced reluctantly. "This does not sound good, but he's already talked to the police, and he's not a suspect. What the hell's the combination for, I wonder?" She remembered the series of three flowerpots of descending sizes on the front steps of Kirbee's house. "I probably should water those flowers, too."

Em proceeded to finish the research she had in progress in the Library of Congress online catalog, making careful notes to document her search terms. When she'd had quite enough of that, she marched upstairs to her bedroom in search of presentable clothes and shoes for the expedition to Kirbee's house to feed the wise Siamese princess.

Although she felt she could wear anything she had around the house, including the paint splotched pants with the patch on the butt she wore gardening, visiting a client was a different matter. She leafed through her collection of skirts, not often worn, and chose a calf length printed linen then found a white jersey top with a draped neckline. The skirt was actually a size too large, but it would do for the afternoon. She should really take it in at the waist, but she wore it so infrequently since the layoff that it hardly seemed worth the effort. Slipping on shoes with two inch heels, also leftover from corporate days, Em headed downstairs.

Deanna and Sandy were going out to work and wherever after that. Since the appointment with Kirbee was already on her calendar, she reasoned they could find her if needed. Off she went in the aging van down into town to feed the prized cat. Traffic was light. She made a quick drive through the back roads, down Orange Street past the delis and onto Bacon Avenue, considering what could have made Kirbee bolt. Concern for his own safety seemed likely, hunting up a lead on Hussein's killer or possible kidnapping were her three top choices.

Em's lucky day, she actually found parking in front of Kirbee's house. As she got out of the van, she looked around cautiously. The house was close to the corner, and drivers often took the corner at higher speed. Up the street she noticed a green car with a man in running shorts leaning into the window, perhaps giving directions. She crossed the street and headed up the brick walk. All of the lawns on the street were raised a foot or two above the sidewalk paved in very large flagstone slabs. The brick front walk sloped gently up to grade level as it progressed towards the house.

On her way up to the house, Em, with leisure to appreciate it this trip, enjoyed looking at the architectural details of the façade. The terracotta tiles in a rosette pattern formed a band across the front with a large tile that depicted a vase full of tulips. All the terracotta and brickwork, with the gorgeous stained glass window by the staircase, it must be a European style.

As she remembered, the three terracotta flowerpots were there, one on each of the brick front steps that led to the heavily paneled front door. Em stooped to pick up the smallest pot that rested on the lowest step. The pot seemed heavier than she would have expected. It held a rootbound begonia plant with petite red flowers. She hoped to see the key under the pot, it was not there.

Oh shit, she thought. She looked at the bottom of the pot itself to see if the key stuck to it but saw only a raised triangle shape, one point towards the edge. The bottom of the pot looked as if it was a separate piece like a plate beneath a flowerpot to catch drainage, but it turned in her hand. On closer examination, she saw incised lines along the base of the pot itself. What she had at first taken for random lines, now looked like Roman numerals.

Professor Kirbee had a fondness for gadgets, she knew this from her visit to his home office. He was an inventor by trade. Em tried the combination she remembered from his email. Turning the triangle on the base plate to the Roman numerals, the combination worked the first time, and the base of the pot popped open revealing a round metal hiding place containing a ring of two keys. *How cute,* she said to herself. *A portable garden safe. I wonder if I can talk him out of one for the Spring House. It would look nice right by the bench in front.* Em removed the keys, closed the bottom of the pot and gave the plate on the bottom a spin to clear the last number of the combination. She put the potted begonia back on its step, made a mental note to water it and opened the house door with the first key she tried.

Em swung the heavy front door open easily, the hinges were well oiled. Cleome sat directly in front of the door. Greeting the cat, she found Cleome friendly and vocal in her own greeting. It pleased her that Siamese cats talked frequently, not so much to each other as to their human friends. Always curious, Em took the opportunity to look carefully at her surroundings and even poked her nose into Kirbee's study again. On the wall were his framed degrees and awards and pictures of various groups, including a picture of four soldiers in Vietnam era fatigues. Kirbee was in the center. *Now that I wouldn't have guessed. He must be older than I am,* she concluded.

Continuing to the kitchen at the back of the house, Em found Cleome sitting more or less patiently by her bowls. Kirbee had left a note with directions for feeding Cleome as well as cans of her favorite foods out on the counter. Which meant to Em he could not have been in a great rush to leave, and she wondered again what could have become of him. Surely he had been told to stay in the area.

Talking pleasantly to Cleome, Em opened the can of cat food and admired the view from the kitchen window. The backyard garden was meticulously laid out and maintained. A sundial and a pretty stone bird bath were placed in the center of circular flower beds. So unlike the plant riot of flowers, herbs, vegetable and weeds that inhabited the lawns of the Spring House. *I am just not cut out to be the owner of House Beautiful,* Em said to herself with a smile. *Much too neat for me.* She checked the litter box before she left, finding a cat carrier next to it in the small hallway that led to the securely bolted back door. It was a surprise there was no security system apparent, but then Kirbee must have kept what he valued most in his lab.

After giving Cleome more friendly attention and a few well-placed pats, Em locked up the house. The weather continued to be fine, but clouds moving in promised rain soon. She decided to water the flowerpots tomorrow if they needed it. As she approached the sidewalk, Em saw the man in running shorts she had noticed earlier. From a distance, he looked familiar. She stepped onto the sidewalk and took several steps along it, staying close to the yard side to allow him to pass her. Out of the corner of her eye, she perceived he seemed to increase his speed.

Suddenly she felt a hard thump to her shoulder that sent her off balance. Her heel caught in the flagged sidewalk. Her legs flew out from under her. To avoid falling, Em grabbed the jogger and tripped him as well. They fell back on the raised grass lawn. Em fell flat on her back with a cry. The jogger came down directly on top her, knocking the wind out of her lungs. She opened her eyes, gasped for breath and found a warm sweaty man staring down intently at her. Warm dark brown eyes, full head of brown hair with the beginning of grey and a sun bronzed face. Still trying to catch her breath, Em could feel his heart beating against her chest strong and steady.

"Are you alright? Oh my God, I didn't mean to hurt you!"

"My ankle," she gasped. She closed her eyes and swallowed hard, trying to catch her breath.

Down the street, in the green car, a man and a woman, both in uniform watched with rapt attention.

"What the hell is this guy doing?" the woman in the car asked her companion. "He goes any farther and she can have him up for assault. What did you tell him to do?"

"I said make her acquaintance, bump into her in a public place," was the gruff defensive reply from her partner in arms.

"Where did you get this guy?" she queried.

"Geology department. We needed someone legit and well-known around here. We've used him for his technical knowledge before. I showed him her picture, gave him the time of her appointment with Kirbee from his calendar, and he came up with the rest."

"Geology, it figures, it looks like he's channeling his inner cave man. Stop 'em and drop 'em." She was not convinced.

"I didn't tell him to knock her down and straddle her."

"What did he do, win a Noble Prize? Or an Oscar?"

"Not really, not yet. Did a three year stint with us. He's not a loose cannon."

"You surprise me," she replied.

"It's not all that bad, she hasn't kicked him in the balls yet," the man in uniform growled, but the woman accompanying him on this assignment did not agree with that.

On her back on the lawn, the scent of clean male sweat and a high volume of pheromones nearly overcame Em's sense of dignity. He was breathing deeply from running, and he pressed down on her in what might have been agreeable ways if he'd had the sense not to lean so hard.

"What do you think you're doing, get off me Professor!" Em needed a lungful of fresh air.

"I, uh, are you hurt?" For an attractive man, he was not quite verbal.

"I scraped my knee and twisted my ankle. And I can't move because you are on top of me. Get off!"

"Oh!"

Several students who were passing by stopped to watch this new scene with interest. They'd seen the fall and initially come to see if they might help and were staying now for the entertainment value.

"Move it, Professor! If I were a student you'd be hearing from the President's Harassment Committee." Em tried one last time to talk sense into him.

"But you're not a student. I'm Jim Stevenson. Let me take a look at your ankle. I can get you over to the infirmary."

"D.U.H.? Department of University Health? I don't think so." It flashed through her mind, *I have got to get this guy off me before I roll him over and hop on him myself. If it smells good, and it tastes good, it might be good.* Wrapping one leg around one of his, digging one heel into the ground, Em used all her strength and her weight against his shoulder. The professor went flying over her and landed on his back.

Em sat up and rubbed her ankle. "It's not broken folks," she said to the small group of onlookers.

The students laughed and moved on. Em heard one say, "Wow, Professor scores a touchdown."

Stevenson pulled himself up next to Em, stunned. "Here, let me see your ankle. It's starting to swell, it needs ice. Can I get you back into the house?" On his feet, the professor attempted to raise Em from the ground. Her first step with the twisted ankle was not a happy one. Stevenson attempted to wrap an arm around her to pick her up and carry her towards the house. A struggle between them ensued with Em trying to keep both feet on the ground.

"Let me carry you in." The professor made a valiant attempt at a fireman's carry. Em felt bound and determined not to be thrown over his shoulder like a sack of laundry.

"I can walk, dammit," Em hissed.

"No you can't!"

In what looked, from a distance, like a version of a children's three legged race, they made it up the walk to the front door. Em used the key to unlock it.

———◆———

The Army officer in the olive drab car said, "I'll be damned, he's in the house with her."

"Looks like he played football in college. That was some tackle." The ranking officer shook her head. "She got him off pretty handily, that took some training, and practice. Is he wired?"

"No, we didn't think he would get this far," the man said with regret.

"A shame. The man makes his own opportunities," she said.

"Yeah, he blew up his lab a couple years ago on a project."

"Our kind of recruit," she observed dryly.

"No, that was the point. The experiment worked. He used a low intensity laser to detonate a controlled charge from a distance. Part of geology is mining, and that could have broad use for some of our applications. But you didn't hear that from me. The professor said he'd been trying it for months and the last thing he tried worked." The man in uniform laughed. "Looks like this worked, too."

———◆———

"Nice! Is this your house?" Stevenson asked as he looked around the hallway.

"No, I'm cat sitting for the person who lives here." She thought quickly, *I need to find out what this guy wants.* She recognized him on the lawn and was not alarmed by his presence in the house. "The kitchen is back through the hall. Hello, Cleome."

The cat surveyed the new guest and voiced a polite inquiry as if to say, *Who's this and why is he clutching you, lady?*

"It's okay, Cleome," Em meant to reassure the cat.

One cat look said, "Mmm, so you say." Cleome turned on her elegant tail and hopped up on the sofa, claiming the best seat in the house. Em gave her a pass on that one and headed for the kitchen with Stevenson following along behind her.

Stevenson searched the fridge for ice and came up with a chilled bottle of Pouilly-Fuissé.

"Very good, I was going to invite you out for a drink by way of apology, and here we have it!" He spotted a lump of cheese near the wine. "We have goat cheese to go with it. Now we need to find some crackers."

"Put that back, I don't live here. I told you I'm only taking care of the cat," Em exclaimed.

"Tell them it was an emergency. Think of it as recompense for hazardous duty. Besides, it will give us something to do while you sit there with ice on your ankle. I'll put some ice in one of those plastic bags and wrap it in that dish towel for you. Sit yourself down, madam. I will replace the wine if you insist." Em took a seat at the scrubbed pine table in the center of the kitchen and put her foot to rest on another of the four kitchen chairs.

As good as his word, Stevenson wrapped up the plastic bag of ice in the dish towel he pulled off the rack and placed it on Em's ankle. His hand lingered there longer than necessary. "Fifteen minutes on, fifteen minutes off should do it. Now let's see if I can find those crackers."

Stevenson proceeded to search the kitchen cabinets starting at one side of the refrigerator and systematically working his way around. He found the tall standing cabinet that served as a food pantry. "Ah, success! You know who I am, I did introduce myself outside." He found the drawer containing the corkscrew for the wine and opened the wine bottle with practiced skill.

"Yes, you did after you practically tackled me," she admitted.

From the dish drainer he pulled two wine glasses. "Dusty these! Need a rinse. You do look as if I should know you. Faculty, staff, faculty spouse?" he asked, his eyebrows raised in inquiry.

"Not any longer. The Geology faculty member decamped for Texas with my best wishes," she said, a sharp tone in her voice. "I'm Travis Huber's ex-wife, Em."

"Trav. No kidding. Took off for the oil fields. A legend in his own time. Came back all buffed up. People hardly recognized him. What's the story with that? Tenure not enough? A man's got to be crazy to walk away from that. He almost had that appointment."

"Yes, really. We're not discussing him now. I've had enough of that and don't need any more." Em was in no mood to raise Trav Huber as a topic of conversation. Her ankle ached under its pack of ice.

Stevenson lounged against the counter with a wine glass in his hand, balancing it by the stem, giving her a good view. "Nice to meet you again. Huber always ran interference between you and any man under eighty who approached you."

"Until the last year or so after they announced the Perrelli appointment, after which it seemed all downhill. Surely there would have been other endowed chairs to come along," Em wondered out loud.

"Actually, not for several years. The incumbents in the other chairs are all still alive, well and professionally active. Geologists are a hardy bunch. You know, he was my bet for the Perrelli chair. I'll say that to anyone. But what have you been up to since then? Surely not just cat sitting for that beautiful feline out there in the living room." Seeing her reluctance to answer he continued. "This is Frank Kirbee's place, isn't it?"

"Yes, it is."

"Friends? Significant? Longstanding?" Stevenson asked her, his voice suggesting a close connection.

"Recently met." Em smiled at him, her smile giving nothing away.

"Serious?" He passed the plate of goat cheese and crackers he'd prepared.

"Not that I'm aware of," she admitted.

Stevenson stared at her speculatively. "His partner was murdered recently. Did you know him, too?"

"I only met him once, briefly, in passing. He seemed very nice, and I know that Professor Kirbee thought a great deal of him and his work. Kirbee said he considered him a good scientist, meticulous and accurate in his work. Not afraid to be wrong, and that ensured his results could be trusted."

"His work? What was that? I've lost track of Kirbee."

"Solar energy, I believe, but I'm not technical, and it wasn't discussed with me." She gave him the truth, more or less, depending on how you were inclined to stretch it.

"What's your specialty? I believe Trav said you hugged volcanoes for a living," she countered.

"Geysers, actually, geothermal energy sources. Not finite and polluting like fossil fuels." Stevenson had a trace of disapproval in his voice for Travis and his oil bearing assets.

"Sounds promising," Em rejoined pleasantly.

"Takes research money, and there's precious little of that to go around. Kirbee is fortunate that way. He could talk his old buddies in Washington into supporting solar flypaper if he wanted to."

Em finished her wine, which was indeed refreshing, and polished off the last of the goat cheese and crackers. "We should go," she said. "I have dinner to fix at home. I have two college kids with me for summer vacation. I'll tell Kirbee I developed a terrible thirst when he gets back. The bag of ice can go home with me."

"Let me do the glasses." With a smile on his face Stevenson searched the cupboard below the sink for dish detergent. He washed the wine glasses and the cheese plate, and replaced them in the dish rack.

"Expect Kirbee home soon?"

"No clue, he asked me to care for the cat, and I haven't heard from him since."

Em did her best to usher Stevenson out of the house in front of her. Cleome looked askance as they passed her on the couch. She made no attempt to object to being left alone again or to scrape an acquaintance with the new guest. Standing on the front step, Em locked the door behind them.

"Are you sure I can't drive you home? Here, take my arm down the steps." Professor Stevenson was all easy courtesy, which confounded Em. It seemed habitual to him. They walked arm in arm to her car. How could such an apparently well-mannered man have bumped her flat on her ass and refused to get up when repeatedly asked to do so she wondered.

"May I call you tomorrow to ask how your ankle is doing? Perhaps ask you out to dinner by way of apology?" Stevenson smiled at her with boyish charm as he handed her into her car. His arm rested on hers, warm and strong.

"Why, yes, you may. Thank you, Professor." This piqued Em's curiosity. As he turned away, she saw him give a long appraising look towards Kirbee's house. It struck her, *He's even more interested in Kirbee's house than me and my ankle.* That thought did not console her.

Sure enough the following morning Professor Stevenson called to invite Em for dinner at one of several private clubs in the city. The club he mentioned served as a quiet haven frequented by university and academic business people. This was well frequented turf for Em in her past life as Mrs. Professor Travis Huber. She begged off his invitation for a day or two pleading previous commitments. Professor Stevenson offered to meet her again the next afternoon to help her feed Cleome, which she declined. The professor encouraged her once again to accept his dinner offer, and they agreed on a tentative date early the following week.

Em decided to time her visit to Kirbee's house that day a little earlier in the afternoon to miss Stevenson's run. The geology department office was after all a few blocks away from Cleome's domicile. Em judged that Stevenson was most likely a creature of habit and would probably take his exercise at about the same time each day. By avoiding Stevenson, she would step away from the reach of one inquisitive man and unknowingly into a house party of still more determined investigators.

11

CLEOME'S HOUSE GUESTS

———◆———

E M ARRIVED AT KIRBEE'S HOUSE that afternoon a good hour before she anticipated Professor Stevenson might take his daily run. The light early morning rain watered the pots on the front steps, and the flowers were looking cheerful. Em let herself into the house. Cleome again sat right in the center of the hall and greeted her with a pleasant call. The house was quiet, and growing dusty, the way old houses did when left on their own for a while.

"Professor Kirbee? Are you here?" Em called out in a voice she hoped would carry up the very elegant stairway. Hearing no response, not even a creak of a floor board, she gave in to her temptation to go up the stairs a ways to better appreciate the beauty of the stained glass window that graced the wall half way up the stairs. Certainly that was a blameless thing. After admiring the intricate pattern and the glowing blues, greens and rose colors of the window, she turned her attention towards the second floor landing. Perhaps if she went up to the second floor, she could call out for Kirbee there as well.

But on the second floor she gave up the pretense of calling and quickly made the rounds of the four bedrooms and a sizeable old fashioned bathroom. Three of the bedrooms had only the simplest furniture. Kirbee's own room near the head of the stairs was neatly put together, but there were few personal items in view. She drew the line at searching his drawers or touching anything, in part because she hadn't provided herself with gloves.

Her last stop on the second floor was the bathroom. She believed she could take the liberty to pay an innocent visit, and so she shut the door. The floors were white marble. The sink was set in a slab of muted purple granite with an elegantly beveled ogee edge. Around the top of the porcelain basin was a hand painted ring of purple pansies. The taps were antique brass. An oversized tub with finely detailed ball and claw feet stood next to the sink on the inside wall. A dark wooden box with a pull chain hung high on the wall above the toilet. Using a tissue to cover her fingers as she opened the medicine cabinet, Em searched the bathroom thoroughly. It truly seemed that Frank Kirbee had checked out of his house. His comb, brush, toothpaste, toothbrush, and electric shaver or razors, along with soap were not in evidence.

Feeling slightly guilty for exploring Kirbee's house, she decided to leave the attic and the cellar for another day. If anyone watched the house, it wouldn't do to spend too much time there, only to feed the cat. Em stood at the top of the stairs admiring the carving of the sturdy banister and the substantial spindles that supported it. It was all she could do to resist the impulse to slide down the banister as she had done so many times as a child in her grandmother's house. The long descent of the banister, curving around at the base of the stairs ended with a high newel post that would stop her slide safely. Reluctantly she put that idea aside for another day, perhaps when she wore jeans and not a straight skirt.

Walking with dignity down the stairs, which creaked loudly like old bones, she heard the noise echo through the house. She was greeted at the base by Cleome who voiced impatience with her guest. The cat headed off towards the kitchen and her bowls.

"Alright m'lady, lead on. We'll get your dinner," Em said to the cat, who seemed to expect a response.

Em washed Cleome's food and water bowls. She prattled away to the cat who sat companionably by her feet. She selected a can of gourmet cat food from the stack that the professor had left on the counter, twelve cans, plus a bag of dry cat food. She surmised that Professor Kirbee planned to be away for more than a day or two. Locating the can opener placed right by the canned food, Em was opening a can of shrimp dinner when she heard a sound from the front hall, followed by heavy footsteps and men's voices.

She turned around from the counter to find herself face to face with a uniformed city policeman. "What are you doing here?" he asked in a voice of accusation. She and Cleome looked at each other. The cat chose to answer first with a low throated feline growl. Cleome's lips curled up showing impressive fangs.

"What does it look like I'm doing, I'm feeding the cat. The professor who owns this house is away," Em replied simply, very glad she had not been caught up on the second floor when the police arrived. She placed the bowl of cat food on the floor for Cleome.

"Yeah, we got that. That's why we're here." The policeman took in Em's calm response.

"What's wrong with the cat?"

"She objects to the smell of that very large dog. You have dog hairs half way up your pants legs. German Shepherd?" Em conjectured.

"Police dog."

Cleome added an unprintable comment, seeing no need to hiss since the source of the offensive canine scent was not present. She turned her attention to the shrimp dinner while keeping a wary eye on the policeman.

"Does that cat ever say meow?" The uniformed officer asked, still regarding it with suspicion.

"Not that I've heard," replied Em.

"We will need to ask you for identification, ma'am."

Em sighed and slowly reached for her handbag, making sure that the officer could see she only took out her wallet. She handed him a driver's license and answered his routine questions simply. Em added no information other than that which he requested. The sergeant seemed to lose interest and returned to the active scene. Em refreshed the water in Cleome's bowl and drifted towards the living room, too.

Police filled the front room of the house, tracking dirt on the Oriental carpet. One waved a warrant at Em. She stood in the archway between rooms while the police made what they thought was a comprehensive search. Em noticed that their knowledge of turn of the century domestic architecture was distinctly limited. They neglected to pull open the pocket doors, common in houses of this age, which could be used to close off one room from another. They did not pull up the Oriental rug or thoroughly inspect the custom tile work around the fireplace. The police personnel were joking among themselves and heading off to survey the rest of the house when the front door closed with its distinctive solid thunk.

A tall, lean, distinguished man of her own age entered. He walked in slowly, using a carved wooden cane. His well-tailored business suit was wrinkled in a way not often seen with modern fabrics, and his shoes were covered with the fine grey sooty dust which suggested a long trip commuting by rail rather than car travel. A handsome, serious face was guarded, lightly tanned, with a vigorous five o'clock shadow and his short dark hair was shot with grey. After a murmured greeting, a nod to the lead detective, he sat down on the couch where he proceeded to watch, saying not a word. The tenor of the room changed, the search became more focused, and the jokes became fewer.

She sensed he was someone in whose presence they did not speak unless spoken to. The Siamese cat brushed by, rubbing against Em's leg. Cleome promptly hopped into his lap as the man stretched out his right leg, wincing. To Em's surprise, he began petting the cat, who looked quite satisfied with herself.

Em stood watching, listening and calculating. Although she was not aware that the new arrival looked directly at her, he had taken in the scope of the search. Em decided to do some investigation of her own. Walking around the officers who were now conferencing in the middle of the room, she approached the man on the couch cautiously, standing by him until he looked up. Cleome welcomed her with a sound of greeting.

"Friendly cat," said the man by way of an opening.

"No, actually, she's not. She is very discriminating in her taste. Which means you have been here before, and often. She nearly took the sergeant apart on my behalf." Em grinned at him with raised eyebrows.

The man laughed under his breath. "The professor and I had a working relationship. I'm thinking he had one with you as well. He hasn't been in touch. It's a matter of concern to us." To an observer, his attention would seem absorbed by the cat, who gave the feline grin of pure pleasure, but Em saw his steady grey eyes fixed in middle distance. The hands that stroked the cat were long fingered and looked well used, capable of work. *This man is not a just an office denizen, like most of us,* she thought. He wore a gold shield partially concealed by his suit jacket.

"And you are?"

"Michael Halloran, Ms. Huber," he responded as he moved his jacket back to expose the badge. "Some things of national interest are best discussed in private." The man looked down and continued to stroke the Siamese cat, who listened attentively. His voice barely audible, he said, "You and I need to talk. Not here. Where are you headed when you leave?"

"I could use a snack. A light lunch. I was thinking of going down to one of the delis on Orange Street. Would that be good for you?" Em suggested quietly. Cleome looked up at her and spoke dismissively.

"Too close, too public. Come down to my place. It's a family restaurant down by the harbor, close to the hospital." He mentioned the name and address.

"Are you sure about that?" Em recognized the address as located in one of the areas local residents determined best not traveled after dusk. Friends who lived around there did not invite evening guests and made it a point to stay indoors when shots rang out. One of her friends had abandoned a house in that neighborhood, unable to sell it. The bank had been unhappy when they were told if they liked it so much, they could move in.

"You'll be perfectly safe. Park in back of the building. Think of it as guarded parking." He smiled at his own joke. "Go into the Café, order and pay for what you would like at the counter. Then take it to the back. Go up the stairs to the loft. The cross bar that says 'Closed' will open for you. Turn to the left. Go down the short hall to the restrooms. Find the door that says 'Employees Only.' Look up and to the left. Wait a minute. The door will slide back."

"That's a lot to remember. How do I know…?"

"You won't know until you get there. Be there in thirty minutes. I'll meet you in the conference room after I check in. No questions. Just do this Ms. Huber. We need to find Professor Kirbee and you could help."

Halloran put Cleome down on the couch next to him, gave her a parting pat and used his cane to get up. Em noticed the finely crafted cane of a deep red-brown Briar. *Stout enough to hold a man's weight, or hold a good blade*, Em reflected. *The head of the cane looks rather like a sea serpent.*

"Nilsson. Are you done with her? Can she go?" Halloran queried the detective in charge.

"The cat sitter? We have her contact information. She can go if you say so." The younger detective was a well-built fellow, but off the beat growing a little heavier with longish, rather unruly light brown hair in need of a trip to a good barber.

The detective spoke aloud to Em. "Ms. Huber, thank you for your cooperation. You can go. Please call us if you hear from Professor Kirbee. Also if you can think of anything else that might help us to locate them. Here's my card, call us." The detective nodded his head, which shook his long mustache. Em put aside the notion to giggle. She nodded, smiled and headed out the door as quickly as she could reasonably do so.

Once in her car, she took a deep breath. She tried to decide whether to go as planned to a deli on Orange in the heart of the Yale ghetto, or to try to find the federal agent's place somewhere down on the south side of New Haven near the railroad station. That locale would put it close to the Interstate on the west side of the harbor

The local police were wrapping up their less than comprehensive search inside the house. They determined it was not a likely scene of the crime. As soon as Em cleared the front door of the house, Halloran approached Detective Nilsson, who twirled his mustache, absorbed in thought. Drawing him off to the side, he asked, "So what did she tell you she was doing here?"

The detective looked up from his note book. "Said the professor sent her an email yesterday afternoon asking her to come by to take care of the cat. He would be away. The key was in one of the flowerpots on the front step. When we got here, she was in the kitchen opening a can of cat food. That damned cat nearly ripped into Gianelli. We ran her plates and checked her ID. She is who she says she is. She's apparently the ex-wife of a well-known university professor. Rich guy now. Texas oil. She was at a concert in Woolsey Hall with three friends that evening. Half of town was there. So was I. After the concert they went out to an Irish pub for coffee and dessert. It's right around the corner. Said they're just friends, she and Kirbee, and she's no one special."

"And you believed that? She's an attractive woman. Did you ask her about her relationship with Kirbee?" Halloran looked down his not quite straight nose at the younger detective.

Detective Nilsson looked skeptically at Halloran. "He's in his sixties for cripe's sake."

"But he isn't dead. At least not last week," the federal man replied with acerbity.

"Wait a minute, you think she's in bed with the guy and knows where he is? It's not likely she'd kill him and then come feed the cat," said Nilsson, the city detective, who assumed anyone over fifty must be pretty much done for. His khaki pants were bagging around his knees after a long shift and a running pursuit across the New Haven Green.

"I've got this. I'll take care of it," the older man replied. "See if you can find a second body in the river."

"Yessir," acknowledged Nilsson with attitude.

Halloran left the house, climbed into a black fleet car, which drove off in the opposite direction.

Following him back was an option Em was sure he would not appreciate. She weighed other options including a fast trip to the Florida Keys. *I suspect if I don't show up as requested, he'll send someone after me. Probably more than one, and that could be embarrassing depending on where and who,* she concluded.

12

VISIT TO HALLORAN'S OFFICE

———◆———

EM DROVE SLOWLY DOWN THE narrow back street. The buildings were flat-roofed, red brick three story inner city commercial. Shops on the street level were surmounted by a floor of offices with converted low rent apartments above. The address given was close to a corner of a longer building with a singularly undistinguished façade and tinted windows on the second and third floors. The Café occupied the right front end with a shoe repair shop and clothing store featuring black leather and metal chains on the other end.

The parking lot in the rear of the building was half full. Several of the cars looked suspiciously like junkers. She parked next to a battered Civic that looked like it had not been moved this age. Em got out of the car, warily scanning the yard, and especially regarding the high brick wall around it. Razor wire topped the wall, its twisting metal prongs gleamed in the light. The green dumpster smelled ripe in the afternoon sun. The back of the building looked as if it had been refaced in newer tempered brick. There were no windows on the first two floors and tinted glass windows on the third floor. Three solid battleship grey metal doors accessed the parking lot. The two doors in the center were each wide enough and high enough for a fire truck. The roof appeared to be sprouting a variety of metal excrescences that were antennas of some sort but were certainly not microwave. She learned later that this was referred to as the antenna farm.

Seeing no obvious hazards and only one, probably decoy surveillance camera, she shrugged, slung her bag over her shoulder and trudged up the alleyway to the front of the Café. A red and white striped awning shaded the sidewalk. Plants including an out of control variegated Philodendron vine and a Wandering Jew of immense proportions hung in the front window. Second thoughts occurred to Em. *Amateur!* she said under her breath. *I am going to feel totally foolish if this turns out to be some sort of trap and I've told no one where I'm going.* Nevertheless, Em pulled open the door. The atmosphere in the Café was not what she expected.

Two muscular cooks in white tee shirts, pecs on display, tattoos visible up their arms, were working over the grill on the left wall. Both glanced at her briefly. Red stools lined the counter, like a classic diner. The stools seemed to be the favorite of neighborhood regulars. Booths lined the right wall, occupied now by hospital and university office staff, med and nursing students, and neighborhood families. Free standing tables were arranged at the back of the room. The walls were sand blasted brick, no art, no framed posters. Business looked steady for a Thursday afternoon, a good sign in the current economy. The smell of grilled onions, steak and peppers reached out over the counter towards Em, who resisted the temptation.

Standing in front of the counter, as instructed, Em read the menu posted on the chalk boards above the grill. Along with the usual local Italian, vegetarian and Greek specialties were infrequently seen delicacies such as Chipped Beef on Toast, also known as that perennial U.S. Army WW II favorite Shit on a Shingle, and fried Spam, scrambled eggs and Spam. *They have got to be kidding. Maybe I am in the right place.* Em approached the counter to order.

The counter man was a compact Puerto Rican with a self-possessed mien and a distinctive service tattoo.

"Your order, ma'am?" he asked with a respectful and softly accented voice, perhaps reserved for expected guests.

"What would you do if I said Spam, Spam and more Spam?"

"Ma'am?" the counterman said with a puzzled look on his face.

"That's what my father said they ate in the Army during the War. He swore he'd never touch the stuff after he got home. My mother tried to serve him chipped beef on toast once to save money. That did not go over well, I'll tell you."

"Which war was that, ma'am?" The doubt was clear in the counterman's voice.

"The Second," Em replied.

One of the cooks snickered and went to work vigorously chopping and frying steak with a smile on his face.

"She got you on that one, José," commented the cook closest to the counter.

"What can we get for you today, ma'am?" the counterman asked, conscious they were being overheard.

"I'll have an orange chicken salad, a large latte with cinnamon. How are the cannolis?"

"Mrs. Maresca makes them herself. Fresh today. Filled on demand. Super."

"Fine. I'll have six of the little ones with the chocolate bits." Em was eyeing the truly impressive display of Italian pastry, cakes and cheesecakes in the refrigerator case and missed the look that passed between the staff.

"For here or to go, ma'am?"

"Better pack them to go. It's a lot of cannolis to eat at once." Em grinned at the young man behind the counter who invited her to take a seat to wait for her order.

Finding an open booth, she sat down to listen to the

conversations going on around her and to watch the staff. The cooks worked in unison. One fried on the griddle, the other prepped the dishes and cooked on the stove. Both cast their eyes around at intervals. The counterman watched the front. A blonde and husky looking waitress patrolled the tables in the rear, her hair pulled straight back. Her white tee shirt and jet black jeans were spotless, and she wore no jewelry. *This may be a real working restaurant,* Em thought, *but the employees are not exactly off the street hires.*

It appeared they rushed her order because it arrived quickly. The counterman called her number. Em smiled at the sight of the salad, asking for raspberry vinaigrette dressing.

"You will find the cinnamon and the sugar down towards the back and to the left," José told her. She paid him for the food and left a tip in the large glass jar stuffed with bills and change labeled, "All tips donated to services for Vets."

Em smiled at José, wished him a good afternoon and walked carefully towards the back to the find the condiments, plastic bag with the cannolis and salad in one hand, and large paper cup with the latte in the other. Her strategy was to appear as much like the rest of the customers as possible. She tried to act slightly absent-minded, to be unassuming and somewhat clumsy, to fit in. University staff, of course, being a lesser sub-species of academic person. No one paid her any special attention.

Behind the counter, one of the cooks stepped up to José. "What's the deal? We don't usually have visitors come through the front door."

"The boss wanted us to recognize her, and he's is going to have his hands full with that one, my friend. You have to have stones to come in here on your own," José replied in his scratchy and softly accented voice.

She spotted the condiments station, and a narrow wooden staircase with the "Closed" sign. After sprinkling the requisite cinnamon on her latte and gathering up the natural sugar packets, Em turned to see the waitress watching her. The bar popped open barely enough for Em to negotiate through it and up the stairs.

The loft floor covered roughly half of the back of the dining room and was set with additional chairs and tables. The half-height wall that overlooked the dining room shielded the loft from view. It surprised Em to see a man and woman in their late twenties seated at a small romantic table who appeared to ignore her completely, which made her suspicious. They were practicing their Urdu and argued about directions to the Ajmeri Hotel. The man's accent was too flat, Em thought he missed the music of the language entirely.

Looking over her shoulder quickly, Em headed down the short dark hall as if in search of the restrooms. Light bulbs seemed to be at a premium, and several had been removed from the fixtures meant to light the hallway. With the restrooms at her back, she turned to face a plain black metal door with a dingy sign that read "Employees Only." She looked at it doubtfully, jostled her bag, and then remembered the instruction to look up to her left. When she did so, a small white pencil point of light appeared at ceiling height and blinked three times.

The door slid open to reveal a small dimly lit room the size of an elevator car. "Step in please," announced a disembodied male voice with a timber like the baritone voice of Paul Robeson. Em stepped in, praying she had not made a ghastly mistake, and that her children would be able to find and execute her will. The door slid smoothly back in place behind her. Lights came on and she found herself standing in a room with stainless steel walls covered with shining sides of Plexiglas. She felt the air change around her at least twice. After a brief pause, which she assumed was taken up by analysis of the air, an upright rectangle outlined in blue light appeared before her on the left side of the wall ahead of her. "Place your left hand in the box." Em sighed.

Easier said than done, she transferred the latte to her left hand and placed her right hand on the wall. "Your other left, ma'am."

Now this was a sore trial, and she juggled the latte to her right hand to free her left to touch the wall in the lighted box. The blue light vanished. Another blue box appeared on the right. "Oh, don't tell me, let me guess. This is for the right hand," she said aloud, assuming that if they could speak to her, she could talk back to them. She glared at the walls indiscriminately as they appeared featureless. As Em sucked in the first taste of the latte, visions of the trash compactor scene in the first *Star Wars* movie gave her a shiver. Concentrating on breathing helped the wave of anxiety and claustrophobia to pass. The wall before her slid open.

Em faced a console in a brightly lit hall. Behind the desk sat a young African American man with the bass voice, regulation short cropped curling red hair, medium complexion and quiet blue green eyes. The name on the uniform read Garvey, and he smiled at her with good humor.

"Good afternoon, state your name please," which Em did begrudgingly.

As if he doesn't know perfectly well who I am, thought Em.

"Now, please drop that very large purse right here on this scanner," the agent directed. "And let's take out some of those sharp objects I see here." Em, who should have expected this and left certain things in the car, delved down into her bag to dig out the Swiss Army knife and the old Scout knife. She paused to rummage around at the bottom of the bag.

"Keep going, ma'am," he directed. She came up with a box cutter she had forgotten and a small, elegant antique mother of pearl lady's pocket knife. "I guess that'll do, you can have this collection back on your way out, ma'am. Are these all necessary?" he asked.

Deciding to have some fun Em answered, "Gibbs rule number 9, 'Always carry a knife.' In times of national emergency, we could live out of this bag for a week."

Garvey grinned at her, a kindred spirit. "Ms. Huber. Right on time. We are running late. Please make yourself comfortable in the conference room on the left. Eat your lunch if you wish. The airlock is standard procedure for everyone. Sorry about the need to pass things hand to hand."

"Right. Conference room on the left," she said. She thought, *I must look like a crazy old lady with a paper bag of food and the latte.* Em passed through the open door of the conference room and parked herself and her stuff on the opposite side of the table, facing the door. The décor looked one step up from an interrogation room, seemingly without windows. She wondered about that, put her bag on the table and pulled out her cell phone. *No bars. No service. Why am I not surprised?* she thought. With a determined leap of faith, she opened up her salad and began lunch, fresh mandarin oranges, grilled chicken served over a bed of mixed greens sprinkled with Feta cheese.

Outside, at the console, Halloran walked up behind Garvey. "She finished with lunch yet?"

"Just about, sir. She's pretty calm. Usually people are bouncing off the walls by now if you leave them alone that long. Had quite a few tools in her bag. Can I ask, how did you get her to come in voluntarily? People don't generally like to do that."

"Her curiosity. That's quite a collection of stuff. Schwartz and Agarwal will be observing, give Joel a call. Let me know when they're here."

Her salad almost finished, Em was chasing the last bit of orange around the container with her fork when Halloran walked into the conference room favoring his right leg, moving more slowly than before. She waited quietly as the tall man pulled a chair away from the table and eased himself in the chair across from her with apparent relief. Halloran swung his right leg straight out. The cane was tucked under the table.

"Thank you for coming in." Halloran sat and studied the woman in front of him. Em looked him straight back in the eye, calm and steady, not in an antagonistic way, but firm, alert and observant. It gave her a chance to examine his face. Irish of course, but something else as well. His cheek bones were high, and the planes of his face flat. His nose deviated above the slight hump below the bridge. Em could see a scar line visible through his left brow. He impressed her as someone comfortable in a tailored suit, who had taken a right cross to the eye in a fight earlier in his life.

Most Americans will fill silence with speech. This woman seemed fully prepared to wait him out. He sensed she might be a formidable opponent, watchful, patient, at ease. From his ear bud, he heard Joel Schwartz's encouragement to get on with it. "She's got you, Mike."

Sensing a change in Halloran's concentration, Em decided to open first. "Something happen to your leg recently?"

"Fell."

"Off a horse?" she ventured.

"Fell off a dock."

"I'll bet there's more to the story than that."

"We're not here to talk about me, Ms. Huber." He looked over his glasses and frowned.

Em changed tactics. "I hate to be trite, but have we met before?"

"Actually, we have," Halloran admitted with some surprise. "Down in Texas at Robert Albrecht's funeral. I met Travis Huber as well," he added dryly.

"Sad time. I liked Uncle Robert. Were you there as a friend of the family?" This seemed highly unlikely to her.

"No, it was business. Investigating rumors Albrecht had

war souvenirs that should go back to France and Germany. Would you know anything about that? Would your ex-husband have them now?"

After a deep breath, to give her time to organize her response, Em sighed audibly. "Very touchy subject in the family. Before we were married, we visited Uncle Robert and his wife for dinner at the ranch. I let him know at the dinner table I thought things should be returned. He had this soft Texas drawl. He said, 'Honey, if I thought any person or family or institution had rightfully owned anything that I had, I would search 'em out and return it. But nobody's gonna care about a few *playtes* and cups and little vases. Maybe a beer stein or two. Marlene likes that china stuff.

"'Now what some of them did, dis-grace to mankind. Like what General Eisenhower said, made you ashamed to be German. And I'm damn glad he said that. It was what many of us felt. Our family had to stop speaking German at home during World War I. We had to call sauerkraut Liberty Cabbage. Good ol' American frankfurters became hot dogs. And damned if they didn't start another war. No call for that unspeakable horror. No, I'm not givin' them back their *playtes* and cups. Spoils of war.' That's all he would to admit to, and I never saw anything. You're not looking for china, are you?"

The corners of Halloran's mouth tugged, resisting a smile. "No mention of bars of Nazi gold?"

"My opinion? What's down in Texas isn't going back. Did you really call me in here to talk about Uncle Robert and that myth?"

"If Albrecht had anything of significance, could the family be persuaded to give it back?"

"Are we back to this again? Threats won't work," Em enjoined Halloran. "I've already told you, he would have returned anyone's personal property. He was a religious man, but not devout. So, if he'd had a religious piece, he wouldn't have kept it for personal devotion."

"What about, say a couple, two or three bars of Nazi gold?" Halloran was not about to give up the quest.

"Good luck with that one. If, and I said if, he brought back gold, it's buried so deep in the Texas hill country, you'll never see it. You really aren't interested in his 'little china *playtes*' are you?"

Halloran frowned, as far as he was concerned, whatever WWII GI's managed to smuggle back into the U.S. paled in comparison to the systematic theft of art and assets, both personal and civic committed by Hitler's war machine, including that later captured by the Soviets. But there were certain missing assets and works of art that needed return and restoration. Their existence had grown into legend. The GI generation passed with every day, and every death obscured the trail and dispersed the clues. If Albrecht did not have the loot, likely he had been in close enough proximity to have heard or seen or even surmised what had happened to it. Perhaps loyalty to his Army buddies kept him silent during the long years that remained of his life, perhaps something more threatening. To keep a secret like that could be a dangerous thing for a man, for a family.

"As for me, I would have been the last person in the family to know," Em continued trying for a light tone of voice. "For a wedding present, he sent a beautiful old blue and white Meissen vase." She held her hands out to sketch a round shape in the air, "Like this. Actually, it's for starting tulips in the spring. The card said, as near as I can remember, 'Honey, we bought this one for you because we know you like this kind of thing. Papers are enclosed. Love and best wishes, Uncle Bob and Aunt Marlene.' The certificates showed purchase and export date that year. He knew how I felt about replevin, the return of artifacts to the rightful owners. I would be the last person he would tell if he had anything else." She smiled.

Halloran reflected if Albrecht ever wanted it returned,

she would be the first to know. "Unfinished business. Worth trying," was Halloran's chosen answer. He noted her lack of surprise at the mention of the missing gold.

From his ear bud he heard Joel Schwartz remark, "Unlikely that Albrecht would trust the wife of a nephew with that kind of information anyway." Halloran had his own opinion on that question but decided to put it aside for a time when he could better think through what he had just learned. Albrecht had admitted to family members he collected objects that had been transferred to the U.S. He had reason to believe the objects most likely did not belong to private individuals or institutions that might have a legitimate claim on them.

"I believe Uncle Robert. He would never hold onto someone else's property." Her expression let him know the subject was now closed. Em knew she had told Halloran nothing he could not have learned from half the people in the Texas town where Bob and Marlene lived. If he looked back far enough, he might even come across an article in the now defunct local newspaper that covered the start of Bob's collection shortly after the War.

Halloran tried another tack. "Most people are surprised to find this here," he said, gesturing around the room.

Welcoming the change in direction she hoped without perceptible relief, Em picked up the conversation readily. "I can see why. It's a very logical location, halfway between New York and Boston, sub base in Groton out along the east shoreline, down the west shoreline the Gold Coast with Greenwich and Stamford. Transportation hub, two main Interstate highways meet in a T intersection at the head of a harbor lined on the east by oil tanks and on the west by railroad yards. Strategic bridges across the harbor. And of course there is Yale. During the Cold War we had missile defenses at a Nike site in West Haven. I'd be disappointed if there hadn't been something here." She smiled at him, gauging his reaction to her analysis.

"I meant this side of the city," was his dry response.

Testing his patience for female verbal facility, Em charged off again, trying to talk him to death. "I did think the menu downstairs unusual. Do they actually serve Spam and eggs or chipped beef on toast? U.S. Army gourmet food. My father taught me some names for those, and they aren't pretty. The staff all looks like they would be more comfortable in fatigues and carrying weapons. Of course, that could be a decided asset in this neighborhood."

Halloran put on his stern "enough games" face. "The management has a policy of hiring returning veterans with relevant experience. The food's good."

"Yes, good salad," she agreed. "Have a cannoli?"

Schwartz and Agarwal laughed in Halloran's ear. He decided to accept the peace offering. As Em and their boss each selected a cannoli, the hooting in Halloran's ear, encouragement to share the cannolis with his senior staff was consciously and carefully ignored.

"Is there really a Mrs. Maresca who makes these?" was Em's conversation starter.

"Yes, but it's not always the same person" replied Halloran, who savored the last of his cannoli.

"Well, here's to Obi Wan Cannoli." She raised the cannoli in a salute. He has a sweet tooth, she noted. "This is your date, what's next on the agenda?" Em queried, back to the task at hand.

"We need to know what you didn't tell the New Haven Police. All of it. Without exception Ms. Huber." Halloran determined not to crack a smile.

Em paused to consider, she was determined to see her client's project through regardless. She could give him the runaround, fib outright, spin him a tale, shuffle the details unmercifully, pretend absent-mindedness, incompetence or sheer stupidity, or plead the Fifth. Or none of these, all of which would piss this man off big time, which judging from her reading of him so far, she did not want to see.

Interpreting her silence as decision making, Halloran moved to clarify what he needed to hear. "Last time I talked to Frank Kirbee, he said he planned to hire an outside consultant to check questionable business activity by a competitor." He paused for a response, getting none, he continued. "From your online résumé and employment history, I would guess that would be you. What exactly did you do for your former employer? The company simply confirmed employment and referred us to their legal department."

"As for what exactly I did, I forget. Actually, I have a very selective memory." She looked him straight in the eye. "If you have a job like that you leave it at the door on your way out. If you can't do that, you prove you shouldn't have had the job in the first place. But I expect you know all that yourself."

Halloran accepted the rebuff with satisfaction. It was the right answer. "Frank Kirbee said the consultant came highly recommended by an old friend. He sounded anxious, seriously concerned, and wouldn't tell me why. Which was unusual for him.

"You need to tell me exactly what the email said. His partner is dead. Kirbee is missing. We only believe he intended to leave because of an email you said you received. I will need a copy of that email. Tell me." Halloran watched her gather her thoughts. He could be patient, but testing was over. "Now would be a good time."

"Okay, long story short. Professor Kirbee hired me to investigate potential patent infringement resulting, quite likely, from sophisticated industrial espionage." Em repeated the text of Kirbee's email to the best of her memory.

Halloran shifted his weight in the chair, the ear bud remained silent. Schwartz and Agarwal were standing stock still in the viewing area.

"As you may know, his company is developing new solar technology for small scale applications. Excellent market potential." Em looked up at the federal man who nodded.

"Professor Hussein, his friend and trusted business part-ner, was doing due diligence research in preparation for their patent application for the fifth generation of Sun-Sprite technology. He discovered that three small regional companies were selling what at first appeared to be products containing similar devices to an earlier Version, number 3, of their SunSprite. These companies were scattered around the country, away from major cities."

"Names," he barked. This was news to him and not what he had been expecting. Washington would not be an easy phone call.

"Alagash SunShyne in Maine, Prairie SunFyre in Kansas, and River SunShyne in Missouri. To find them online, you need to know that the 'i' in the name has been replaced with 'y.'

"Being a careful engineer, and a cautious man, Professor Hussein ordered products from each of these companies to take a look inside. Each product was designed to appear different and positioned for a different market segment." Halloran looked guardedly at Em as she continued. "One was blue plastic on the exterior and marketed through magazines to boaters along the Mississippi River to provide evening lights. The Kansas version had a different hous-ing and was for backyard lighting sold by mail order. The Maine version was smaller, with a metal base for emer-gency lighting, and it was sold through hardware stores.

"Here's the thing, Professor Hussein reverse engineered them. He took them apart and found they all had the same internal components manufactured to the exact specifi-cations for SunSprite Version 3 and had exactly the same flaws. These flaws are corrected in Version 5, along with significant technical advances, according to Kirbee."

"So someone could have found Hussein through his return address," Halloran ventured.

"I asked that, and Kirbee told me that Professor Hussein rented mail boxes in both New York and Connecticut and in different venues. Even though they didn't consider Version 3 a marketable product, its innovations have the potential to serve a wide range of northern latitudes, even Arctic latitudes. However, depending on latitude, it has a very short life span, only eighteen months or so. He feared they would lose control of Version 5. They were stunned their work could have been stolen without their knowledge."

"Ali Hussein reverse engineered the product. What's your part?" Halloran's brow furrowed. She could tell she had broken new ground for him.

"First, I was asked whether any of these companies had patents for the technology. They did not, no one had. And, there were no registered trademarks, either. Second, to figure out how these seemingly unrelated companies came to be using the same components to produce different products."

"Could you?" he asked quietly.

"Yes. It was a simple basic nineteenth century capitalist monopoly tactic, interlocking directorates with the manufacturing entity Transaxia of West Virginia. Two or three different individuals from Transaxia are officers or directors of the other three smaller companies. Now that I've given you the company names, your people can verify it."

Schwartz and Agarwal were in agreement. "Same old, same old. This lady's good," Joel Schwartz remarked. Halloran nodded to them, casting his glance away from Em.

"And third, I suspect this may be where you all come in, to prepare documentation for a federal lawsuit," she paused, "to be given to Dr. Kirbee's contact in the federal government." One look at the man's straight face told her all. "I guess you didn't get it. I'm telling you this because my client wanted you to know."

"You didn't tell this to the police because?"

"At first, I believed Professor Hussein's death could be

attributed to a random mugging in the park. My client told me the technology of Version 5 is classified. To me that means need to know only. I didn't have his authorization to tell them, and I was not going there with a whole room full of cops."

Em stopped but continued to pursue that reasoning with, "This is a small town. News spreads quickly. Everybody knows somebody, who knows someone who is sleeping with somebody, whose grandmother is buried next to someone else."

Halloran stroked his chin. It had grown late, and his beard scratched. He stalled to listen to Schwartz and Agarwal discuss what they needed him to ask her next.

Across the table, Em watched him thoughtfully out of the corner of her eye. *The man needs a hearing aid. They should all just troop in here and ask me their questions themselves, whoever they are,* she reflected.

"Next question. What was your source and how did you find it?" Halloran asked dutifully.

At last, they had come to the procedural level, this one had to be from the backroom. She explained, "In competitive intelligence, it is common procedure to follow the money. I couldn't do that, so I followed the people and the component parts. Each company has officers and a board of directors. These are small privately held companies, little financial data has to be reported publicly, none to the SEC. It can stay buried in the LLCs. Although lying to the SEC has been done before, too. Credit reports show principal officers. Local business newspapers cover company events with names. It can be pieced together. The larger company manufactures the parts, and then ships them to the other three for cover."

She looked up and around the room and raised her voice, "You could have a forensic accountant go over the books. But any good researcher should be able to verify what I've said." *If they've taken careful notes,* she was tempted to add.

"You told Frank Kirbee this? And gave him the documentation?"

"Yes, are we almost done?" Resting her chin on her hand and her elbow on the table, Em gave the universal I'm tired can I go home signal. Her hair fell down around her face, and she ran her fingers through it impatiently, causing it to fly out still farther. Her interrogator found he rather enjoyed the sight, but from his carefully controlled countenance, she would never have guessed it.

Recapping, Halloran queried, "You created the documentation. You gave it to Kirbee. When and where did you give it to him?"

She looked askance at him, his technique was sound. "Who, what, when, where, why and how?"

"Something like that. Go on." Halloran tried to flex his sore leg discretely under the table, guessing that if she sensed his discomfort, she'd move to close the interview before he felt ready to do so himself.

"I delivered it to my client, Professor Francis X. Kirbee on paper and on disk as agreed at his home three days before Hussein's death. Kirbee didn't trust thumb drives." A deep sigh followed. "What I could not do was tell him who stole the technical specifications. I couldn't find the thief without more information about who had access to their lab at the time Version 3 was in development. The thief obviously missed out on Version 4, which I understood corrected only production issues. Kirbee said he and his partner would handle that." She raised her eyebrows, and her face plainly showed she understood how that must sound.

"I was asked not to keep a copy. For your purposes, for evidence, I think you need Kirbee's copy," she concluded.

"How did Kirbee react to what you told him?" Halloran said, back on his own track.

"He was stunned, of course. But his mind is so quick he came to believe it. There was something in the way he spoke. Quietly. He was angry and afraid the situation could get worse." She paused for breath and he interrupted.

"Worse how?"

She shook her head, "I think he was afraid that Version 5 might be stolen, to be sold to the highest bidder. Version 3 is flawed and not worth it."

"Give us a copy of the report, we'll check it out." Halloran was firm on this point.

"Can't do it. Professor Kirbee made me promise to destroy mine. I used a DoD standard program to overwrite the file on my computer. I wouldn't walk around with that in my pocket anyway. You have what you need."

"That's why you came in, isn't it?" he asked, sounding frustrated and tired.

"Yup. Not good to carry that kind of thing alone. My client is missing, maybe dead. Version 5 is a go and a valuable property to any number of organizations," she lowered her voice, "even countries." Em and the federal investigator stared at each other across the table.

With hesitation, Em made the next opening. "If you're done with your questions, I have another problem. I could use your advice on something. Something unusual happened yesterday afternoon at the professor's house."

"Go ahead." Halloran's voice deepened to bass.

"After I got the email from Kirbee asking me to take care of the cat, I went to the house, found the key and let myself in. Nothing seemed disturbed. I fed Cleome and locked up the house." Em, who had been sitting quietly, hands in her lap, suddenly became more animated. Her hands came up above the table. She gestured as she spoke with open hands, her palms towards her body.

"You kept the key?"

"Yes. His note said to do so," she said, gestures emphasizing her point. Her eyes brightened and her speech came more quickly.

"But, here's the thing. A geology faculty member bulldogged me outside Kirbee's house. As I was heading down the front walk, right as I stepped onto the sidewalk, he was running, bumped into me and he knocked me down on the grass." She pantomimed the attack. Halloran's eyebrows shot up.

"Runners bump into people every once in a while, but they don't usual knock you down, then land on top of you." Em paused to gauge his reaction. It was not easy interviewing a man whose countenance only changed when he allowed it to do so. "He insisted on taking me back into the house to put ice on my ankle. It was not all that bad, really." She shook her head.

"What time?" he asked sharply.

"A little before five o'clock. My appointment with Kirbee was supposed to be at four-thirty that afternoon.

"You said, Geology faculty member. You recognized him?"

"Sure." she nodded. "My ex-husband, Harley Travis Huber, was in Geology. Professor James Stevenson is younger. I'd seen him at various geology department functions."

"So he could be expected to recognize you?" Halloran's eyes darkened in suspicion.

Em nodded again in agreement. "He's not working for you?"

"Not that I am aware of. Not Kirbee's department. Why would you think he would be working with us?" Halloran sensed that the woman must have a good reason for telling him this.

"A few years ago talk was over the sherry at faculty parties that Jim Stevenson was doing some interesting work. Wink wink, nudge nudge," she said humorously. "Stevenson disappeared down to Washington or there abouts for three years. Some of us assumed he was doing a stint at DARPA, those lovely folks who gave us the Internet."

The two practiced investigators, Em and Halloran, stared

at each other across the table and considered this for a few moments.

"Huber's into the oil business, Stevenson may be geothermal, and Kirbee's developing advanced solar technology. They have energy resources in common. Or, financially, in competition. It's a conjecture," Em suggested seriously.

"Anything else you are willing to tell me?"

"Can't think of anything." She rolled her eyes away from him.

"Then we're done here. Your part in this is done. Thank you for your cooperation." Halloran finally felt the benefit of a good stretch. "Go home. And don't go back to Kirbee's house alone."

Em stared at the man across the table with a darkening brow. "I can help."

"I'm serious. Go home. We will find Kirbee." Halloran put the tone of command in his voice, a major tactical error.

Halloran heard Agarwal say in his lightly accented voice, "Oh my, sir, I wouldn't say it in that way exactly…."

"You think because I spent my career in that padded envelope we call corporate life I can't be of any possible use outside of it," Em fired up.

From bad to worse Halloran sharply replied, "Leave it to the professionals." Em took this to mean him and his men.

"I am an intelligence professional." Her undertone conveyed, "you jackass."

"Field agents, I mean. Can you handle a gun? Hussein was murdered with one. This isn't a simple corporate fiddle."

"I'm not into the gun thing. Not everything is solved in the field." She gave an exasperated sigh. "Don't look at me like, go home, little girl. Intelligence is a very suitable job for a woman. Men duke it out. They shoot it out. Women spend their lives outwitting their opponents. Very few resort to outright violence. *Or need to,"* she spoke with a little female growl.

They were at equal odds with each other, and if they stayed together any longer that evening, it would only become more intense. She managed to get behind his professional persona and aggravate the hell out of him, and he was not quite sure why.

Halloran stretched his injured leg again. This time he let her see his wince with the movement.

"Oh, I should be going home, I'm late already." *Halloran must be in pain and on edge because of that,* Em realized.

His ploy worked. She rose to leave, and he hauled himself up more slowly, getting both legs under him to rise to thank her for coming in. Halloran kept his tone of voice conciliatory. One lesson learned.

13

ON HER WAY OUT

———◆———

E M SAID A PROMPT GOODBYE to Garvey at the front desk, who informed her that her things would be in the air lock waiting for her. Inside the sealed chamber, she felt the air change several times, and a security drawer opened out from the side wall in front of her. The drawer contained her knives, nail clippers and box cutter. Scooping them into her bag, she waited for the next air exchange.

Standing with nothing to do but wait, Em wondered what would happen if anyone came to work with the flu, or even a cold, probably not a done thing with this organization. The door slid back. The couple seated at the table in the corner were still there practicing Urdu with little sign of progress. Signs of frustration were showing. They studiously ignored her as she passed carrying the brown paper bag of cannolis.

As she passed José, her voice carried over the counter. "The cannolis were excellent. We enjoyed them. Please compliment Mrs. Maresca for me."

José gave her an understanding smile. "Will do ma'am. Thank you for coming in."

At the Security desk, Garvey and Halloran watched the exchange between Em and José on the built-in monitors.

"Hey, Mr. Schwartz." Schwartz, a smaller more compact man, moved in between them. A good looking man with black straight hair and sharp dark eyes, he wore a blue pinstriped Oxford button down with the sleeves rolled up. Joel Schwartz had begun to show a slight mid-life paunch that enforced office work could bring on.

Garvey addressed Michael Halloran. "She's a handful. I can't believe she just came in."

"Curiosity, I told you," he replied. "She was an intelligence analyst. The best ones are insatiably curious. I gave her detailed directions quickly and let her puzzle them out. Made it an invitation for a visit. If we'd brought her in for questioning, she'd have lawyered up fast. Beyond fast. That's one thing that we don't want in this town. One call to a friend in the Yale Law School, and there'd be a willing candidate for Attorney General down here with her."

"Sir, you were a lawyer, weren't you?" Garvey asked.

"International Law, Georgetown. It's a different mind-set," Halloran replied. "Now everyone knows what she looks like, if we have to go out and find her. Garvey, how did you do?"

"Oh, we'll know her again, sir. Voice prints are good. Both handprints match the federal database. She's not camera shy so I got three good pictures for facial recognition, matches the driver's license and passport photos. Biometric scan is incomplete, she was carrying too much stuff. All we need is a retinal scan and DNA. That will be harder without her cooperation."

Halloran replied with a sub verbal growl. "I've heard that before. We may know who Ms. Huber is, but we certainly don't know what her capabilities are and what she can manage to do with them. She sure as hell isn't telling us everything."

"She walked out with her coffee cup, I noticed. They all watch too much TV," Schwartz chuckled.

"That's good enough for now. How about the car?"

asked Halloran.

"Clean. Nothing on it. I had to promise to give back her collection of knives to stall, or she would have gone to her car and walked up on the guys. That van's so old there's no way to ping a GPS. They added something, as you wanted. One emergency beacon on the larger knife and on the box cutter, too. She's bound to find one if she's that curious."

"I'm counting on it. I'm hoping she will use it if she needs it. Ms. Huber will find the professor if anyone can. We've lost two people on this project already, one dead, one missing. Let's not go for three. Surveillance team ready to go?"

Garvey nodded in the affirmative.

"You told her to leave it alone," Schwartz pointed out.

"That's not going to happen if we can believe her ex-husband. No reason not to believe him. She's got 'Does not take orders' written all over her. She's given us four leads to check, and a clear motive. That's a hell of a lot more than we had before she came in. If we relay the leads concerning the pirated solar products to the local police, they'll think we're genius, and she's the cat sitter. Safer for her that way. That's an analyst's ploy. Figure out the moves, then get the field agents to execute them. You're on Joel. Have V.J. Agarwal work on it, he'll serve as the forensic accountant she suggested. Follow the money like the lady said. Get V.J. to call his contacts. I want the information by tomorrow morning."

"V.J. will like that, he thrives on finding creative account-ing. Makes his day, the more exotic the scheme the better he likes it," replied Schwartz.

"Good looking woman, sir," Garvey said to his boss under his breath.

"A taste for pretty women is a dangerous thing." Hallo-ran had reason to know.

"That bad?"

"I didn't say it was a bad thing, I said it's dangerous. Not all dangerous things are bad. Just some of them. Find Andy Vargas, tell him I have a job for him. Send him to my office." Halloran headed back through the glass doors that led into the offices.

"What's gotten into the boss?" Garvey asked the man standing next to him.

"Did you see the way those two looked at each other? Sizing each other up. He's still sore and limping after the last one tried to kill him. At least this one was a professor's wife and worked in an office, she should be different," Schwartz suggested.

"All due respect Mr. Schwartz, any woman who carries that many knives is not your average chiquita. I need to find Vargas."

"Try Gladys's desk," Schwartz advised. Not a lot got by Joel Schwartz inside the building or out. His former career conditioned his instincts and reflexes. Submitting to desk work was an expedient he hoped would not be too prolonged. Schwartz took himself off down the hall to roust out his right hand man and best money tracker, V.J. Agarwal.

———————

Andy Vargas presented himself to Halloran who sat behind his desk. Not for the first time, the field agent wished that their boss had a bigger office.

"You wanted to see me? We going out? I'll get the car." Andy Vargas, a fit and active man in his late twenties had known hardship as a child. Vargas's people had called Mexico home for generations beyond counting. His shirt sleeves were always worn long to hide scars received in his young years. He liked driving the boss around. They went to unpredictable places and saw more action than a man of Halloran's rank expected to see. After the last exceedingly close encounter on the dock, Washington had made it clear to Vargas that the major responsibility of his job was to keep Director Halloran alive, and preferably uninjured. And, by the way, thanks for pulling Halloran out of the water after the attempt on his life.

"You're going out Andy. I'm staying in to do the report on the death of Professor Hussein."

"You want me to watch the lady? That could be good." To Andy surveillance out in the countryside would be a welcome diversion.

"Being done."

Halloran had his custom street map of New Haven projected on the wall monitor in full view. GIS staff had fussed and fumed over his special requirements. It showed both streets, elevations and underground assets including tunnels, conduits, fallout shelters, command posts and special features like the underground river that ran beneath the university library out to the harbor. A large cover could be closed down and locked into place to conceal the monitor from guests, whose visits were rare indeed.

"I want you to do some leg work in the Fair Haven section. This spot shows Professor Kirbee's house down towards the center. This is the murder scene, in the park along the west side of the river to the north, short of the edge of town. The park on the other side of the river is used by the residents of the east side of town, part of the Spanish speaking community. Go out, try the park and the shops around there. See if anyone heard or saw anything the evening of Hussein's death. We've heard from one side of the river, closest to Yale. There's a chance that the perps crossed the river or ran around the park into Fair Haven to disappear."

"You think someone from the neighborhood killed him?" Andy questioned.

"No, actually I don't. I'm thinking this is not a mugging. I'm hoping someone has seen or heard something but not come forward."

"Won't the New Haven Police check this out?"

"Illegals may not talk to them. We know that as well as they do. Go in and find out what you can. I want to be the first to know. We have the same problem all law enforcement does in this country. People come here wanting to live free from fear, if they are without papers, they're scared to report a crime or to admit witnessing one. They are more likely to be victims of intimidation, theft and worse." Halloran paused. "But we are still responsible for their safety. Any terrorist attack on a soft target will harm anyone — whoever they are, legal or illegal."

"We have over two thousand reasons to know that, sir," Vargas agreed with regret. He'd lost friends on 9/11, and a family member. He'd watched TV news in shock as the second tower fell.

"This is a case of national security. We have a distinguished scientist with security clearance dead. Another well connected one with high level clearance among the missing. We need the residents' help if they've seen anything. Some folks forget to ask the people who stay in the background. Often they are the ones who are on the alert, and who observe the most. No checks on papers," Halloran concluded.

"I understand, sir. I earned my citizenship by serving in the Army." Andy Vargas stood straighter.

"And a few decorations to go with it. Get going."

Vargas hesitated. "My sister is deployed. We are lucky. I worry about the others, so many people want asylum here. I'll be back in time to drive you home. He was your friend, right? I'm sorry," he added.

"That could be late tonight. And yes, thanks. Kirbee is, too." Halloran continued to stare at the map.

"Andy, see if anyone works at the industrial park. See if they saw Hussein there the night he was killed. We don't know why they found Hussein's body in the city park to begin with."

"Most likely lured there. Not a place too many people go alone late at night, down that path by the water." Andy Vargas ran his hand through his hair. "Man, I need a haircut. I don't like it this long."

"No buzz cuts for street work. You'll look like a fed," Halloran replied without looking up. He'd heard this complaint before.

"I could be back from Afghanistan." Receiving no response Andy said, "Right, I'm going."

"Send in V.J. on your way out."

14

V.J.'S REPORT

———◆———

V.J. AGARWAL, CALCUTTA UNIVERSITY, BA, MS, Wharton MBA, parked his long legs in the chair vacated by his colleague Agent Andy Vargas. "Good afternoon, suh, with the limited time, I've done a quick financial check on the subject." V.J.'s voice reflected his education in his native West Bengal. His English retained the intonation of the language as spoken there, musical and in usage more correctly British than some of his American colleagues could manage. In conversation he often used the continuous present adding 'ing' to his verbs. Under pressure, during presentations especially, his English became impeccable, which could be intimidating.

"Good, tell me what you've found, then we have that other issue of yours to deal with." Halloran drummed his fingers on the desk for emphasis.

V.J. knew that the director would not rest until the pending issue was settled, so he proceeded to give his report as succinctly as he could. Pakhi, his wife, would have dinner waiting at home. "Ms. Huber's finances are in order. Bills are paid on a regular basis several times a month. Only once in a very great while is one overdue by several, two, three days only. This seems to happen at the same time each year. Income though, it is not high, and it requires withdrawals from savings to meet bills some months, and for any big bill. Car repairs, doctors, inexpensive vacations. No large outstanding debts."

"Credit?"

"Cards have moderate running balances and are never quite paid up." V.J. sighed. "People should never really charge what they cannot pay off. The interest is too high on these things. Can't be helped, I know. She is retired after all.

"All very dull and ordinary. Now, sir, here comes the interesting part," V.J. said, having warmed up his audience. "She is divorced from this Professor Huber person. And not a nice one. Connecticut is a no fault divorce state, so there are not many details in the record. However, I did manage to learn that the professor pulled a fast maneuver financially. He left the university, took up a job with the family oil business at a similar salary. That was the amount used in the divorce calculations. Pretty soon after the divorce was final, Professor Huber gets a big promotion, a raise and a title. I called a friend to learn this. It was something of a scandal, you know."

"She got stiffed?" The boss shook his head.

"Well, I wouldn't quite say that, sir, her lawyer negotiated a lump sum payment. She did her best, I am sure of that, you know, considering the opposition." V.J. paused to wait for a question then continued. "Ms. Huber took the lump sum payment and bought that Spring House place. It was a good deal after all. Very interesting. Spring House was a hard place to sell, and easy place to buy for someone with cash down. The house comes with the business, Blackmun's Wintergreen Springs and Ice, which is basically inactive, but a source of potential revenue should it be revived. The land is not subdividable according to the deed, to protect the quality of the spring water. It is classed as agricultural land, and the development rights were sold to the State of Connecticut by the previous owner, who kept that money." V.J. showed he was pleased to be able to give the details on such short notice.

"Agricultural? Because of the spring?" Halloran questioned.

"No, sir, not entirely. It's the trees actually. They are quite old now. I understand that you can see these great huge, sugar maple trees along the road in front of the house and in the woods on the hill above the spring. They were planted years ago by New England custom. The land with the trees is rented for two or so months in the spring to a farmer who makes the maple syrup. Rent is minimal, part of it is paid in 'best grade' maple syrup. It is supposed to be quite fine. Not a big income producer." Both men laughed.

"No large payments, no offshore accounts that I could find, no failed investments. But there is one more thing you might want to know. Mr. Robert Albrecht's will is being probated. And, Professor Huber is contesting, he had the expectations that he would be inheriting a controlling interest in the family business. He will not. Rumor has it that grand old lady Mrs. Marlene Albrecht retains control. Seems the gentleman, Mr. Robert Albrecht took issue with some recent behaviors of his nephew, Professor Huber." A very sociable man, V.J. enjoyed a good soap opera, one with lots of romance and action. Bollywood films were his secret passion. The Hubers's divorce had the delicious scent of scandal around it. "Shall I continue to look for more, sir?" V.J. said with obvious relish.

"Good job, yes, keep digging on the Albrecht will. Ask your contacts about indications that any material possessions might be passed along. Watch for any influx of cash on Ms. Huber's accounts," he directed.

"Now, V.J., we have the other issue to deal with." Halloran put on his stern taskmaster face.

V.J.'s shoulders slumped noticeably.

"Target practice. You've got to do it. We all, every one of us, has to re-qualify every year. In an emergency, we could need you in the field."

"But sir, my workload."

Halloran cut him off. "V.J. I know all about your workload. You have until 5:30 on Friday afternoon to get it done. I'll call Joel and tell him to give you the time." On inspiration, knowing his man, the director continued. "Besides, we know how good you are at this, and we need you to raise the team's score."

V.J. sat straight up. "What team, sir?"

"Home Office, here. You know some of the analysts can't shoot worth a good damn. Practice for a couple hours, then nail the test for us. I know it's not cricket, but do your best. Tell Joel."

"Right, sir. I'll tell the rest of them, too." V.J. spoke with enthusiasm.

"Good evening, thank you for staying. Best to Pakhi. Tell her I'm sorry for delaying you." Halloran said to himself, *Now, what have I done. The whole crew will be down blasting away on the range, and I'll have to justify the bill for the ammo. Worth it in the end, I suppose. Gladys will have to give Bertha a heads up.* Before he left that evening, Halloran drafted an email announcing the team competition for Gladys Rodriquez to distribute to all Regional staff.

15

DEANNA AND SANDY
IN THE KITCHEN

———◆———

"MOM SAYS WE'RE TAX AND insurance poor. She used her divorce settlement to buy this barn of a place that nobody else wanted. We've been here two years already. Remember when the basement was all full of cobwebs and mouse turds and broken windows? The floor in the sunroom had buckled because the rain and snow got in one of the windows. All of us scrubbed it and painted it, and Mom hired some crazy guys to sorta clean the basement. Something's always leaking and the wiring needs to be replaced. It's drafty in the winter, and the mice still think they own the place." Deanna washed the leaf lettuce fresh from the garden, Boston Bibb, Butter Crunch and the reddish Oak Leaf lettuce, splattering water all over the counter.

Sandy scrubbed down the old Mexican tiles on the counter in preparation of chopping the vegetables for the dinner's salad. She and Deanna were waiting for Em to arrive home, unaware of her inquisition in Halloran's office. The warm late afternoon sun shone in through the kitchen windows, which faced due west. The kitchen casement windows looked down on the neatly stacked pile of firewood and on down the hill through the trees to the meadow.

"I counted three different species when we moved in, deer mice, field mice and domestic house mice. You know, the deer mice live down the front hall and they're actually kind of cute. They have long noses, beady black eyes and big ears." Deanna wiggled her wet hands over her ears in imitation of a famous mouse. "Sandy, we could give them names, we see them so often. Watching the cat chase them around in front of guests is kinda fun, too."

Always the practical one, Sandy replied, "We probably should have another cat, I don't think one's enough for this place."

"But we kinda like it here, if you climb one of the trees in the backyard high enough, you can see Long Island on a clear day." Deanna had fond memories of climbing the younger sugar maple.

Sandy chuckled as she chopped the carrots for the salad. She'd heard all this before and still enjoyed it. Each time Deanna told it, she mimed it differently, sometimes she mimed the mice, sometimes the cat chasing them. Although Sandy spent much of her time living with the Huber family, she often missed summers. She tried to be as little burden as she could to her adopted family and to earn as much as she could by being a sleep away camp counselor. During the school year she often held not one but two part time jobs.

"The crazy old professor who owned it said he wouldn't sell it to just anyone. Probably had to find a soft touch like Mom. He left most of the furniture in the living room, said his kids didn't want it and it needed to be appreciated. Whoever heard of Stickley anyway? He said it belonged here."

"And then there's the basement, the freakin' place is like a sports museum, nothing new. Some things are really old, who ever used wooden blades for ice skates? I'm surprised

the canoes aren't made of birch bark. There is some seriously funky stuff down there, too." Deanna paused here,
judging it best not to expand on the "seriously funky stuff."

Seeing Sandy reaching into the fridge she said, "Watch
out, the milk on the left is sour. She keeps it for baking.
You'd think this was 1929 or something. Grandma said
they had to can their own vegetables, make their own
wine and everything back then."

Sandy laughed outright. "We did that last week, we froze
the fresh peas."

"Don't even remind me, she's looking forward to making Grandma's chili relish in August. Do you have any idea
what that smells like cooking? Knock you over." With a
flourish, Deanna threw the now thoroughly washed leaf
lettuce into a large turned wooden salad bowl.

"You weren't here when my father saw this place, he
called my mother 'plumb crazy' to think about buying it
'all by herself.' My mother grumbled. Of course, it was
absolutely the wrong thing to say. Dad never learns. Times
have changed. You tell a full grown woman not to do
something she has her heart set on, because she's a woman,
and she'll bite your arm off."

Deanna tossed the dried cranberries into the salad with
the fresh vegetable crunchies prepared by Sandy. She set
about scrubbing the potatoes, passing them to Sandy to be
pealed. "Of course, I can't blame Dad too much for what
he said. Mom hadn't seen him in quite a while, and she
started yelling." This was Sandy's favorite part, she'd heard
it before, and she'd been waiting for it. Deanna puffed up
her chest, threw out her hands and overacted her imitation
of her mother, voice and all.

"'Harley, what the hell happened to you? What happened to your nose? It's straight, did you have an accident?
Where are your freckles?'" And now suspiciously in a
deeper voice Deanna said, "'Did you get them buffed off?'
When he starts to deny that, she says, 'You had your front

teeth fixed, too. No boots? Those shoes may look fine in Rome, I don't know about San Antonio. Are they going to let you back into Texas looking like that?'" Both girls went off into fits of laughter, endangering the progress towards mashed potatoes for dinner.

Eight Years Previous

IT WAS NOT A DARK and stormy night when Sandy came to stay, a chilly drizzle fell that afternoon in mid-October. The middle schooler stood in the light rain on Em Huber's doorstep at what came to be known as the "old house" on a tree lined street in a fashionably academic neighborhood in town. Sandy had been expected on Friday evening, then Saturday morning, and finally arrived at 4:30 on Sunday afternoon, in time for Sunday dinner. Only her mother came to drop her off, and the former Mrs. Waitely didn't stay long and barely set foot beyond the front hallway. The plan was Sandy would stay with the Hubers to attend school until a new apartment could be rented for her family, beginning the first of November. When Em asked for a cell phone number to enable her to contact Sandy's mother, the woman seemed reluctant to give it and left quickly saying Sandy could always call her.

For Em, the lack of willingly provided contact information was only the beginning of the paradox of her scanty relationship with either of Sandy's parents. The bright blonde petite, well dressed, well put together woman of her memory no longer existed, it seemed. Sandy's mother's hair color had reverted back to a darker ash blonde, her eyes were bracketed with deep wrinkles, and she was bone thin. Her expression seemed hardened. Eye contact was refused to both her daughter Sandy and to Em. Deanna's presence went unacknowledged. The woman appeared to be in nothing but a rush to leave Sandy there in the hallway. There was no hug, no word of encouragement or endearment on parting. Sandy's mother simply walked away.

Sandy stood on the hall rug, damp from the rain that had been falling all afternoon and bedraggled from lack of care. Her honey blonde hair, plastered close down to her head, hung in lank and tangled strands. It was mid-October in Connecticut, days and nights were chilly. The central heat was on in the houses around town. The young girl shivered in her faded black turtle neck, several sizes too large, and frayed jeans, ripped at the knee. She brought with her a black plastic garbage bag of clothing and a school backpack that had seen better days. Her expression was forlorn, as if she had been a castaway. Her complexion was sallow and without the glow of youth and health that Em remembered seeing in Sandy's elementary school years.

Deanna had really, seriously, tried to prepare her mother. Looking at Sandy, Em's heart clenched in her chest, but she kept her feelings to herself. The previous week, Deanna brought home a letter written by Sandy, one of several that were given to her friends, saying her family had lost their apartment. The short note asked if anyone had room to take in a family until they could find a new place to live. Deanna asked her mother if they could help. Em had not enough room for a family, and Harley Travis Huber would not have acquiesced to such an arrangement. But she did have a spare bedroom, once the province of a grandparent. Mother and daughter agreed that they could take in Sandy for two weeks. Huber would be gone to attend a convention for part of that time. Sandy would go to school on the bus with Deanna. The girls were then in eighth grade. That was the agreement, two weeks.

Em welcomed Sandy as a much anticipated guest, which she was. Sensing that they needed to get the girl into the shower first off and into clean clothes before dinner, Em composed a tactful inquiry about this subject and was

promptly cut off in no uncertain terms by Deanna. Deanna's first priority was to get her friend something to eat
and drink. They had been sharing Deanna's school lunch
every day since the beginning of the school year.

"Drop your stuff in the hall. I'm hungry! Let's get something to eat," Deanna told Sandy. She dragged her friend
by the hand into the kitchen at the back of the house,
leaving her mother standing alone in the hallway her arms
crossed and with a smile of appreciation for her warm
hearted daughter. The kitchen was the crowded haven of
the family women, decorated with hanging pots and pans
and yellow chintz. Celina, her older sister, was pulling her
experimental rosemary and candied ginger scones out of
the oven.

Celina watched with delight as Sandy ate three of her
still hot scones, slathered in strawberry jam and dripping
with butter. It was gratifying to Celina when one of her
creations received enthusiastic response. Her newest blend
of hibiscus tea was just the thing for a chilly afternoon
though. She was developing into a fine cook, and a better
baker. However, her herb and spice combinations once in
a while left a tang as an after taste. It was possible, really, to
put too much black pepper in chai, and too much baking
powder in biscuits. Deanna reflected it was fortunate this
new batch of scones was not half bad and had no unidentifiable ingredients that she knew about.

When Em came to watch them through the hallway
door the three girls were laughing. Sandy looked distinctly
brighter. Not one to stand on ceremony with a guest in
obvious need, Em forged ahead with her first impulse.

"Sandy, we're so glad to have you. It's Sunday, we're washing clothes for the week. Do you have any that you would
like to wash? Oh, also, there will be a line for the bathroom
this evening. Would you like to take your shower, or a bath
now, before dinner? To avoid the rush." Her daughters
looked at their mother, they did laundry in the evenings

and on Saturday.

To Em's relief, Sandy's eyes lit up. "A shower? Can I take a shower right now?"

"Of course. Plenty of towels. Shampoo. Soaps. Upstairs." With a look directed to Deanna, she said, "Why don't you two start a wash first, then take Sandy upstairs to her room to get her settled." Deanna received the hint and took her friend off to the front hall to collect her belongings. She had her own plan though. As usual she took her mother's directions rather as guidelines.

While the two friends climbed the stairs, hauling the black plastic garbage bag and the disreputable backpack, Celina turned to speak to her mother. "I can't believe that's the Sandy we knew. She looks so different. She's half starved and scared and very tired. Mom, what happened to her?"

Em sighed and looked on her oldest daughter, who was in many ways a mirror image of herself. "As far as I can figure out, it's a case of divorce that isn't working out in favor of the children. Which is odd in this state. Your father and I used to see her parents at school open house each year. They seemed to be very comfortable financially. Her mother was always dressed in expensive suits. And her father, you know he is a big man, always dressed in tweed overcoats and a business suit. Fancy Rolex watch, BMW to go with it. Then they stopped coming. To me, her mother looked like a very pretty younger woman who was scared silly of her husband. He always spoke for both of them. She would start to speak, and he would interrupt to finish her sentences. Not in a kind way. She barely got to speak a word of her own."

Celina shook her head. "I remember they used to have sleepover parties for Sandy's friends. They owned a big house with a long center hall and a crystal chandelier. I wished we had one."

"Yes, now Sandy and her mother and the two younger

children have lost an apartment and not in the best part of town, either. From corporate executive's daughter to homeless. Hard to believe. I'm sure we'll hear some of the story. Let's take care of Sandy, ask as few questions as we can, and repeat nothing she tells us."

"She ate half my scones! I was going to save them for supper." Celine was pleased, obviously, and she shook her short curly brown hair.

"Why don't you make some of your rosemary cheddar cheese biscuits instead? I have plenty of chicken in the Crock-Pot. Let's see if we can fill her up. Do you have an extra sweatshirt or two you could lend her? She came in all wet with no coat on."

"I noticed, Mom, I noticed. I'll go up and get her some stuff. Then I'll bake." Celina was an organizer who planned and acted on her plans, seemingly without the necessity of further consideration.

Celina took off towards the stairs, almost tripped by her sister who was heading down towards the laundry room in the basement.

"Sandy's taking a shower, and I stole all her clothes. They so needed washing, Mom. You won't believe this. She doesn't have any pajamas or anything else to sleep in! And she forgot her toothbrush and stuff like that. They packed up so fast one night," Deanna said in a rush of words.

"So you stole all her clothes. What's she supposed to wear when she gets out of the shower, smarty? I'm on it, I've got stuff that will fit. You do the wash." Celina gave her younger sister a mostly playful shove towards the basement door.

"We have extra toothbrushes and personal supplies in the linen closet, top shelves," Em reminded Deanna as she considered the possible reasons for a hasty late night move from an apartment.

At the supper table that evening, it was the three girls, older brother Joshua, Em and Huber. Sandy ate chicken, green beans, a great heap of mashed potatoes with gravy, as many cheese biscuits as she dared and said very little. Once washed and dressed in clean clothes, Em reflected how remarkably similar Deanna and Sandy looked, similar height, hair color and features, only Deanna was the more athletic of the two. Sandy had a fuller figure and a more reserved manner. They could almost be family. Huber, already distracted by outside interests, consigned Sandy to the status of his wife and daughters and barely noticed her. He and Joshua talked football and the effects of glaciation on the local hills, which the family had heard a million times before. As it turned out, Huber's lack of notice was a blessing in disguise because he forgot when Sandy had arrived, and only occasionally inquired, absently, when she was to leave.

After dinner homework was the agenda item for the evening before television could be turned on. At first, this appeared to be a new idea for Sandy, who rummaged around in her backpack and finally did manage to find her work. Shortly, after 9:00, growing visibly weary, Sandy asked if she might go up to bed. Long about the family's usual bed time, Em and Deanna looked in on Sandy together. They found the young girl curled up on her bed in borrowed togs, holding a small well-worn stuffed animal, species now unidentifiable. Em noticed Sandy was sleeping between two blankets. The next morning, Em gently suggested to Sandy that she could crawl into the bed and sleep between the sheets. Before they left for school, Deanna let her mother know Sandy's family had been sleeping on mattresses in the apartment with no sheets.

Over time, incidents were mentioned, details came to be known gradually of Sandy's family situation. Two weeks grew to two months, and then an indefinite stay. From that time forward, the Huber women had a project, provide shelter, care and support for the neighbor at their door in certain need.

16

HALLORAN'S DIGS

———◆———

HALLORAN PREFERRED A CROW'S NEST to a man
cave. On the third floor of an expansive old Victorian
house on the east side of the harbor, on rising ground,
he found the vista he wanted. His apartment had been
converted from the sizable attic, walls primed in white and
left that way. It had a captain's walk on the roof above, and
new deck out on the harbor side. Security features had been
added as a matter of course. With his injury, he had found
it beneficial to have a stair lift installed that wound up the
back hall stairs. At first reluctant to admit he needed a ride,
Halloran found the elderly Naval officer and his wife, who
were the second floor tenants, were grateful for it. They
used it for carrying groceries upstairs. The ground floor
tenants were a Coastie's young family. His duty station was
right down the avenue at Fort Hale Park. The view from
their choice location spanned the mouth of the harbor, the
bridges, all the way to East Rock, a mountain of basalt on
the east of the city. Telescopes were a feature on each floor,
Halloran had two lined up against the sliding glass doors
to the balcony deck.

A tired man rode the stair glider to the third floor attic
apartment and entered the security code on the key pad

camouflaged in the woodwork. Once inside the door, he entered a different code into the security panel that hid behind a small framed etching of an 18th century sailing ship fully rigged, sailing into the wind. Halloran gazed around, in threat assessment mode. Nothing seemed amiss, the bright white walls, the sleek Danish modern furniture, even the waves on the dark seaweed green and deep blue shag carpet seemed in order. He glanced over at his work-table at the balsa wooden ship model, the galley *Whydah,* Black Sam Bellamy's pirate ship, wrecked in a violent storm off the coast of Cape Cod. Almost half finished, the galley would have to wait for another night. Halloran was working on a model of the controversial pirate ship for a historic exhibit. A finished model of the *U.S.S. Arleigh Burke,* the class leader of guided missile destroyers, rested peacefully on a shelf over the worktable.

After surveying the harbor and finding nothing either interesting or suspicious, Halloran pulled the To Go containers of Mrs. Maresca's lasagna out of the warming oven. He grabbed a bottle of Harpoon from the fridge and settled down on the couch, leg elevated, television news on in closed caption mode. Dinner was eaten as Halloran read through the transcript of the afternoon's interview with Em Huber. Interviewing officers needed to review, correct and make any additional notes on interview transcripts, then sign off.

Draining the Harpoon, regretting the absence of a cannoli for desert, Halloran loaded the audio file of the interview from a jump drive. Using a single earpiece, he listened to the file, comparing the printed transcript to the audio. He listened for the changes in tone, inflection and volume, especially for the pauses and the hesitations. As with many good investigators, his memory was excellent, amazing really, the envy of his staff, and it had been the terror of his three now grown sons. The WAV file of the interview brought him Em's voice, clear, with a distinctive local accent, a blend of Boston vowels, the clipped speech of New York, and the influence of Yale.

Curiously, Ms. Huber's accent varied with the subject. Certain words were pronounced more correctly at one time than another. Most individuals were more consistent in their speech. A note on her resume listed basic knowledge of several widely disparate languages. He made a list, first note. "Good ear for languages, wide vocal range, mimic?"

Halloran found he liked the sound of Em Huber's voice, the vibrant low notes resonated for him. He found himself listening to one section three times. With another Harpoon in his hand, he listened as the tone of her voice rose and diminished, expressive, and for him enticing. From the hesitations in the section of the file concerning Albrecht, which she worked to keep quite brief, he felt she was more comfortable discussing Kirbee and the murder.

With time to think, the investigator remembered the well-attended funeral of Robert Albrecht almost two years ago in Texas. Em Huber, already divorced from Travis Huber, seemed genuinely grieved. During the service, she sat in the family pew with the widow and her two daughters. It was Travis Huber who seemed on the outside fringe. Halloran hadn't liked Travis Huber and suspected that the rest of the extended Albrecht family were beginning to have reservations about him as well.

Halloran made it a point to listen to conversations around him while seeming to focus his attention elsewhere. He'd overheard one of the deceased's Army buddies referring to Travis. The older man said he himself had learned his own lessons about certain French women during the War and believed Travis was too old to be trying out those parts. Halloran had done his best to identify all the old war buddies at the funeral as part of his investigation, but the identity of that particular gent remained elusive. Something there, but he suspected it was more complex than just the trail of missing bricks that could never be displayed, never be legitimately sold, whose possessor risked prosecution.

Over the harbor, dusk had grown to the deep black of an early summer night. Lights ringed the harbor, highway traffic streamed around and across, the towers of the city stood out, airplane warning lights on top. A corporate jet, following the highways up from New York, circled the city, heading for the airport out in the marshlands of the east shore.

Halloran found himself anticipating the multiple ways Em Huber could disobey his request to stay out trouble and to stay away from his case. It occurred to him that she might stir up no end of speculation by contacting everyone who had ever even heard of Frank Kirbee and Ali Hussein. Would she be canny and cautious enough not to bring down the ire of the local FBI office or still worse the university or city administrations? Surely she would burn the wires searching the Internet for clues and making innumerable phone calls, which they could track. It would be best to leave the investigation in the field to his agents, yet he had his doubts she would understand that. Thinking about it was not an unpleasant exercise, but not even Halloran could accurately predict her next foray.

17

V.J. SEEKING SANDY

THE NEXT MORNING FOUND HALLORAN in his office even earlier than usual, but he did not remain alone for long.

V.J. Agarwal planted himself in the chair in front of Halloran's desk before the customary start of their working day.

"Good morning, V.J., we're both early this morning." Halloran looked up from his habitual first thing in the morning bout with paperwork.

"Yes," V.J. launched his topic without waiting. "So I thought I had best inquire about the household of Ms. Huber. It is this, one hears that Ms. Huber often introduces the girls 'my daughter Deanna and Sandy.' People may assume that they are both her daughters. Indeed they are not. It was an understandable mistake, looking at the photos, the girls do have what is called a passing resemblance to each other. However, Ms. Huber's elder daughter has the name of Celina and is not at all looking like these two young ladies."

"What is your point V.J.? The girl's a friend, a college roommate?" asked Halloran, knowing there was likely to be a good reason for this early morning interview.

"Now there it is," V.J. pronounced with pleasure at surprising his boss. "She is more than this. She is Allesandra Waitely, who has been taken in by the Hubers and is living with them since she was but a young teenager. However, things are not all on the up and up.

"Not all of this is known by many people. Some of what I am telling you I found out through asking one friend of Pakhi's who is a middle school teacher. The Waitely family went through some sort of problems, and the attendance and whole behavior of the child Allesandra changed. One year all is good, the child is happy, doing well, showing good promise. The mother and the father come to all the events and the PTO meetings, then not a thing. With each marking period the child's grades and attendance are getting a little worse, and her clothing worse still. The teachers cannot reach either parent. No one will come in to school to speak of these matters. If she becomes sick in the school, they cannot reach anyone to pick her up. She is arriving with no coat in the winter." V.J. paused to observe the effect of his words. "In the cold New England climate here, a winter without a coat means staying in the school building. No field trips."

"Go on." Halloran's tone indicated he knew there should be a point coming.

"All of a sudden, as if, one would say overnight, things begin to change for this young person. She begins to ride a different bus to school and to be arriving on time with homework done. Pakhi said it was as if she had been taken in hand. Her hair, her clothes, her teeth, everything was clean once more. Teachers could tell this by walking up and down the aisles next to her. Someone was giving her math help. Gradually her clothes became newer, not perhaps brand new, but clothes made for a girl. The teachers knew that she came to school with Deanna Huber and could be said to live in the town for school residency. The young lady is very bright, and the teachers choose not to ask questions. They left the signing of papers and things to the administrators. The young lady caught up for those couple of years of inattention until she was receiving the school honors as a regular thing."

"So she is living with the Hubers, who get her help with math?" Halloran prompted V.J. to continue.

"Here is the thing that you might wish to know. Looking at tax returns, Ms. Huber does not claim Miss Waitely as a dependent. Her father Mr. George J. Waitely, who has been divorced these many years now from Allesandra's mother, shows child support in the amount one would expect for three children based on the state's usual amounts. Allesandra is the oldest of three children from that marriage. Her mother, who now lives out of state, shows the full amount of the child support on her income tax and claims Allesandra as a dependent. There is no sign that Ms. Huber receives any of this money, or ever has."

Halloran frowned. "Allowance to the girl?"

"The young lady has worked every summer since she was fifteen years old and able to get a state work permit. As she became older, even two jobs. She is not likely getting extra money. I have reviewed the tax returns," V.J. concluded.

"Dodgy. Em Huber will have figured this out. There has to be a reason. Good job, V.J. She has two other children, what are they up to?"

"Well, here is another thing that you might wish to be knowing. The eldest child, Joshua Huber is through with grad school, married and employed in the maritime defense industry in the Boston area. Engineering is his field. When I called the company, they were not at all welcoming my call. The HR man asked me who the hell we were and what the hell I wanted to know for. Yes, Joshua Huber was employed by them. Had he been applying for a job with us, and no, we could not have him. Why would they think we would want him, I ask myself."

Halloran nodded.

"Then he asks me who the hell I work for, meaning yourself, sir. I did tell him your name. There was a rather long pause in the conversation. He came back to say that someone named Sam Hatch says, 'How the blazes are you, thought you were dead, would you like to go fishing?' And to tell you he has a new boat. Something very special."

Halloran laughed. "You won't get anything more out of Hatch, but you don't need to. His specialty is electronic surveillance and remote sensing. We sailed together years ago."

V.J. could easily figure that out, there were few people of interest in their line of work with whom Halloran had not sailed, drunk beer, argued a case in court, fished, gone to school with or otherwise heard tell of. The man had a companionable way about him when he was after contacts or human intel.

"Well, now for the eldest young lady, Celina, she is in the graduate program in pharmacology at the state university. Her special field of study is the traditional use of plants by various cultures for the development of medicines. She has been to South America, in the jungles recently, and is now in Maine working on farming techniques for herbal medicine. She has already published some well received findings.

"Nothing to send up an alert, sir," V.J. concluded.

Nothing, except the fact that Joshua Huber has a job that cannot be discussed. The apple, Halloran surmised, had not fallen or rolled far from the maternal tree.

18

ANDY'S REPORT

———◆———

HALLORAN HAD LEARNED EARLY THAT "just the facts" didn't work for Andy Vargas, it was about the people, the story. He pulled up his sore leg and positioned it more comfortably to listen to his Senior Agent's report.

Andy Vargas parked himself in a chair directly in front of Halloran's desk, far enough back to give his boss and mentor room to stretch out his legs. "So, it's like this, at first no one knows anything about anything. But I tell them I'm working for a friend of the dead guy. True right? Sort of. This friend is willing to pay money to anyone who can help him find out who killed his friend, and we don't want to tell the police about this because the friend wants to make sure he finds the guy first.

"This was scary for some people. But the guy at the fish market tells me his daughter knows a girl who came home frightened that night. She and the boyfriend were out in the park together. You were right. On the east side of the river. The father doesn't want her seeing the boyfriend because he's Puerto Rican and has no money. If I was her father, I'd worry if he had too much money and I didn't know where it came from. He's from Puerto Rico, he's legal. He's a citizen."

"Andy, what did she see?" Halloran interposed.

"Alright, so people think everyone who speaks Spanish is the same. She's Mexican. It's not the same," Andy continued to make his point. He could see Halloran understood.

"Okay, so the friend calls her and asks her to meet me in the parking lot behind the Dunkin' Donuts where she goes. Most of the staff there speaks Spanish. Twenty minutes later this car drives up. License plates checked out to the boyfriend. Nice girl. They were in the bushes on the east side of the river doing what kids do in the bushes on a warm night. They'd been there about an hour. They were putting themselves back together when they hear a man's voice and two gun shots. The sound carried over the water. Then in a couple minutes, they hear another gunshot and a woman scream, short, like she was surprised, followed by a big splash in the water like she fell in. Or someone fell in.

"They try to stay hidden, but they get curious and sneak down to the edge of the water to see what's going on. The moon is not too bright at this time. Couldn't see much in the woods across the water. They stay down in case there's more shooting. Then they hear a young woman screaming about 'He's dead!' So they decide they'd better get the hell out of there."

"Reliable?"

"Oh yeah, they're good kids. If I were her father, I'd put him to work in the store and make him marry her. Got names and addresses if we need them, but I promised we wouldn't." Andy stopped for a moment to gauge his boss's reaction.

"Basically, you're telling me that these witnesses corroborate the story the graduate students, the Weston girl and Masaryk, told the police when they found the body. Brief call out from a man, probably the victim, two gun shots, pause, third shot, brief scream from a woman followed by a splash, as if someone had gone into the river. All the action took place on the west side of the river. The night was too dark to see much across the water. Still no second body," said Halloran thoughtfully. "Put in for petty cash, I'll sign it."

"I told him to buy her a ring with it."

"Price of gold today he won't get much," remarked his boss.

"You know, there could have been people who were closer. These people I spoke to, they are here legally. There should have been more people around down in the park away from the river, and on the streets, out in the evening walking the dog. I could go to church in Fair Haven for Mass and talk to people there."

Andy Vargas looked off to his right, his brow furrowed, and he rubbed his left forearm, over the long wide scar Halloran knew resided there. This was Andy's tell, when he was troubled, he would rub the old scar. "When I was in school, we learned about the Statue of Liberty. 'Give me your tired, your poor, yearning to breathe free. I hold my light above the golden door.' What happened to that?" Vargas asked earnestly.

"Nothing, it's an ideal, and sometimes people forget their ideals. When my folks came over from the old country, there were signs in the windows that said, 'No Irish need apply.' Despite that, a couple generations later, we had an Irish Catholic President. Every new generation of immigrants has to make its own way. Not always easy. We make, and remake this country every day with every new group of people who arrive, however they come here. Mine came steerage.

Go to church, ask and listen," Halloran directed.

Andy Vargas nodded, he would look forward to it.

——◆——

Two Years Previous

STEFAN RANKEL WAS NOT ANDY Vargas's favorite partner, at first. As Senior Field Agent, Vargas expected the best. His first sight of Stefan Rankel caused a sinking feeling that took a week to dissipate. His first IIA partner, Nash Washington, had been a college athlete, a basketball player and scholar. Nash descended from a family that served in the home of General Washington in colonial Virginia. Agent Washington was a man of stature and intelligence with a solid future in law enforcement that had taken him up the food chain to the FBI after only a few years. First spotted in the hallway coming out of Halloran's office, Rankel couldn't have been more different. Under regulation height, thin to the point that adult men's suits hung on him, he wore his dark hair very short and his working clothes snug. There was an intense guarded expression on his narrow face. He appeared to be another one of Halloran's unlikely hires, which truth be told, usually turned out to be trumps.

For their first week together, Rankel observed and absorbed everything. He spoke little and communicated his understanding with nods and changes of posture that Andy soon learned to read accurately. Seen together, the partners seemed a mismatched pair. Rankel, although only slightly shorter than Andy, took up much less physical space. Andy Vargas a man of medium height had a hefty build enhanced by military training. Although the new recruit followed Andy's lead, he wasn't above commenting and acting on his own.

That first week, during their attempt to apprehend a federal fugitive who headed into a public housing project in Bridgeport hoping to avoid them, Andy watched in astonishment as Rankel outpaced him in their chase through the hot and crowded streets. Rankel could run like the very devil and he could climb. He proved his speed chasing the fugitive into a three story apartment building. The man ran through the apartment of an elderly lady who watched *Ellen* on TV, out a window and down a fire escape into Andy's clutches.

Handcuffing his capture, Andy had his back to the entrance of the alley below the fire escape when he heard Rankel yell, "Drop it!" A shot rang out from over his head. When Andy looked up he was amazed to see his new partner hanging from the fire escape ladder by one arm and a leg, with a gun in the other hand, looking for all the world like something out of *Spider Man*. Rankel jumped down and sped by Andy and his prisoner to bring a second man over twice his size to the ground. It soon became apparent that Halloran had hired himself a Ninja from CCNY, City College of New York.

The partnership of Andy Vargas and Steve Rankel grew on the pattern of their first pursuit. Andy was in charge. Rankel did what he deemed necessary and had his partner's back at all times. Rankel listened well and spoke his mind as he deemed fit. While Andy Vargas, a naturalized American with a strong family background, with true faith and allegiance obeyed the letter of the law and followed department procedure, Rankel varied it and was a little more flexible in his interpretation, shall we say.

Stefan Rankel was a second generation American, whose family lived in Hungary during both World Wars and suffered under two occupations. After the student inspired uprising against the Soviet-backed government failed in the fall of 1956, at long last, Rankel's family fled Hungary. Rankel grew up with a sense that laws and procedures were guidelines that could be honored, respected or disrespected as necessary in the service of humanity and justice. He had a freedom fighter's heritage buried deep within him.

Growing up as a boy of shorter height in a New York City neighborhood on the fringe of gang territory, Stefan learned early that it was imperative he find a way to survive his childhood without becoming a victim. Challenged by a gang of boys in a park one afternoon after school, he discovered he could use his smaller size to twist himself from their grasp, his wits to find a way out and his legs to outrun them. His father was understanding, self-defense and the defense of others were strong family values. Karate lessons followed. New running shoes became an annual birthday gift. Training for marathons became little Stevie's hobby. In high school, classmates called the tough little guy by his last name, and Rankel came to prefer it that way.

So it was late one dark, damp night on the Connecticut shoreline, about a year after Steve Rankel was hired that he and Andy Vargas found themselves attempting to chase down the man who hired them, Michael Halloran. Assigned to provide backup for an undercover sting, the partners were hidden from view of the marina dock on Long Island Sound where the meeting was to take place. The lighting was bad, several of the dim orange overheads appeared to be out on the shore side of the dock that extended into the sheltered harbor. It was almost like an Apogee low tide, a seasonal tide drawn out low by the phase of the moon. The sharp distinctive odor of seawater drained from mosquito laden salt marshes and storm sewers, blended together with the black mud of the salt flats rose in the air. The sailboats, small yachts and motor boats hung low from their moorings in the secluded inlet.

Halloran had gone in for a meeting, posing as a prominent local businessman desirous of bringing a Russian business partner, who had been denied a visa, into the country. His carefully cultivated target was a European woman suspected of managing a sophisticated organization smuggling high value merchandise in and out of the country, and most especially significant personnel. To their frustration, the field agents lost Halloran in a warren of buildings down on the docks. Sail boats, motor boats and

yachts lined up in the harbor, not one of the best managed marinas on the Sound. Barely maintaining the Coast
Guard standards for waterways, the marina was perfect for
the inconspicuous movement of boats at all hours of the
day and night.

Searching each dock, they came upon Halloran who
had been held at gun point. Trying to get the gun away,
Halloran wrestled with a woman who almost matched his
height but was heavier. She succeeded in forcing Halloran
to lose his footing on the slippery wooden planks, trip over
a cleat, and catch his right foot. This enabled her to send
him crashing down onto a boat deck and into the murky
salt water. As she raised her gun to shoot the injured man
in the back, Rankel and Vargas charged down the dock
yelling "Federal agents" at the top of their very healthy
lungs. The woman turned and fled towards a speedboat
moored in deep shadow at the end of the dock. With the
understanding that the partners developed, Andy Vargas
dove into the water to pull the unconscious Halloran to
safety. Stefan Rankel outran the woman, who gave him
quite a fight before she found herself in handcuffs that
looked like white twist ties. Rankel's lean profile offered
little room for concealed metal cuffs.

The driver in the speedboat made a successful escape.
And that was how Halloran acquired the limp, and a
renewed respect for dangerous women.

19

CRUISING DOWN THE RIVER

———◆———

EM SLEPT FITFULLY THAT NIGHT and was awake early. Her mind was active well before Deanna and Sandy stirred. The house was chilly as it was shaded from the warming sunlight of dawn by the ridge to the east. She dressed and went downstairs to the living room to wait for the girls to rise for breakfast.

"Hey, Mom, what'ya readin'?" Deanna found her mother on the blocky Stickley couch with her feet up on the wooden bench in front of her. A small warming fire was lit in the fieldstone fireplace. A large old leather bound Bible was on her lap. In the background, Mark O'Connor fiddled "Moonlight on the Water." Em wondered if he played it on his Vuillaume, a fine 1830s French violin with a distinctive sound.

"I'm reading about the spies. I like that part," Em replied. "Nothing like a good spy story. I think I may understand how they won the battle of Jericho. The directions are clear in the Book of Joshua. He sent two spies into Jericho to assess the town's defenses. The spies were hidden by a woman named Rahab, who is said to be a prostitute. Perhaps she felt victimized by the people of Jericho and helped the spies to save her whole family. Suppose that the spies determined the walls were vulnerable based on their construction of mud brick."

Em sang, "'Tramp, tramp, tramp.' When soldiers march in step they create ground waves and need to break up their stride when they cross bridges so that the vibrations don't damage the bridge. In the Book of Joshua, all able bodied male Israelites were called up to fight, now that had to be an army of men, say 10,000 or more. So following directions, they take the Ark of the Covenant, seven priests with seven ram's horn trumpets and they *march* around the city of Jericho once each day for six days. The army of the Israelites is silent, the priests blow the ram's horns.

"It could be that on each of the six days the ground vibrations caused by a large army *marching in step* crack and weaken the city walls more each day. On the seventh day they march around the walls seven times, the whole army led by the Ark and the Priests. At the end, the Priests sound the seven ram's horns and the army of the Israelites give a great war cry. They have created their own earthquake with sound and vibrations, and the weakened walls of Jericho fall before them. Joshua had faith and just followed the directions given to him. That's the message."

"Why am I not surprised? Their own earthquake. Is there a part in there you don't like?" Deanna stood before her mother on the rather faded Turkish carpet in front of the hearth.

"So much I wish I understood better. You can learn a lot by listening, and you can learn a lot by reading. But understanding what you learn takes time and thought. Reflection. Do you know there are parts of the Koran, Surah 3, that are very similar to the stories in Luke?"

Seeing the expression on her mother's face, Deanna asked, "What's bothering you?"

"There's something I'm not understanding about this case. Time for a field trip. There's a time for thought, and there's also a time for action. Let's go get a canoe."

"Oh no, last time you talked us into one of your adventures, we stayed up half the night." Deanna moaned, she favored giving her mother a hard time before acquiescing to any request, no matter how beguiling the scheme.

"You like canoes. It'll be fun. We can take lunch. You two can paddle down the river." Em grinned, nothing like a good book to settle the mind.

"I call shotgun on the stern," Deanna cried.

"Fine. You can steer, and I'm going to search. Go roust out Sandy."

"You always give me the hard part. Sandy's not that easy to persuade. She's always got some reasonable objections." Dee shook her head.

"It will give you practice in overcoming objections," Em replied. On second thought, not one to miss a teachable moment, she added, "Tell her it's in the cause of justice. A worthwhile goal can almost outweigh reason, good sense and good taste. Almost. Do your best, then threaten to go without her. She'll be worried enough about the trouble we'll get into without her to come along."

Deanna reflected she had become inured to having unusual parents. If she lived long enough she might inherit a piece of a Texas oil patch. However, their family was recognized for producing men who lived to great age, if they didn't get shot first. A distant cousin bought it at the Alamo. One died in a Flanders field. One ran up San Juan Hill cursing TR because he joined the U.S. Cavalry to ride and had one leg and his life shortened (to eighty-five years). If her mother had her way, by the time her inheritance might arrive, they'd all be using solar power.

"Come on, it's a beautiful day. We'll enjoy this!" Em was all pep and energy in the kitchen of the Spring House. Sandy and Deanna sat at the table in what passed for pajamas, old tee shirts and baggy flannel drawers, looking weary. Em required less sleep than the two younger women and was anxious to begin her next project.

Oatmeal buttermilk pancakes were in the cast iron frying pan with bubbles starting to appear around their edges. Em poured spring water into the base of a small espresso pot, good dark roast coffee grounds into the metal basket and screwed the top and bottom together. She set the pot on the gas stove. In a small enamel sauce pan she heated fresh skimmed milk from the dairy until almost boiling and whisked it to raise foam on the top. She stopped to flip the pancakes. When the little pot finished perking its intense brew, she poured the hot coffee into the milk and whisked it a bit more. Pouring the café latte into the waiting mugs, she divided the foam evenly. The pancakes were ready. Em flipped them out of the pan onto their plates and ladled the next batch into the pan.

The smell of hot coffee and pancakes seemed to renew the girls' interest in life. Em delivered the pancakes, mugs of latte, a jug of Spring House Maple Syrup and farm fresh butter to the table, hoping her bribe would work. She returned to the stove with a sly smile on her face to repeat the process for her own breakfast.

Em no sooner seated herself at the breakfast table than Deanna, who was now fortified asked, "So when do we leave?"

"As soon as I finish my breakfast. Why don't you and Sandy get dressed for the river? Find the camera, get a sketch pad, pencils and plastic bags for everything."

"Are you sure we should do this? Wouldn't the police have found any evidence by now? Suppose someone sees us?" Sandy was always the voice of reason and restraint.

"We'll be on the river by nine o'clock. No one will be around. I need to see the murder scene for myself. I need to see it from the river and search the river bank." Em said this as if it was the most logical thing in the world to do on a bright, late spring morning.

Deanna finished her pancakes, wiping up their house special maple syrup with the last bite. She pointed her fork at Sandy across the table. "You know she'll go alone if we don't go with her. She's getting too old to do this stuff all by herself." This was an argument that Sandy understood. Em had a long history of taking them on more adventurous travels than a short canoe trip down a river in the city. "What can happen?" Deanna and Sandy looked at each other. Sandy shook her head doubtfully.

In the cellar of the Spring House, the three women looked up at the joists. Two canoes were hung up using a system of ropes and pulleys. It took Em a moment to make her decision. The newer green canoe was good looking with wooden slats and a narrower frame than the older aluminum one. The aluminum canoe had a rather disreputable look to it with its two overlapping metal patches at the prow. Its virtue was in its broad flat bottom, with the lengthwise seam sealed in a ridge on the inside. The old canoe was designed to have a shallow draft and an ability to slip over muddy patches and weeds.

"Let's take the 'Pirate.' The tide was going out early this morning, I checked." Canoes were not generally named, but the 'Green Dragon' and the 'Pirate' were christened years ago by another family of children.

"It's embarrassing, Mom, all the patches and the dents," Deanna said as she and Sandy used the ropes to lower the aluminum canoe.

"Nobody's going to notice us, nobody is going to care. I'll get the paddles and the life jackets. Are you ready? I'll get the cellar door."

Em opened the side door of the cellar. The girls hoisted the canoe over their heads and carried it out to put it on the roof of the van waiting in front of the house. Em stayed behind to lock the cellar door. When all their gear was stowed in the van, Em gave in and let Deanna drive. This ensured a fast trip with a few brushes with the tree branches by the side of the country road. Further along they passed a speeding black car with New York plates.

"Probably scared of the woods," Deanna remarked about the fast retreating vehicle.

———— ◆ ————

The river by the boat launch below the dam was of a reasonable depth. The river contained fresh water here, and there had been enough rain to provide a good flow over the wide spillway. Deanna parked the van on the gravel as close as she could get to the launch site. They could see the river rolling sinuously over its few rapids.

No one else was anywhere in sight. Em checked around her continually. She attached a float to her car key and put her cell phone into a tough re-sealable plastic bag. Into the pockets of her cargo pants she put a waterproof disposable camera, more plastic bags and non-latex gloves. A small pair of binoculars went around her neck. She strapped on her life jacket, ready to go.

"So what's the plan? We paddle down the river to look for what? A dead body? Cool!" Deanna approved of the idea, without considering the look and smell of the reality.

"Dee, I don't think I really want to go if that's what we're doing. Shouldn't we leave it for the police? Anyway, wouldn't they have found anything like that by now?" Sandy registered her concern again as they took the canoe down from the van roof.

"Well, yes, they might have found a *dead body*. Perhaps the woman survived. That's what we will be looking for down by the park. They were searching at incoming tide in the dark. We'll paddle around down to the Interstate and stay within the marshes." Em was quite used to coaxing Sandy along, she was a good sport once convinced. Sandy enjoyed their adventures together best in retrospect, preferably when back safely at home.

They launched the canoe with their usual splashing and laughter. Since Deanna had insisted on steering, she took the seat in the rear of the canoe with Em in the middle seat and a reluctant Sandy in the front.

The water was faster here through the woods, and it took little effort to propel the canoe forward. It took more skill steering to avoid rocks and the occasional hazard of a fallen tree limb in the river. Around a bend the channel widened, tall marsh grasses and rough barked willows lined the banks. The water turned from clear brown to the cloudy grey green of a brackish mix of fresh and salt water. The river was tidal here. The exposed banks were the muddy brown of dark chocolate and full of all sorts of living wriggling creatures and tiny bubbling air holes.

"Get in as close as you can, please." Em raised the field glasses to her eyes and examined the west bank for signs of disturbance. "Go slow!" Deanna and Sandy obediently dragged their paddles in the water, slowing their progress. The sun was bright. It was a pleasant feeling to be drifting down the river. Sandy relaxed. The canoe nosed its way under a cut stone bridge. Deanna hooted and hollered and enjoyed the echoes.

"Okay, down to business, we're almost to the spot where the professor was killed on Tuesday. Sandy help me search. Dee, steer the canoe towards that break in the reeds." Em spotted what looked like a gap in the tall grasses. Deanna angled the canoe in as close as she could to the bank. "It looks like a herd trooped down that path into the water. From what I can see it's boot prints and flipper prints. We'll keep going slowly down stream." Deanna back paddled, pulling the canoe away from the bank. As she positioned it to head down river, a noise like a loud pop sounded from the east shore, and something whizzed past Em's face. Initially stunned, Em froze for a second.

"Gunshot!" Deanna yelled as a second round tore through first one then the other side of the canoe not far above the water line between Em and Sandy.

"Get down and scream!" Em yelled, and they did. Three heads went down as far as they could in the canoe. Em sucked in a great breath and screamed as loud as ever she could, joined by a shrieking Deanna and truly frightened screams from Sandy.

The sound of a third shot came from the east bank. The bullet went overhead missing them.

"Capsize the boat! Rock to the right." It took them several tries but they succeeded as they had in practice, flipping the canoe over and getting into the smelly water. Staying low, using the floating canoe for a shield, they swam in four feet of water. It was deep enough to keep them out of sight.

"What the freakin' hell was that? Mom, what have you gotten us into?"

"I knew it! There's something around here. We need to find it!"

"We're all going to be sick, this is so gross." Sandy came bobbing up in her life jacket covered with salty water, twigs in her hair.

"Just don't swallow any of it, dear, the rest will wash off." Em hung on to the canoe and crouched, trying to reach the cell phone in her pants pocket. "This muck is the least of our worries."

"Over there! It came from over there!" Two graduate students with a shaggy dog materialized on the lawn of the park above the west bank of the river a hundred feet or more ahead of them. They were calling and pointing. Their dog yapped furiously.

The sound of wheels spinning on gravel and then the whine of a car burning rubber peeling out on the road from the east bank reached them.

"Look! They're getting away!" the young woman yelled. Her companion was busy calling the police on his cell phone. The dog on the leash jumped up and down, dragging her closer to the edge of the lawn down towards the river.

"Sounds like they've gone." Deanna swam back to the

end of the canoe and peered around it. "Getting back into the canoe's going to be tough."

"Looks like a launch site down there. Near where that girl's waving to us. See if you can grab the paddles." Three paddles were found. Em always brought a spare although it wasn't used in the middle seat. They flipped the canoe back over to make it easier to guide it through the water and threw the paddles into it. They headed downstream riding the gentle current. Em tried to watch the bank as they went along for any place else to beach the canoe, but there was no sign of one, and no sign that anyone else had come ashore recently.

The path down to the water was narrow, not meant to be a boat launch. The three travelers emerged from the water and squelched across the mud flat in their water shoes. Struggling and slipping in the mud, they beached the canoe. They turned it over to get most of the water out of it. A young woman waved to them from the lawn.

"We've called the police!" Indeed, a siren could be heard on the other side of the river nearing the departure point of the fleeing car.

"Ew! This is so gross. I itch all over. I think there are bugs in my hair!"

Em couldn't help but smile. They'd been shot at, there were holes in her canoe that would need patching, and Sandy was worried about the water bugs. "We'll dry out quickly in the sun. It's a good thing it's warm."

"How are we going to get back to the car, Mom?"

"We'll have to wait here for the police, and then paddle on back up the river." Em shrugged. She turned to wave to the young woman with her dog. They left the canoe in place and walked up the muddy path that led through the salt marsh grasses with head height tassels. Em looked at the well-trodden path as she walked slowly behind the two girls. In the short grass next to it, she found the prints of a small boot with a very definite two inch heel.

Deanna turned back to see her mother bending over looking into the grass. "What did you find?"

"A small woman's boot print. Not what I would expect here. Keep looking at the ground!"

It was Sandy's sharp eyes that found it, mashed down in among the grass roots close to the path where it could easily be missed. A sodden square of good quality note paper, folded several times to wallet size.

"Do you think this is anything? It looks like it's soaked through and it's been stepped on." Sandy pointed to the wet paper. "I can see writing coming through from the inside."

Em dug into her cargo pocket, pulled out the water-proof disposable camera, and took a picture of the square of paper, including a woman's boot print next to it. She crouched low, turned and took several other pictures in quick succession of the same boot prints along the path. Em hoped her movements were screened by the tall grasses around the narrow path. From her pocket she took a plastic bag and put Sandy's find into it.

"Good work. We won't know what this is until we get it peeled apart. You never know, let's keep looking. Maybe we'll get lucky." Em passed the beer bottles and soda cans and usual park litter thrown deep into the weeds. Other than those, the area around the path was remarkably free of debris.

The young woman with the dog watched them with a puzzled expression on her face.

"What are you all doing down there? We called the police, and they said they had an officer in the area who would be right over," she shouted in a friendly voice.

Em laughed a disarming laugh. "We're coming." Under her breath she said to Deanna and Sandy, "Keep looking, I'll go meet the policeman."

Em trudged along the path through the high grass, up the short incline to the park lawn where she came face to face with the long white nose of a very tall Clydesdale police horse ridden by a young woman officer on patrol. The horse had very large bones and was dark reddish brown with white feathered stockings on her legs and a broad white blaze down her nose. The horse was not as showy as the Budweiser Clydesdales and on the shaggy side. The mare, whose named turned out to be Daisy, looked at Em with composure, ignoring the frisky barking dog.

"Problem here, ma'am?" the mounted officer asked.

"Somebody shot a hole in my canoe. We were out on the river, back up there by the other path down to the water when I heard a bullet go right by me! I was in the middle of the boat. Then another bullet went right through both sides of the canoe in front of me. We started to scream, and then there was a third shot. We capsized the canoe and went into the water for protection."

"We saw it all. We were taking the dog for his morning walk. We do it every day." The young woman was joined by her companion, a slender man in his mid-twenties.

"And you are?" the officer asked. She dropped her reins on the horse's neck and took out her notebook. The pair identified themselves as Ginny Weston and Tim Masaryk, university biology graduate students who lived together a block away from the park. The officer paused to look carefully at the students. "We've talked to you recently, haven't we? It's alright. Just tell me what you saw today."

"They were turning their canoe to head down the river when we heard the shots. Three shots, like she said. We yelled and then we heard what sounded like a car speeding away on the other side of the river," her male companion picked up the story.

"That's where the shots came from," Ginny Weston added.

"Could you see the car?"

The two graduate students looked at each other. "Maybe a dark one, possibly black. It's shaded over on that side, hard to tell from here," he said. The young woman nodded her agreement.

"And what happened then?"

"Nothing. We could see them in the water. They had life jackets on so we weren't too concerned. They were floating down river towards us so I called 911. Ginny went down to meet them."

"And you, ma'am. Your name and address, please."

"I'm Em Huber, and this is my daughter Deanna Huber and Sandy." Em gave her address and contact information.

"Anything to add, ladies? Either of you?" Deanna and Sandy had joined the group to stand behind Em. "Can you think of any reason for someone to shoot at you?"

"Not that I know of, we were just cruising down the river," Em said helpfully.

"Bird watching?" The officer asked, noting the binoculars still hanging from Em's neck. The policewoman wore her hair short and ran her fingers through her bangs like a comb, thinking.

"We saw a really beautiful blue heron standing on a stump in the marsh and a bright red male cardinal back in the woods." Deanna made her contribution to the discussion to her mother's satisfaction. "I was hoping we'd see a white one, an egret. I know we have to be careful around the swans 'cause they can be really nasty and chase you if you come near their nest."

The officer looked doubtfully at the three thoroughly soaked women. She thought, *Something's not right here. They've been shot at, and they're worried about the swans, and they are nowhere in sight.*

"I took a picture of the holes in our canoe with my phone, would you like me to send it to you?" Deanna offered.

"That would be fine. Do you know that a man was killed right up there by the path?"

"Yes, we saw it on the news and read about it online.

Who would want to hurt a professor? Was it robbery? The news coverage didn't say," Em asked in earnest.

"We're not releasing any further information. You didn't go on shore there did you?"

"No, we stayed in the canoe, we just looked," Em admitted. She determined it was best to tell at least partial truth.

"Can we pet the horse?" Deanna asked and received permission to pat Daisy's soft white nose.

The officer put them down as local curiosity seekers. Still it was a shooting in a sensitive area close to a crime scene, and it needed attention. Since no one was hurt, when she received another call, the officer passed out her business cards and turned Daisy's head towards downtown. She planned a report to her superior as she rode off.

The women stood watching the departing backside of the mounted unit. "Well, that was an adventure. I'm Em Huber," she introduced herself to the students. "My ex-husband was in the geology department a couple years ago. Do you walk here often?"

"Oh yes, we poop and scoop twice a day. Our landlady doesn't want him in the backyard. We had to convince her to rent to us at all with the dog. Two months security deposit, can you imagine! We convinced her it would be good to have a watch dog."

The dog was medium sized with straw colored rather curly longish hair and a humorous and friendly look on his face. He licked Deanna's hand.

"His name is Chinle. I don't know why, we rescued him. He's a Tibetan Terrier."

"Is he a good watch dog?" Sandy asked, thinking having one was a good idea.

"He's good, and I'm glad we have him, especially now. This isn't the first time we've heard gun shots in the park."

"No, really?" Em asked. Deanna looked down at the dog to hide the expression on her face. Sandy sat down on the park bench next to them to pet the dog, leaving Em free to pursue her questions.

"You'all were lucky this morning. We found the professor's body, or Chinle did."

"Are you one of the students in the paper? I read that they were out walking a dog when they heard the shots. Where was that?"

"It was right over there," she said, pointing north. "We were on the walk going towards the end of the park, right before we got to the hiking trail that goes through the woods. We heard two shots, right together. A man cried out. I was so scared. You could tell someone had been hurt. I didn't know what to do so I stayed to call 911. Then we heard a woman scream sort of. My friend Tim said we needed to do something. We couldn't just stand there. So, Tim went tearing into the bushes with the dog barking like crazy."

"Is that when he found the body?"

"No, not at first. It was pretty dark so he had to find his way through the bushes to the hiking trail. When he got to the trail, he said he heard someone running away up the trail, but the dog was barking and pulling him towards the river."

"Oh, good dog." Deanna rumpled the dog's ears. She and Sandy listened now with rapt attention, trying hard to keep still and let Em do the questions.

"He is, he really is. He pulled and pulled until he found the professor. Tim had a small flashlight. We're biology students. He could tell that the man was dead. He called 911, too, to tell them he'd found a body. They told him to stay right there. He's brave like that."

"Did you see the woman?"

"Neither of us did. I heard a splash and then kind of a short scream like she fell into the water after they shot her, too. Tim said it sounded like a man running away, heavy footsteps, but only one person. We told this all to the police. There were reporters everywhere. They must listen to the police calls." The young woman seemed relieved to be able to talk about it to the older woman and the two girls.

"I would have been so scared! Are you alright coming back to the park?" Sandy was sympathetic.

"Oh, yes, both of us have lived in cities before. I hate to say it, but gun violence is everywhere. We make sure we walk the dog earlier in the evening now and stay away from the woods over there." All three heads turned towards the clump of bushes that hid the hiking trail from view.

"They haven't found the woman yet. Did she scream like us?" Em joked.

"Oh no. You were all really loud! I could tell you were doing it on purpose. Her scream was short, like a surprised scream. More like an 'eek!' then a splash, but not a big one."

Em considered this for a moment. "You must have a good ear. We intuitively tell a child's cry from a teenager's screech and from an older person's call. You've said it was a woman, was it an adult voice? Did it sound like an adult older than you?"

"It sounded like an older adult, but not elderly. You're right. I played the flute so I did have to listen to the other band members around me."

"Then I'll bet you could tell the pitch, too. Women's voices become lower as we age. Men's voices come up a few notes. Let's see if we can guess her pitch. Sandy has a very nice soprano voice," Em said with an encouraging gesture to Sandy. "Please sing the scale from your highest note to your lowest."

"Say when, Ginny, if you hear the note of the woman's scream."

Sandy complied with a carefully modulated note by note run down the musical scale.

"No, not that high," the young woman shook her head.

"Here goes cocktail alto," Em took a deep breath and sang "Oh" from the lowest sound she could produce. Deanna rolled her eyes as if Em's singing was painful to her ears. As Em approached her mid-range the young woman signaled her to stop.

"That's it! She had a lower voice, but not a strong one!"

"That's why you assumed she was an adult, the tone seems too low to be a younger person. Good one."

"I hadn't remembered it that way before. That's so interesting." The biology student was surprised and pleased. "I work with mice, lots of mice, not people!"

Chinle whined, and yipped. He'd had enough sitting still and was anxious to get going on his walk.

The possibility of facing reporters spurred Em to make a quick nod towards the hiking trail to Deanna, who promptly said, "Do you suppose we could go look at the crime scene? We did a crime scene investigation workshop when we were in school."

"If you want to, it's up there." Ginnie pointed towards the woods. "The police have been all over it, I don't think there's much to see. The professor's body was dragged off the trail. There might still be tape around it. I'd rather not show you, but you should be able to find it. Nice to meet you all, my boyfriend's waving at me to come over." She took Chinle's leash firmly in her hand, and the terrier made his best attempt to drag her across the park lawn to his master who stood in the shade talking to two of his friends.

"Let's go, Mom." Deanna was on her feet and ready.

"I think I should stay with the canoe, so it's still here when you get back," Sandy volunteered practically. Leaving the canoe unguarded was not a good idea after all.

"Fine, we won't be long, but we need to look casual, Dee. Take it at a walk."

"Scream if you need us and don't talk to any reporters until we get back." Dee laughed back to Sandy.

Walking across the lawn talking and smiling, Em and Deanna gave their impression of a casual visit to the park until they reached the bushes.

"Looks like someone crashed through here. We should stick to the path. There's a short cut to the trail right over there, he must have missed it in the dark." Deanna reluctantly followed her mother through the undergrowth along the narrow path to the wider one beyond. The trail that followed the edge of the marshes and the river was well used. It showed the marks of bicycle tires, dog prints and scuffs from running shoes. Deanna spotted yellow crime scene tape fluttering in the light breeze among the young trees to their right, towards the river.

Looking both ways up and down the trail and seeing no one, Em signaled to Deanna to head towards the tape. They were far down the trail when Em stopped short.

"Poison ivy! Look at that, they dragged the body off the trail right into the poison ivy."

The poisonous plant at their feet, common to moist areas along trails, showed its three shiny leaf clusters borne on woody stems. Most potent in early spring when the leaves were a shiny maroon, oil from poison ivy irritated the skin producing itchy watery blisters that became infected easily.

"Jeez Mom, they mashed it all down. They're going to be covered with it. What kind of an idiot would do that?"

"Someone desperate without a flashlight, who's never hiked, or who's not from around here. We can go around this patch. It looks like an army trampled through there anyway. Maybe the police and EMT's, looks like heavy shoes."

Finding their way around the poison ivy, avoiding the low growing plants and their vines creeping up the trees, Deanna and Em arrived between the site where the body was found and the river bank. Unlike the path where they landed the canoe, the bank dropped off straight into the channel of the river, not into the muddy shallows.

Deanna was practicing her crime scene skills, and Em let her do it uninterrupted. "The professor gets shot on the path. Two people are there, a heavy man and a woman.

Maybe the man Tim Masaryk heard running away on the trail, dragged the professor through the poison ivy to hide his body. The water is so close. If the woman was standing there," Deanna pointed to a disturbed patch of ground, "she could have turned and gone the wrong way in the dark. The river bank drops off right over there. It looks to be two feet at least. One misstep, she'd be in the water. Or she could'a been shot or pushed," Deanna conjectured as she pointed her index finger at an imaginary target, made a pop sound and shot it with her thumb.

"She cried out so she was alive when she went into the water, and they haven't found a body. She could still be alive. We need to get back to Sandy."

"Before she freaks out!"

Back in the sunlit park, Sandy sat on the bench thinking about their trip home. She was sure Em and Deanna would want to go back to the car in the canoe. Having to port the canoe all that way was an onerous task. Getting it back on the roof of the van was enough work, much less carrying it back. Leaving Deanna here with the canoe while they walked back to get the car might be best. But as she sat there, Sandy watched the activity on the other side of the river. Policemen were searching through the high grasses as a TV news van appeared. She looked anxiously towards the hiking trail and was relieved to see Deanna and her mother emerge from a path and walk towards her. Em and Deanna reached Sandy in time to watch the TV van parking.

The possibility of being caught out on land by the TV crew caused them to hustle down the muddy path and to launch the canoe. The two new holes were well above the water line. Deanna observed it was hard to put a bullet below the waterline of a boat with such shallow draft from the distance across the river. The shooter was probably on drier land above the marsh at the widest part of the river basin, and that was the location of the active police search now in progress.

Launching the canoe proved an easy task. The river bottom was deep enough for them to slip the boat into the water and to push off into the channel with their paddles. For the return trip, Em sat in the front seat, with Sandy in the middle watching the bank for signs of disturbance, and Deanna sat in the back. Once they'd renegotiated the side on which they each would paddle, and synchronized their strokes, Em and Deanna sent the canoe skimming across the water.

Em insisted on continuing their search down towards the mouth of the river, down to the Interstate Bridge. They were going only so far as it was safe to do so. Seeing no signs anyone had climbed out of the water, and no signs of a body, they turned the canoe back north. Aided by the now incoming tide their return was easy. They stayed well away from the east shore, close enough to see the edges of the water, but not close enough to run aground. The police search was wrapping up and the TV truck had driven away.

Alone out on the water, the three companions relaxed. Although Deanna reminded them they should probably watch the shores on either side for anyone with a gun. The tide raised the water level gradually erasing the muddy beaches. The tiny white seabirds abandoned their hunting in the mud flats and flew off towards the Sound. Paddling back up into the fresh water river, they passed stands of native cattails, their soggy habitat not yet seized by the invasive plant Purple Loosestrife. The warm sun reflecting off the water baked their hair. Sunscreen on their noses was a thing of the past.

All seemed well until they came within visual distance of the boat launching site. Parked right next to their van, the TV truck stood out like a great white bread box. Next to it stood a camera man and a screen ready TV reporter who was waiting for them. It was too late to flee back down the river.

"Oh shit, they must have gone around the lake." Em was chagrined, she'd never faced media before.

"What do we do? We can't exactly pretend nothing happened. We've got two freakin' holes in the canoe," Deanna remarked from the back of the canoe.

"We can stick to the bird watching story and say we're too upset to say anything else," which was true for Sandy as she spoke. "I wish I had a hat to hide my face."

"Good idea, Sandy. Keep it simple and say little. Okay, here we go! Deanna head us in sideways."

They were self-consciously aware that the TV camera was capturing their landing and then their not so graceful disembarking from the canoe. Sandy stayed on the far side away from the camera, and Deanna did her best to stand in front of her, blocking her from view. The well-dressed TV talent, a thirtyish woman, approached Em for a comment. Em appeared flustered. She was good at that ploy.

"Oh, we were out for a morning ride down the river looking at birds in a mixed aquatic environment." To Em, that sounded dull enough. "When we heard one shot and then someone shot holes in our canoe. Can you please not show us? We tipped the canoe over, and we're covered with mud. *We must look just terrible.*"

This was all too true. Em's naturally curly hair had taken the opportunity of sun, salt and a breeze on the water to go wild. Sandy's straight honey colored hair was plastered to her head and sticking. Deanna's pony tail hung down her back in lanky strands. Their clothing was drying unevenly in the warm sun. Some strategic spots stayed stubbornly damp, including their back sides as the metal seats of the canoe kept them wet. Deanna stood awkwardly behind her mother, tried desperately not to scratch an embarrassing itch in front of the camera.

"No, we have no idea why anyone would shoot at us. We want to go home and change and get clean. Of course you can take pictures of the canoe. The holes are right there. Could anyone help us take it up to the car?" Em asked brightly.

Of course, that was not possible the camera man said. The TV talent backed off as three recently soaked women, now smelling like denizens of a salt marsh, picked up their canoe and carried it back to their van. The women hoisted the canoe up, tied it securely to the roof rack, stowed the paddles, waved and drove away. Sandy kept her face averted through the process and only raised her head when they were safely away.

"Whew, that was a close one." Deanna turned back to look at the TV truck.

"Do you think we'll see ourselves on the evening news?" Sandy worried, she was always shy of drawing attention to herself.

"Something smells in here." Deanna wrinkled her nose and made a face at Sandy.

Em sniffed. "I do believe it's us."

"Open the windows."

20

RECRUITING ASSISTANCE —
OFF TO THE GYM

———◆———

IN THE ROCK GARDEN, DEANNA climbed up on a bench and threw the garden hose over the bracket of a hanging planter to make an outdoor shower. Dancing like wood sprites in the improvised shower of cold well water the girls rinsed their clothes and hair. They took the outer layers off and threw their clothes on a bench in the warm mid-day sun. They stripped down to their two piece bathing suits with skimpy tops, the ones Em forbade them to show on the river for fear of attracting unwanted attention.

Deanna sported a vivid jungle print bikini, and Sandy's two-piece was a deep rich royal blue that accentuated her honey blonde hair. They laughed at Em's old fashioned idea of modesty at the time and laughed again after their adventure on the river since they were destined to end up looking absolutely sodden in jeans and tee shirts on the evening news. Taking turns under their makeshift shower, Deanna gave an imaginary interview to the TV reporter.

"Oh my dear, of course it was too exciting, being shot at on the river," Deanna mugged, water from the garden hose streaming down her face. "I said honestly," she spit a mouthful of water up and away like a fountain, "What could happen…?" Sandy burst out laughing and tossed her a bar of soap. It slipped from her friend's grasp landing in the flowerpot of fire engine red geraniums. Water from their bodies splashed against the side of the house and spattered the living room windows with soap bubbles.

Clean and still damp from a very short hot shower, Em relinquished the upstairs bathroom. She could hear the girl's cheerful voices from the garden. She brought old beach towels out for them. Deanna and Sandy did rock, paper, scissors four times before Sandy easily won the next turn in the bathroom for a hot shower. Deanna drew the task of watering the flowerpots and starting lunch.

From her desk in the living room, Em retrieved a long pair of tweezers with wide spatulate blades, the kind used by stamp collectors to pick up delicate items. On the kitchen table she arranged a baking sheet and covered it with plain white paper towels. She filled a small squeeze bottle with boiled water left in the kettle from breakfast. Her camera was at the ready.

Using the tweezers and a dull bladed kitchen knife, Em began the careful process of unfolding the damp and smudged paper Sandy had found along the path. She fought back the impulse to clean up the paper by drenching it with the water. It carried the distinctive smell of salt water and decaying plant life of the marsh land. Working the dull knife between the folds and then grasping the edge gently with the tweezers, she gradually teased two folds of the paper open without ripping the creases. Handwriting appeared through the paper, the folds protecting the note written in dark blue ink from the mud of the path. Em changed the paper towel which carried away some of the mud and tiny particles with it. She put the towel aside and went on working cautiously. The inside folds were sticking together and one of the creases ripped despite her careful handling.

"Whatch'ya doin' Ma?" Deanna came to stare over her mother's shoulder.

"I'm trying to be careful and not always succeeding. Would you please go get a hair dryer?"

"Why? You're almost dry."

"Yes, but the note isn't. This thing stinks and it's going to grow mildew and things if we don't dry it out. I was about to put it in a low oven to bake dry, but that's probably not a good idea. If we still had the old photo print dryer that might work. But I'm afraid that's long gone. Your father ditched it when he moved out. That and a lot of other things."

Deanna sensed it was best to avoid the subject of her father and said, "I'll get it. Don't start without me."

Em heard a brief argument taking place in the upstairs hall as Deanna confiscated the best hair dryer in the name of science. She managed to work the last fold open and to lay the note flat on its bed of paper towels. Deciding that documentation was necessary, she carefully measured the piece of note paper and photographed it. On her first examination of the note, she could tell they had found more than a bedraggled bit of castoff paper, but a piece of evidence. The paper itself was of good quality, of the kind and size bought for letter writing. Its color was cream. What had appeared to be a ripped lower edge proved to be a tattered deckle edge, a feature of expensive stationery.

The note was addressed to "Al" in a sloping woman's cursive handwriting. Although the contents of the note were splotched where the water had penetrated the folds and the dark blue black ink had run, most of the few words were clear. Trying to hold her excitement, Em took the hair dryer from Deanna. She gave her hair a once over until it warmed up and then methodically passed the dryer over the note, working from top to bottom.

Deanna surveyed the note. "I think we should have given this to the police."

"Now how was I supposed to know what it was without opening it?" Em continued passing the dryer back and forth across the paper. A few more letters became clear but the text of the note was brief.

———◆———

Al,

Arrived this afternoon, staying in Room 306. We can meet this evening to talk business. I'll call you.

———◆———

"No signature, not even an initial. That would be too easy. No question mark. She's telling him she can meet him, not asking him to meet her. Professor Kirbee called Professor Ali Hussein, 'Al' the afternoon I first met him. She knows him that well, too."

"Where's the rest of the note? It looks ripped," Deanna asked.

"We don't have it if there is any more."

"We assume Professor Hussein was shot in the park. What were they doing in the park? She's got a room. Why didn't they use it? If they were talking business in the park, I'll bet it was shady business. It got him killed anyway." Em finished drying the note to her satisfaction.

"Maybe that was the point. Lure him out to the park. Kill him. Dump the body in the river. But they got interrupted by Chinle walking his biology students," Deanna suggested. "I gotta go. Sandy's out of the shower. Will you fix lunch? Any luck with the map?"

In the car on the way back from the river, Em consulted an old city map. On it she marked the spot where the body was found, where their canoe was shot at, her best guess as to the location of the shooter, and where they came ashore. She spread the map out on the table beside the cookie sheet with the note on it.

"Kirbee's house is here. Let's see where Professor Hussein

lived. Hand me the phone book?" Em found that Professor Hussein was traditional. He had a listed wire line number. The address proved to be quite close to the north end of the park where he was shot and was nearly in a straight line from their lab in the industrial park." Em marked the approximate location on the map.

"He was killed close to home. It was a beautiful evening. Maybe she said let's go for a walk and talk it over. We may need help finding the right Room 306." Em ran her hand through her hair, which immediately sprang back, seemingly invigorated by its dunking in salt water. "I need to make a phone call."

"We have gym classes this afternoon," Deanna was quite definite. She was not about to give up her lesson.

"It will work out perfectly, you'll see." Her mother smiled at Deanna in a way that said, *Don't worry dear, I have something else up my sleeve.*

"One thing. Why would she write him an actual note? Why not send him an email or text him?" Deanna was a puzzled, definitely a child of her generation.

"If she were young, she might do that. Some people find a handwritten note more personal. In this case it doesn't seem threatening. Also we may have the only copy. Once you digitize information, and especially if you send it, it can be trapped and traced. It's easier to destroy a single piece of paper," Em reminded her.

"Or lose it in the marsh," Deanna surmised.

"Good point. That was bad luck for her. Hurry up with that shower."

<hr>

Sitting on the desk in front of him, Halloran's medium rare cheeseburger and hand cut fries were getting cold. The ketchup pooled on the bottom of the paper plate. He scowled at his computer screen. His lunch could wait. The head of the Analysis group, down the long hall from his office, had sent him a report for his immediate review with audio files of police calls attached. An intercepted, live unedited video feed from the local TV station's news truck followed. He heard the 911 call reporting the shooting on the river and the mounted officer's report to the station. It was vexing. Em Huber had been searching one side of the river and he had Andy Vargas deployed out on the other side, and they were both right.

Gladys Rodriquez and Garvey heard a hearty laugh all the way out in the main office area.

Halloran watched the unedited news feed of Em's interview with the always meticulously put together newswoman. Em was disheveled and wet, but she still managed to outwit her opponent handily. *Oh miss, I am so innocent,* he said to himself. The cameraman panned to capture the two younger women standing by the canoe, trying to stay out of view, seemingly self-conscious. He picked up Deanna's quick sideways glance at her friend, and her agile step to shield her from view. *Something there,* he realized.

Halloran picked up his phone. "Get Vargas and Rankel in here. I have an assignment for them." He picked up his burger, grilled rare, and took a large satisfying bite.

———◆———

Lunch was over at the Spring House, too. They gathered their gym bags. Em slipped the note, now dry, into a plastic bag and sealed it closed. She placed it into her gym bag in between the folds of the clean towel. Deanna insisted on driving, and the conversation centered on the implications of the note. Consensus was reached that the handwriting was that of a woman of a certain age who had been well trained in penmanship, possibly in a private school as this accomplishment was a rare thing in recent generations and not stressed in public education.

They arrived at the gym in one piece, with only a single white knuckle experience for Em who sat in the back. The gym's sign was small, and the facility located in a converted industrial building set back off the street, away from the high traffic area. The parking lot was not visible from the busy road in front. All of this was probably a coincidence of low rent and an accessible location, but it served to promote the privacy of the members.

Once inside the building, the three women went their separate ways. Em was early for her class and went in to the locker room and the shower rooms to change. Deanna and Sandy had no compunction about arriving in sweats and tank tops, or in leaving the gym in them for that matter. It seemed perfectly natural. Em insisted on changing, so the girls were not surprised when she went off by herself. Em greeted several of her acquaintances in the locker room and headed for the individual shower rooms. A red hand towel hung on the handle of one of the doors. Looking around behind her first, Em knocked on the door.

"Are you decent?" Em spoke to the red towel.

"Give me a minute," replied a muffled female voice.

"I'll meet you in the break room." Em walked off to fix herself a green tea and to wait for her friend.

In a few short minutes, a tall woman in her thirties walked into the break room. She emerged from under the towel she was rubbing vigorously to dry her dark auburn hair.

"Nancy, good to see you!"

"So what can the FBI do for you today, m'friend? I need something stronger than that green stuff. It's been one of those weeks." After pouring herself black coffee that looked aged in the carafe, she dropped down into the chair next to Em. Nancy was over six feet, and although not heavy, she carried solid weight on a well set up frame. Her nose was covered with freckles and her eyes were a sharp green and crinkled at the edges. College basketball gave a start to her career and a law degree furthered it.

"I'll have to make this quick. Class starts soon. Here's

the note we found this morning." Em pulled it out of her gym bag.

"We have no proof it was directed to Ali Hussein, but it sure looks like it to me. And somebody didn't want us looking around that crime scene. We got shot at from across the river."

"So you said. I've seen the preliminary report. Professor Hussein was a real loss." It was one of those trying events for the local FBI office that week.

Em kept her voice low. "Would you be willing to go out looking for this Room 306 with me tomorrow? Another federal agent named Halloran warned me off, had me into his office to question me about my work for Professor Kirbee."

"Hussein's partner, right? Wait a minute. You went to Halloran's office? Are you sure?" The younger woman turned to her in wonder. Her short red hair gradually began to stand on end as it dried.

"Yes, he showed me his ID. I read it carefully, tall man, about my age, walks with a limp and a cane. Scares the crap out some of the local police. He gave me directions to come to his office. It's really kind of..."

"Don't say it! We're not even allowed anywhere near it. It's like the Bat Cave." Nancy lowered her voice. "The fewer people who know about it the better. You must have security clearance, right?"

Em shrugged her shoulders and rolled her eyes.

"That's alright, don't answer that one. I wouldn't. So you want to go looking for this Room 306 on the odd chance that whoever wrote the note met Hussein? And you called me."

"Halloran warned me off. He gave me the go home and be a good little woman lecture. I can't work with that," Em fumed.

"Few of us can. They're in my office too, fortunately not as many as there used to be. Okay, I'll send this to our lab, and I'll meet you tomorrow. We'll have to set up a time then."

"Great, thanks so much. I've got to go to kettle bells class. If I'm late all the good ones will be gone!" Em took off through the locker room, pulling off her tee shirt as she went to reveal her exercise top. Changed and ready she headed towards the main exercise area where her class was about to begin.

Nancy Dombroski looked at the note, safely placed in its plastic storage baggy. With care, she slipped it under her tee shirt. It was worth a try, the murder of the scientist Ali Hussein was their case, too. What Halloran and his elusive organization wouldn't listen to, they wouldn't know until she filed her report, which she decided on the spot could wait until tomorrow. She unrolled her towel, extracted her gun in its holster and strapped it to her ankle, pulling her sweatpants down to cover it.

———◆———

A small black fleet car backed into an inconspicuous parking spot near the front of the gym ready for a fast getaway.

"Boss, we have a situation here. They've gone to a gym, but it's not one of those $10.00 a month all the machines you could want gyms. It's a boxing gym." Vargas grinned into his phone as he gave Halloran the name and location. "They took gym bags in with them."

"What the hell are they doing there? Are you sure?" Halloran was fast losing patience, first the women damn near get themselves shot full of holes on the river by the crime scene. Obviously not a coincidence. Now what could Em Huber be up to?

"Yes, I'm sure it's a boxing gym. It says it on the sign, and I've heard of the place. If you want us to talk her into coming into the office, we'll have to go in. We could make like we're interviewing for a new trainer." Vargas paused for effect.

"Okay, find out what they're up to. Andy, you keep the gloves off and stay out of the ring. And keep Rankel off the high ropes. You've got half an hour. Call me back." Halloran muttered "Kids in a toy store," ended the call and stretched his right leg out in front of him. He'd lost interest in the weekly videoconference call on threat level assessment currently visible on his monitor. Under his desk, he kicked over the almost empty waste basket to use to elevate his sore leg. Most of his trash was of the shred it, incinerate it or forget it type.

Vargas heard the call disconnect. "We're good to go. He told me to stay out of the ring, and you're supposed to stay off the ropes. Let's go *investigate* this gym."

"Yeah man, that means you get the ropes and I get the ring, right? We haven't had a good workout since we scared off that last trainer," Rankel enthused.

Vargas and Rankel left the fleet car and walked through the parking lot observing the cars as they passed through. "You do that side, Rankel," said Andy Vargas as he set about memorizing the license plates on his left. "Nothing familiar over here. Looks like solid citizens, nothing on the hot sheet. Not yet anyway. Not much here to tempt a thief."

"Something familiar here. I used to date that one," Rankel remarked as he passed a bright blue electric car.

"So much for going under cover," Vargas growled.

"She thinks I'm lazy, marginally employed and play a mean guitar." Rankel laughed regretfully at her appraisal of him.

"Good for her, sounds about right," said his partner with a chuckle. He'd yet to see Rankel stay with one woman for more than a few months, often much less.

The front entry way of the gym led off in several directions. No one greeted them at the door. From the entry the agents could hear the activity around them, the smack of boxing gloves on bags, the clang of weights lifted and dropped, the slap of feet on a treadmill and the regular rhythm of a rowing machine. One of the boxers did hot pepper with a jump rope. Occasionally there was a heavy thump on the floor. Several coaches gave short staccato directions. From a large room came laughter from a mixed group who were talking loudly in bursts the way people do when they are lifting hand weights.

In a far corner of a corridor lined with a few exercise machines, the agents recognized Sandy. Head phones in place, she was walking on a treadmill with a well-worn library book propped up in front of her. She appeared oblivious to her surroundings. Avoiding the machines, Rankel and Vargas were drawn into a large open area in which a dozen or more punching bags were suspended in rows from the girders supporting the roof. The rhythmic sound of fist to bag lured them on. Thick ropes hung from the girders, some with knots at handy intervals for climbing. Rankel gazed upwards and rubbed his hands.

"Something's wrong here. It doesn't smell like a boxing gym." Rankel looked around for his former girlfriend.

"It doesn't smell at all. You can tell a woman owns it," was Vargas's considered opinion.

In one corner of the gym a petite young woman with her hair pulled back energetically pounded a bag with her pink boxing gloves. An older man in a muscle shirt with tattoos covering his arms and a kerchief wrapped around his forehead worked up a sweat punching a bag in the next row. Rankel managed to pass the high ropes without climbing. They rounded a corner as a huge rubber truck tire landed on its side in front of them. A slender young woman, who he recognized, in often washed black work out shorts and a small grey top picked up one side of the huge tire and flipped it over. She continued to do this in a straight line across the gym floor.

Across the open space in front of them, the agents saw a class of mixed ages, both sexes, in various stages of physical condition. The class was working out on thick mats under the supervision of a woman trainer. Each person had a selection of weights, including a pair of dumb bells and two or three kettle bells of different sizes.

"I assumed she'd be in a Zumba class or something. She's doing Sumo Squats holding a kettle bell the size of a large cannon ball. Look at the kettle bells on the rack behind the class. The smallest is eight pounds. The whopper on the floor is over a foot high, it must weigh sixty-five pounds if it's an ounce." Andy Vargas itched to get his hands around the horn, the curved round handle, of the of the largest steel kettle bell. Rankel was not so enthusiastic, he preferred wind sprints.

Em Huber was towards the middle of the class. It was easy to pick her out because Sandy leaned over to whisper in her ear. Em moved to pick up a kettle bell for the next exercise. She had anticipated pursuit by Halloran or his staff and was greatly relieved she had successfully passed off the note to Nancy. Vargas realized their arrival had been spotted and reported by the forward observer. Sandy retreated back towards the exercise machines with a quick glance at the two agents standing in a corner trying not to look like they were watching her.

The class trainer called for alternating single arm swings using one kettle bell, to be followed again by lift and chop. Em picked up her heaviest weight in one hand, swung it down between her legs and up to above waist height and let it go. The kettle bell seemed to hang weightless in the air. Then she reached out with her other hand, caught it and brought it down between her knees and up again above her waist. Vargas noticed that not everyone in the class was as experienced as the woman they came to see.

As Vargas and Rankel watched the class change exercises every two minutes or so, a tall man in boxing gloves and long baggy yellow and red boxing shorts walked cautiously around the class. The boxer was careful not to look at the activity. He stopped in front of Rankel and Vargas.

"We're just checking out the gym," Rankel offered.

"Good place. I wouldn't stare at the class though. We don't. They don't like it, and with all those kettle bells, it could get ugly if you get them mad." The tall man continued his trip to the lockers

"Right. Thanks." Vargas turned around, away from the class. His attention was drawn to a pair of women now climbing into the padded boxing ring in the center. He was surprised to see a short solidly muscled woman boxing coach with large flat red mitts on her hands who was accompanied by a young woman. It was the slender form of Deanna Huber, her hair in a ponytail, wearing boxing gloves.

In response to her coach's commands of "Jab! One! Two!" Deanna hopped nimbly on two feet and punched first one of her coach's mitts and then the other. From where he stood, Vargas could barely hear Deanna's gloves hit the mitts. To him they were little girlie punches. But he had to admit she was fast, her timing was excellent and her aim was good. Since she was not wearing a mouth guard or a helmet, Vargas suspected this was good exercise for Deanna, not preparation to fight in earnest.

While Andy Vargas's back was turned, Rankel took the opportunity to find a set of ropes lying on the gym floor. A long heavy rope of a size to tie up a battle ship was secured in the middle of its length to a standing beam. Checking to make sure Andy's interests were elsewhere, Rankel picked up the stout white rope, one end in each hand. He made wave forms in the two ends of the long rope by raising and lowering his arms with speed and strength.

"Show off!" The young woman who had been flipping the tire came up behind Rankel. "I didn't know you could do that. What are you doing here anyway?"

"My friend's a boxer and he's looking for a new gym." Rankel nodded towards Vargas.

"I didn't know you had friends," she said speculatively.

"One or two." She had never met any of his friends and drinking buddies who were mostly in law enforcement.

"If you want to work out together sometime, you could call." She stood with her arms crossed as Rankel continued to work the ropes in an intricate alternating pattern.

Rankel gave her a toothy grin, like a man caught in the act. "Okay, Amanda, maybe."

"Maybe I'll answer if you call. I'm doing the Workout of the Day and have to finish up and get to work."

She pointed to a white board on the wall next to them. The headline on the board read Workout of the Day — Firemen's Workout. Underneath there was a list of exercises and activities with the number of repetitions to be done and a time limit of 30-45 minutes. Rankel read the list and turned around in astonishment, but Amanda had moved into her next set of exercises and was no longer in view.

Around the corner, Amanda met a friend who expressed her interest in Rankel. "Who's that little bit of muscle out there? Is he new?"

"No, actually that's my ex, Steve. I told you about him. He's the one who never seemed to work much, mooched dinner often and played the guitar."

"He can mooch dinner off me any time!" her friend teased. But now Amanda was not so sure. Rankel was too good with those ropes never to have seen them before. His pal looked like a boxer alright, but his hair was too short. Taken together they looked like men on a mission. It certainly gave Amanda something to think about.

The kettle bells class cooled down with stretches done on the mats. Seeing the agents out of the corner of her eye, apparently waiting for her, Em scoured the gym. Nancy was standing near the ring, in discussion with a man in boxing gloves and sweats. As Em stood up to walk to the locker room, Vargas and Rankel approached her. She was careful to keep a few feet of space between them, and a weather eye on Nancy in case backup was needed.

"Mr. Halloran's compliments, ma'am," said Vargas, who Em remembered as Halloran's driver from her first encounter with the man. He showed her his ID, carefully screening from anyone else's line of sight. "Can we talk for a minute?"

"Nice gym," Rankel said. "You come here often?"

"Every week, sometimes twice. What's up?"

"The boss would like to invite you to come back in. He's got a few more questions…" Vargas let his sentence hang.

"Well, it will just have to wait. I have to be home soon to sign for a delivery. How about Monday? I'm free on Monday." Her eyes widened, and she smiled in a way that was meant to be disarming.

"He said today, ma'am."

"Oh good grief, I can't go into his office like this. I'm dripping wet! And I need to get home."

It was now clear to Rankel and Vargas why she kept backing away from them, her face glistened with sweat.

In a soft emphatic voice the woman said, "I'd set your sensors off from a block away. Besides, I have the girls with me, and you wouldn't want them dragged down there, would you?" Em looked around. Nancy watched this interaction carefully. Rankel followed Em's glance.

"Tell your boss, Monday," Em said firmly.

"What's wrong with tomorrow?"

"I have things I need to do, and I'm giving a Rent Party in the backyard on Saturday. I'll be busy all weekend." Em looked pointedly at both men, picked her head up and said, "I'm going to take a shower. Tell him, Monday. He can name the time." Em walked off leaving Rankel and Vargas standing by the ropes and Nancy trying to hide a smile.

"Let's go call in, and see what he wants us to do." They could hardly drag her into the office.

Rankel nodded his agreement.

They contacted Halloran from the fleet car, briefly interrupting him in a virtual meeting with his counterpart on the West Coast.

"So how'd it go? When is she coming in?"

"Monday, sir, time at your convenience. She said she's busy through the weekend and has the girls with her now. She's giving a Rent Party, whatever that is. Something else about this gym, the place looks alright, but it's crawling with local talent." Vargas anticipated an abrupt response.

"What kind of talent? Boxers?" Halloran wasn't quite following.

"Local police boxing, firemen trimming down to pass their physical exam, and feebs hanging out around the ring. And Rankel's old girlfriend," Vargas couldn't resist that comment and was rewarded by a sour face from Rankel.

"So they're at the gym, Andy, spit it out. Why is this important?" Halloran did need to get back on his call.

"Because that woman FBI agent, the one with the red hair is here. The one they call Nancy Dr…"

"I know her," Halloran replied.

"She was giving us the hairy eye when we talked to Ms. Huber, like she knew her. Rankel saw it too. We had to back off. She looked like she was about to come right on over to us. Then Ms. Huber stalks off to take a shower, said she was, uh, not dressed to come into the office today."

"Okay, good job, worth a try. Get back to the office. You kept the gloves off and Rankel stayed on the ground, right?"

"Yessir, we'll bring back some stuff for you to read about the place."

Halloran sat at his desk with his foot on the waste basket and paused for a minute. *I tell her to drop everything, but she heads for the crime scene. Em Huber gets shot at, any normal person would have been tempted to call it a day, but she hares off to a gym for a little exercise. Or to make contact with her red headed friend. What a pair, an analyst and an armed federal agent. Sounds like they have plans for tomorrow. We'll have to watch what those two are up to.* With those interesting thoughts resolved into a mental note for his agents' assignment, Halloran jumped back on his video conference call.

21

BOUTIQUE HOTEL

————◆————

ON FRIDAY MORNING, EM AND Nancy questioned hotel clerks across the city, working from the least expensive upward to the most exclusive. Coming up with no new leads, they decided to finish with the most discrete, least likely boutique hotel New Haven had to offer. Celebrities, persons of influence and notoriety, along with the wealthy graduates and parents of graduates, came to stay at the Alcorn Inn. Located in a renovated late 19th century building with a storied history of a theatrical and musical nature, the hotel hardly needed to advertise. Years ago Broadway bound shows tried out in New Haven bringing life to the saying "We bombed in New Haven," as many tryouts failed as succeeded. The hotel staff at the time was quite used to the cast and private partying, aspiring stars running half dressed down the halls pursued by ardent producers, or errant leading men or women. Working life has been duller in the hotel of late.

The hotel lobby was a mélange of faded grace and glory and new age slick. The white marble walls retained their fluted half columns, now edged in a faded yellow. Black marble with a cast of forest green paved the new floor in diamond diagonals. Oatmeal beige sofas and chairs surrounded the requisite potted palms. Em was reminded of the Biltmore's Palm Court in the late 1960's.

As Em and Nancy entered the lobby, a young person dressed in rumpled yellow sweater and jeans headed out past them, a determined expression on her face. The girl's jeans were tight and not in a good way. A muffin top was not a fashion accessory unfortunately, Em reflected with a sigh for her own waistline.

The desk attendant in his dark suit looked upon the two women entering the massive glass hotel doors with something bordering on contempt, with an edge towards pity. He pegged them as lost, certainly out of their proper element. They were casually dressed and without a designer label between them. The taller younger woman with the wavy red hair wore a loose fitting grey pinstriped suit jacket that bulged slightly under one arm. Obviously not a made to measure suit. Both women looked ordinarily respectable. At least he did not have to be concerned with showing professional ladies without special invitations, the door.

"Good afternoon, we're inquiring about a person you may have staying in Room 306." Em spoke in her cultured accent, usually reserved for university matters.

"I cannot give information out about our guests." The man behind the desk, the day manager, raised his red nose and pointed his rather flabby chin at Em.

"Nancy, it's time to flip the badge." After a long afternoon trudging around the city, Em was in no mood to dally.

"FBI." Nancy hauled out her ID.

The manager gave careful scrutiny to the ID and the women. "Nancy Dombroski," he read. "Any relation to Nancy Drew?" Bored with his day job, he most certainly thought himself a wit.

"She gets that all the time. It's not funny. Remember she's armed. Nancy Drew was not."

This of course explained the bulge under the jacket, in a way that the man behind the desk was not prepared to doubt.

"We'll ask the questions. Who do you have in Room 306?" Nancy took over the lead.

"Right. FBI. No sense of humor. It's an urban legend."

"Save the legends, we need the name and specifics." There was a hint of growl in Nancy's voice.

The manager, whose name tag read Evanson, shook his slicked back mouse brown head. He made a show of checking the computer console hidden down below the level of the desk front. "Ms. Marla Eisenstein. Ms. Eisenstein checked in two days ago. Paid in advance for a four day stay."

"In advance. Is that unusual, in your professional opinion?" Em tried flattery. She stopped short of batting her eyelashes. In women over thirty that seldom had the desired effect.

"Yes and no. Plenty of people find it more convenient, shall we say, to avoid the use of credit cards. Discretion, you know, can be a valuable thing. No credit card, no trails." Evanson paused to look worldly wise before these two local women. With sleight of hand, he passed a pen down through the fingers of his right hand and back again.

"Did she reserve in advance with a credit card?" Nancy took over, all business.

"I told you she paid cash, not traveler's checks. Ms. Eisenstein called in that morning to see if we had availability and told us she would be arriving in the late afternoon on a quick business trip. Staying perhaps three or four days. It was the middle of the week, nothing special going on in town, so we did have a single non-smoking room available for her."

"Did she present ID when she checked in? Address?"

"She must have. Here's the address and her license number." Evanson wrote down a number on Bleecker Street in

New York City. "She presented a New York driver's license. Check in time was 4:54 p.m. She must have come straight from the train station. She did not use the Valet park."

"Bleecker Street is in Greenwich Village." Em looked at Nancy.

"What did Ms. Eisenstein look like? Can you describe her?" Nancy made notes in a small diary.

"She was a thin woman, shorter than your friend here. Also middle aged. Wore sun glasses. I would say dark hair. She wore one of those new knit hats, so it was hard to tell. Polished. Attractive."

Em was not yet satisfied. "Right. Now let's do this again. You see many people in your position, you are an observant man. I can see that from the way your eyes move. You watch the lobby, you see the activity around you, and then you focus back on us without missing a beat. I'll bet if you blocked out everything around you, perhaps even closed your eyes, you could describe what she was wearing, right down to the jewelry."

His eyes dropped to half closed, to think.

"Here we go, head to toe, start with her hat. What did it look like?" Em prompted.

"It was one of the new beanies that we see in the news, in paparazzi photos. Hand knit in natural cotton."

"Cheap?"

"Oh, no, Ms. Eisenstein looked like she had money. Very well dressed. Everything well fitting. Polished."

"Now we're getting to it," Em said quietly to Nancy, who was trying her best to keep patience with this line of inquiry, which was not in her style at all.

"Earrings? Necklace?"

"Gold earrings. Very distinctive, I admired them. Three oval honey colored stones, matching ring on her right hand. She signed in with her right." Nancy took notes, she had never asked about jewelry.

"Amber?" asked Em.

"No, more like a faceted cut, topaz, or citrine. The ring had a larger stone and unusual oval shape. Very pretty, good taste, simple gold chain necklace."

"Oh, very good! You noticed her hands. Polish? Color?"

"Very well cared for, no colored polish."

Em was truly pleased. "Professional manicure?"

"I would say so, yes."

"This is all very helpful, Mr. Evanson. Did you notice a watch?" Em was convinced people who wore expensive or highly distinctive watches, came to think of them as part of their identity and seldom left them off.

"I'm afraid I couldn't see one. She had on a long sleeved black sweater, very plain, fashionable design, matched her pants."

"Now Mr. Evanson, this is key, and I know you will be able to assess this. Was she comfortable here in your milieu?" Em waived her hand gracefully, and a trifle theatrically, to indicate the hotel around her. She rose in Evanson's esteem, she understood the Inn. Surely she must be a person of note, although rather inadequately dressed.

"Yes, I see what you are about. Ms. Eisenstein had a presence, as if she belonged here, but very understated, as if she was someone who was reluctant, shall we say, to be recognized. The hat, the sunglasses. *Please.* And there was the designer fragrance*, trés chic, trés expensive."*

Falling in with Monsieur Evanson, Em embroidered. "It is as we hoped, you do remember. Her voice, did it, too, have the distinction?"

Evanson encouraged, warmed to the topic. "Her voice was cultured, low in tone, as if she was used to excellent service. But perhaps not used to traveling alone."

"Why do you say that, sir?"

"My impression. Ms. Eisenstein seemed as if she was used to having a personal assistant. She was a tad awkward with her luggage as if she was not used to towing it around with her. She almost left it at the desk. We have no bellman on at that time of day during the week. You understand, the economy."

"Of course, what can one do? Tell us about the luggage."

Nancy fidgeted, she could sense the direction of Em's questions, but not the purpose.

"Not what I expected, one of those less expensive department store pieces. Appropriate size for a three day stay. The laptop bag and the handbag were top quality leather though. Coach handbag, Hermes for the laptop, but showing use. Perhaps she picked up the roller for a quick trip." Em nodded, it was a likely possibility. She and Nancy exchanged looks. The manager used the past tense when describing Ms. Eisenstein.

"How would you sum her up, Mr. Evanson? Brief impressions…."

The manager cocked his head. "Business woman on a mission. Rushed. Executive type. Did not want to be recognized. Not in the fashion industry."

"Academic?" Em gave the word a full four syllable treatment.

"Heavens, no, too well dressed, too polished."

"Meeting someone, would you think?" said Em with innuendo in her voice.

"Not here. She checked in, ordered room service for tea, and then a light supper. Had her supper tray picked up. She went out shortly after that. We haven't seen her since early that evening. I presumed that's why you're here. Of course, she could be staying with friends."

Or she's split town after a meeting, or she might be floating out on the tide heading for the City by the water route, thought Em wryly and tried not to betray her concern on her face.

"That's why I was surprised to see that young woman who said she was Ms. Eisenstein's assistant come to pick up her things. Not at all what you would expect. You passed her on your way in."

"What?" Em and Nancy chorused.

"Of course we wouldn't let her into the room. She had no identification and no authorization from Ms. Eisenstein, either in writing or over the phone. And that's what I told her, too. She just did not look right, more like some kid right off the street. *Not dressed,* hair all this way and that. Looked like she slept in her old clothes. Odd though, I could swear I've seen her before." He tilted his head and looked off to the right, remembering.

"How long do you keep your security camera footage?" Nancy asked, taking over in relay with Em.

"This is a high quality establishment, we can't release that information. Alright, a month, but you'll need some sort of an order for that. You can never tell what you might see, even in the hallways, and who you might see doing it."

"We'll need a week to start. Now we need to see the room."

"What if Ms. Eisenstein comes back?"

"Call me, immediately," Nancy ordered, passing over her business card to him. "We have a few more questions for her if she does show up. Call, don't mention our visit to her."

"The girl who claimed to be her personal assistant, where might you have seen her?" Em was back on track. The hotel was not exactly doing a flash mob worth of business, and no one else had approached the desk. Several guests strolled in and out, but no one seemed to distinguish Em and Nancy with any special attention.

"To me, she looks like one of the kids who hang around the corner near the Korean grocery and the noodle place. The boutique on the corner caters to them, but it's not cheap."

"Did she give you a name?" Nancy anticipated that any personal assistant would have announced herself straight off.

"We stopped her in the lobby, here at the desk. That's why I'm out here myself. I sent the desk attendant to the back office so I could handle any unpleasantness she might create. The young woman announced she was here to pick up Ms. Eisenstein's things. We were not about to let her upstairs. Before she left she did say she would be coming back with someone else. One moment, I'll call Gisele to the desk so I can take you upstairs myself." The tone of his voice suggested Gisele was the source of his interest in French culture.

The new chrome elevator car was tiled with the black and green marble that matched the lobby floor. It rose with a bare minimum of sound or sense of movement to the third floor.

I wouldn't like to be trapped in this small box, Em thought, suppressing the tendency to look for a means of escape. The halls of the third floor were marble lined with new fire rated carpet down the center, patterned in swirls of black and green.

Evanson knocked on the door of Room 306 first, and then popped the master card key in the door handle. The room looked undisturbed. The manager backed out into the hallway leaving the door open.

The bathroom to the left of the door was done in caramel marble with veins of white. Around the bathroom was a chest high band of cream ceramic tile embossed with a chrysanthemum motif. The natural silk textured shower curtain repeated the chrysanthemum pattern in a tone on tone woven design and was wrapped around a gently curving bathtub. A soup plate sized shower head, multiple water jets and a hand held jet on a long hose were on view. The wall paper was a green and beige repeat pattern of single bamboo stalks. The washstand was an open ebony finish table on which a gracefully shaped glass bowl rested. The polished taps and the elegant faucet were shaped to suggest bamboo. Thick natural cotton towels and a hotel robe, all apparently unused hung with precise neatness over the ebony rack. The shag rug of natural cotton seemed several inches thick.

At a glance, the mini-spa of a bathroom appeared immaculate. There were, however, several personal toilet articles, toothbrush, Tom's toothpaste, an expensive face cream and co-branded body wash arranged by the taps. The bathroom was of a size to include a black lacquer dressing table with a bamboo framed mirror. A tortoise shell comb and brush set were aligned perfectly on the dressing table, seemingly waiting for use.

The elegant makeup case on the table gave an indication of personal taste and the occupant's coloring. A tortoise shell compact contained custom blended face powder in a shade to match a light complexion. A brand new tube of lipstick from a top European brand was in a tasteful neutral shade, a practical choice to match a range of colors. An expensive facial moisturizer and a new bar of rose scented French milled soap completed the contents of the makeup case. Em noted the lack of eye shadow or mascara, probably omitted for a business trip with no formal evening engagements.

Em retreated from the gorgeous bathroom. She pictured her own bathroom at the Spring House, its nearly ancient ball and claw footed tub and its narrow band of stubborn rust stain around the drain. It gave her a case of the envies. Not even the mural in her bathroom at home and its risqué mermaid seemed to console her.

"You could check me in here just for the shower alone. Since she paid in cash for four days of this, we might want to ask the denominations of the bills she used."

"A roll of small bills might indicate something. But, I think we would have heard that from your friend Evanson," Nancy remarked as she walked around the room, giving it a thorough preliminary examination. "Put gloves on."

The room was a luxury single, French vanilla walls, khaki carpet with ebonized wooden furniture of contemporary

Asian inspiration. An original oil painting in a gold leaf frame of an urban cityscape with lights of red and yellow, counterfeiting the style of the French Impressionists hung over the King sized bed. The bed was covered with a quilted spread in a chrysanthemum print highlighted in gold, similar to that found in the bathroom. The armoire and the desk were ebony. The room designer was mixing metaphors, or the person who chose the furniture was at odds with the art consultant.

On the desk, a polished brass lamp with double lights and an oblong black shade sported data ports and additional power outlets on its base. A cream desk set wireline phone sat on the nightstand by the bed. There was no sign of a laptop or a tablet.

The three day roller lay unzipped on the luggage rack, Louis Vuitton, or a knock off. Three dresses, one black, one mocha, one charcoal grey, linen jackets, skirt, blouses and black linen pants hung at even intervals in the armoire. Shoes to match were on the floor below. Em separated the dresses to better examine them. Puzzled, she removed the first one from the hanger. Admiring the cut, the fabrication and the seaming, she looked at the label and exclaimed, "It's an Issey Miyake!"

Nancy looked up from her search of the desk, with a "so what" expression on her face. "Who's that when she's at home?"

"Not she, he! An innovative fashion designer. The other one looks to be a Badgely Mishka. Here's a Vera Wang. No one would walk off and leave these, they're works of art. Not to say very expensive. At least for me." Em paused to remember for a moment, "You know, she might leave these. I haven't seen these styles in three or four years. The dresses are model sized. Smaller, shorter woman, as Evanson said. The average American woman is a size 14." Em herself was battling to stay down to a 14. Nancy was a full figured, tall, athletic size 14. "The shoes are also designer,

New York favorites. They cost a few hundred a pair, but they are not new either. Small size, too."

"Not much in the luggage," Nancy replied. "I did notice the silk undies, PJs, all small, and actual stockings."

"Panty hose are back in since the Duchess of Cambridge's visit." Em examined the jackets and the linen trousers. "It's a good thing these are too small for anyone in my house, or I would be tempted to protect them for the owner. Any jewelry in the luggage?"

"None found. The laptop and the purse are gone." Under the beds, and all drawers checked, their search was almost complete.

"If we can find the imposter of a personal assistant, we may be able to figure out if these were left intentionally. The girl didn't have the room key card so her visit is probably someone's improvisation," Em surmised.

"Someone else may have the card key. Can we pack all this up and take it back to your office?"

"Not yet, no sign of a crime here. We can document with pictures. I'll ask the manager to disable the room key so anyone trying to access the room will have to return to the front desk. The staff can be alerted to watch the room as well." She took cell phone pictures of the items.

"The hairbrush in the bathroom may provide us with a little something to take back. Do you have evidence bags?"

"Does a cat have fleas?"

Nancy pulled a plastic zipped case from her pocket, an evidence kit of her own design. Diminutive enough to fit in a suit pocket, it was full enough to ruin the line of a jacket. The case contained gloves, evidence bags, eyebrow tweezers, flat bladed tweezers, a tiny pocket knife, clippers and short blunt pointed scissors, a small envelope of fingerprint powder, felt-tipped pen, a six inch flexible ruler, and a flattened section of paper tape, among other useful objects.

Heading for the bathroom with an evidence bag and

tweezers, Nancy reminded Em to check the clothing for hair strands as well. Nancy teased out several strands from the brush. Em called her to come remove a single hair from the inside of the Issey Miyake dress. Nancy removed it with a satisfied smile. "Looks like we have enough to ID the occupant of the room."

The minibar contained bottles of beer, California wine in small bottles, soda in cans, bottled waters and flavored seltzers. The fridge contained fruit juices that neither woman had seen before. While Nancy finished searching the minibar and fridge hidden in the console under the TV, Em gazed around the room taking mental snapshots to remember the placement.

"Nancy, this picture is all wrong for this room."

"Am I investigating this with Martha Stewart?"

On intuition, Em went straight to the wall and lifted up the edge of the painting with a gloved hand.

"The picture has been replaced recently. The wall paint's faded around a smaller picture. The room décor is Asian, the painting is Paris at the turn of the century. Not right. This whole place is matchy matchy as Tim Gunn would say." Em turned around and poked her head out the door to call Evanson back to the room. He remained in the hallway to answer her questions, seeming reluctant to enter.

"Mr. Evanson, we can't help but notice that the art in this room. Well, it doesn't match the décor." Em cast a critical eye at the painting on the wall.

"Oh, you would notice that. Ms. Eisenstein had us change the painting. Who ever heard of that? It was such a nice Japanese watercolor seascape. An original, too. She said if she was going to stay in the room for four days, she wanted something with more vibrant colors. Something she could actually see."

"What colors were in the Japanese seascape?" Em asked although she could anticipate the answer.

"The colors were soft blues and greens, grey sky. When

we replaced it, we choose the brightest painting we had in storage. She seemed to like it. Although it's not nearly as good a piece of art. Very derivative, don't you think?"

"Yes. Thank you, that's very interesting and explains the unusual choice. We'll call you if we have any more questions." Em was done and Evanson retreated gladly.

"So what was all the art history about?" Nancy asked.

"Ms. Eisenstein may be color blind. Although this type is rarer in women, it sounds as if she has an issue seeing blues, greens and greys accurately. Those colors may look so similar to her she couldn't appreciate the watercolor. The staff replaced it with a bright oil painting assuming she wanted more intense colors, not understanding she simply needed different colors."

"Interesting theory, she could be developing cataracts," Nancy commented.

"We'll know when we find her. Alive, I hope."

22

MISSIONARIES ARRIVE

———◆———

"I'M DONE HERE, MARTHA!" NANCY was both thorough and quick with her work and ready to move on to the next task. "Next we need to trace the so-called personal assistant."

"If we can't trace her right away, we can put our heads together with Evanson for a description. If we borrow a good sized piece of paper and a pencil, I can try to sketch her from what we remember," Em offered.

"Not a bad idea if you can do it. I don't usually get to travel with my own sketch artist," Nancy replied good naturedly.

Em laughed to herself as she slammed the hotel room door behind them.

As it turned out, Em's talents with a sketch pad were not to be tested that day. As the elevator deposited them in the lobby, they immediately recognized the rather poorly dressed young woman approaching the front desk. She was accompanied by an older man dressed in worn but clean clothes. He had the look of retirement, bald rather than in the process of balding, pants now too big, out of date, and not quite appropriate for the season, fall rather than spring. Both the young woman and the elderly gentleman had an air of earnestness about them that perplexed Em and Nancy who walked up behind them.

Evanson backed up by the faithful Giselle, were behind the desk together. "Mr. McVeety, sir, please do understand that yours is an unusual request. We simply cannot release personal belongings without a written or verbal request from Ms. Eisenstein, no matter how worthy and respectable your cause. The Homestead Mission is so well-known and we value the good work you do in our community." The elderly man took in Evanson's speech with a profound mildness. The young woman shuffled her feet and looked rather downcast and disappointed.

Nancy began her questioning circumspectly. "Are we to understand you have come for Marla Eisenstein's possessions? Is she known to you?" She showed the elderly man her badge which caused the young woman to take two precipitous steps backward. She turned right into Em who had placed herself directly in back of the young person in anticipation she might turn tail and run for it. They came up face to face, nose to nose.

"Excuse me, but we need you to stay here with us. We need answers to a few questions concerning Ms. Eisenstein." Em put the tone of command in her voice, and a professional excuse for smile on her face.

The young woman assumed from her tone that Em, too, was a federal agent. Em didn't enlighten her.

Nancy got out her notebook, Em stood rear guard. "Mr. Evanson is cooperating with us in an ongoing investigation. It is imperative we locate Ms. Eisenstein. Tell us how you came to request her things."

In the mildest of manners the elderly man responded, "Why, my young friend Shelli here took the phone call this morning. Shelli is one of our young people who came to stay with us at the Mission and is now working with us for the good of others." Mr. Evanson nodded, this was where he remembered seeing her. "Shelli was not sure how to respond to the person's request, so she asked if I might speak with them. It's alright Shelli. You've done nothing wrong," he said over his shoulder.

Shelli wrung her hands anxiously.

"The person on the phone asked if we would send someone here to the Inn to pick up Ms. Marla Eisenstein's personal things. She'd had a death in the family and would not be able to return soon enough for them." At this Em raised her eyebrows at Nancy who was writing in her notebook. "The person on the phone said that we should tell the manager one of our own people was her personal assistant so the Inn would release the things to us." He paused to catch a breath, then went on to say, "We were told we might keep the clothing for our thrift shop, anything that we could sell, and use or discard the rest. For this we would receive a donation of $200 to be used for our infant nutrition and assistance program."

"A very worthy cause," Em added.

"Indeed, we were grateful for the offer of support. It's hard to convince people to donate money to buy diapers for new mothers in need. It was unusual, but the Inn itself has been so generous with donations of food left over from banquets, especially during the holidays, and with gifts of gently used sheets and blankets. It seemed as if they must have referred Ms. Eisenstein's person to us. Isn't that right, Shelli?" he asked the young woman, whose given name turned out to be Sheldine Saunders. Relieved, she nodded yes enthusiastically.

"Mr. McVeety, you have said repeatedly, the 'person' on the phone. It was not Ms. Eisenstein? Was it a man or woman?" Nancy inquired.

"To tell the truth," the Missionary replied reluctantly, "we have the least expensive phone service we could find, and the sound quality is not what I remember having years ago. With that and the static on the line it was hard to tell, but I had no indication it was the lady herself calling. My own hearing is not what it was either."

"Please try!" Nancy asked with some urgency.

"More likely a man, what would you say, Shelli?"

"Yeah, either a man or one of those old women with a raspy voice. He's right about the sound, Mr. McVeety is. If someone calls us on a cell phone, it's not so good. You can tell the difference."

"Please tell us when you received the call, Shelli. What puzzled you about it that you went to Mr. McVeety for assistance?" Em tried to be firm but patient. Nancy was about to take a much more direct approach, but Em spoke more quickly.

Relieved that the women were not inquiring about the funny cigarette she had stashed in her pocket for later, Shelli's intuition told her the fastest way to get out of there was to fess up. Cooperation seemed the best diversion. She became suddenly vocal. "You see, I answer the phones at the Mission, that's part of my new job. I've got to know who's on the phone and what they need. 'Cause we could have an emergency and they need help right away. There's always a person for me to call if I think that." She looked around and found herself the center of attention and almost faltered.

"Go on, Shelli, you're doing fine," Mr. McVeety encouraged her.

"There's never been a call like this one so when whoever said I could keep the makeup, I got scared. You see, I didn't want anyone to think I was stealing nothing. So I got Mr. McVeety real fast." She brushed her bangs back off her face with a shaky hand.

"It's alright, my dear, we believe you. A while ago Shelli had an experience in a drug store, and the police were called. It was a small matter, and she's been talking through it with one of our counselors." McVeety was about forgiveness, but he was about personal responsibility, too. Shelli looked gratefully at McVeety. It seemed to explain the young woman's case of nerves.

"Shelli was understandably concerned then. You think it was a man?" Em saw the doubt on Shelli's face. "Would you recognize the voice if you heard it again?"

"I might, I don't know. Seems a man wouldn't think about the makeup." Shelli grew agitated again.

Nancy thanked both Mr. McVeety and Shelli, took down their contact information at the Homestead Mission a few blocks away. She gave them each her business card with the request they call her immediately if the person called back and a warning that no mention should be made of their talk with her.

After requesting that Evanson keep Room 306 as it was left, and not to allow anyone at all to enter until she could arrange for paperwork for a formal search, Em and Nancy hit the street. Em's feet were sore, and she was beginning to appreciate Nancy's choice of less than fashionable footwear.

"I need to send requests in to the office." Nancy surveyed the street as was her habit, watching passersby, vehicles, windows and roofs of surrounding buildings, assessing the threat level. She caught a fleeting movement as if a figure withdrew from her line of vision around a nearby street corner.

"That hotel has a good restaurant," Em pointed out. It was now later in the afternoon, Em's instinct was to search out the nearest café. "But we would be an object of interest to the staff. How about Claire's?" Em named a local favorite vegetarian restaurant within an easy walk from the Alcorn Inn. "We could be two women in for a quick nosh," she joked. "I'd feel safer with more people around."

"There's a point. You can give me the benefit of your analysis, and I'll provide the security." Nancy slipped back into professional mode.

Em was not about to let her off. As they passed the corner she said, "Okay, Drew, whatever you say."

The figure of a lightly built man in dark clothing followed them at a convenient distance, concealing himself adeptly behind groups of shopping women, or knots of laughing students as he moved through the crowded sidewalk traffic.

Once inside the small restaurant, the women stood in line along the counter to place their orders. Em spent the waiting time feasting her eyes on the tall cakes made in Bundt pans, oversized muffins and large scones of several flavors. Em came away from the counter with a cup of tea and a thick slice of carrot cake slathered in fresh butter cream frosting. Nancy ordered a platter of nachos that would be delivered to the table when ready. With sharp eyes, Em spotted a table in the corner and outdistanced a distinguished Professor of Philosophy for the seats. The woman looked daggers at Em, who smiled back at her.

"What was that about?" Nancy asked. She'd seen the silent interchange between the two competitors.

"Interdepartmental rivalry. It's not enough that they're the brains of the place, they need to take fitness more seriously."

"So much for anonymity in a crowded place," Nancy huffed at Em.

Nancy planted herself behind the small table in the corner, back to the wall, and moved her chair for the widest angle view. She encouraged Em to place her chair so she could see around her, enabling a view of both exits, the counter and the kitchen door. Em's position in front of Nancy at the table was also calculated to block the view of any passerby at the satellite connected handheld device into which the federal agent rapidly typed information and requests.

The platter of nachos loaded with toppings arrived at their table hot and steamy. Em was already halfway through her hefty sized chunk of carrot cake. Nancy completed typing and made determined progress through the heap of nachos on the very hot platter.

"Your deductions, Martha. Stop if I raise my hand like this," Nancy raised several fingers off the table just enough to be seen.

"Okay, woman probably in her fifty's, over 5' feet tall under 5'4", wears a model's size 6. Hair likely dark, white business woman with financial resources, manager or executive, used to having a personal assistant. Conservative taste in colors, likes expensive designer clothes and shoes, and distinctive jewelry. So she is knowledgeable about fashion and has access to New York brands."

"Could be consignment shop or a thrift shop." Nancy suggested.

"It would have to be one hell of a consignment shop, and she'd have to be blessed lucky to find her size. She probably only brought what she considers to be old clothes with her.

"To continue," Em replied. "She wears expensive makeup, but understated, and has fair skin, light complexion. Wearing the jewelry was a strategic mistake by the way. It's too identifiable. From the description Evanson gave us, we could identify the ring and the earrings even if they turned up in a pawn shop."

"Good point." Nancy made research notes for herself, unlikely to catch one of her male colleagues asking a witness about jewelry.

"Her vision issue may be blue/green color blindness or cataracts. She does carefully look at the pictures on the wall, some people don't even notice them. Sounds like she was used to having art around her. She was comfortable in the most expensive place in town. Everything we've learned about the woman from the hotel room indicates money and position."

"I would agree. Even the offer of the $200 gift to charity indicates resources because the donation would be confidential. If there was no follow through and the money was not received, there would be chatter about it that might eventually reach the local police. I'm not liking the whole donation pick up the stuff issue either." Nancy cast her eyes around the restaurant, with a glance or two out the window at the street.

"And she paid a good sized hotel bill in cash and was anxious not to be recognized or traceable. We have a name and address, but I'll bet you it isn't her own. She is among the missing. We only found her trail because of the accidental loss of the note by the river and prompt follow up today."

"Dead or alive?" Nancy confirmed Em's analysis with her notes.

"I'd say it's a toss-up right now. We need to find Kirbee or his lab assistants to see if they recognize the description. Try Missing Persons in New York State. She's the woman who went into the river at the time Hussein was killed.

"Can you get the Mission's incoming call records? You know, Shelli thinks it was an older woman with a raspy voice on the phone. Might check on Shelli Saunders as well, Sheldine sounds more like a last name than a first name. I wonder if the caller tried to bribe Shelli with the $200 first. The Inn is so close to the Mission, I can't believe a New Yorker would know that. Local knowledge, local connection?"

Nancy dredged up salsa, melted cheese and guacamole with a large tortilla chip ready to take a bite when the screen on her device changed. She held the nacho suspended in mid-air in front of her. The nacho stayed suspended for quite some time as she read the information forwarded to her screen. After what seemed an age, Nancy took a healthy bite out of the nacho.

"You know, when you first approached me about this, I thought, hey, let's humor her. Now Martha, I think you're onto something that the rest of us missed." Nancy looked up, from the corner of her eye she caught the movement of a figure backing away from the restaurant window. She frowned.

"Quit calling me 'Martha.'"

"They ran Eisenstein's New York driver's license number for me. She's a teacher who lives in the Village and who had her wallet stolen in the subway station two weeks ago. Credit cards, license, all forms of ID and most of the cash were taken. Wallet was recovered from a trash bin close to the subway exit."

"Suggestive…" remarked Em.

"Wait, it's more than that. Marla Eisenstein thinks she was targeted for the theft. She rides the subway regularly to and from work and keeps her wits about her when she does. It's New York. She noticed a woman watching her, she felt as if she'd seen her at least twice. The third time, the woman was with a man, an older white guy. The woman walked by her and got off at the stop before Marla's. As Marla gets off the man bumps into her. When she got up to the street level, she realized her bag was lighter and her wallet was missing."

"So the woman tagged her, and the man robbed her."

"Yeah, Marla's got a good head on her. She looked around, spotted the man and ran after him. She actually saw him ditch the wallet in the trash, but the sidewalk was packed with commuters so she couldn't see where he went. She reported it to the nearest policeman."

"Cute setup."

"It gets better, and you are really going to like this. Ms. Eisenstein swears the woman looked enough like her to be her sister, only she doesn't have one."

Nancy scrolled down the screen. "Description of the woman on the subway is very similar to the one we're developing. We'll have a picture of Marla herself from the driver's license photo."

"We have a long range planner on our hands. She may not be a victim." Em's tone was serious.

"Bingo! This is not good," concluded Nancy.

"She was looking for someone who resembled her to have the ID stolen, probably by a hired hand. She's used to having personal assistance after all. Someone like that is going to take precautions and not get dead real easy."

"No kidding. I've got to go do paperwork for an evidence team to pick up her stuff and get an order for the Missions phone records. Are you done? You know we're being followed?" Nancy glanced out the window again. "Who do we think this is?"

"Oh, let me guess. Short man?" Em laughed out loud, drawing disapproving looks from the philosophy department table.

Outside the restaurant, the women parted ways. "I'd walk you to your car, but I think I can leave you in care of the colleague behind us," Nancy said under her breath.

Out loud in a bright clear voice Em was heard to say, "Let's do lunch again soon! I do enjoy a good gossip, don't you?"

The figure in the dark clothes, who was now lounging against one of the historical reproduction street lampposts, brought out a cell phone and placed it next to his ear. He spoke into his collar. "They've had crumpets and tea, making like two lady friends out for the afternoon. She was with the woman fed, the one the guys call 'Drew' when they're a couple blocks away and they're sure her back is turned."

"The whole afternoon?"

"That's right, the whole afternoon. They hit almost every hotel, motel and dive in the area. Looks like they found what they were looking for at the last one, the Alcorn Inn, the ritzy one. They were in there for almost an hour. Then they headed for the restaurant. Lady fed types a bunch of stuff. Our friend does most of the talking."

"Doing analysis, right," a voice in his earbud replied.

"All of a sudden the fed stares at her screen. They talk it

over, and she gets all business. Leaves the rest of her nachos and they head out. The fed heads across the Green in the direction of their office. The other one is getting in her car."

"Anyone else interested?"

"Not that I saw. Do I follow?"

"Not necessary. Get back to the office, Rankel."

23

RENT PARTY —
THE CONCERT BEGINS

———————

CLEAR, BRIGHT AND BUSY, SATURDAY morning started early at the Spring House. The eco-friendly portable toilets had arrived the previous afternoon. That was the delivery that postponed Em's meeting with Halloran. The portables were placed in a clearing downhill and on the opposite side of the road. They were a good two hundred feet from any water source. In case of a spill, Em placed them well away from the spring and the brook. High on the day's to do list was a quick stocking of the biodegradable toilet paper for the portable conveniences, details, details. "The Fred," their backyard outhouse with a composting toilet and no running water, was to be off limits to all but the handicapped. The bathrooms in the house were off limits as well. Too many flushes might overwhelm the elderly septic system. There were other reasons for restricting access to the house, too.

In the kitchen, the family breakfast was eaten standing up and quickly. The first volunteers arrived to begin setting up tables for food, chairs for sitting on the lawn behind the house, and the borrowed gas grills. Two of the best long tables were placed on the stone paving in front of the house for donations of money, non-perishable food items for the town's food pantry, and another special collection of books. The guest of honor, for whom the "Rent Party" was being given, violinist Mai Lyn Chen, would be receiving the donations to assist her in funding both an apartment of her own and to launch her professional career by entering an international violin competition. Then, there was of course, the hidden agenda.

Mai Lyn's friends and family were laughing and speaking in Chinese at the check in table. Two youngsters were making signs in English and Chinese for the directions to the portable johns, parking in the lower field beyond the brook and food choices, with the postalized rate of a suggested donation of $1.00 per item — negotiable. If the person had limited or no money for food, he or she would still be welcome to a good meal. An uncle was carefully correcting the Chinese characters. The donation for admission was $15.00, or whatever, reduced to $10.00 with a food donation, or donations of certain books.

In the backyard on the downward southern slope, Mai's roommate's family helped to set up the mics and amps and were carrying Jamaican specialties into the kitchen. A family from down the road brought in coolers filled with ice, though no one was sure who they were.

Sandy was down in the spring room with friends. They were filling new water bottles of various sizes. The bottles were ferried out through the cellar door on a child's wagon and in a garden wheelbarrow. They were headed for the area of the upper lawn where the bottles would be given out for a cash donation.

Em and her friend Tina, a strikingly handsome woman of African and Cherokee heritage, were trying to organize the food donations to keep the hot food hot and the various potato and pasta salads chilled. The large tray of fried rice and another of homemade egg rolls shared the oven with the Jamaican meat pies. The Puerto Rican pulled pork sat on the stove joining its tantalizing aroma with the smell of Em's vegetarian chili from her largest Crock-Pot on the counter. Basmati white rice filled a rice cooker. Still another of Em's Crock-Pots held a mixture of brown rice and crunchy wild rice. Mint tea, made from leaves harvested that morning from the garden, sat cooling in a large brown and white stoneware crock.

Deanna was out near the rock garden, on the lawn in front of the terrace by the living room door. She set up her grills and tables for the food in the shade as best she could determine where it would be shadiest by lunchtime. She despaired that all would be in full sunlight by 3:00 in the afternoon, when a crew of family and friends arrived with two tents on long poles that would provide the desired shade. After some moving and hauling, tables were arranged along the uphill edge of the lawn. From the cellar came sheets of plywood that were hammered onto the steps up to the Fred to make an accessible ramp. The coolers of ice appeared. Water bottles, soda and seltzer cans went into the coolers to be chilled.

The children who made the artful signs, decorating them with flowers and musical notes, moved from the front of the house to the backyard. There they took requests for signage, including a big "Off Limits!" sign for the house's back door. A newly arrived group of children went around and systematically added Spanish to all the signs.

Amazingly, out of chaos and laughter, and some cursing heard from the musicians and their roadies who were setting up and testing equipment, by 11:30, all was as ready as it ever would be. The volunteers stopped for an early lunch served in the kitchen and eaten outside in the garden. One must always be prepared to feed starving musicians.

Em took a deep breath and left Tina in charge of the kitchen. She could hear Mai tuning up upstairs. A soprano could be heard warming up in the sunroom at the far end of the house. Each performer trying to keep as far away from the other as possible. There was no such thing as quiet practice space that day. Em headed down the cellar stairs to the spring room where she found Sandy and her crew finishing up with the bottles of water. Congratulating them on a job well done, she encouraged them to get up to the kitchen to get something to eat before the opening at noon. Em secured the spring room door and headed out through the cellar, latching the ground level cellar door behind her. Like many New England farm structures, the Spring House was built accessible from two ground levels, and the stout wooden cellar door opened out on the lower south side of the house.

Out on the lawn, Em walked past the musicians and their crew, turned and headed up the slope. Halfway up, she placed her favorite lounge chair with a towel draped across it to show that it was reserved. From this vantage point, close to the wall of the house, she could see the improvised stage area at the base of the lawn and up the gentle slope to the food tents. To much laughter, she let everyone know that this was her spot, her very own spot, where she might be found if needed. Sound checks were becoming more satisfactory. Power cables ran out the cellar window, and from the outside plugs, and no one was happy about it. The trenches to carry the PVC pipes for the cables needed to be deeper. Friends were dispatched for the garden tools kept in the Fred to dig them deeper to protect them from the footsteps of the crowd.

The Spring House gardens were coming into bloom. Bright orange daylilies, planted generations ago, were massed against the building at irregular intervals. New daylily cultivars in a variety of colors were displayed in the yard, joined by large flowering daisies, Black Eyed Susans, lupine, with several varieties of hostas in the shaded areas. The herb and vegetable gardens had been marked off as forbidden territory to ward off two legged predators.

After surveying the lawn and gardens, and finding the

signs charmingly misspelled in two of the three languages she could read, Em went up to the food tents to check on Deanna. She found her waving a long handled grilling fork dramatically, yelling, "I am the Grill Master! Get your hot dogs and veggie burgers here. My father's a rancher and my mother won't let me serve hamburgers!"

"That's enough of that Deanna," her mother reproached, dodging the very long wooden handled fork. Deanna's audience of volunteers faded away, returning to their tasks. "You are already sopping wet. Go change before you serve anyone. Quick before I close up the house."

Deanna knew better than to disobey when her mother used that tone of voice. She looked down at her already sweat stained tee shirt, let out a playful shriek, handed her fork to another young volunteer and headed for the house. Em stayed to admire the setup, the first hot dogs and veggie burgers were grilling. Drinks were ready. Several women set out bowls of ice to keep the salads cool and hot plates for the dishes from the stove. Em preferred to do her organizing work well before the event, so that on the day of the event she could be free to coach and be available if needed for any problems that might come up.

Em could hear new voices and laughter from the front of the house. Despite using a few fliers and word of mouth advertising, people were beginning to arrive. The best spots on the lawn in front of the stage area were taken up quickly by the friends and families of the musicians. The foodies chose the spots close to the tents. Tina's helpers brought forth lunch. Watermelons arrived and were stowed away to be kept cool for dessert, and the second annual rent party and benefit began in earnest.

———◆———

Not long after noon, a rather non-descript, beige, mid-size American car drove up the road towards the Spring House. It hesitated at the lower field, and then continued on up towards the house. Finding the handicapped parking sign designation at the driveway in front of the barn, it pulled in smartly. A tall man with a cane emerged from the car. He removed a compact gunmetal grey racing wheelchair and placed it by the open car door.

A robust young man with a shock of undisciplined blond hair threw himself out of the car and landed in the wheelchair with practiced ease. Spinning his chair around, he faced his boss who nodded and said, "I'll put this on the expense account. No need to save your receipts." Anson was not sure whether Halloran was joking or not. The younger man reported to work dressed for an undercover operation in beat up jeans and a comfortably used jacket and his best wheelchair. He was still stinging from their argument that morning about using his feet.

"You're going out into the field. Put your feet on." Halloran used his tone of command voice as they were readying themselves to leave for the Rent Party.

"I'm fine without them. I'll be undercover, right? No one will think I look like I'm there to…"

"It's not about how you look. It's about what you can do," growled Halloran patiently.

"I can do surveillance in the chair," Anson had said positively.

Halloran decided reasoning with the younger man might work. While he respected Anson's differing abilities, he knew the man could do more with the abilities that he had.

"If I need you to pursue a suspect, you will be faster on your feet than I can be on mine. There are some places that the chair cannot go easily." Halloran shook his head.

Anson had no reply to that and wisely kept still. He was no longer in discomfort himself, and he appreciated that the older man still did not walk very far without pain.

"Are you armed?"

"Yessir!" This order Anson could do well.

"Fully armed, with a vest?"

Anson looked up at his boss from his favorite wheelchair. Halloran sighed, he'd seen that look from one errant son or another quite often.

"Don't ever go out into the field without your gun, a knife and your vest on. Got that, Lieutenant? I don't care if you are going to the supermarket, if you're on duty, wear them. Go get your feet and get that vest on. And I can see your badge, so conceal it."

His back stiffened, Anson felt as if he was a kid who'd been told to tuck in his shirt, or else, and he was not happy about it. Taking direct orders was not one of those things he liked to do.

As he wheeled across the country road, slowing to match the older man's pace, Anson was fully armed and ready if game was afoot. At the check in table at the front of the house, Halloran and Anson read the signs taped to the tables. Two large cardboard boxes were placed beneath one of the tables. On one box was a sign for donations of non-perishable food items. The second box was labeled: "Bibles, any version, any language, or religious text of your choice." The two men were cordially received and tactfully made aware that the handicapped accommodations were called something that sounded very much like "The Fred." Halloran asked where Em Huber might be found and heard she would most likely be out in the yard by the food tents. "Keeping eyes on daughters."

With Anson following his boss, who set too slow a pace, the two men followed the crowd along the length of the Spring House. They passed the band warming up on the back lawn. A growing crowd was laying down blankets, setting up chairs of all sorts, and negotiating for personal space on the lawn. Off to the side, along the house and slightly up hill, Halloran spotted a lounge chair. Selecting the perfect spot, he headed for the chair. A young man who had perched himself on the very end of the lounger to talk to two laughing girls rose promptly. He saw the tall man approaching slowly followed by a man in a wheelchair heading his way. "Here, sir," he said, knowing that the person whose chair it was would approve.

Halloran thanked him and settled down with relief into the lounge chair, swinging his injured leg up carefully. Watching the older man walk on the grass with some difficulty, Anson understood Halloran's temper at his own reluctance to use his legs. Across the yard, Halloran spied out The Fred. He turned to Anson, "There's your answer! The Fred is the John." Traditional quarter moon cut into the door, the composting outhouse stood there in all its glory, stairs repurposed as an accessible ramp. "Beats walking all the way down that hill." Halloran laughed for the first time that day.

Anson's head came up, the aromas of foods, blended and wafting in his direction called to him. Breakfast had been hours ago at the Café. José was taking his turn as weekend staff and made Western omelets for early morning clientele.

"Would you like something to eat? I'm going to investigate the food tents." He had been given strict orders not to address Halloran as "sir" undercover, so he covered his almost slip with a cough.

"Maybe some spring water later. I assume that's what they'll be serving," was the reply. His boss was more intent on observing the moving tableau before him. The lounge chair was excellently placed and quite comfortable for this.

Under the food tents the lunch rush was upon them. Deanna was singing as she cooked veggie burgers and Kosher hot dogs as fast as she could. Volunteers served individual portions of food which guests paid for at the end of the line. Sandy hauled out water bottles, cans of soda and seltzer. Em, who'd organized the day with Tina and the Chen family, stood near them with her plate full, lunching on fried rice, egg rolls and pulled pork.

Sandy caught Em's attention. "Some man's sitting in your chair. Maybe you should let him stay. He has a cane, and he came in with a man in a wheelchair." Em swung around to look and was stunned to see Michael Halloran in casual clothes wearing wire rimmed glasses, dark grey hair rumpled as if combed with his fingers. He sat propped up with his cane, calmly surveying the crowd down the hill.

"Well, I'll be damned," Em muttered loud enough for Sandy to hear. Em took in the sight of Anson wheeling uphill towards the food looking around him with eager interest. He headed directly for the grill station. "That man has chili dog written all over him," said Em as she headed down the slope towards her chair, leaving Sandy in surprise.

Of course he spotted her right away out of the corner of his vigilant eyes as she advanced on him. He kept his glance at the crowd, a study in casual. It would be so much easier in the typical dark glasses he mused.

"Welcome to the Spring House. I am surprised to see you." Em picked up the towel meant to save the chair for her. Halloran had placed it on the foot of the lounger. She placed it on the ground next to him, on the downhill side, and sat down plate in hand. "I can recommend the food. It's all very good. By the way, this crowd is building, it won't last long. Why are you here?"

"You didn't have time to see me yesterday. Now I understand why. Nice crowd. The yard's filling up," he said pleasantly. There were people seated all around them, and they were both aware they could easily be overheard.

"Yes, the portable johns arrived yesterday afternoon, and I had to be here to sign for them. Last year was a success, I'm hoping now we won't be too successful. I do have more hot dogs and veggie burgers in the freezer, but when the rest of the food's gone, that's it until dessert." Em nibbled on a homemade egg roll.

He paused, and in a lower voice replied, "You got yourself shot at this week. I thought that you and the girls would benefit from some company today. You've opened up your place. Do you know everyone here?"

"No, of course not."

It was obvious she hadn't considered any risk.

"I invited the neighbors, it's always better to do that when you're having a noisy party. Even my lawyer's here with her husband. Just in case." She grinned at him. "But the invitation was posted down at the university, so, no, I don't know everyone."

He nodded. "Seemed like it might be a good idea if we came to hang out with you for the afternoon and enjoy the music."

Assuming that he would not come alone she asked suspiciously, "Where are the Hardy Boys?"

"They have the afternoon off."

"The man in the wheelchair, who is he?"

Anson waited in line, working his way up towards Deanna.

"My new driver."

"How's that working out?" Em asked with concern.

"Anson drives too damned fast, but he's a good man, he'll be good with the girls," Halloran assured her, letting her know the division of assignments.

"The girls will be good with him, too. I have kind children. What happened to him?"

"He drove over something that blew up, managed to get himself and the other guy out but further damaged his feet doing it. Worked hard to become a wheelchair athlete, but that's the problem. He's fine from the knees up they tell me. The challenge is to get him up on his feet again, to get him to stop considering himself as disabled, to think of himself as an able man in the field with a different kind of feet."

Drawing closer to him, shielding her lips with her napkin, Em asked quietly, "Is he armed?" Halloran nodded to her.

"Are you armed?"

"Always," he said under his breath. The two of them looked straight into each other's eyes. Em felt her chest tighten, in a good way.

"I have the house locked and two friends in the kitchen." She laughed briefly. "We had some problems last year. An unauthorized incursion," she joked. "I told them, that's what the woods are for." Em was smiling and blushed slightly. It seemed to him there was more to that story than she was willing to tell with so many people around her.

Halloran found another topic interesting. "Question for you, why the Bibles and religious texts?"

"Ah well, you see there are places where Bibles, Hebrew and Christian, Korans and any other religious texts, are not published. It varies place by place, of course, but when governments forbid them, there's a reason. These books give readers a sense of the core values of humanity, a separate moral compass, different from government decrees. Governments come and governments go, in constant change. The books represent collective wisdom of the generations. Thousands of years." Seeing that she had his attention, she continued. "It's not a coincidence that the U.S. Olympic team was only allowed to bring one Bible for personal use to the Beijing Olympics."

"What if someone brings a Koran?" he asked.

"Then it is treated with equal respect and goes to people who can best use it."

Halloran took a moment to reflect. He was a strict believer in observing Christmas and Easter and had seen that his boys were acquainted. When it came to confession, he'd long ago come to the conclusion that his own, especially in matters of National Security, was best done directly and in total privacy. The extent of his religious practice was to go into a room alone, shut the door and get it off his chest.

"I hesitate to ask how these things get where they're going." He grimaced.

Em polished off her lunch. "I expect they could fly or maybe sail," she said lightly. More seriously she said, "Some head for the nearest correctional facility."

"The State Department would take a dim view of that flying and sailing."

"Possibly, but who do they work for?" she asked him, implying the old "we pay their salary" argument.

"Smuggling's not a good thing."

"There is good smuggling though. Think of the Underground Railroad," she countered. This was not an argument she would let him win, and jurisdiction wise, it was not his problem.

The Concert Begins

THE OPENING BAND WAS ON deck, the lead singer welcomed everyone. With prompting from event volunteers on the side, he pointed out the handicapped Fred and reminded the audience of the comfort stations across the road and down the hill. Also, in a jibe at Harry Potter, in an imitation of Dumbledore, the lead singer stated that the house was off limits "to those not wishing to meet a most painful death." He also remarked that a real rock band shouldn't have to do public service announcements, which provoked cat calls from friends and family. Em and Halloran sat together and listened to the boys' band do their set, to be followed by three girls singing with a guitar player and a drummer for accompaniment.

Up on the hill, Anson waited patiently in line for his lunch selections. By the time he reached the head of the line for the grill, he was fantasizing in his mind how much he could load onto those long hot dog buns from the assortment of toppings on view. It seemed the organizers would make more in donations if they weighed the finished hot dogs he saw going by.

As he wheeled up in front of the grill station Deanna again waved her grill fork over the sizzling hot dogs, amusing those around her with a humorous incantation to promote speedy cooking, *a la Shakespeare*. Deanna turned to face the next person in line to find Anson looking at her with a lopsided grin on his face. He was amused and discovered despite his initial reservations, he was going to like this undercover assignment. Although he had been shown pictures of Em Huber and the girls standing by their canoe with its bullet holes, he could not immediately identify which one of the girls was before him flailing the air with her grilling implement.

"Oh, hello, how are you? The hot dogs will be ready in a minute. I've put more on the grill."

The humor in Anson's expression, together with the sight of a husky blond man with an athletic build and eyes the color of warm honey, gave Deanna immediate pause. She panicked, her train of thought ran, *Oh no, he thinks I'm acting like an idiot, and I am a total mess,* this was followed by a short litany of unsaid words and descriptive phrases best left out.

"Ah yuh, I can see that," Anson decided to play up the Maine accent, just a fellow from out of town. He was pleased to see that it worked immediately.

"You sound like you're from Maine. Are you?"

Anson nodded.

"We love it up there. Have you ever been to Red's in Wiscasset?" Without waiting for an answer Deanna forged ahead to get past her nerves, "It's the stand on Route 1 right by the bridge near the mud flats. They make the best onion rings and fried shrimp. We camped on Mt. Desert, then headed down to Boothbay for dinner at the Lobster Dock. They had a Bobby Flay Throw Down there. They won for their lobster mac and cheese, but we missed it."

"Ahm from Portland. Been to Reds, like the lobsta'roll." Anson knew the accent wasn't quite right, but it was less interesting than admitting he grew up in Bath, Maine. Heading up U.S. Route 1, towards Wiscasset, she would have seen the view of naval ships at Bath Iron Works.

"Lobster! Break my heart. My mother makes us do veggie burgers and hot dogs." Deanna's obvious tone of dramatic regret answered Anson's question about who she was. The apron provided by her mother had been cast aside. Her once clean tee shirt was smeared in several places with charred grease from the hot dogs. Her hair was pulled back and a stray lock of damp hair hung over a sweaty brow. She smiled at him, and Anson saw her as utterly charming. Go figure, sometimes it's not about the wardrobe.

"Why no hamburgers?" he asked her the question everyone else in the line wanted to know.

"My mother worries about that pink slime stuff they've been putting in ground beef. She says she can't afford to feed everyone in the yard Black Angus or Bison burgers. Buffalo's delicious, have you had it?"

Behind Anson, the line of hungry concert goers was growing restless. But seeing a young man in a wheelchair ahead no one grumbled aloud, "What's going on up there?" Instead, the line of people grew closer and leaned in so they could better see and overhear the conversation. A man towards the back said hopefully to his wife, "Do they have Bison?"

"How many?" Deanna asked.

"Huh?"

"How many hot dogs? Do you like yours hot, crispy or burned black all around?"

"Two crispy, please. I'm Dave."

"Nice to meet you, I'm Deanna. You get your choice of stuff to put on the dogs. Watch the chili, though. It's half beef and half soy crumble, and really spicy." She grimaced. "The onions are sweet Vidalias and the sauerkraut's homemade…."

"Miss, I'm sure he can read the little signs. The rest of us are starving to death," came a voice from behind Anson's chair.

Anson and Deanna laughed, and the young man in the wheelchair headed out to load up his prized hot dogs. He proceeded to heap his plate with coleslaw, potato salad and a marinated salad of fresh tomatoes, carrots, onions and different colored peppers. He took a pass on Em's popular vegetarian chili and rice. Anson cruised down the tables to meet his second target, Sandy, who was handing out drinks and looked calm and clean in the shade of the tent. Anson was again the personable guest to good effect when he introduced himself.

On the stage down the lawn, the three young female singers were accepting applause and making contact with the audience by wisecracking about each other. Standard fare for live concerts, including everyone in the jokes. Anson went through the line and parked himself in the shade of a specimen gingko tree placed out in the center of the yard with his back to the trunk. It was not a large tree, and its shade was not deep as its branches had the look of being stuck onto the tree at odd angles. His attention was directed towards the girls, which anyone watching would have found quite natural.

There was another presence watching, quietly, in hiding, concealed in the bushes by the Fred. Waiting, watching for an opening, biding time. An unwanted guest had arrived through the woods.

Em sat in companionable silence with Halloran during the music, but at breaks between the groups they talked. Halloran looked up the slope, occasionally checking on his new recruit. Caught in the act by Em, he asked if those were her daughters up their serving the food.

"Some yes, some no. The one by the grill is my youngest daughter Deanna. Celina is in Maine this summer working on a farm."

Observing two college age boys approaching Deanna, Halloran asked if the one giving her the hug was "the boyfriend."

"No, actually his boyfriend is the other boy with him. They are old friends from grade school. He came out to the girls in high school. I think there was some disappointment on the part of one of the girls, but both have been supportive, so are his parents." She watched for the man's reaction.

Without looking at her he said, "Both parents?"

"Yes, as far as I can tell. They love him. Why?" she intoned quietly.

"It's not always that way." He paused.

Oh, here it comes, Em thought, but she was wrong.

"One of my three sons is gay. My ex-wife couldn't accept it. We still make sure one of us is with him when he sees his mother. Avoids hurt feelings. He's out in California in grad school for film, digital editing. One thing is sure, if he wins an Oscar, she'll be right there in the front row," the man said dryly.

Seeing his expression, Em touched his arm gently with her hand. "I'm sorry I didn't mean to pry."

"It's alright. With Jamie, he's smart and funny, there were choices I made differently based on his needs and talents. I felt my sons were my sons. They deserved to be accepted for who they were. You parent differently for each child in any case." Halloran looked at her and smiled, he was not about to shake her hand off his arm.

"What does he do?" she asked in a softer voice.

"Computer graphics, animation, games, special effects, simulation, and the like." They let the topic rest between them at that.

24

HALLORAN'S NIGHT VISITORS

———————◆———————

14 Years Previous

HALLORAN WISHED HE WAS HEADING out to sea, just leaving port, a great grey warship beneath his feet. The wind off the Atlantic had been calling to him all day. Instead of sea duty, he had opted for a land based job to be nearer to his family, three young boys and the shrew of a soon to be ex-wife. Leaving the office each night, heading out towards the small apartment within a few miles of the family home, he felt bereft of his family and the sea. He loved the sea, he loved his children. Not an enthusiastic cook for one, he made his new habitual stop at a deli for groceries and containers of prepared entrees. Tonight's choice was meatballs in marinara sauce.

On a tree lined suburban street, across town all was not well in the Halloran family house. Gillian Mashall Halloran had had a tiresome, aggravating and utterly unsatisfying day in the office of the PR firm where she ruled a team of corporate consultants. One of their corporate clients insisted that truth was an important component of public communications and risked years of effort creating and polishing a more perfect and highly desirable public image.

Reaching the house later than usual, she found a frustrated sitter who was an hour and half late heading home.

Regina, the after school sitter, threatened to give notice if Gillian ran late, and she was not called in time to arrange for the pickup of her own daughter from the magnet school bus stop. Regina's daughter walked home in a downpour that day. Gillian, as a matter of course, could not be bothered to apologize. Her work always came first. And then she was told that James, also known as Jamie, had been playing with the girls across the street again.

The three Halloran boys could sense the thunder in the air. There was no dinner on the table as she had neglected to call ahead. The boys were in the kitchen, hungry, having demolished the supply of chips and salsa. Matt, James and Peter learned to run for cover when they heard that tone in their mother's voice. Mostly, they were successful in the past. However, since their father moved out several months before, there was no one to run interference for them. More often than not, James, the middle child came in for his mother's wrath. Matt, at twelve tried to step into his father's role, with mixed success. This evening, as soon as Regina's car left the driveway, Gillian berated ten year old James for his choice of playmates and his penchant for imagining and illustrating scenarios for live action computer videos, which she termed "a total waste of time."

The boys tried to retreat to their bedrooms, but Gillian blocked the doorway from the kitchen to the hall. Peter, the youngest at eight teared up, knowing pretty well what would come next. First the thunder in his mother's voice, then the cloud burst of invective. Nothing his father had done was ever right, and this was often followed by the hail of what small objects came to hand. After the storm, there would be quiet and relative peace for a week or so while the family tip toed around Gillian.

Now, more than ever Gillian was a sly hitter. The flat of her hand, the ruler or the yardstick were her weapons of choice. Timing was key, the boys knew they were safe when another person was in the house. While Halloran lived at home, there were never any bruises. In recent weeks, this had changed. James's teacher noticed a change in the outgoing, funny boy, now withdrawn, almost silent. Once she noticed he winced at contact during routine passing in the hallway. When challenged he replied he had fallen out of a tree in the backyard and convincingly described the fall. He had indeed fallen out of the backyard tree but bounced up triumphantly unhurt. Peter had bruises on his arm that looked like the finger marks of a forceful grab. Matt was tall like his father and had a serious demeanor that had so far deterred Gillian.

This evening was different. Facing off in the kitchen with three male children who looked so like variations on their now detested parent, it was too much for her to bear. To Gillian, every pang in life was someone else's fault. Her voice rose with her emotion. Why did she have to be stuck here in the home alone with them? Why couldn't Halloran stick to the law? Why couldn't he accept the opportunity her father presented to him? Then they would all be comfortable and more, and she wouldn't need to work with those idiot bastards. Why did he stay in the Navy, and why did he ship out and leave her?

Jamie edged in front of Peter, keeping the butcher block island between them and his mother. This was old ground for the boys, but they knew this was not the only source of her grievance. Voice raised in frustration and seeming disgust, she berated Jamie for playing girl games and spending his time on useless fantasy. "You can just go back to your father! I don't want you!"

Peter, already seriously frightened, clung to Jamie. "Please don't hurt him again!" implored the little brother.

When she looked around the kitchen and paced away from the doorway towards the sink, where the dishes and silver were waiting to be placed on the dinner table, Matt signaled to the younger boys to make their escape behind him. Catching his gesture to them in the corner of her eye, she whirled around at him, screaming, "You're just like your father, you always defend them!"

The two boys ran past Matt down the hallway to the stairs. Gillian struck out with the flat of her hand, landing a resounding blow on the tall boy's face. The blow knocked him to the side. Agile and spirited, Matt caught himself and broke his fall in mid flight. In tears, he came up with fire in his eye, and his fists raised in defense. "Don't ever hit me again. Don't ever hit Jamie again! I'm telling Dad. I'm telling the social worker, and I'm telling the Judge," Matt yelled in a newly deepened male voice that did not break under stress.

Gillian saw immediately what she had done. The boy's face was flame red, blood was beginning a slow trickle from his mouth to his chin. She had marked him. "Don't you dare call your father. Get out," she hissed. He took her up on her order and made for the hallway door. Matt could see that her business suit was torn at the back of the shoulder with the force of the blow she had struck him. He vowed never again would he and his brothers come within her reach.

Dashing up the stairs he formed a plan. Sending Jamie back to his father, leaving Peter to the mercies of his mother was not going to happen on his watch. After a quick search of the upstairs bedrooms, he found his brothers hiding in his own room, in the closet on the floor behind winter jackets and his hiking frame backpack. Retreating from the closet quickly, he locked his bedroom door. Kneeling down in the closet he attempted to coax his brothers out of hiding. In the semi-darkness the younger boys could barely make out their brother's face.

"Listen, we're leaving. Right now. Tonight. We're going to Dad's."

"What if he's not home?" Peter sobbed.

"He gave me a key and told me to use it any time we needed it."

"How are we going to get there?" Jamie asked, more than willing to go.

"We're going to call a cab to meet us at the corner. My cell phone is on my desk. Come on, we've got to move it. Stuff some clothes in your backpacks, take your homework." Matt edged out of the closet into the light of his room. The younger boys got their first look at his face.

"Wow, that'll be a shiner. She hit you hard. We could hear it." Jamie was serious, he knew how it felt to be hit without warning.

"Yeah, well, she won't do that again. Once Dad finds out, she'll lose custody fast," Matt replied as he jammed clothes into his school backpack. Remembering the number displayed on the side of the local cabs, he called in his most adult voice, arranging to be met in fifteen minutes at the corner of the next street. He was told it would be at least twenty minutes until pickup. Thinking it best to leave the house as soon as possible, he rummaged quickly through his sock drawer for his stash of money kept there.

"Come on, let's get your stuff." Matt opened the door of his room with caution. Finding the coast clear, he guided his brothers down the hall to the room they shared. Once inside he again locked the door behind them. Assisting his brothers to gather pajamas and at least a semblance of a change of clothes and especially underwear, which they were inclined to forget, the boys packed up quickly. A favorite sleep buddy for Peter, and sketch books and thumb drives for Jamie went into their backpacks.

"What if she catches us?" Peter asked anxiously.

"She's probably hitting the bottle. That's what she does after she yells a lot," Matt responded. "She'll be in the dining room. Depending on where she is, we'll go out the front door or the back door and down the alley. Follow me and be quiet."

Sneaking out the bedroom door, leaning over the stair railing, the boys could hear the clink of glass and bottle coming from the floor below, along with a turbulent murmuring. Gillian was working on the spin she would put on the incident that was likely to produce a black eye on the face of her eldest son.

Matt judged that the shortest way out of the house was to go down the front hall. But they might be seen as Gillian moved into the living room. With practiced stealth that the young mastered early in a troubled home, the boys worked their escape carefully to coincide with their mother's migration to the front room. Sneaking through the kitchen, Jamie grabbed the bunch of bananas from the fruit bowl on the counter and kept on going. Quietly and carefully, Matt made sure the backdoor locked behind them. Staying low, the three boys ran through the shrubbery that lined the yard, being careful to avoid the center where at any moment they feared their mother would flood the yard with light and discover them.

Once in the service alley that ran behind the houses, the boys stopped to get their breath. The back gate squeaked, a neighbor's friendly dog barked, but there was no sign of pursuit. Although they could not know it, Gillian assumed wrongly that the silence in the house meant her triumph. The boys had gone to bed without supper, and it served them right for being disrespectful. It was not long before gin and fatigue put her to sleep in the armchair. She was confident she could talk her way out of anything the boys might claim.

The alleyway was dark and at the end, the boys were half way down the block to the corner where the cab was supposed to pick them up. Their alternate plan was a two mile walk in the dark to the apartment building where their father lived. Staying hidden in the shadows until the lights of the cab appeared, the boys managed to finish off the bananas and to hide the skins in the neighbor's neatly trimmed boxwood hedge.

At first the cab driver was dubious about his assigned pick up. When he saw three children and their backpacks emerge into the circle of the streetlight, they looked like runaways. He shook his head, *American children*, and worried his own would grow up willful here. But as he drew up beside the boys, about to give them a lecture and insist they return home, he saw the littlest boy had a face streaked with tears and scratches. The oldest sported a swelling eye that gave signs it would be an impressive sight in the morning. The middle child was shaking as if from cold, although the evening was mildly chilly. A father himself, his sympathy was immediate. They were afraid. The Sadharji, a Sikh man in a turban, got out of his cab to investigate. A tall hefty man with a black beard, he towered over the three boys as he asked them where they were going at this time of night.

"Please sir, something has happened and we need to go to our father's house. We have the money to pay for the cab," Matt said.

"Have you your parent's permission to go there?" The cab driver could plainly hear the entreaty in the boy's voice, the youngest cried, and that decided it. "Who is your father and where does he live? You must call him now." He offered his cell phone to Matt, who promptly produced his own. He called his father's cell, hoping and praying for a response.

Halloran nearly dropped the groceries off the counter as he stretched to reach his cell phone. The ring tone alerted him that the incoming call was from his eldest son. He succeeded in answering at the last ring before the call rolled over to voice mail. Halloran heard a seemingly out of breath voice say, "Dad, we need your permission to come over to your place tonight. Can we go please?"

"Of course, Matt, what's the matter? Where is your mother?"

"We called a cab, but the driver needs your permission. Can you talk to him please? I'll put you on speaker."

Halloran, now deeply concerned, told the cab driver his name and address and that the boys had his permission to be driven the two miles to his building. He would meet them at the sidewalk and pay the fare.

Reassured, the cab driver convinced the boys to let him put their backpacks in the trunk. The three boys piled into the back seat of the cab together. Peter burst into tears of relief. "What are we going to tell Dad? Do I have to show him the bruises?"

"Keep your voice down, little man," Matt ordered, but the child had been overheard. The driver radioed in his pick up of three young boys, with the permission of the father, and gave the destination address to the dispatcher. The boys tried to keep their voices low, but their agitation raised them enough so they could easily be heard. From their words, the cab driver gathered enough of the story to be glad that the children had called and were on their way to a safer place. He drove quickly and carefully through the thinning evening traffic.

The trip in the cab was so short that Halloran was exiting the elevator in the lobby of his building when the boys, their backpacks and the cab driver reached the glass door of lobby. Peter broke from the group, dropped his bag, ran pell-mell to his father, grabbing him around the legs and wailed, "Daddy, Mommy hit Matt hard!" and the best laid plans of the boys for discretion were blown away. Halloran put a sheltering hand around his youngest son. One look at his oldest told the tale. Matt had not stopped to wash his face, blood smeared his chin and the back of his right hand. The eye was starting to change color.

Mr. Singh came forward with the luggage dropped by the child. Heading across the lobby towards them paced a tall dark haired man in the uniform of a Navy officer who was so obviously the boys' father. He received sincere thanks from their father for picking up and caring for the boys. When Halloran attempted to pay with a generous tip, he initially refused. Halloran insisted, saying that it was for his children. In the privacy of his cab, Singh told the dispatcher what happened, for the record, in case there was any concern that he had acted improperly. It was to prove a wise decision.

Once inside the one bedroom apartment, Halloran determined that the best thing to do was to calm the boys down before questions. First things first with growing boys, he asked if they had eaten, which of course they had not. He directed them to wash up, Matt first. While Matt was in the bathroom, Halloran prepared a plastic bag full of ice, wrapped in a towel. He handed it wordlessly to Matt when he returned to the kitchen. Halloran threw a boxful of spaghetti in a pot of boiling water, and while the pasta cooked he heard the first version of the events at home.

"Alright, here's the plan. You all stay here overnight. You can all stay home from school tomorrow. I'll call your schools. I'll call my lawyer, and I will sue for full custody." The boys all breathed relief with thanks. "But here's the catch," Halloran continued. "You have to tell what's happened since I left the house, honestly. Truthfully answer any questions you are asked. Don't be embarrassed or be ashamed. This is not your fault. None of you. You are all my sons, and I love you." They heard the catch in their father's voice. This was especially meaningful to James, as Halloran suspected it would be. He assured them that they had done the right things, say no, protect each other, and tell a trusted adult. "I am my brother's keeper" ran through Halloran's mind, and he was justly proud of Matt.

Halloran spent the night on the couch, sleepless, regretting he left the house without the boys. At the time, it seemed as if he had no choice. Never one on an even keel, since her promotion at the firm, Gillian's stress level and volatility at home had apparently sky rocketed. Now he meant to give her no quarter. First thing in the morning, he fixed the boys a large breakfast using every egg in the fridge and all of the bread for toast then made the calls as promised.

Gillian awoke in the living room armchair after 9:00 in the morning. Finding the boys, the bananas and the backpacks gone, she assumed erroneously that they had gone to school without disturbing their mother. With relief, she showered, dressed and went off to work as if nothing had happened. Since Halloran had called the boys' schools, she received no notice of the true state of affairs until her divorce lawyer called her at work later that afternoon.

Halloran had requested an immediate change of custody on an emergency basis, and she was to be investigated for child abuse. The cab company records and the sworn statement of the cab driver were discovered in the social worker's inquiry. Mandatory reporting was done by classroom teachers based on their observations when the boys returned to school on the following day. These reports, along with statements from Matt, James and Peter, guaranteed Halloran sole custody of the boys and the house. And he was stuck with full custody of the hamsters, too.

Halloran contented himself with successfully teaching his boys to sail and fish on the Chesapeake.

25

LET'S TALK, LADY

———◆———

UPHILL, DEANNA TURNED HER IMPLEMENTS over to another volunteer, gathered up a veggie burger and stacked it high with fresh sliced tomatoes, onions and lettuce. She piled a plate high with green salad and Ranch dressing and headed for Sandy, who left her beverage station, as well, to get another lunch plate. Deanna sat down on the grass next to Anson's chair, which shielded her from the view of the figure in hiding behind the bushes. They were to be joined by the two boys and Sandy who were carrying plates containing selections from the remaining food. There are almost always too many casseroles of baked ziti, but even that was fast disappearing onto plates and into the crowd.

Halloran saw the girls seated under the vigilant eyes of his new recruit.

"Single parent?" she asked. Her hand slipped from his arm.

"Yes, it seemed better that way after what the boys had been through with their mother. We were divorced when they were still in school. I gave up sea duty to stay home. There was another woman for a few years, but I'd go home to the boys. When it seemed long enough to think about more, she suggested that a Navy officer might want to send his sons to military boarding school, then she and I could be together. I realized she didn't want family life, more like a live-in escort, someone presentable for the Washington scene. Not the right choice.

After that, she took a job in Philly, and I gradually declined to provide escort service. I found I had to work weekends, or go to a soccer game, gymnastic meet, baseball practice, whatever the boys were doing. Once they damned well did not want to ride the bus to camp in the Adirondacks so we all took a road trip. She eventually found herself an eminently suitable squire in Pennsylvania."

Em was surprised. Halloran explained rather more than she expected of him. So, following his example, which most probably was his strategy, Em confided, "Me, too. When you have teenaged girls in the house, you have to be careful about the character of anyone you bring in. Much less a date." Em warmed to her subject. Sandy brought her a folding chair and bottles of spring water, receiving thanks from both of them but no introduction. "And dates. A guy who wanted me to dis my ex so he could spend the evening complaining about his, too. Or the one who said, 'The kids are over eighteen, they should be off on their own.' Then there was the guy looking for a tennis partner for mixed doubles. One wanted to go out to dinner Dutch. You just knew that was never going to change. He ordered New York Strip and I'm sitting there with a Caesar salad, without the chicken. Another guy wanted a wife who could write code in Assembler, the programming language. Who does that anymore?"

Halloran laughed outright.

"I mean what the hell?" Em gestured with both hands, and Halloran could see from whom Deanna's sense of the dramatic originated.

People around them who listened to their conversation, or who walked by and caught snatches, and who wouldn't, thought it was good for the old folks. People assumed they were two mature people getting to know each other, not bodyguard and subject, certainly not an armed federal agent in charge and a not quite well enough paid competitive intelligence consultant. Em was, after all, the event's host and principal organizer.

Shaded by a golf umbrella of elephantine proportions, Mireille, newly delivered of a brawling baby boy, sat in state on a LaFuma lounger. Em's divorce lawyer watched her client and thought how nice for her to have a gentleman friend and wondered how she met him. Not one of the many lawyers who inhabited the local Bar association certainly, or a university type like her husband Philippe. But so observant, the grey headed man seemed to take in all around him, yet so casually. She hoped he would be a new interest for Em, and not the new client. *Clients and romance, never a good mix, mais non.*

"You and I should talk. Is there any quiet place around here? You wouldn't come into the office. Of course, now I understand why." He caught the inquiring eye of the reclining woman under the umbrella and gave her a fleeting smile.

"Let's wait for the Bluegrass band. Someone I know wrote one of the songs. They're performing it for the first time here."

Five men of assorted ages and a variety of instruments including fiddle, bass, harmonica, banjo and guitar took the stage. The oldest man with the longest grey hair introduced the group with jokes about the very able banjo player, an MD in practice, including references to the reputedly low intelligence of banjo players and the general lack of tuneability of the banjo itself. "When is a banjo in tune? Maybe never!"

The youngest member of the group switched instruments to play the mandolin and gave the group leader an argument concerning the key in which to play the next song. The young mandolin player then proceeded to tape a small sheet of music to his mic, to the obvious disgust of the other players.

The third song was the new one called "Chili on the Table." Em scrunched down in her chair, Halloran smiled. Quite fortunately she had remembered to feed the musicians first. It was their bribe to sing the song.

"Know the song writer, do you?" Halloran quipped.

Men over a certain age should never smirk, it's unbecoming, really, Em thought. *Makes him look like a wiseass teenager.* She frowned, which made him laugh.

The lyrics to Em's song were well received, although it was hard for a man to sing with anything like the Dixie Chicks' edge.

———◆———

"Chili on the Table"
(a fiddle tune)

——

There's a special dinner on the table,
You say, 'Oh, it's okay.'
You play solitaire on the computer
For hours and hours.
While your lover waits patiently,
Until she leaves.
Along comes some fiddler feller,
Looks her in the eyes and says,
"Honey, you feelin' alright tonight?"
There's that winnin' chili on the table.
There's music in the parlor, laughter in the den,
And when the lights go out in Austin,
The laughter doesn't end.

8

Well, if I were you my friend,
I'd think twice about that woman
Sittin' across from you at the table. [pause]
'Cause you're gonna lose your wife.
But again, maybe not.
Keep on doing what you're doing,
'Cause I like it mighty fine here.
There's that winnin' chili on the table.
I play my music in the parlor.
There's laughter in the den.
And when the lights go out in Austin,
The laughter doesn't end.
Keep on doing what you're doing,
Boy, and you're going lose your wife,
To me!

———◆———

"HE'S NOT BAD," HALLORAN COMMENTED about the singer, nodding his head.

"He's one of Mai's teachers in the Music School. Personally, I think he keeps his Grammy in his sock drawer," she replied with her cat-ate-the-canary smile. "We can go into the house after they finish this set."

At the break between groups, Em stood up, waved her thanks to the Blue Grass group. She offered her hand to Halloran as he hoisted himself out of the lounger and draped the towel over the two chairs to save their places. The grill was closed. The lunch dishes had been cleared with a few leftovers still on the tables. Watermelon, fresh fruit, home baked treats and punch appeared. Lines were forming for dessert. Trash and recycling barrels were looking very full. Em guided Halloran around the food, asking him if he would like some dessert.

Em waved to the girls who were seated not far away in the shade of the gingko tree. Deanna was engaged in seeing who could spit watermelon seeds the farthest. Eyeing Anson, Halloran admitted to a taste for watermelon. Em sighed and turned to him. "I'm not sure that girl will ever grow up. Try to bring her up to act like a lady and she's spitting watermelon seeds like she did when she was seven. You have to be careful with those things, you know, or we will be pulling up watermelon vines all over the place next spring. Her older brother claims we'll have trouble marrying her off."

Halloran, in one of his rare perceptive moments concerning love and marriage, replied, "I wouldn't bet on that yet." He could see one set of eyes very much taken with Miss Huber.

Em handed him a plate brimming with juicy pieces of watermelon and motioned him on. "Time to go in."

From his new vantage point at the top of the slope, Halloran's sharp eyes caught a furtive movement behind the Fred. Tugging on his ear, he murmured into his collar, "Anson, behind the outhouse. Can you see anything?" The younger man swung around in his chair, scratching as he moved. "No."

"Movement back there. Check it out when you can. I'm going into the house."

"Roger." Anson contemplated excusing himself for a trip to The Fred.

Halloran reckoned that the best way to break Anson in as a field agent was to give him an assignment and trust him to handle it. With some lingering reservations, he followed Em as she led him through the rock garden to the back door where she pulled out her keys from the pocket of her jeans.

"Tina, it's me, Em," she called out.

"Good to see you, lady!" A woman dressed in a bright African print dress, who was close to Em's stature, although taller, came out of the kitchen. The vivid colors of her dress set off the clear deep red brown of her skin. Her features were fine, and her cheeks were flushed with the heat of the kitchen and the activity of the day. "About time you showed up, my son's on next!"

From the kitchen a tall slender young woman followed her mother. She was quiet, reserved and moved with a dancer's grace, her *café au lait* complexion glowing. "Max is here, too!" Maximilian, the front man for her brother's group, was the man of the hour for her.

Em introduced them as her friend, Bettina Wallace, and her daughter Avril. "Go ahead. We'll stay in the house now. This is…" said Em, unsure how to introduce, or much less explain Halloran.

"Mike," the tall man supplied and stuck out his hand to Tina, who shook it cordially with a firm grip.

"Good thing you came in. I swear someone's been trying to get in that front door. We could hear it rattle all the way in the kitchen. And there's a sign on it, too. I'm glad you won't be alone in here." Tina eyed Halloran, who returned her direct gaze.

"Kids again?"

"Didn't seem like it, Em. Too quiet like, no laughing. Just the knob being turned and the door rattling."

Em looked at Halloran, who said, "We'll be here. Don't worry. Enjoy the concert."

"You got the security system on, right?" Tina asked. "You should let me goose it up, living out here in the country. Battery backup longer than two hours, please. For fun, we could do little cameras outside so you can see what the birdies and the beasties are doing all night," she teased. "You could have off-site streaming backup."

"No thanks, Tina, this is not your data center." Em laughed out loud then turned to Halloran to explain, "Tina's a disaster recovery and computer security expert with the company where I used to work. She cut her professional teeth on Y2K software issues years ago."

"Oh, good. Looking for a job?" He was surprised but

also saw an opportunity.

"Behave yourself, no recruiting today!" Em came back at him with good nature. He shrugged.

Tina looked sharply from Halloran to Em, who grinned at her. She'd pegged him for Em's new client, which was not far off the mark, and wondered why her close friend had not mentioned him. Determined to learn at least more about him, she made a foray. "You know you are a fine looking man, would you be Native American by any chance? We're part Cherokee."

Avril tugged on her mother's sleeve to get her to stop asking personal questions of the guest.

"Actually, some, a great grandfather was Eastern Band Cherokee. Otherwise Irish and French," he said.

Em thought, *I knew it, it's the cheek bones.*

"Oh, the Hell No We Won't Go Cherokee. I shouldn't say that because some people might be offended." Tina explained to Em, "The Army was supposed to move the Cherokee tribe out to Oklahoma, that's the Trail of Tears when so many people died. But some folks didn't want to leave so they hid out and stayed on their own lands. They are known as the Eastern Band of the Cherokee and number about 10,000 now."

"My great grandfather was married to a white woman, so he got to stay," Halloran acknowledged.

"Well, well, it is nice to meet you, brother." Avril was shooing her mother towards the door. "You can keep this one, Em."

As soon as Tina and Avril closed the living room door behind them, Em said, "Sorry about that. Cherokee?"

"Yes, surviving something like that, it's always there in a family, although we don't get to talk about it much. It isn't always recognized. We played a different version of cowboys and Indians. The Indians chased the cowboys until my mother told us to stop," Halloran said, arms crossed.

With a smile Em replied, "One of my aunts was French

Canadian, Irish and Native American from Quebec. She had broad flat cheek bones, bright blue eyes and freckles. Once your family has been in this country long enough, you can have a whole bunch of different people behind you.

"You know, if someone was trying the front door, it's probably not the kids. Last year five or six of them snuck in the back door while we were bringing out the food."

Halloran gave himself over to appraising the house. He stood towards the center of the living room and looked around him at the fumed oak furniture, the richly patterned but somewhat worn Oriental carpets, the delicate twisting vine patterns of the summer curtains, looking for motion sensors, sensors on the windows and doors. Through the open casement windows in the kitchen, the band could be heard tuning up. He spotted the security system panel on the wall behind the dining area table, closet to the front door.

"Security system on?"

"It's zoned so some of it is. The Blackmun's Wintergreen Spring office at the front of the house is always on. Everyone is out of the cellar so the spring room and the cellar are alarmed. The motion sensors upstairs aren't on. You can see everything in here from the kitchen, so it's not armed now."

"Thorough. Any cameras?"

She shook her head, and as if reading his mind, replied, "My son did it for me," which told him more about her son's line of work and about the system itself than she could have guessed. If her son built the system to protect his mother and sisters, it would not be surprising that the system had some capabilities beyond those Em listed. The system might even have a few additions her son neglected to mention to his mother.

"Is there a panic button or two?" He made a guess, referring to hand held remotes that could be carried around, perhaps even outside.

Em brought a unit the size of a small cell phone from her pants pocket. On it were recessed buttons labeled Fire, Police, Emergency, System and Talk, with a tiny speaker/microphone inside.

"Good," he commented.

Anson guardedly watched the movement in the crowd around him and tried not to be obvious. Noticing Deanna's mother unlocking the house door, Anson turned to her to ask why the house was locked. His query sent her and Sandy off into repeated waves of laughter that gathered the attention of those around them.

As soon as she could speak, Deanna explained in gasping breaths. "Last year, we had some problems." More laughter. "Mom went into the house to bring out the watermelon. She was in the kitchen when she heard thumping on the ceiling coming from the bathroom, and the sound of the shower on full blast."

Sandy continued. "So she goes upstairs and stands outside the bathroom door. She hears laughing and sounds like there's dancing and more than one person in the bathroom. Somebody starts singing!"

"Being my mother, she couldn't leave well enough alone. She bangs on the door and tells them they have five minutes to get dressed and get out of the house. So she's really pissed when she goes down the hall and sees the beds in our rooms all messed up." By now, half the upper yard was listening, and several of her hearers rolled their eyes and looked guilty. "And she was really mad later when she found out they used all the clean towels and left them in a heap in the corner of the bathroom." Deanna paused for breath. Sandy grinned, she knew what was coming.

"When she gets to her bedroom, the door is half closed, so she whips it open! There are two people doing it in her bed. Opposite sexes, okay? She yells at the top of her lungs, 'What are you doing in my bed? This is not a two bit motel. Use the woods, that's what they're out there for!'" Deanna dropped her voice to the tone of a conspirator. "Makes you wonder what they did in the olden days, doesn't it?" Guffaws all around, but some folks looked at the trees with new interest, especially as it seemed permission had been granted to wander there.

Deanna and Sandy were struck with the guilty pleasure of having company on the lawn. So, they decided to return to assist with doling out Pina Colada and red raspberry punch with fresh berries from the garden. Seeing that the girls were surrounded by other volunteers, Anson excused himself to head out to continue investigating.

Using the excuse of needing clearance for the wheelchair, Anson tooled around the edge of the crowd. Rolling down the slope to the outhouse, he gave himself an unobstructed view of the structure. Approaching The Fred by the woodland side, from his lowered vantage point in the wheelchair, he spotted a string. It led from the bushes to a small canister duct taped to the underside of the building. Anson promptly parked his wheelchair on the string so it could not be pulled taut from the bushes. Working quickly he sliced through the string with his army knife and pried up the duct tape with the knife blade. He recognized the canister as an older, obsolete smoke grenade. Peering into the woods, he could see no sign of movement. Reaching into a concealed utility pocket on his chair, Anson fished out an evidence bag and hurriedly stuffed the smoke grenade into it.

Speaking into his collar, he said, "Boss, you were right. Found a smoke grenade secured under Fred here, tied to a string. Can't see anyone around. Probably waiting for some little old lady to use the latrine to create a diversion. I'm not sure..."

"Stay there, don't pursue. Someone tried front door of

the house, too. Probably wants to get inside the house. Check out the building. Make sure it's secure. Stick with the girls. I'll call in for backup. You have an evidence kit? There's a full field kit in the car if you need it," Halloran replied.

Anson did as he was told, he thoroughly searched underneath the small building. Wheeling around to the ramp, he first surveyed the spaces between the makeshift ramp and the steps, then he got it in gear to wheel up the ramp. On the deck in front of the door, he was faced with the challenge of getting the door open and wheeling in. Swearing to himself, he hoisted himself to his feet, hung onto the railing that surrounded the deck and took his first steps of the day. With a plastic bag of evidence collection supplies jammed into the pocket of his jeans and the smoke grenade concealed as best he could he made it into the Fred. He was not about to leave the evidence outside on the chair.

The interior of the Fred was compact and neatly organized. Latching the door behind him, he slipped on gloves from the kit. Practicing long unused skills, he searched for ordinance of any kind. He checked all of the stored rolls of toilet paper and inside the boxes of plastic bags stored for re-use in the trash bucket, which was fortunately close to empty. Finding the inside of the outhouse clean and free of anything suspicious, he decided to give it one final test. After checking under the seat, Anson stood before the composting toilet and took careful aim. Not exactly a scientific test, but in the field you used what best came to hand. He looked around with relief and realized it was good to be standing up again.

26

RANKEL PLAYS A TUNE

HALLORAN WAS NOT BEING STRICTLY accurate when he told Em he gave Andy Vargas and Steve Rankel the afternoon off. He assigned them to work another case with Peter Leonard, his lead field supervisor. Leonard was tracking the same group of smugglers and people movers Halloran met the night he was thrown off the dock, injuring his leg. Vargas and Rankel, having made a pit stop, were driving down the Interstate from Hartford in an unmarked car (which is all they ever drove) heading back to the office when they received Halloran's call for backup. Hot, tired, hungry and bored after a less than successful stakeout behind a hangar near the airport, the Rent Party gig sounded like a hot ticket to Agents Rankel and Vargas.

Already conversant with the back roads around the Spring House, they headed the car off the highway, approaching from over the hill. Seeing Halloran's car in front of the barn, in the area designated handicapped parking, they parked nearby. Since Andy was driving, they avoided parking in the poison ivy that grew quite vigorously in the shade. Calling Halloran as soon as they arrived, the partners were told to take up positions on either side of the stage area, one by the power cables and one halfway up the hill on the woodland side.

Two older people were left at the check in table at the front of the house. They were playing Mah Jong amicably and enjoying the music from the backyard concert. The boxes of books and food donations had already gone on their separate ways. The two agents presented themselves at the table. "Too late! Too late! Food almost gone. Enjoy concert! Just go!" For the money was on its way to the bank as well.

Andy and Rankel shambled their way along the Spring House into the concert, stopping short of the stage. "Jeez Andy, I could use some food and water. Anson's up there on the hill. Think I should go up?"

"Yeah, alright, you go first. Then come back," Andy Vargas replied. He was in the way, standing there by the PVC pipe that carried the electrical power cords. Vargas had a hard time keeping his post at the corner of the house where he could see in both directions, up the lawn to the food tents and back towards the street along the side of the house. Musicians and roadies were changing equipment frequently it seemed. He felt as if he stood out like a security guard at a high school dance.

Rankel, who had been to enough concerts to be quite the habitué, sauntered up through the crowd as if he belonged. Bluegrass wasn't his thing, but you never knew. He managed to score some leftover salad and ziti with vodka sauce for free. He made sure Anson the rookie knew he was there. Seeing him surrounded by Deanna and Sandy and their friends, Rankel reflected on the intimate relationship between luck and women, something along the lines of some guys have all the luck. Carrying his plate and two bottles of spring water back down the hill, he relieved Andy, who moved off through the crowd. Andy and his bottle of Wintergreen Springs took up a position between the Fred and the stage back towards the trees where he had a clear view of the edge of the woods.

Looking to find a creditable reason for standing around by the stage, Rankel spotted a "For Sale" sign on a Fender Stratocaster electric guitar. A violinist may need only one Stradivarius violin, or a Guarneri del Jesu violin, if he or she was an adventurous player. But it was a truth, provable and verifiable, that a man could never have too many guitars. Rankel had a perfectly fine vintage Les Paul, but the Stratocaster might be a useful practice instrument, or so he reasoned to himself. He decided to investigate by asking a roadie who he might see about the guitar and was told that Max had come off the stage.

Rankel found a warm welcome now, and Max readily joined him to answer questions. Rankel's eyes glowed when Max offered to hook it up to a small portable amp for him to try. Andy looked across the lawn at Rankel, amazed to see his partner was very much in his element. With the volume down reasonably low, because an electric instrument was meant to be heard at a distance after all, Rankel played one of this favorite riffs. Jimi Hendrix was his idol, and he had been working to learn his style from several old vinyl recordings. As he played, he listened to the sound and judged the responsiveness of the Fender to his fingers. A young woman in a white silk blouse and black dress jeans approached to listen. Sometimes it was the music.

"You should play that on stage for us. Everyone will like it!" she said to Rankel. Rankel was surprised by a pair of smoky black eyes and was about to protest when she said, "Don't worry. It's my party. I invited the other musicians, too."

Max agreed. "Yeah, man. Go for it! Come on, we'll get you wired into the big speakers. I'll introduce you. The next group can't seem to get it together yet. What's your name?"

"Steve."

Back in the house, Em and Halloran were watching the concert from the south living room window when a man with a bright blue electric guitar took the stage.

"Isn't that Agent Rankel?"

"Yes, and that isn't his assignment. He is an event waiting to happen unless he finds an outlet," Halloran remarked in a rare moment of candor concerning his staff.

Rankel began to play the famous piece slowly to get his audience with him, then ramped up the sound and the tempo and gave the crowd his interpretation of Jimi Hendrix playing the *Star Spangled Banner*. The crowd went silent for the first time that afternoon. Rankel gained volume and confidence as he went on. The rising wail of "land of the free" was punctuated by a variety of sounds that few people could produce on a single instrument. He even included the notes of "Taps" that Hendrix added towards the end of the four minute piece. There was a pause, and applause washed over the audience, some of whom stood and hooted their approval. Rankel bobbed his head and waved to the crowd, anticipating that a pink slip might find his desk on Monday, but it was worth it.

"That guitar," Halloran said to Em, "it sounded like sirens and gunfire."

"It's supposed to sound like that. Jimi Hendrix played in a time of social upheaval. It is our national fight song, all those bombs bursting in air. Much as I love *America the Beautiful* and *This Land Is Your Land,* they represent our peaceable side, and we haven't been able to express much of that lately."

"Not hardly. He's not bad either." Halloran was surprised, the guitar was not on Rankel's resumé.

"You were concerned about him, but I think he's found his outlet in music," Em said.

Outside on the lawn the crowd asked for more, but Rankel declined. Many of the older people in the group remembered the original Hendrix version and were telling the rest all about it with their own enthusiastic impressions.

Rankel stepped off the stage and said to Max, "I'll take it!" Mai smiled her approval, and Steve Rankel smiled back.

The end of the concert was approaching. Mai was the closer. The next group finally stopped arguing with each other and quit punishing their sound equipment. The lead singer insisted she needed a vocal mic, and that she wouldn't sing into a mic designed for instruments. She was right of course but earned herself a reputation as a thorough going diva. "Lady GaGa, you're not honey!" Her side man moaned.

Up on the hill both Andy Vargas and Anson were separately thinking the same thing, that Steve Rankel had taken undercover work to a new level.

27

FIELDER'S REVENGE

———◆———

AFTER RANKEL'S UNEXPECTED STANDOUT PERFORMANCE the next group had difficulty capturing the audience's attention. Their task was to prepare the audience to appreciate Mai's classical violin solos, set the mood, set the tone, do it right. It appeared that was not going to happen straight off. The crowd, long seated without a seventh inning stretch, roused and actively sought more food, drink and more rock and roll. The group's first number was lost in the murmur, buzz and movement of the crowd, so they hastily changed their playlist to tunes with more energy and a good driving beat.

Anson was made uneasy by all the excitement and movement of the crowd. That made watchfulness a challenge for him. Instincts tested in battle gave him a heightened sense of their vulnerability. When the crowd finally began to settle, Anson felt, rather than saw, a quick movement in the woods behind him and down towards his left. Another canister came flying out of the woods to land at the edge of the crowd not fifteen feet from him. Anson exploded out of the wheelchair in two long stiff strides as if leaping on peg legs. He scooped up the canister. With a fielder's precision he shied it back into the woods, aiming it to fly as close to its source as he could. There was the sound of a pop, and a cloud of smoke rose through the woods. A man's voice cried out in astonishment at the unpleasant and unexpected surprise. Anson heard the sounds of a rapid, disorderly retreat, branches snapping, bushes pushed forcefully aside.

"Serves him right," Anson muttered to himself, standing up straight.

Andy Vargas loped up the hill, signaling to Anson as he headed into the woods in pursuit.

The situation was well in hand. Anson made a half turn with the intention of getting back to his chair but stopped short, looking down at his feet as he realized what he'd done. He felt a stunned expression come to his face *"What are these things, and how did they get there? I can run on them."* Mastering the surprise, Anson looked up towards the waiting wheelchair, only to see Deanna standing in front of it watching him.

Deanna had a teenage Halloween prankster's familiarity with smoke bombs so she had no difficulty identifying what she'd just heard. While not always being the first person to be aware of happenings around her, she was often the first person to act. She'd been up and after Anson quickly.

"You can walk," she said.

"Not very well, yet." Anson sighed, caught out.

She reached out her hand. "Come on, we should go tell my mother what happened."

Anson gave her a rueful look. She wiggled her fingers at him. He could see the dare on her face. Now that she had seen him run, she was not about to let him refuse to walk. So, he took several short hesitant steps towards her. Deanna held her ground in front of the wheelchair, blocking his access to it.

"Let's go in the house." Deanna was gentle but firm. Sandy rose to stand next to her friend.

"I'm not steady on these things." Anson was not sure how to handle women not reluctant to be seen with a fellow with his perceived level of disability.

"That's okay, you can lean on us." Deanna stepped up to capture him. She linked her arm through his arm on the right side. Sandy came around to take his left arm.

"Watch my chair?" Anson asked the college friends of the girls who had been engrossed in a debate about the influence of Jimi Hendrix on all subsequent American electric guitar players and had missed the action.

The girls guided Anson around a family with rambunctious children who were wrestling with each other in front their grandma. She scolded them good naturedly. They passed the food tents with under the breath comments that there was bound to be more goodies to eat and drink in the house. Once into the rock garden and onto the flagstone patio, a difficulty arose. Anson hesitated in front of the fieldstone steps that led up to the small porch. The steps were old, uneven and worn, and even Em had twisted her ankle on them more than once. Several large terracotta pots containing flowers and herb plants lined the sunny side of the porch, further narrowing the path towards the door.

Deanna asked Sandy if she would unlock the house for them, which she did, leaving Deanna to support Anson on his right side. As Sandy turned back to see if her help was needed, she saw Deanna slip her arm around the blond man's waist.

"Come on, let's go, you can lean on me." Deanna looked up at him with a smile, and that's what did the trick. There seemed to be no way out for Anson, so he draped his arm around Deanna's shoulders determined not to lean on her any more than was absolutely necessary. After that it was easier and not unpleasant at all. Deanna tried to make it through the door first without tripping Anson, who was after all a big guy. Sandy had two hands on his back to steady him over the last step. Three new friends made it through the door into the living room and ended up laughing out loud as they crossed the threshold together.

And Anson set foot in the Spring House for the first time.

They stopped short on the carpet in front of the fireplace. Standing together staring at them from across the living room were Em and Halloran, truly a formidable pair. Em had her arms crossed, never a good sign.

"Mom, this is Dave." To Anson she said, "She's not as ferocious as she looks."

Anson didn't look as if he was convinced. In a momentary lapse, possibly the result of his rookie status, he addressed Halloran directly. "Another smoke grenade, sir. I tossed it back into the woods." He did not relinquish his hold over Deanna's shoulders. Wearing a grin like a good wing woman should, Sandy moved around her friends to face Em.

"So I've heard. Rankel was impressed. Fast on your feet." Halloran gave Anson his first feedback on his exploit.

"Need some practice," Anson acknowledged.

"Get it. Good job."

Em looked from one man to the other, both of whom were standing up straight staring each other down. Young buck and the old bull moose she thought. Breaking in, she said to Halloran, "These are my research assistants, my daughter Deanna and our friend Sandy." To the girls she said, "This is Mike, he's here with…"

"The 'Hardy Boys,' we saw them. One of them went off chasing whoever it was in the woods. Wow, and the other one played the guitar on stage. Did you hear him?" Deanna piped up. "'Hardy Boys.' That's what Mom calls the other two guys. This is about the professor, isn't it?"

The expression on Anson's face showed he was not quite sure what to make of Ms. Huber's calling his boss "Mike."

Halloran raised his eyebrows in surprise at the sound of

his name.

"What's this disruption for?" Em turned to the man quietly leaning on his cane, rather close to her.

"Testing. Trying to find a way in to search the house. Create a diversion, draw anyone in the house out onto the lawn. Slip through the crowd and gain access to the house. Not a very professional effort, I would say. Vargas says he found signs of only one man." Halloran paused to chuckle. He listened to a report in his ear bud. "He says he ran through a small clearing in the woods. Two young folks thought they could enjoy a little privacy on the grass there. By the time Andy arrived they were pulling on their clothes. They were able to give him a brief description of the man who passed by first. The suspect then drove off up the hill towards the highway in a dark car with New York plates. Similar to one seen in the vicinity of the river about the time someone put two holes in your canoe. So, we are one step further along, and nothing bad happened," he concluded.

"Dave," he intoned, indicating this was not his usual form of address to his rookie. "We'll need a fingerprint check on the front door handle and that canister you collected, right?"

"Yessir, it's secured in an evidence bag," Anson replied, fervently praying it was safe in the pocket of his jeans. Casting his glance sideways at Deanna he asked, "Should we keep the girls in the house now?"

Deanna nixed that idea straight off. "No way. Mai's on next. We're going back outside. He can protect us," she said, referring to Anson.

Halloran recognized it would be useless to argue this point. The immediate threat seemed to have been removed from the area. Andy Vargas was back in position. Rankel was there. He nodded his permission. "Good to see you on your feet. Keep it up."

"I'm going to need to sit down at some point soon,"

Anson said to Deanna in a low voice.

"We'll find you a bench," she replied.

Having received their dismissal, Anson, Deanna and Sandy beat a hasty path out the living room door before someone should change his or her mind. They left the house with more confidence than they came in with.

As soon as the living room door closed behind them, Em turned in towards Halloran whom she found standing close beside her. "Did you see what I saw? Are you alright with that? I don't usually see my daughter wrapped around a man she's just met."

"No? He is supposed to be watching out for the two of them. Although they did seem to be doing the same thing for him. My staff does seem to be taking an unconventional approach to undercover work this afternoon. Probably best for him. It looks like it took pretty young women to get him out of that chair. He hasn't really needed it for some time I understand."

"Why was he using it then?"

"It seems that while he was in the hospital in Ramstein he got a Dear John letter from the girl back home saying she couldn't face his injuries. How could a man with no feet provide for a family? I expect that's why he's down here, away from his home in Maine." Halloran paused.

"That's dishonorable. She could have waited." Em's voice was hoarse.

"This war, with the use of body armor, we have more people coming home who might not have survived previous conflicts. But they come home with injuries to the arms and legs like Anson's injuries."

"At least they come home." There were tears in Em's eyes.

Halloran looked at her. "What happened?"

"I was only a kid towards the end of the war in Vietnam. I had a crush on an older boy. Joe wanted to be a journalist. His father remarried a younger woman. She didn't want him and his younger brother at home, so they were sent away to an expensive prep school. Instead of going to college as they expected him to, after Joe graduated, he was eighteen and joined the Marines." Em hesitated, obviously having difficulty continuing.

"And then?" he asked quietly.

"It was that very next school year, it didn't seem long at all. We heard he was missing in action. At first I thought sometimes they find people alive, but months went by. Then I thought maybe he was taken prisoner and would come back, like Senator McCain did eventually. A year went by and we didn't hear anything. The relationship with his parents was so bad his friends didn't feel they could call to ask about him." She looked up at him.

"For a while I even hoped he had deserted and was living in the hills with the tribes. At the time, anything seemed better than thinking of him in pain, dying alone in the jungle. They had no body armor to protect them." She wiped her eyes with the back of her hands like a child, openly mourning her friend.

Halloran thought, *It's over forty years and she's still crying over his memory.* He was about to reach out for her when she continued, pulling herself together.

"So right from high school I was very clear that not everyone who goes to war comes back. I'm no fan of war. I'm with Eleanor Roosevelt who visited an American cemetery in the Pacific after WW II. She said something like, 'How many young women's hearts are buried here?'"

"The way you remember him, if he'd come back, I think he would have been a lucky man."

"He probably wouldn't even have remembered me, I was just a kid to him."

"But you still remember him. I'm sorry for your loss."

Em sniffled. "Thank you. That's the first time anyone has said that to me." She gathered her reflections to share.

"My family and I, we're only here because an American soldier came home." She gestured towards a framed photo on the wall by her desk. It was an enlargement of a black and white photo, now faded to sepia. Halloran could see the resemblance. A man in U.S. Army khakis sat posed on a manicured lawn in front of a reflecting pool filled with water, with the unmistakable beauty of the Taj Mahal in the background.

"CBI China-Burma-India Theatre. As a child, I remember meeting one of my parents' friends, a woman who never married because her fiancé was killed in Normandy.

"Please excuse me. I guess I'm not very good at the stiff upper lip thing. It was seeing Dave and Deanna. It didn't look to me like his feet were her principal interest." She smiled in spite of herself. "She is a handful, though."

"So is he. Do you want me to talk to him?" Halloran was prepared to warn Anson off if requested to do so.

"You said he is a good man?" Em was checking references.

"From all I've learned, clever, brave, a good leader, otherwise I wouldn't have hired him. If he works at it, he could do this job very well. He'll have much to learn, but they all do." Halloran was not a man to hand out praise lightly. He didn't tell Em at this time that his Navy contacts knew of Anson's father, and both father and son came highly recommended.

"Then let's let them work it out or not between them. He got out of the chair, and she's not going to let him climb back in on her watch," she said kindly, willing to rely on Halloran's judgment. "Watchful waiting. Who said that?" She smiled at him, her tears were dry, and he liked her better for it.

In fact although he said little, he liked her a great deal, which posed even more concerns than any friendship between Anson and Deanna. Not an impetuous man, he was clear why he had chosen to come to the Spring House himself that afternoon. He could easily have sent Andy Vargas and Rankel by themselves.

28

DINNER AT THE CLUB —
LADIES IN WAITING

———◆———

MONDAY MORNING, CRACK OF DAWN, or near enough, Em attempted to reach FBI Agent Nancy Dombroski. She left several messages here and there. Since Nancy checked her messages obsessively, Em could surmise the answer was "no." Em was anxious to make a visit to the Homestead Mission. Her intuition prompted her that the girl Shelli had more to contribute than she was willing to say in front of the venerable Mr. McVeety. Hard to live with the saintly, Em reflected, when you were young and more than a little bit foolish, or at any age really. She smiled as her own transgressions at that age loomed up before her.

In a rare bout of caution, since she couldn't reach Nancy, Em decided to postpone the excursion to the Mission and to go with Plan B. Rallying Deanna to go with her, Em set off for a stint at the public library for research followed by a day of culturally uplifting shopping and gallery hopping, on a limited budget.

———◆———

Andy Vargas and Rankel stood elbow to elbow in Halloran's small office in front of his desk to report their lack of new leads, and the merry chase Em Huber and the girls led them on that day. Their assignment was to watch Em Huber to see if she and Professor Kirbee contacted each other, and it had foundered.

"Okay, so they get up early. Like dawn early, at least one of them does. Somebody lets this black cat out. Ms. Waitely gets picked up at 7:30, probably heading to work at the hospital. Car is full of college girls all dressed for work. We let her go because we figure that leaves the two Ms. Hubers who are more likely to be the ones to make contact with Kirbee. So far so good right, Andy?" Rankel turned to Vargas for support. He showed he intensely disliked talking through a day's report, which was exactly why Halloran and Vargas made him do it.

"Awhile later we're in the bushes down across the road, and we get busted by the black cat. We're eating breakfast we brought with us. We hear this noise, it sounds like a cranky baby, and we look down and there's the black cat standing in front of us, kind of yowling at us. Is there such a thing as a watch cat? We were afraid they'd hear him, so Andy gets the idea to share some scrambled eggs. The cat takes the egg and cheese and takes off." Rankel paused. He could see the look on Halloran's face said speed it up.

"Why is the cat important enough to tell me about?"

"It is important boss because we almost missed them coming out of the house. They got in the car and drove off over the hill away from us. The cat delayed us. We had to sprint back down the hill to the car to follow them."

Andy Vargas came to his partner's assistance. "We think they knew we were out there. They almost gave us the slip by taking the river road down into town."

"Let me get this straight. You two can tail drug dealers, terrorists and smugglers, but a couple of ordinary women are giving you a hard time?" Halloran looked askance at his team lead.

"I don't think they are exactly ordinary, sir. They know

those back country roads. We could have lost them. When they got into town, they parked in the most exposed spot and walked down the middle of the sidewalk in the open to the public library. If they wanted to make it harder to follow them without being seen, I don't know how."

"What were they doing in the public library, returning overdue books?" Halloran looked thoughtful. He rubbed his chin, suspecting she was up to something.

Vargas and Rankel could see the boss was onto it. "Yeah, that's what we said. What's the rush about?" Vargas lowered his voice. "After today, I'll take a drug dealer with business to do. Have you ever chased two women shopping all day?"

"Back to the library, what did *she* do?"

"Here it is, first thing they don't return the books. They sign up for something on a clipboard. Then the girl sits down at a computer. Right out in the middle of the room, in front of the Reference Desk. In full view of everybody. She starts typing. Her mother stands in back of her." Rankel warmed to his subject.

"Like she's keeping lookout," Andy Vargas added.

"They do this for half an hour straight and print some stuff, not too much. Maybe three sheets. They get up and go to return the books, so I sit down at the computer to see what I can tell about what they were doing, and this little old lady swats me on the shoulder. She says it's her turn, and I have to go sign up on the clipboard for computer time." Rankel shared his frustration.

"What do you conclude from this?" Halloran directed his question to the speaker. Vargas stood by silent, waiting.

"They needed to get to the library early so they could use the computer first. We know they have Internet access at home, so unless the service is down, they are using a public IP address to avoid exposing their own. I learned that the library PCs are configured to delete the history of sites visited, and that the girl knew enough to reboot the machine to make sure it did."

"They are certainly being careful about their digital trail, although you think they knew you were following them." Halloran considered the implications of this.

"Any sign of Kirbee at all? Could you tell if they were picking up or sending email?"

"No, sir, we couldn't get close enough to see the screen. Ms. Huber was in the way."

"On purpose, of course. Then what?"

"Shoe shopping. I hate that. How many shoes can women wear? And purses," Rankel complained.

"They stopped for lunch and then kept on going. They picked up Ms. Waitely down here at the hospital and went to the Farmer's Market. We found them buying yellow beets the size of golf balls and some green leafy stuff we don't even know what it was." He could see he was about to lose Halloran again. "Here's where it gets good. We spotted that guy Stevenson in the crowd, all of a sudden we're not the only ones following them. He goes up to them, says a nice hello, how you doing kind of thing, and takes off."

Vargas crossed his arms and nodded at their boss. "So I told Rankel to follow him. Then I finally get lucky. The sidewalk is crowded and I can get closer. They stop at a café with outdoor tables for cold drinks. The two girls are teasing Ms. Huber about having a date tomorrow night with Stevenson.

"Sir, what are we going to do? We can't follow her in there. She's going to dinner at that fancy university club with that guy who knocked her down." Andy was not about to tell the boss anything he didn't need to know, especially how close he'd come to getting caught again by Em in the process.

"Yeah, wonder what he's really after," Rankel added, his tone caustic. He'd observed Professor Stevenson out for his afternoon run and seen the exaggerated courtesy he exhibited to the young women in his way on the sidewalk. Stevenson was agile and fit. The likelihood he'd knocked Em down accidentally faded measurably each time the professor carefully skirted around pedestrians and pets of all shapes and sizes. Rankel was not a fan.

Halloran found this interesting. "Did you happen to hear what time they are meeting for dinner?"

"Six thirty tomorrow evening," Andy's replied.

"I think I may be able to get someone inside. I'll make a phone call to a contact of mine. Anything else I should know?"

"Yes, Stevenson runs an easy workout. He's good on his feet, no way he knocked her down accidentally." Rankel expressed his natural skepticism.

"If we know that, she knows that, too." Halloran stretched out under his desk and his eyes narrowed. "Women."

Rankel and Vargas laughed.

———◆———

Ladies in Waiting

THOUGH EM'S CLOSET OFFERED LIMITED choices for evening wear, she dressed with the intention to be ready early for her dinner date with Professor Stevenson on Tuesday. She tried on and rejected the classic little black dress as a bit much for dinner at the club. Likewise she rejected a long batik purple and white print spaghetti strap sundress gathered at the waist as too reminiscent of Mama Cass. A softly flowing designer ready to wear dress, in a blue on black print with a deep neckline was her final choice. She added her best black strappy sandals. For a casual dinner at the club, makeup was not required.

She looked herself up and down critically in the full length mirror on her closet door. The fit was not quite perky, *If only I could get rid of these rumples in the middle,* she thought. Off came her chosen dress. In haste she searched through her underwear drawer for black shaping garments, found a very good bra, put it on, hiked it up and pulled on a long slimming pair of underpants under her slinkiest black slip. Back in front of the mirror, she was now reasonably satisfied with what she saw and ready to go out. Clothes may make the man, but good foundations could make the woman.

The girls were out, so Em could escape their scrutiny with the low neckline. Her children insisted Em dress to their image of a mother in her fifties. Em preferred to show a little of her very pretty cleavage, gym toned legs and well-shaped ankles as a distraction for her hopefully no longer sweaty date.

Arriving at the club's miniscule parking lot in the city, Em found it full and needed to circle the city blocks to find a spot on the street over a block away. There was a fair walk to the club's back entrance, but Em had arrived twenty minutes early in anticipation of this difficulty. The walk took her past stately homes, many now converted to apartments or to university offices. She continued towards the back entrance to the club through the colonial garden with its old brick walk, wisteria and raised beds of herbs and flowers laid out around a tiny fountain. It was always an enjoyable walk, although she had not been to the club in several years, not since her ex-husband dropped the family membership under duress. The membership was a pre-divorce casualty of Huber's early indiscretions.

Membership in the club was by application and recommendation, annual fee and an agreement to make use of the facilities at a certain level. This often led to family dinners, entertaining friends and business acquaintances or stopping in for lunch when in town to run up the required tab. Em suspected her invitation to dinner at the club fell into that category.

Several years before, Huber stopped bringing family to the club and instead brought a succession of younger women, most especially one administrative assistant. After a particularly cordial dinner, he made the mistake of asking the manager if he might have use of one of the upstairs rooms usually reserved for visiting scholars of distinction. This request was declined, and shortly thereafter he received notice his membership would not be renewed for the next month. The club was not interested in being used for a place of assignation, or words to that effect. The antics of visiting scholars aside, really, members should know better and take their fancy elsewhere.

A very short time later, in the following month to be exact, Em and two of her lady friends decided to lunch at the club. The manager was surprised but made a quick decision. He gave Mrs. Huber a cordial welcome and accommodated the ladies to a most pleasant lunch. Several days later Em received a discrete phone call letting her know her husband declined to renew his membership, but that she and the children were most welcome to continue as members. This was one more item on a lengthening list of complaints and reports Em received concerning Huber's behavior. That very next semester Huber took a leave to lend his geological expertise to the family oil business in Texas. Em had not been back to the club since that phone call.

Had Professor Stevenson been privy to any of this she wondered as she approached the back door. Was this a play to make her aware of the contrast between his good standing relative to Huber's fall from grace? Stevenson was one of the three competitors for the appointment Huber missed. He was younger than both of the other men and took his more senior colleague's appointment as a good sport and even liked the guy for it. The winner proposed he and Stevenson work on a project of interest together, funded by his new budget. The Chairman applauded the selection committee's decision.

Em summoned up her dignity, grasped the polished brass

door handle and gave the heavy wooden door the customary shove. The door opened to a hall paneled halfway up
in white with Robin's Egg blue walls above. The scent of
garden flowers from an arrangement in a cut glass bowl
resting on a small side table met her as she entered. All was
soothing and understated, as she remembered it.

The club manager who happened to be at the reception
desk spotted Em immediately. "Why Ms. Huber, how very
good it is to see you! It has been much too long. And how
are the children? We still talk about the humorous song
they sang at the Holiday Party years ago. Might we ever
have a copy of the words to their version of "Twelve Days
of Christmas"?

Em couldn't help laughing with pleasure. "Mr. McArthur, I'm afraid that has been lost to the sands of time
and lives only in fond memories. I'm meeting Professor
Stevenson."

"Ah yes, we were expecting you." McArthur showed his
approval with a warm smile. Professor James Stevenson
would be eminently suitable for her, not like Huber at all.
"Professor Stevenson called, he is running a bit late. We are
to offer his apologies. He took a group on a field trip and
they're stuck in rush hour traffic. Road repairs. He will be
here as soon as he can."

Em wondered how they defined, "a bit late."

"Please let us make you comfortable in the lounge."
McArthur abhorred the idea of a woman sitting alone at
a table in the dining room waiting for a man. Stevenson
should know better than to keep a lady like Ms. Huber
waiting, even if she was fifteen minutes early.

"Mrs. Howell Weiss is also waiting for her dinner companions. I believe you must know each other. She is the
widow of Professor Howell Weiss, the Emeritus Aspinwall
Professor of International Law. She is having tea."

Knowledge of proper titles and a good memory for faces
were nonnegotiable prerequisites for McArthur's job. Tact

and discretion and a firm hand with staff counted highly as well. McArthur retired early due to health with his professional standing intact from a major hotel chain, so there was little he hadn't seen. The club was his idea of a rest spa.

Em allowed herself to be gently guided into a seat in the club's lounge, a quietly decorated room with walls of the club's signature blue, printed summer drapes and a now cold white marble fireplace. Seated next to her in a comfortable chintz upholstered chair was a lady with clear sparkling blue eyes and the pure white hair of the truly elderly. Her summer suit graced a still ample but trim figure. Before her on a circular mahogany table sat a china tea pot and several cups in the university china pattern. A plate of shortbread cookies dipped in dark chocolate rested next to the tea pot. McArthur made sure to introduce the two ladies, although from their smiles they obviously welcomed the sight of each other. He then wandered away to greet a family of three generations newly arrived for dinner.

Em recognized the doyen of faculty wives, a woman of distinction in her own right, a historian always a little ahead of her time.

"Do join me for tea. I'm expecting guests for dinner. But I finished my research in the Archives early and felt the need for light refreshment. McArthur was kind enough to set me up with tea in here. So much nicer than sitting in there at a table on those hard wooden chairs. They have been here forever. You would think they'd splurge on cushions."

Em had to agree that the traditional Windsor chairs in the dining could be uncomfortable for long meals.

Mrs. Howell Weiss put aside the book she had been reading. Em saw the title on the lightly worn volume, *World War I Paris Peace Negotiations, President Wilson and Col. E. M. House.* Seeing Em's interest in the book, Mrs. Howell Weiss remarked, "Fascinating man, Colonel House. He carried a pretty little pearl handled Belgian pistol when he met with his friend Wilson. He believed he could protect him better than the Secret Service because he was closer. For a Texan, you would think he'd prefer a more sizable revolver."

Em laughed. "It must be in the Branch Water."

"Do forgive me, dear, but is he coming? Are we to expect the presence of Texas oil this evening?" The elderly lady rested her spoon precisely on the saucer of her teacup. Her hands were small and her fingers now thin with age, but she wore her nails long and impeccably manicured. A ring of diamonds and blue sapphires on her left hand flashed in the afternoon light.

"No, Harley's in Texas for the duration I believe. He's expressed a disinclination to set foot in New Haven again. Of course, he's not the most reliable of reporters, so who only knows. I'm meeting Professor Stevenson this evening."

Em was trying to pass off Huber's reluctance to visit his children lightly. She accepted a cup of tea and sat quietly for a moment, sipping the now rather strong "Constant Comment" tea with its infusion of citrus flavors. Quite an old fashioned pleasure, the shortbread cookies dipped in chocolate were also a treat. Searching for a neutral topic of conversation Em asked, "How are your son and his family?"

"He's teaching Law at Georgetown. Like his father, he ultimately prefers the classroom to the courtroom. The Supreme Court can be so trying. The family is enjoying all the sights and activities of Washington. The boys love the Air & Space Museum the best. I worried about the younger wife you know, but it's turned out to be a blessing, or multiple blessings." The professor's widow smiled.

"Would that be Professor Stevenson of Geology you are meeting? Weren't he and Huber at odds?"

Em nodded her assent.

"Dinner with the opposing party? How did this come about?" Mrs. Howell Weiss asked in her very direct way as she stirred sugar into her next cup of tea.

"It seems Professor Stevenson, of Geology, has a remorseful conscience. He was out for a run and knocked me down flat."

"Do tell! It sounds romantic. I hope you weren't hurt. How did this happen?" Mrs. Howell Weiss raised an inquiring eyebrow.

"I am cat sitting for a friend in the physics department who lives on Bacon Avenue. He was called away unexpectedly and asked me to take care of his very special Siamese cat. Her name is Cleome." Em hesitated. "You know, I don't think it was romantic. More sort of an absentminded error in judgment, either that or it was staged somehow."

"Oh, how so?" Mrs. Howell Weiss stared at Em over her teacup.

"As I was getting out of my car in front of the house, I looked down the street. I think I saw Stevenson leaning into the window of a strange dark green car parked on the opposite side of the street as if he was talking to the people inside."

"Why was the car strange? Psychedelic paint?"

"Not at all, it was a dull dark olive green, almost like some sort of government car."

"Could you see the license plate?"

"I didn't look that closely, and it was too far away to see it clearly. I don't remember if it was still there when I came out of the house.

"Now, when I finished feeding Cleome," Em resumed her narrative, "I locked the house and started down the front walk. As I reached the sidewalk Professor Stevenson came running up the sidewalk towards me. He was all sweaty and looked as if he had been running for quite awhile."

"Was he looking where he was going, dear?"

Em seemed truly puzzled. "I could swear he speeded up, and he bumped me rather hard on the shoulder. I'm not exactly a light weight so the impact caused him to stumble. I caught my heel, twisted my ankle and went down. You must know the street."

The elderly lady indicated she most certainly did.

"Fortunately the lawns are raised a foot or two above the sidewalks. I ended up flat on my back on the lawn." Em took a breath. "And he landed on top of me. Perhaps I grabbed for him, although I don't remember doing it. I can't think how that could have happened."

"It does seem a rather unusual occurrence. Every year we have casualties, the usual run-ins with cars, bicycles, students and faculty on Chapel Street. Not usually on the lawns of one of the nicest streets." Mrs. Howell Weiss mused. "One of my favorites. May I ask whose house it was?"

"Professor Frank Kirbee."

"Dear man. What did Professor Stevenson say? How did he excuse himself?"

"Not at all, at first. I asked him to get off at least twice. When he made no move to do it, I flipped him off myself. I was tempted to turn around and pin him down and ask for submission, but my grappling moves are limited to self-defense."

"Grappling moves? Self-defense? My dear woman, did Huber abuse you?" The elderly lady sounded the shocked listener.

Em laughed out loud. "Not in that way certainly. How I came to take self-defense classes is a good story though."

"What happened after you 'flipped him off?'"

"He did say he was sorry and insisted on taking me back into the house to put ice on my ankle. It's not my best joint, I've strained it a number of times. We struggled into the house, me trying to stay on the ground and him trying to pick me up and carry me."

"Sounds like a wrestling match."

"We did draw an audience out on the street," Em

acknowledged. "Once we got inside he did seem more interested in the house than in my ankle. Professor Kirbee is a minimalist when it comes to furniture, and there isn't all that much to see. We put the ice in a plastic bag to put on my ankle. Then I convinced him I was fine to drive myself home and got him out as soon as I could. The next day he called to ask me to dinner by way of reparations so here I am."

Wishing to divert the conversation away from Professor Kirbee's house, Em lowered her voice. "Would you like to hear the story about self-defense?"

"Tell me!" Mrs. Howell Weiss took another shortbread from the china plate.

"Well, it began like this," said Em lowering her voice to ensure the attention of her sole audience. "Two years ago, it was our first spring season at the new house in the country. I bought it after the divorce. My daughter and her friend Sandy were home for a short break from college. Sandy asked if she might have a high school boyfriend over for the afternoon. Deanna and I planned to be out, so she could have the house to herself. They were sophomores in college, for heaven's sake." Em regarded the older woman who placidly sipped her tea. The Howell Weisses had once lived in college, so Em knew not much about undergraduate behavior would surprise her hostess.

"Did you ever have the feeling you should be somewhere, not where you planned to be and not know why? I had that feeling that afternoon."

"Hmm."

"So I headed directly home instead of stopping for a cappuccino or a latte. When I got there, you will never guess what happened!" Em's tone was light, so Mrs. Howell Weiss was prepared for humor rather than tragedy.

"When I stepped in the front door I almost fell over a pair of very expensive and rather muddy high tops. He'd dressed up for the occasion. There were raised voices in the living room. When I got down the hall, what did I find?

"He's half naked. She's half dressed. He's preparing to climb over my Stickley sofa after her. Sandy's holding a chemistry text book up in both hands, making like she's going to swat him with it!

"I yelled his name and, '*What do you think you're doing!*' Well it was perfectly obvious what he was thinking of doing. I swear I saw his winky hanging out of his shorts. He says, loud, '*She said she liked me, then she changed her mind!*'

"Sandy yells back. She's usually so reserved. '*I do like you, you silly ass! I said no because I'm not ready for this yet. We haven't seen each other in two years!*' There's nobody else around here, is there?" Em dropped her voice still lower.

The two women surveyed the lounge and the adjacent hallway. Seeing no one, Em hurried on with her story, now afraid Stevenson might show up before she had a chance to finish it.

"I said to him, '*You have to take* No *for an answer, like a gentleman.*'

"'*But the boys in the Frat said…*'

"'*I don't give a damn what the boys in the Frat said, you're the one who's bucking for Father of the Year honors here.*'

"He looked at Sandy, who was shaking her head yes hard.

"'*They said everyone takes…!*'

"'*No!* Sandy yelled. '*I did like you but not now!*'

"'*Sometimes* No *is* No, *sometimes it's not yet, and if you behave like an idiot it could be never! And you Mister have to take* No *for an answer. She gets to say when and if!*' While I'm saying this, he's tucking himself in."

Em narrated dramatically, "So I did what any mother would do, I took his shoes. I told Sandy, '*Get his jeans and hold on to them. I'm going to call his parents.*' But I didn't, not right then. I did it later. I went back down the hall, grabbed up his shoes and headed out the front door, around the house to the side yard. There's a spring-fed brook that creates a swamp down the hill in the early spring. Lots of healthy big skunk cabbage plants, rich black muck and insect larvae of all kinds growing in it." Em paused for effect. "I have a fair arm. I played right field as a kid. So I threw his high tops, one by one into the swamp."

Mrs. Howell Weiss gave a lady like hoot of appreciation.

"When he came running out of the house after me, he was in his shirt and skivvies. He yelled, '*What did you do with my shoes?*'

"'*Your shoes are in there!*' And I pointed to them and said, '*Oh look, I think they're sinking! You'd better hurry if you want them!*'

"He scrambles down the bank to the swamp. The kid is no outdoorsman. He didn't think his way through the swamp. First you step on this big tuft of swamp grass, then you step on that stump. No, he plunges in, literally, bare feet and all. Squish! He gets both shoes, and turns back towards me. I'm standing on the bank above him with my arms crossed. I said, '*Watch out for the water snakes!*' That set him off!"

The elderly woman laughed discretely behind her hand. "I'll bet that did!"

"By this time Sandy's standing next to me grinning. I wondered where she was. As he's climbing up the bank from the swamp to the lawn, she has her cell phone out taking pictures. He's hiding behind his muddy shoes, and his 'tighty whiteys' aren't near white any longer. I did make her stop taking pictures," Em acknowledged. "And I told her specifically that this was a private matter, and I didn't want to see this on social media. She knew that was a serious threat because I don't do it for reasons of personal privacy."

"My dear you certainly do have an ingenuous way of handling things."

"Wait, it gets better. At the top of the bank he says, '*Where are my jeans?*' to Sandy who replies with a certain *je ne sais quoi, 'They are on the bench in front of the house.'* He takes off at run. She tugs my sleeve to get me to come with her and runs after him.

"She stops at the corner of the house. We watch him as he finds his jeans. He picks them up and turns to face Sandy with a horrified look on his face. *'What did you do to my jeans?'* he yells, probably loud enough for the whole neighborhood to hear him.

"Sandy yells back, *'A little ketchup and mustard for you, Hot Dog!'*

"After that Deanna and Sandy decided all of us, myself included, should have self-defense training because you may not always have a heavy chemistry textbook handy."

"Did you call his parents?"

"I did indeed. I reached his father at work and let him know he should have a man to man with his youngest son. Maybe get him out of the Frat. It took a few minutes to persuade him, but he finally saw my point. He asked what they could do by way of making it up to Sandy. I suggested *his son* could write a note of apology and accompany it in person with peace offering. That might be acceptable. No flowers. Chocolate and not the drugstore kind either. The boy called, came to the house with a note and a five pound box of Godiva chocolates. We feasted on that for a month. Damnedest thing, she still likes him."

The two friends laughed so loud the staff came to check on them. Once their laughter quieted down, a man's pleasant voice could be heard in the hallway towards the reception desk.

"Oh, I think that's Professor Stevenson." Em attempted to stifle another wave of laughter.

"Shall I have the waiter hold the condiments, dear?" asked the elderly lady in her most innocent tone of voice.

"I'm only dangerous when I'm provoked. I promise to be on my best behavior. The rice pudding here is excellent, which means I'll have to make it through dessert. I'm

determined to find out what this is about."

"Best of luck. Let me know if I can be of any assistance. So nice to see you again, dear, and to find you so well. You were looking quite sad the last time we met."

Em held her seat. Stevenson was a good half hour late for dinner, and he should come to find her and not the reverse.

29

DINNER IS SERVED

———◆———

PROFESSOR JIM STEVENSON FOUND EM Huber
seated comfortably in the lounge of the club with
the most respected of faculty wives. She looked utterly
charming for a woman who was somewhat older than
he was. Seeing Em Huber so pleasantly chatting with
the widow of a former College Master gave him another
inspiration for dinner. To be Master of a College, one would
best have a spouse as the Colleges had been co-ed for many
years now. And of course there was the opportunity to one
up that bastard Huber.

Stevenson's wife, a *Parisienne*, never quite adjusted to life
in a university town. Monique enjoyed his three year stint
in Washington where the social and cultural life hummed
and world events swirled around her. But life in a dreary
little burg like New Haven, *mais non*. Monique, whom he
met while he worked on a project in the renowned caves
of the Dordogne region of France, was an artist on holiday
at the time. She was now back with family and friends in
her native Paris, leaving him unattached and prospecting
for a wife suitable to his role in the university.

"Mrs. Howell Weiss," said Stevenson, addressing the
senior lady first. "Ms. Huber, good evening. I am very

sorry to be late. My students and I became so engrossed in the rock formation we are studying we practically had to run down the mountain to return on time. And we had several of the Forestry School people with us. You know how they are on the subject of climate change. Apparently they found something of great interest, young trees of species growing farther north than previously observed. Very significant, they said. Everyone came back happy. Lots of good material for papers and further study." He stopped for breath.

"Field trips are always such a challenge but so enriching to the learning experience, don't you think?" pronounced Mrs. Howell Weiss with a sly smile. "I'm sorry you had to do all that running, no trips and falls, Professor?"

"Uh no." He considered for a moment. "Ms. Huber's told you how we met? Again my apologies. How is your ankle?"

"It's better now, thank you." Em hid a smile.

"Perhaps some wine before dinner to ease any lingering discomfort. Ms. Huber might appreciate that. You know the wine cellar here is highly regarded," suggested the elderly lady who was bound that Em would enjoy her evening at the club.

"Why, yes, Mrs. Howell Weiss, would you care to join us?" Professor Stevenson remembered his manners but was not at all sure of the results.

"Thank you very much for asking, I do have friends who should be arriving at any moment to join me for a quiet dinner. Pleasure to see you again, Professor Stevenson and delightful to chat with you Emmie."

Taking his dismissal gallantly, Stevenson extended his hand to Em who took it and rose gracefully from her chintz covered armchair. As she and Professor Stevenson walked towards the lounge doorway, Em turned to wink at Mrs. Howell Weiss. The elderly lady smiled conspiratorially in return.

McArthur provided a table for them by a window that looked out onto the street side of the building. A small place card with the name Stevenson marked the spot. On their way through the dining room to their table, Em noticed a similar place card for Mrs. Howell Weiss at the prime choice table in an alcove with two windows on the garden and a view of the fountain. She smiled to herself, seniority had its privileges.

McArthur held the chair for Em once at the table. The wine list appeared. Stevenson remembered Em's taste in wine and ordered well. Em was quiet, which seemed to suit the occasion. She was not used to consideration from an escort. Huber spent years treating her as if being with her was nothing special to him. She smiled appreciatively at Stevenson who became solicitous of her dinner selection.

The club menu was a selection of simple New England favorites with an admixture of French, Italian and Greek specialties that evening. Fresh scrod, salmon, trout, roast beef, herb crusted roast pork and the proverbial oven baked chicken were the main courses. Creamy New England clam chowder, Italian wedding soup and consumé were the featured soups of the day. A variety of potatoes, couscous, rice and pastas were available. Fresh vegetables and a house salad completed the meal. A basket with a selection of warm breads and mini muffins appeared while they were still consulting their menus.

Em decided to make a meal of it. She gave the Boston Baked beans and brown bread a miss. She chose the Consumé Madrilène, roast beef au jus, Duchesse Potatoes, and young string beans sautéed in garlic. Her choices pleased Stevenson who recognized a woman who enjoyed a good meal might enjoy other pleasures as well. A first date with a woman who ordered a scrawny salad was not generally a favorable augury. Stevenson opted for roast beef rare with gravy and a large baked potato. The beef was a treat for Em and when it arrived she was doubly pleased. It was a thick slice done medium rare and it was tender to cut.

"Professor, I should thank you for the invitation to dinner. It's kind of you. I haven't been to the club in several years."

"Call me Jim, please. You're welcome." Stevenson raised his wine glass, "Let's drink to seeing you here more often in the future."

Em smiled demurely, wondering what interested this man — her company or her access to Kirbee's house. She thought, *surely he must realize I'm older than he is, but that's not the way he's looking at me.* She could see the interest in his eyes and pretended to be absorbed in the food on her plate, exercising care with her knife and fork.

It was written that one should never have meat with gravy at meals where business is to be discussed. This was not a recognized paradigm in academic circles, at least not for Professor Stevenson.

After a series of conversation starters that were well received but produced little of interest, Stevenson had exhausted his short list. He made directly to the point. "One of my contacts, a friend actually, told me you've started your own business. We all knew, suspected really, that your research for the corporation was not just literature."

"Oh?" Em paused, holding a forkful of sleek green beans.

"Would you be open to an offer of project work?" Stevenson popped the question right out there.

Em put down her fork. This was not what she'd expected, but she decided to go along with it.

"Some professional friends of mine have a venture that we could use some expert research skills to complete." Stevenson returned to cutting his roast beef.

"Would that be the DoD, by any chance?" Em said blandly.

Attempting to cut a rather large piece of rare roast beef

covered with gravy, his knife slipped. The piece of roast beef took a flying leap, did a back flip and landed on the white linen table cloth gravy side down.

Em grinned and said, "Feisty beef, perhaps well done next time. Not quite so rare." She laughed pleasantly.

Stevenson looked abashed, but his guest smiled at him with such good humor he was forced to laugh at himself. He retrieved the piece of meat, leaving its print on the table cloth in gravy.

"It'll be our little secret," said Em softly. She smiled sweetly at Stevenson who was fast making mental recalculations. He'd heard it said that Huber's wife was capable of giving back better than she got but hadn't experienced it himself.

"Really, if you and your friends are interested in hiring a competitive intelligence professional, you can hardly expect me to be surprised. Three years in Washington where geology is a little thin on the ground. Aren't you into geothermal energy, and aren't half of the world's geysers in Yellowstone on government property?"

"But that could be Department of the Interior. You know the National Parks Service." Stevenson tried a feint, but the diversion didn't work.

"Could be, but the uniforms are different, aren't they?" Em grinned wolfishly.

"Alright Em, Ms. Huber, something valuable's missing along with your friend Professor Kirbee. We need to find it. Other people are looking for it, not all of them good people. We'd like to hire you to help us find it."

"Professor, I already have a client."

"That would be Kirbee, right? Em, if he's out there on his own, he's in danger. Anyone who has it is in danger. This is major league type stuff."

"The McGuffin?" Em quipped. "The Mysterious Thing that everyone wants. That's what Alfred Hitchcock called it when he used it in his movies."

"It's not funny. We're not exactly sure what form it's in. It could be a model, could be data, documents, executable code, or it could be all of these." Stevenson was in earnest now.

"In other words, you don't know what you're looking for."

"Are you going to eat the cucumber in your salad?" Stevenson asked as a server walked by their table. Em pushed her wooden salad bowl closer to Stevenson who promptly stuck his fork into the thickest slice of cucumber. His rather furry eyebrows raised in pleasure. Em put her elbow on the table and rested her chin on her hand. She watched him finish the rest of her salad with obvious relish. Although his eyebrows did not quite meet in the middle of his face, they might be left wild on purpose. They helped to conceal a prominent brow ridge. Exploring caves looked to be a natural instinct for him, resembling as he did one of our cave dwelling ancestors.

"Do you like rock art, by any chance?" Em asked on speculation.

"Love it, absolutely love it. Best use of geological structures until the quarrying of stone for the pyramids. And the Greek temples of course," he replied with professional enthusiasm. His eyes lit up as he launched into a spirited description of the Paleolithic cave art of southern Europe, from Altamira in Spain to the caves along the Mediterranean coast of France, which could be accessed by diving underwater into the sea and swimming up into the caves.

All in all Em learned enough to write a term paper on the topic. "Compare and Contrast the Paleolithic Cave Art of Chauvet, Lascaux and Altimira," and to get an A on it. Even Em's interest in the subject flagged after the description of too many early hand prints, paintings of cave bears, pregnant horses, rhinoceroses, mammoths, ibex, auroches, which were the ancestors of modern cattle, lions, reindeer and the single engraving of an owl on the walls of the best known caves.

"Over thirty thousand years of cave art, so many different images so beautifully painted as if they knew each animal first hand. But the animals would seem to be from different climates, all pictured in the same or similar caves. There are paintings of cold weather beasts, reindeer, cave bears and mammoths and warm weather lions and rhinoceros, sometimes painted in the same cave. And one owl. If the images could be dated, would it show that the artists documented climate change in their era for us to find? Perhaps they painted the animals as a way of remembering them," his attentive audience suggested.

"Documenting climate change, interesting theory but not my field. Cross disciplinary topic when it comes to cave art," Stevenson demurred.

Abruptly Stevenson changed the subject. "So will you help us? We'll pay your going rate. We understand from informed sources you are now in the information consulting business full time."

Em had no idea what to charge or how promptly she would be paid. She had a client, even if he was currently absent and possibly dead. "I'll give it serious consideration, Jim. Is it time for dessert? I'll go and freshen up." Em rose from her chair to seek out the ladies' room. Stevenson poured the last of their bottle of wine into his glass. They were at a standoff, yet again. But he was now sure of her relationship to Kirbee, and she felt she knew who put him up to scraping her acquaintance. A simple phone call wouldn't do for a project like this one.

Em followed a path across the club dining room, skirting the tables with other diners, and walked down the hall to what was still called the ladies' powder room. The ladies' lounge was a suite of two rooms, paneled in white to half height with a pretty small print blue flowered wall paper above. In the first room two upholstered chairs flanked an elegant small table. Across the room were two very old sinks set in white marble with brass taps and faucets that stood up quite high. The twin mirrors above the sinks were tall ovals framed in dark wood in the ogee molding style. The inner room contained the toilets which although old were quite efficient and were housed in stalls of polished dark wood. Em proceeded directly to the second room. As she did so she heard the door behind her swing open.

In a few moments Em was back at the sink washing her hands and splashing water on her face. She wiped her face carefully on one of the small linen towels provided for guests. There was no longer an attendant to assist the visiting ladies. Used towels were to be disposed of in a closed wicker basket for laundering. The covered tip jar remained for occasional use when large parties required constant attention to the lady guests' comfort. Em guessed that Graduation Weekend and the weekend of "The Game" might require the extra expense of staff for both of the rest rooms.

As she finished washing her hands, Em was joined by a second woman. To her surprise and pleasure, Mrs. Howell Weiss washed her hands at the second sink.

"Well, dear, how goes dinner with your new friend? Is he as romantic as he looks? Those dramatic eyebrows!"

Em laughed pleasantly. "Oh, Mrs. Howell Weiss, it's not that at all. He offered me a job, a research project. He seems to be all caves and business."

"A research project? I didn't know you were geologically inclined, dear." Mrs. Howell Weiss gave her an arch smile.

"I'm not. Too many rocks make Jack a very dull boy, and I've lived with that. He had business research on his mind, more my specialty than his," Em replied in kind.

"Is he going into business for himself? So many of the science faculty do, you know, exploiting their discoveries for the benefit of others, and themselves, too. Is he planning to rent out geothermal wells or the odd geyser?" Mrs. Howell Weiss speculated merrily.

"Hardly that. Although it is a thought, isn't it? I already have a good client and he who signs my paychecks buys my loyalty. And I am careful whose paychecks I accept." Em found Mrs. Howell Weiss well informed.

"Quite right, my dear. In the world of business, one cannot be too careful." The elderly lady peered at Em closely. "Do be careful. You've heard the rumors about Professor Stevenson's government work? Grant money comes through many channels and may have, shall we say, requirements for performance attached to it. I hope you remember what Ike, President Eisenhower, said in his speech about the Military/Industrial complex in this country."

"Yes, I expect it does come with conditions. On some projects it is possible the researcher might not know the ultimate source of the funding or even the use which might be made of the research." Em was pensive. Actually she could not remember what Ike said, if she had even known at all, but she made a mental note to look it up on the Internet. It could not but be good advice from the commanding General of the D–Day invasion of Normandy during World War II and later an esteemed President of the United States.

"Perhaps like the reverse of *caveat emptor*, let the buyer beware. How would one say in Latin let the employee beware?" Mrs. Howell Weiss finished drying her hands and tossed the linen towel in to the wicker basket with a practiced aim.

"I think saying it straight out in English is the best way." Em took the warning seriously.

"Very sound approach. I hope you have knowledgeable friends to advise you. Do call me if I can be of any help. 'Better a lawyer before trouble, than after.' My dear husband used to say that. Of course if more people followed that there would be less work for both lawyers and the courts. He was a wise man, but not always a practical one."

"Thank you. I will be both cautious and especially careful of Professor Stevenson and his grant partners." Em smiled. She was chastened and ready to return to her table. "Now for dessert!"

"Em, you are both single-minded and determined." Mrs. Howell Weiss led the way out of the ladies' powder room. She linked arms with Em and whispered, "I fervently hope they haven't run out of rice pudding."

Dessert was uneventful in the extreme. New arrivals were seated quite close to Em, so close that her chair barely had clearance. She looked uncomfortable and Stevenson was both apologetic and unable to continue any discussion of the proposed project. He appeared so frustrated that Em, who was enjoying her Earl Grey and rice pudding, suggested he walk her to her car. Taking the hint, Stevenson signed his tab and left a generous tip for the server.

Professor Stevenson guided Em down the main hall of the club and out the wide front door. The steps down to the street were broad and well-worn brownstone. It was a nice evening for a walk. The trees along the narrow street were in full leaf, and their gentle movement diffused the light from the street lamps, creating moving patterns and constantly changing shadows. Em intuitively checked around the Escalade for the figure she glimpsed from the window. Seeing nothing, she turned towards Stevenson who took her arm companionably. They walked in silence for a moment or two.

"I enjoyed dinner and I hope you will think about what we discussed. Here's my card with the office, home and cell numbers on it. I hope you will use it soon. You know there's a good Irish pub around the corner from here."

"Thank you for dinner, it was nice to be back in the club. I'll take a rain check on the pub, and I'll think about the job offer."

"Promise? Can I call you next week?" Stevenson gave

her arm a gentle squeeze, and she nodded pleasantly in return.

They rounded the street corner proceeding at a leisurely walk in the direction of her car. Cheerful voices could be heard. Em saw movement between cars ahead of them and was about to say a word to Stevenson when the back gate of the club's garden sprang open with a high pitched squeal. A tight little knot of four senior women emerged onto the sidewalk in front of them.

"Really they should fix this! How are we to get out of here without waking the dead on the Green?"

"Don't you mean buried in the Green, dear Mabel."

"I assumed they dug them all up and moved them when they opened Grove Street Cemetery."

"Hildy, sorry to be so disappointing but they couldn't find all of them. It was the nineteenth century after all, so they had no ground penetrating radar to assist them with the process." Mrs. Howell Weiss was quite firm on the subject.

"Never give a historian an opening to show off, that's what I say," Mabel Van Arsdale teased her longtime friend.

The ladies laughed together. The sharp eyes of Mrs. Howell Weiss spotted Em and Jim Stevenson. She held out a hand to Em and drew the pair into her group. Introductions were not necessary as everyone had at least a passing acquaintance. They chatted about the dinner and the staff changes. New servers did not yet know everyone's preferences for tea. The group progressed down the street. Em stared off into the darkness between the cars but could identify no moving shapes. As they came to a very sleek little mini, three of the ladies broke formation and climbed in after wishing everyone repeated goodnights.

The three friends continued on in the scattered lamplight. Only one other couple, graduate students, intent on each other, were visible on the street. When they reached Em's van, Mrs. Howell Weiss apologized and asked very sweetly if Professor Stevenson would continue on with her to her own car. She confessed to some uneasiness in the dark. As it turned out they both were parked in the same university lot. Stevenson had just a moment to plant a friendly kiss on Em's cheek ostensibly behind the elderly lady's back. He exchanged Em's arm for Mrs. Howell Weiss's arm, and they walked off down a driveway into a university lot reserved for Faculty and ranking administrative staff. Stevenson saw the elderly lady safely into her car, waited for her to start the car successfully and followed her out of the nearly deserted lot.

Em took the most traveled way home and saw nothing that could indicate anyone was following her. She drove through the streets to the center of her own town. It was as if they rolled up the streets at ten p.m. There was not another car for two or three blocks. Perhaps the watchers, if they were there at all, had no need to follow her.

———◆———

Mrs. Howell Weiss had a shorter distance to go up the hill to a meticulously kept white wood frame house with deep green shutters. The center hall 1930's gem of a house was designed by Alice Washburn, a locally famous woman architect who specialized in the New England Colonial style. She shared this with an old family friend. It was not good for adults to live alone she reasoned.

Mrs. Howell Weiss had been tempted to call in from the road, but her conscience smote her about cell phone use while driving. She satisfied herself with sitting down to the phone immediately as she reached the kitchen.

"Michael, good evening, dear. How nice to hear from you today. Such a nice idea, we had a lovely dinner. I'll send you my bill. Thank you.

"You were quite right. Stevenson did have something on his mind. He offered her a research project but didn't specify what it would be, as near as I could tell. Em was not eager to jump at it. I did take the opportunity as you suggested to caution her about grant money from the military. Oh, they got along quite well. He is so different from that man Huber."

"Hmm. Did it look like they were close?"

"No dear, I wouldn't think so. He may have an interest in her. But it does not seem she takes him at all seriously. No war paint." Mrs. Howell Weiss smiled to herself.

"War paint?" he asked.

"No makeup, dear. A very nice dress with lots of leg showing, but no makeup."

There was a silence on the other end of the line.

"There is one other thing. Did you have someone watching outside the club?"

"Why?"

"On our way out to our cars, Emmie kept looking into the shadows across the street as if she had seen something."

"I'll check on it. Did you see anything?"

"No, I can't say that I did. I had too many ladies all chatting around me!"

"Thank you very much, I'm glad that it went so well. You're a natural. My best to Marc and the family," Halloran said, his tone warm to the mother of an old friend from Georgetown Law School.

"It's not as if I haven't done it before. I'm sure they would love to see you the next time you're in Washington." Mrs. Howell Weiss smiled to herself. Michael might be an even more suitable match for Emmie, and it would serve that man Huber right.

30

SECRET IN THE ATTIC — KDKA

———◆———

DRIVING EACH DAY TO FEED Cleome was fast becoming a ritual. Em expected she might hear from Frank Kirbee at some point, at which point she was not sure. Twelve cans of cat food suggested he would check in. It was Wednesday, the day after dinner at the club. She carefully varied the time to avoid another chance encounter with Stevenson. As she drove around the corner onto Bacon, on the spur of the moment deciding to scope out the neighborhood, she continued past the house. Looking to see who might be watching, she regarded each vehicle parked on the street with suspicion.

It was early afternoon, just after lunch hour. Street traffic was quiet, no olive drab car was in evidence, nothing to arouse her interest. Coming around the block again, she parked several houses away from Kirbee's address, on the opposite side of the street in the shade of a tall and graceful elm tree. Em walked across the street and up the sidewalk to the house. She always felt underdressed for her visits in that neighborhood, even more so that day because she was wearing jeans and a form fitting clear red V-necked tee.

Bacon Avenue was a street of meticulously groomed

lawns and flower beds, meticulously shaped hedges and several fancifully clipped specimen bushes. Bright flowers, often exotic ones to suit the owners' tastes, presented spots of high color to the street. On certain days, the sound of lawn mowers, edgers, backpack leaf blowers and the occasional tree saw enlivened the streetscape and broke the quiet as landscaping services worked through the spring and summer to maintain lawns and gardens. Workmen patched and painted and roofed here. Today was one of those active days in the neighborhood. The professor must have a lawn service, the grass was neatly cut, and the flowers in the pots on the front steps were watered. It also explained the perfection of the garden in the backyard of Kirbee's house.

Cleome met her at the door. The cat was cordial but looked bored. She had the most dignified of cat manners but asked to be petted and pampered. In the kitchen, Em fed her gourmet tuna with a side order of dried cat food. Seeing Cleome satisfied with her victuals, Em opened the door to the basement located under the main staircase in the small back service hall. The smell that greeted her from the stairwell made her wrinkle her sensitive nose and sneeze sharply. The odor was musty, the classic mixture of damp old cement, hint of mold, laundry soap, home heating oil, perhaps a residue of coal and another chemical scent she couldn't readily identify. It was not inviting. Em closed the door firmly, saving that adventure for another day. The anticipation of being trapped in the smelly basement with its variety of odors while alone in the house was not heartening.

Em spent some time looking through the ground floor of the house. She did think to bring her disposable gloves. She assumed the police had been through everything at least once, so she wasn't sure what she hoped to find. Cleome followed her loyally until they reached the living room where she hopped up on her favorite spot on the couch. Em judged it useless to shoo her off as she would return as soon as she was alone again.

With renewed energy, helped along by the fresh air in the wide hallway, Em headed to the staircase. Pausing at the foot of the stairs, she briefly considered calling out, but the house gave echoes to every loud noise. Instead, she took the stairs as quietly as she could while trying to minimize the creaks and groans. Several steps showed horizontal separations between the boards and protested loudly when stepped on. Em pulled on her gloves as she climbed the stairs, trying to remember which steps were the loudest.

After a quick survey of the bedrooms and the bathroom, seeing nothing noticeably changed, Em went into Kirbee's own bedroom. It was not the largest master bedroom, but the one most conveniently located next to the bathroom. On this visit, she did search Kirbee's quarters, working neatly and quickly. Going through his bureau drawers top down, she noticed that although the clothes were organized by type, socks, underwear, polo shirts, crew neck tees, and so forth, his clothing drawers seemed half empty. Not having met the man often, she was not able to discern what specific clothes might be missing.

Surveying the contents of the walk-in closet, it harbored a number of upscale brand name tailored suits, better sports jackets and good quality tweeds, slightly out of style. There were no empty hangers. Again it was not possible for her to tell exactly what he might have taken with him. A clean spot in the light dust on the shelf above the clothes racks was an oblong shape that might have been created by a piece of luggage designed to hold a week or so of clothes.

This survey of Kirbee's bedroom took a short time as she wished to disturb it as little as possible. She stopped to pull open the small drawer in the table under the window by the bed. But for a few much used pencils, it was surprisingly empty. Em pulled out the drawer, turned it

over, found nothing on the bottom and looked into the
open drawer space. At the very back, she spotted a tightly
crumpled piece of paper, as if it had become inadvertently
wedged there. The paper was ripped across the top, the
numbers and letters meant nothing to her, so she jammed
it deep into her jeans pocket.

Em looked around the second floor carefully and stood
at the head of the formal stairs listening intently. Hearing
nothing but mowers on the neighbors' lawn, she moved
back down the hall to her secondary target, the attic door.
To her surprise it opened smoothly and quietly revealing a
plain wooden staircase leading up to the sunlit third floor.
The attic smelled of old house, old wood, dust and warm
sunshine. On the left wall at the base of the attic stairs there
was a curious black box with a circular knob. Em guessed
it was an original light switch from the time the house was
first electrified. A hanging bare bulb fixture was visible at
the top of the stairs. The possibility of shorting out the
light caused Em to give the switch a miss. At the top of the
stairs, she recognized the light bulb as a true antique, its
delicately shaped hand blown elongated globe was drawn
to a sharp point and unfrosted, showed the filament inside.

———•———

Back at Halloran's office, in the Control Center, David
Anson was doing his obligatory training with a stint in
front of a large split screen monitor. He'd called Halloran
directly, which was not generally done by the new recruits
in that office. Together they surveyed the unmoving green
blips on the monitor as they appeared on a portion of the
street map of the city.

"She drove around the block slowly, parked three houses
away from Kirbee's. She's been in there almost thirty minutes. How long does it take to feed a cat?" Anson asked
rhetorically. "The cell phone is in the house but hasn't
moved either."

"Shouldn't take that long. Call her number," Halloran directed. Anson brought Em's cell phone number to a pop-up on the monitor. The cell phone rang out to voice mail. The men looked at each other, the look on Halloran's face darkened. "Keep calling. Get me Vargas and Rankel."

KDKA

STANDING UNDER THE HANGING LIGHT, Em found herself in the very center of the attic. Light from windows of various shapes lit the high space. To one side were two roughly finished rooms. They contained a single metal bed frame, no mattresses, old bureaus and assorted boxes. The heat registers were very small she noticed, most probably maids' or the cook's rooms. Old chests, trunks and storage boxes were placed under the eaves and apparently left for generations, at least long enough for a thick veneer of gritty dust to form on them.

Looking at the floor with the white light of her flashlight, in addition to the golden ambient light, Em could see a path of use in the dust. She followed the path to the back of the house past a storage area jammed with Christmas decorations and a bristling artificial Christmas tree made before plastic.

The path continued around one of the chimneys. Children's toys lined up along another roughly framed wall. There under the eaves she found it. Shelves lined the enclosed area right under the peak of the roof. A broad shelf nailed to the outside wall formed a workbench, now swept clean. The light switch here was more recent, also the light overhead, but neither was new. The three electrical outlets over the bench, however, had been upgraded, and included reset switches indicating equipment use.

But the little workshop showed its age. Books on the

shelves concerned electricity, electrical engineering and early radio technology. Their copyright dates placed them in the 1920's. One of the books was a bound note book with the name of the owner. Its title was "Radio Log," and it documented the reception of the earliest public radio stations in the Northeast, starting with KDKA out of Pittsburgh, PA. Very old vacuum tubes of bizarre shapes and sizes were displayed as a collection on a set of shelves along one wall with a set of suspiciously dustless empty shelves next to them. In one corner two brand new banker's boxes and their lids had been haphazardly cast aside.

On the wall by the back window, which was directly under the peak, a small black metal telephone box was nailed to a wall stud. It had a half round metal bell at the top and an empty switch hook beneath it. A hand held receiver should have hung from the hook. Em had noticed a complete unit affixed to the wall in the back hall closest to the kitchen door. Wires with clasp ends hung from the wall unit, presumably for the batteries. The house must have had a very early intercom system, perhaps installed by the workshop's original owner.

The high metal stool had been pushed neatly under the workbench. All recent work looked to have been removed. She had lost track of time and been more engrossed in her find than she meant to be. With one last look around the workshop, she was ready to leave. Then she heard a distinct bump that sounded to be on the back of the house. The noise startled her. At first she thought it might be someone at the back door. Standing close to the window, she edged over cautiously to look down. First the sound of steps, and then came the sound of a window opening below her. She looked down out of the attic window in time to see what appeared to be the legs of a man disappearing none too gracefully into the window of Kirbee's bedroom.

The quiet of the house was broken by the scrapes of furniture moving and thuds as if things were being thrown onto the floor. The noises startled her. *We're being burgled. But, aren't burglars quieter than this? It sounds more like an active search, and it is the middle of the day. With the price of silver, certainly any burglar would head downstairs for the candlesticks in full view of the windows on the dining room table.*

Em felt the first flush of panic at the possibility of being trapped in the attic with an assailant. The adrenalin rush served to clear her mind. Being somewhat claustrophobic as a child made her into an escape artist. She took off her gloves and stuffed them into her pocket. Leaning against the workbench, she pulled off her rather large cross trainers. Holding her shoes in her hands she walked as silently as she could out of the workshop, timing her steps to coincide with the noises coming from the bedroom below. Once out of the workshop, Em moved quietly across the attic and crept down the attic stairs, preparing to spy out the intruder, hoping no one would pay the attic much attention.

Opening the door to the second floor hallway, she could hear sounds of drawers being pulled open in Kirbee's bedroom. She slipped down the hall, her shoes in her hands. She looked into the room to see a man in light colored overalls with his back to her. His dark hair was greying, rather long and not especially clean.

Taking advantage of his absorption in Kirbee's sock drawer, Em crept forward. Her cell phone was in her bag in the kitchen. To call for help she needed to reach it. The man pulled the pairs of socks apart and felt each one carefully, then threw them down in a heap on the floor. Walking as carefully as she could, up on her toes, a floor board creaked unexpectedly under her tread. The burglar wheeled around and seeing Em he took a fast step towards her.

"You…" he growled. As hard as she could, Em threw her shoes at his head one right after the other and set off at top speed in her stocking feet for the stairs.

She was in jeans, now dusty, but why run when you can ride? On inspiration, she grabbed the newel post at the head of the stairs. She turned around to go down backwards, put one foot on the step close to the banister, swung her other leg over the banister as if mounting a horse and planted her fanny heading down. She raised her feet, let go of the newel post, bent forward and let her weight slide her swiftly down. The man in the painter's pants made it out into the hall in time to see Em's head disappear from the head of the staircase as if she'd been sucked down the stairs. He turned and ran back to the bedroom. None too fast on his feet, he could see that giving chase was not in his best interest at that moment.

Using her hands for brakes towards the bottom of the stairs, they made a squeaking sound as she finished a quick sweet ride around the corner at the base. She hit the newel post at the foot of the banister more solidly than planned, but she was well padded on the bottom. Em sat up quickly with grin on her face in spite of herself, ready to dismount in a hurry. Then she looked over her shoulder to see a tall grey eyed man leaning on his cane.

Halloran had been searching the kitchen when he heard heavy footsteps in the room above him. Em's all-purpose overly large bag sat on the kitchen counter, her cell phone buzzed angrily inside it. The cat cocked her head and ran down the hall towards the front of the house, with Halloran following right behind her. He arrived at the base of the stairs to see a shapely bottom heading down the banister directly towards him, a sight he enjoyed. He had a difficult time controlling the smirk on his face and instead decided to relax and let it be.

"Second childhood?" he asked, amusement in his voice.

Em came up looking him straight in the eye, her seat on the banister giving her height.

"But, I'm not sure you've left your first one yet."

She saw the lopsided grin on his face and groaned

inwardly. Of all the damned people to find her like this, it had to be him. "We're being burgled! There's a man up there searching Kirbee's room!"

"Get in here. Intruder, second floor, back room," he ordered into his collar. The sounds of two pairs of running footsteps approached the house. Rankel, followed by Vargas, charged up the steps across the porch. The front door was thrown open. Halloran pointed unnecessarily up the stairs, and the two men continued up without breaking stride. The steps groaned and creaked in protest.

Em, still seated comfortably on the banister, hoped the agents wouldn't notice. As she moved to dismount, one foot touching down on the stairs as the other neatly cleared the newel post, very much like a rider dismounting her favorite horse, Andy Vargas looked over his shoulder and grinned at Halloran.

"You don't have to put the banister thing in your report do you?" Em asked as she attempted to tuck one of the disposable gloves back into the pocket of her jeans. That task of concealment was useless as she had picked up dust and a few cobwebs in her journey around the attic. There was a wide smudge of dust across the bridge of her nose.

"In my report I can write came down the stairs expeditiously," he joked. "Find anything interesting, in the attic, was it?" He reached up and tugged gently. "You have cobwebs in your hair."

The sound of a van engine revving up and speeding out the driveway, squealing as it turned sharply onto the street interrupted them. The van sped off. Although they couldn't see him, Rankel took off on foot after the vehicle.

"Sounds like he's getting away."

"Maybe not." Halloran knew his men.

Halloran was making her nervous, and she prattled to give herself time to recover her wits. "There's a nice ship model, a sailboat almost three feet high with a green hull, various trunks, pretty much empty rooms and a workshop with old electrical radio and telephone parts. Interesting, it's been used recently, probably by Kirbee. Nothing new there that I could find quickly, empty packing boxes in one corner, looks like things have been removed." She stopped for breath.

"And?"

"I was in there when I heard a noise. At first it seemed it must be outside, but it turned out to be a ladder bumping against the house. I looked out through the window and saw a man on the ladder climbing into the bedroom window below me. Actually only the legs of the man. After he cleared the ledge into Kirbee's bedroom, I saw the paint can hanging on the ladder. I thought he was going inside to raise the windows so they wouldn't stick when he painted them. Instead I heard heavy footsteps all around the room and thumps and thuds as if he was turning over furniture and slamming things around in the bedroom. That's when I decided to get out of the attic."

"So you took off your shoes so he wouldn't hear you walking across the attic floor…" Halloran provided.

"…and down the attic steps to see what was going on," she finished his sentence.

"No thought of staying put, staying safe in the attic until the intruder was gone? No cell phone to call for help?"

Cleome observed them from her choice seat on the couch. The cat looked like she was laughing.

Em failed to see the point of inaction, for how was she to find out who the heavy footed intruder might be, and what he was after if she stayed hidden like a frightened little mouse (who was indeed afraid to be caught) in the attic. About the cell phone thing, her jeans were snug and her cell too large to be comfortably wedged into one of the pockets.

"Too large for my pockets," she replied defensively. She hadn't anticipated the situation correctly and knew it.

"Get a case for your waist like the rest of us. Tell me what you saw."

"From the hallway I could see a man in light colored overalls like painters wear. But clean, no paint stains. I always get paint all over me, most people do. I didn't see any brushes either. He was going through the bureau drawers pulling things out, taking things apart. He'd heaved the mattress off the bed. That may have been some of the noise I heard."

"You saw him, what did he look like?

"About 5'10", kind of heavy set, maybe fat not muscle. Longish greying black hair, like a comb over, greasy looking. Dark eyes, hairy eyebrows and heavy features. Not Frank Kirbee if that's your next question."

"Did you see him full face?"

"He turned towards me. That's when I threw my shoes at him and ran."

Halloran paused, he had to get past the image in his mind of Em flinging her shoes. "Gun?"

"Not that I saw."

"He saw you and he knows you saw him?"

"Yes, and yes again." It pained Em to admit it.

"Could he be a housepainter who decided to rob the house?" Halloran floated a conjecture.

"His pants were clean, he had no brushes and he was searching inside the pairs of Kirbee's socks for cripe's sake. This is a high value, high maintenance and high anxiety neighborhood. I think he snuck in as a painter to avoid suspicion," Em replied. Her nerves were settling down now that the burglar was out of the house and away.

"I agree." Halloran shook his head. Em accepted that as a sign of progress.

Andy Vargas appeared at the head of the stairs. "Boss, he's gone. Rankel went down the ladder after him but he was already half way out of the driveway. Had a small van hidden in front of the garage, couldn't see it from the street. Local police?"

"When we're done," Halloran said.

"I'm going back upstairs," Em announced as she looked at Halloran. "I need to get my shoes and see what he did up there."

"Put your gloves back on, the ones in your pockets. Don't touch anything you don't have to." Halloran looked up the long curving staircase. "I'll be going through Kirbee's office. Both of you come back to tell me what you've found," he said with a look at Andy. "Bring her back with you when you come back down."

"Should I search the room?" Andy Vargas liked evidence gathering, especially finding ingeniously hidden materials. It was a mind game to him.

"Report what you see. I'll call for an evidence team."

Andy and Em set off up the stairs with Andy in the lead. Halloran watched Em's progress. She had an hour glass figure and walked with a little sway in the tail, which he watched with pleasure. Some pleasures were best postponed. He turned towards Kirbee's office before she caught him watching her as she looked back over her shoulder towards him.

Cleome chose to follow her old friend Halloran into the home office on the main floor. Once there she hopped up onto her favorite Barcelona chair to watch him as he made a systematic search with gloved hands, starting with the bookcases.

On the second floor, Kirbee's bedroom until recently acceptably neat, was now thoroughly tossed. Blankets, pillows and sheets were strewn on the floor over rugs that had been pulled up and scattered. Clothes from several bureau drawers were heaped in a pile as if each item had been examined and discarded. The drawers themselves had been pulled out hurriedly and dumped on the floor.

The bedroom had two windows facing the backyard. The window in the middle of house, farthest from the door, stood open with and aluminum extension ladder braced in it. To Andy's surprise, Em stuck her head out the window. She stayed there for so long Andy worried she was about to follow Rankel by climbing out. He wouldn't put it past the woman, from what he had seen on the stairs. Using a gloved finger, she pried up a long thick paint chip from the window frame. The house was unpainted brick, but the trim around the windows was old wood and badly in need of scraping and painting. She leaned forward, looked down at the ground below the window and to the left and to the right.

Finished with her investigation, she asked Andy, "Do we close the window? I'd like to look at the lock." Together they hauled the old window down. The very old lock was basically intact but did show deep scratches where a tool had been used to force entry. The window screen had been cut and lay on the floor in the corner where it had been thrown. Andy put the window back up the way they had found it.

"I'm done. I'll get my shoes and we can go back downstairs if you are ready." Andy took one more, quick look out the window to see if Rankel had returned. Em picked up her shoes, including the one that had landed under the bed. Andy escorted her back down the stairs to the office to find Halloran, who by this time had progressed to searching Kirbee's desk.

"Are you calling the police?" Em started to feel uneasy without knowing quite why.

"After I'm done here," Halloran replied with asperity. "Come and sit down. Talk to me. Andy, go find Rankel. Make sure we're not interrupted." Andy headed out towards the front hall to call Rankel and keep watch. Cleome crossed her paws and prepared to listen.

"Alright, Ms. Huber, tell me what you did before we got here, what you saw, and what you think."

Em took time to put her memories in order. She sat down in the very same carved wooden chair she used during her business meeting with Kirbee.

"Did you search the house? What were you looking for?" Halloran saw she needed a prompt to get her going.

"I did look through Kirbee's room, but I didn't search it the way you all would, inside of this and under that, or item by item the way the painter guy was searching. I only looked through enough to answer my own questions."

"Which were?" he needed patience to interview Em and he knew it.

"Was Kirbee kidnapped or did he leave voluntarily? Was his departure planned or was it hurried? Was there any indication of where he was going based on what he might have taken with him? I wasn't looking for any *thing* in particular."

"Why not?"

"If he left on his own he would have taken whatever with him, not leave it here for anyone else to find. Kidnappers would have searched as well. We now know somebody thinks there's something of interest in the house. I didn't know that before."

"What did you see and what did you think?" Open ended questions might work best he reasoned.

"Personal care items are missing, toothbrush, paste, razor, things like that. His bureau drawers were organized by type of clothing when I got to them, but they looked half empty. He took underwear, pants and polo shirts, shorts, tee shirts, socks, stuff like that."

"Suggests a planned departure." It was obvious to both of them.

"Yes, but it gets more interesting. There's nothing missing from the closet but maybe a couple pairs of shoes and possibly a medium sized piece of luggage. None of the business clothes or the formal clothes are missing. There are no empty hangers. All the clothes missing are appropriate for the season around here. No woolies for Alaska, no fancy Bermuda shorts for the South."

"Conclusions?" He was more interested to see how her conclusions matched his own.

"He's gone off somewhere to hide out in jeans or khakis with boots and shoes to match. Army buddies?" she said to surprise him.

"What?" He snapped to attention.

Em was pleased to be one step ahead of him. "Look at the photograph on the wall. The four guys in uniform. If my father had to escape, to go hide out somewhere, he would have headed for his Army buddies, to men he'd trusted with his life before."

"I like the way you think, it makes sense. We'll track them down." He removed the picture from the wall. Halloran ran his hand down his stubbled chin. It was mid-afternoon. The man could shave twice a day if he wanted to, it seemed to Em, or maybe it was his thinking tell. He stretched his right leg out under the desk.

"So that's what you observed of his room. The attic?" Always a systematic questioner, Halloran was not easily distracted or thrown off track.

Em was beginning to anticipate his line of reasoning and stopped to consider what to leave out and what to leave in her answers.

"Kirbee had a small workshop up there. One that's been there at least since the 1920's. I found an old log of radio stations received back that far, including details of programs, times, dates, station call letters and frequencies. Book collection to match, old tubes and testing equipment for radio repair. The electrical outlets over the work bench have been updated, suggesting equipment use. Anything new has been removed. The rest of the attic is basically unused except for storage."

Halloran sometimes wished Andy could be as brief, but suspected too, that Andy left nothing out. With Em Huber's selective editing he couldn't be so sure.

"I wish you'd had the sense to stay in the attic."

"But now I can help you find him. I don't think he's the killer though."

Patience, Halloran prayed, *give me patience.* "We can talk about that later. Now that he knows you can identify him, it puts you at greater risk. We'll have you look at some mug shots."

"That doesn't work too well with me. The only time I ever did that I identified a guy who'd been in prison for eight years." Em was apologetic.

"Sketch artist then," he suggested.

"Piece of paper and a pencil, I'll sketch him for you," she volunteered readily. "I'm actually not too bad." Em's attention drifted off, a pensive look on her face.

"Alright, I'll bite. Why don't you think the man in the painter's pants is the killer?"

"I get the sense there is someone else behind all this, an insider planning and giving directions. This guy looked like hired help, not quick witted at all. He was doing a thorough search, but he didn't have a paint brush or a paint scraper on him or on the ground."

"The trim on the house needs painting," Halloran observed.

"He chose exactly the right window to enter, one out of five on the second floor on the back of the house. The ground below that window had the least stable footing of any of the windows."

"Just dumb luck."

"Hear me out. The second window in Kirbee's room has a table with a heavy brass lamp in front of it. The back wall of the house is also now in full sun, bad for the paint. It would dry it too quickly. I prefer to paint in the shade myself."

Halloran had finished his preliminary search of Kirbee's home office desk. He had become convinced Kirbee's disappearance was voluntary. Kirbee seemed to have cleaned house there — the pencils, technical rulers, calculators all were missing. "We'll call the local police and get an evidence team of our own to go over the house, basement to attic."

"The basement smells funky, damp earth and some chemical, too." Em held an aversion to searching it.

"I'll have them bring HazMat gear in case it's more than a funky smell. Let's go take a look at the stuff he left behind, see if we can find a paint brush or two." Halloran pulled his sore leg out from under the desk and hoisted himself to his feet.

Walking together, with the very elegant svelte Siamese cat following closely behind, Em and Halloran reached the kitchen as Andy finished his cell phone conversation.

"Rankel followed the van on foot. He found it abandoned about three blocks away from here. It had a painting contractor's number on the side so he called it right away. Seems they reported it stolen from their lot yesterday afternoon."

"Police confirm that?"

"Gladys is going to contact local police to check on the report."

"Seems Kirbee was a client. But they are not scheduled to work on the house until early next week. None of their painters were here today. They are all at other jobs. It's a small business, so they know where all their workers are." Andy shoved his notebook back in his pants pocket.

"Insider knowledge," Em ribbed Halloran, in her I told you so voice.

He frowned, to Andy's amusement.

"He stole a truck from the right painting contractor. Someone knew Kirbee planned to have the house painted. Check neighbors, friends, employees. Did he happen to mention it to you?" Halloran asked Em.

"Not that I remember. He would have no reason to do so. Should we check the outside?"

"The back door is locked with a deadbolt, key access on

both sides," said Andy who enjoyed watching Em and his boss together.

"I may have the key. There are two on the key ring he left for me." Em pulled the keys out of her pocket with an effort. The first key she tried in the back door lock failed to work. The second key, the one she used to open the front door worked easily. "I still have one key left, and I haven't noticed any other locks in the house. How about the garage?"

31

MERCEDES UNAWARE

———◆———

OUT IN THE BACKYARD THEY found only the stained drop cloth under the ladder. Em confessed silently she was not eager to explore the garage for fear of what might be found there. Certainly the local police would have searched it for Kirbee. She was eager to see the garden, to explore the grass paths that led around the circular flower beds. The brick garden wall, about six feet high, had capstone shapes in terracotta. Weathered teak garden benches were interspersed among beds of ivy and newly clipped evergreen bushes. Free growing bushes of laurel and rhododendron of advanced age provided scale as several clumps were now taller than a grown man. The garden was fragrant with the scent of old fashioned garden roses and peaceful in the sunshine. A paved path led to the side door of the oversized double garage.

Em put the key in the garage door before Halloran could stop her. This door, too, opened easily with the right key. Em was through with the men following her before they could exercise their usual due caution. She heard about this lack of forethought later and repeatedly. One car stood rather forlornly. The sight of this vehicle drew Em into the garage so quickly.

"I know this car! Isn't it wonderful!" Em exclaimed in excitement. "I think it used to belong to my elderly neighbor down the road. She's retired from the university."

"Wait." Halloran placed a guarding hand on her arm.

"But I know this car." She pointed to the elderly Mercedes, its dark blue paint dull with age. "When I first met it in the early 1980's, it was parked on the street outside of Mory's restaurant. It belonged to a senior History professor. Women full professors, they are rare. Do you think it could be pre-World War II?"

"Could be ma'am. Certainly close." Rankel appraised the car and advanced towards it to get a closer look. "Keys are in the ignition."

"We could take it out for a ride. After all Kirbee gave me the key to the garage."

"Not so fast. It's not a good sign that the keys are in the car, and we don't know why." Halloran voiced his misgivings.

"Oh, I hadn't thought of that. Can I look to see if it's the car I remember? It had a special polished wooden steering wheel put in by its previous owner. There's a good story that goes with this."

"Tell us later. Don't get too close, and don't touch anything." Halloran motioned to Rankel to keep the curious woman from getting too close to the car. Andy stood behind Halloran, watching out the garage window as rear guard.

For once in their still short relationship, Em did as Halloran instructed. Crossing the space to the truly vintage car, she was relieved to notice fresh oil spots and a wider tire path next to it on the garage floor. This seemed a hopeful sign, Kirbee might have taken the newer car. Her eyes smarted. She halted close enough to get a clear view inside the car. As Rankel reported, the keys were in the ignition. A steering wheel made of a beautifully grained wood showed in the dim light of the car's interior, just as she remembered it. Sniffing for the scent of well cared for leather, instead her nose itched and burned, she could barely speak and sneezed violently. Em had a powerful sneeze. To the astonishment of the three men, she sneezed repeatedly and backed hastily away from the car.

"Rouse! Challoo! Andale! Vamanos! Vite! Vite! Vite! Smells!" Em gasped.

"What the hell does that mean, lady?"

Em grabbed Rankel's arm and hauled hard towards the garage door. "It means get the hell out of here."

Andy flung open the side garage door and hustled his boss out and away from the building. Rankel turned the tables and half dragged the choking woman out of the garage into the

fresh air.

Outside standing in the middle of the lawn, Em worked to regain her breath. "It smells! Chemicals. Like the basement of the house." It took all the breath she could muster to get the words out. Halloran was close enough to her to hear the wheeze in her chest.

"She's right. I could smell it too, but it didn't affect me as much," Rankel agreed.

Finally able to draw in a lungful of air, Em relaxed and breathed more normally. When she did she found Halloran had an arm around her in support. Still leaning against his shoulder, she spoke slowly with an effort. "I smelled an odd chemical smell when I opened the basement door today. I'm sensitive to strong chemicals odors. I sneezed then too. It seemed best not to explore down there." She was certainly to be proved right on that one. "There's no reason I can think of that the car should smell the same way."

"Need an inhaler?" Halloran asked with concern.

Em shook her head no.

"We should maybe call the locals, boss," suggested Andy.

"We might want to mention the intruder and the stolen

van while we have them on the phone, if Gladys hasn't called it in already," chipped in Rankel.

"Yes, Bomb Squad first, then, maybe Arson. Do it!"

"Cleome, we need to get her out of the house," Em piped up, instantly concerned for Cleome's safety.

"Rankel, open the door, don't go in. Let the cat out. Come on Cleo!" Halloran called. The liberated cat bounded joyfully across the lawn towards him with the energy of a cat without exercise in the fresh air for several days.

"Andy, you and Rankel stay on the scene with the local teams. Andy, Kirbee's an inventor. You can coach the locals on the more creative hiding places. Rankel keep watch. See if anyone shows up who might have a special interest we should be aware of. Get Leroy down here. We're the senior agency on site now. Take the car in when they're done. Get him to haul it off under cover. Don't take no for an answer."

While Halloran issued orders, Em's mind was fast reviewing her exploration of the house. Halloran regarded the expression of concentration on her face. The woman seemed to reach a conclusion and looked up to find him watching her.

"Do we need to stay here?" she asked. He'd relinquished his hold around her shoulders to give direction to his agents.

"For awhile, until I'm sure everything is underway. The police will want to know why you were in the house again."

"Feeding the cat. Hello, Cleome." The Siamese twined herself around the legs of the two friends who'd released her from captivity. "Then let's sit down."

Em noticed Halloran leaned on his cane, and her throat and lungs were still feeling sore from the allergic reaction. Together they found a weathered Lutyens design garden bench with its silver wood comfortably warmed by the sun. Halloran sat down and stuck his long legs out in front of him. The cat hopped up on the bench to sit between them and settled herself in to play chaperone. Halloran absentmindedly stroked the back of his elegant feline friend. Em watched his hand out of the corner of her eye, trying not to wonder what it felt like. Cleome certainly seemed content. Em tried to shake off the impression.

"Do you think they're trying to kill Kirbee and level the house?" she asked.

"It crossed my mind. There are things missing from his office. You found things missing from the attic and his bedroom. It looks as if Frank packed up himself and took off in his SUV." His attentions to Cleome produced a sustained purr. For a fleeting moment, Em envied the cat.

"And they're looking for whatever it was he took with him. If they can't find it or if they do, they're prepared to kill him"

"Probably why he left. But Frank is too valuable a human asset, so they may be covering a trail. Maybe even more than one group, too."

Halloran's attention focused now on the house.

Em's hand went to her pocket. "There's something I forgot to tell you in the heat of the moment."

Halloran looked at her sharply.

"Really! It slipped my mind. I didn't think much of it. I found something in Kirbee's bedroom. It's a torn piece of paper from a small journal with notes, actually numbers on it. They didn't make any sense at first. It was jammed in the back of a drawer of the night table by his bed that looked like it had been emptied."

"Where is it now? Don't give it to me unless you can do it without being seen. We're out in the open." He looked away intentionally, to make as if the house was his sole concern.

Em fished around in her pocket. She worked to lodge the paper into one of her disposable gloves. She pulled both gloves out of her pockets resting them on her lap in plain view. After several moments, she shifted her weight and placed the gloves on the bench behind the cat.

"It's in the glove on top, sort of under the cat. Now that I've been to the attic, I think I know what the numbers represent."

"Right." Halloran picked up the cat and one glove, placing Cleome on his lap. She purred happily. He managed to slip the glove into his pocket.

"What do you think the numbers are?"

Em scratched her nose with her hand to obscure any view of her words. "Radio frequencies in the lowest, earliest bands. Calibrations for transmissions a few megahertz above or below those of existing stations."

"FCC won't like that. Pirate radio," Halloran remarked as if to the cat.

"The Federal Communications Commission doesn't like anything. They're not in the business to like or dislike. They're in business to regulate a public asset in the public interest," Em laughed. She found something about that funny.

"It could be the key to Version 5. They fixed the hardware defects, but they needed another step. Individual solar units are adjustable and receive positioning information daily or seasonally by radio. The lower bands may be a convenience for testing, easy broadcasting to test. It could be computer generated information that would vary by latitude since the northernmost latitudes would need the closest accuracy in positioning…." Em scratched her nose vigorously when Halloran cut her off.

"Sounds tenuous. We're not having this conversation out in the open. End of subject. We need to talk in the office." Halloran's tone was suddenly strictly business.

Oh, bull's eye, Em congratulated herself.

"I'll prove it to you. Look at the house, up on the chimney. That's one frickin' big radio antenna strapped to it.

Probably can't see it from the street side," she countered.

"Humph, radio, who would have looked for it." He paused. "I do believe Frank was in communications in the Army." Halloran gave her a meaningful smile.

Oh no, not this guy, her cheeks grew warm, then hot. The look in Professor Stevenson's puppy dog eyes under his furry brows didn't have the same effect on her.

Halloran's grey eyed gaze held hers for a moment, just long enough, and then he looked down. But he'd seen her color and enjoyed it for what it was.

"And if you hadn't found the workshop in the attic and the paper, we wouldn't know to look or listen for this now. That might explain any intentions towards the house itself."

Halloran tapped his collar. "I'll need an evidence courier and a driver. Send Anson as one and my car. Courier to return immediately. Heads up to Evidence and the analysts incoming. Results needed stat."

Andy Vargas and Rankel met Detective Nilsson and Sergeant Gianelli, his side man, on the front lawn of the Kirbee house. The local Bomb Squad van had turned onto Bacon Avenue.

"What the hell do we have now? This better be for real." Nilsson was not a happy detective. "We've already searched this house." His mustache twitched up and down with agitation. The appearance of the local police had stopped all activity on the street like a freeze frame.

"Well, amigo, something new has been added." Andy had a friendly way of defusing tense moments, without coming out and asking why the hell Nilsson hadn't had active surveillance on the house. If he had, perhaps the Bomb Squad wouldn't be needed. Rankel was sorely tempted to be snarky about things like this.

Nilsson dispatched Gianelli, who was actually quite an imposing figure in uniform, to ward off onlookers. If the crowd grew larger or if the TV truck arrived, they would need extra officers. If they found anything, it would mean an onsite visit from the chief and all the rigmarole that entailed, statements to the press, and who only knew what else. Nilsson had a dinner date with the possibility of an overnighter and was anxious to make it on time. Then there was the mayor to consider, his phone lines would be clogged with calls from the well-connected homeowners on this particular street. Why couldn't one of the police commissioners live somewhere else? Fortunately the senator lived on the other side of town entirely. One thing in his favor, Nilsson remembered to contact the chief of the university police to let them know they had a situation developing in their backyard. They would handle any complications on their own patch of New Haven.

"Check the basement first, then the car in the garage. See what you find then yell at us. Front and back house doors and the garage side door are unlocked," Andy continued in a reasonable way. "Access to the basement is closest to the back door of the house."

"Is your boss here?" Nilsson said on speculation, he had not been promoted to detective for no reason.

"Yeah, he's out in the back garden with the cat sitter. She smelled the stuff."

"And she called you all instead of us?" Nilsson wasn't too happy about that.

Andy didn't correct Nilsson's assumption. He just shrugged and walked off.

Nilsson turned away to give direction to the Bomb Squad members who were finishing their preparations to enter the house, and they stomped off in heavy gear. A knot of Halloran's federal agents formed on the front lawn, with Rankel and Vargas who looked like they were out to absorb the afternoon sun. Trying to appear casual, Anson and the young woman evidence courier sauntered into the group. A slight man with slicked back black hair in a nondescript jacket, Leroy walked up behind Andy and Rankel.

In his gangsta persona, Leroy said, "I got a flatbed coming to haul out the car. Guy's gonna stay around the corner with it until we're ready."

Andy instructed the young woman, "Go now. Boss is in the backyard, sitting on the bench far as he can get away from the house and the garage. Don't get stopped."

As soon as Nilsson's back was turned, the courier headed down the driveway towards the back of the house.

"Leroy, boss says check out the Huber woman's car for any unwanted additions. We'll need to drive it in to the office. Might check any of the cars near it, too. Show your badge if you need to."

"Right," muttered Leroy, who had had difficulty finding the damn thing before leaving his garage. He didn't get out of the office much. Hoping not to be recognized by family and friends living close by, especially not in his work clothes, and not by his mother who might be home, he had been hiding behind the field agents. When they turned around, Leroy was already gone.

It seemed a short time before the armed courier found her way back to the front of the house, evidence bag carefully concealed under her hoodie. She smiled at Rankel, wiggled her fingers good bye and left quickly.

The Bomb Squad emerged from the basement carrying their findings into the yard to be placed in secure drum shaped containers for transportation.

Nilsson approached the small group on the lawn. He noticed there were now only three of them, one, a tall blond man whom he had not met. He was not used to seeing even this many of Halloran's agents in any place at one time. It crossed Nilsson's mind briefly to wonder what happened to the other two.

"Looks like you were right. They found two incendiary devices with timers in the basement. They're heading out to the garage now. We've got both ends of the street sealed off, but it looks like the FBI and Homeland are making it through now. The TV truck is holding on Orange Street." Nilsson was actually more comfortable with Halloran's IIA agents. They were more like smoke rather than their bossier higher profile federal kin who were more likely to hold his feet to the fire, or his ass if they could get it.

Again, it was not long until the two heavily protected Bomb Squad personnel came out of the garage carrying pieces, widely separated now, which they placed in still a third insulated drum. They called for their van to be brought into the driveway, loaded the three drums inside, and drove away as expeditiously as possible.

"Come now," Andy said into his shirt collar to Leroy who had made his way past the police barricade through the gathering crowd, past the TV truck from the local station to the waiting flatbed truck.

"Get the garage doors open for us, we're on the way." Leroy flashed his badge at the barricade and said, "Evidence collection detail," to the uniformed officers who saw the federal badge and let them pass.

Leroy was a qualified field agent whose specialties were motors, electronic surveillance and a host of other skills that had to do with blowing up things. Shy of appearing in public, he yarned his friends and relatives that he worked in a no name garage with a less than sterling reputation. His younger relatives said he was cool, and he liked it that way.

Leroy's assistant backed the flatbed into the driveway with professional aplomb, meaning that he succeeded in backing the flatbed right up in front of the garage without taking down the garden wall.

Rankel opened the overhead garage door as the flatbed cleared the side of the house. Speed was of the essence. Rankel gathered a handful of papers from Leroy and took off into the yard with them. By the time Leroy and the truck driver had the elderly Mercedes up on the truck, and were concealing it under a tarp, Rankel came to return one copy of the paperwork to Leroy. The flatbed headed out the driveway, made a wide turn and headed down Bacon Avenue in the opposite direction, away from the TV truck parked on Orange Street. As soon as they were through the police barricade at the other end of the street, and a reasonable distance away, Leroy called in to Andy and Rankel.

Nilsson was conferring with his new law enforcement professional guests on the front lawn when he saw the flatbed go by and noticed Andy Vargas and the hefty new agent studiously ignoring it as it passed by them. His guests were intent on establishing jurisdiction when Rankel casually wandered over to Nilsson and handed him paperwork. Nilsson looked down at a properly completed receipt for evidence custody signed by the man himself, Michael Halloran.

"Shit," Nilsson muttered, "he's stolen my evidence." Then he reconsidered, the other agency was first on the scene and senior. First come, first grab. He realized that if the car wasn't already removed, the two other agencies now present would be fighting him for it. Now it was a signed and sealed deal. No problemo. After all, he had the incendiary devices already on the way to the State lab.

———◆———

"What do we do now? How long do we have to sit out here?" Em asked Halloran, whose pants were beginning to show signs of cat hair. Cleome of course was content in her spot on his lap.

"We wait for Nilsson. Vargas says he's on his way back here to report."

As if on cue, the loose limbed figure of Nilsson loped around the corner of the house on the driveway side, coming rapidly towards them.

"Why is he running?"

"Working off nervous energy. Not a man for a desk job yet," was Halloran's assessment.

Nilsson spotted Halloran, Em and the troublesome cat at the very back of the yard. They were seated on a bench against the brick garden wall. Nilsson came to an abrupt halt in front of them.

Cleome raised her head and voiced an interrogatory call, charitably translated as, *Who goes there?*

The detective, refreshed by his short run, addressed Halloran without the courtesy of a greeting, "You were right. Bomb Squad pulled two incendiary devices out of the cellar. The smell was the accelerant. Not very well made, leaking some. Stuff an amateur could make with directions off the Internet."

"Too damned much information out there."

"We'd all agree to that. Timer set for 1:00 a.m. tomorrow morning. Car bomb same level of minimal expertise, motion sensor. It would have taken out the car, driver and garage if moved. No timer on that one. Not hard to build, not wired into the car."

"Were they missed in your search?" Halloran was skeptical of this.

"I swear on my mother's brisket they weren't there when we searched the house and the garage. No sign of forced entry that I could see."

Nilsson showed his frustration by shuffling his feet, his deep blue eyes moving from Halloran and Em to the cat as if he were preparing for a fight from an unseen adversary. Em saw the detective could use another lap or two around the yard.

"I don't think someone likes pussy here," the detective concluded.

"Point taken," remarked the man with the cat on his lap.

"She'd better come home with me," Em said, looking at Halloran. "Unless you would like to take her."

"I'll help you get her into the carrier. She'd be better off with you."

"Dammit it all to hell. What are we dealing with Halloran?" Receiving no answer, Nilsson fumed.

"Do you know who we have out front?"

Halloran nodded yes.

"Do you know who lives in this neighborhood?"

Halloran let Nilsson tell him what he already knew.

"There's a judge three doors up the street, he gets threats as it is."

"That's all you're worried about?"

"One of the police commissioners lives over across the way there. His wife is home alone with the phone glued to her ear. She has a disabling condition. I had to send a female officer in there to sit with her because I didn't want her out on the street yelling at me."

"Evacuated the neighbors?"

"Yeah, of course. There must be close to twenty workers and pedestrians out on the street. We need to get them a safe distance away without losing any of them before we can question them."

"Good," said Halloran. He approved of Nilsson's care for the civilians in the area.

"Yale's nuclear research facility is practically in the back freaking yard. The mayor's already had his chum the president of the university on the phone, the governor, and half the damned faculty, and all the rest of the town...."

Halloran chuckled. He was petting the cat on his lap.

"Washington chewed out Homeland Security for not calling them first, and their guys are going ape shit on the front lawn. What the hell are we going to do here? My ass is grass if I screw this up," Nilsson finished up.

"Nilsson you are a good detective and you are not going to screw this up. I'd hire you myself, but you are more useful here. For now." Halloran paused to see the effect his words had on Nilsson, who stopped moving about.

"Alright, here's the line — We are dealing with a group, possibly with international connections. They are after a scientific discovery made by members of the faculty. It is in development under government contract, paid for by the people's money. It's crucial that we keep our technology here and safe. My organization received a creditable threat. Before we could act on it, one of the two developers was murdered in your park."

"That would be Professor Hussein." Nilsson deduced from Halloran's carefully limited information.

"Correct. Kirbee, the lead developer, is most probably in hiding against protocol. He should be in a safe location. He is probably not. The cat sitter interrupted a burglary attempt. We contacted you to report the suspicious activity. Okay so far?"

"I'm not liking what I hear. Give me simple murder, plain robbery, a drive by gang shooting. Not this international stuff. That's what we have New York for."

"Here's the thing, if the crew on the front lawn give you a hard time, refer them to me for any questions. Tell them I said it was a matter of national security. That will get you off the hook. We'll all work on it together, each agency acting within their own authority. My agency will coordinate and provide intelligence support."

"That would be a radical change. Should I give them your phone number?" Nilsson recovered his sense of humor. He'd half expected the senior federal agent on the scene to ream him out big time.

"Only if they can't find it on their own, Detective." The two men laughed.

Em considered what she learned from Halloran's briefing that she hadn't already known.

"I suggest you have the best evidence people anyone has go over the house. Use Vargas, he's good. Change the locks, deadbolts this time. Bill us. We'll take care of Kirbee. Don't overlook any of the day workers when the questioning is done."

"There must be fifteen of them."

"It's too easy for investigators to talk only to the influ-

ential people or to people who are like them. The people
who do the work here will know the street life best. They
can tell you if anything is new or different. If English isn't
their first language, get translators. Don't overlook anyone.
Make it clear you are not Immigration. Vargas is good at
this, too."

"Well, let's have him do it then."

"We will all work very hard to find Hussein's killer and
to find Kirbee before they do," Halloran assured him.

"So why did your guys take the car?" Nilsson was puzzled, although he knew he had received his marching
orders.

"Because we have an exceptional mechanic with demo-
litions experience who will get us results fast."

"What about the FBI?"

"If we left it for the FBI there's a high probability they
would spray the interior with glue to lift the fingerprints
and ruin a perfectly good car."

"Oh! Antique Mercedes. Could the owner sue if it's
ruined?"

"Try. We'll take the cat and the sitter back to the office.
You'll have our report and possibly a sketch of the intruder
before dinner."

"Good idea. We're bringing in a bomb sniffing dog. I
don't want to send it back in shreds." Nilsson looked at
Cleome. "A sketch?"

"Don't repeat that until you see it. Watch your cell
phone."

"We'll need the cat carrier, the cans of cat food, the bag
of dry food, the litter pan and the special dustless litter.
She's allergic." Em was now anxious to leave. She needed
to chat. "Also my bag, it's on the kitchen counter."

"Shouldn't we get the witness's statement before she
leaves?" Nilsson felt compelled to advocate for following
procedure.

"Too distraught right now. Nearly blown up," Halloran

answered.

Em looked at Halloran. "Devastated, absolutely devastated."

32

ARTIST IN RESIDENCE

"THE CAT CAN RIDE UP front with Anson." Halloran was now anxious to have his two charges, Cleome and Em Huber out of the backyard of the Kirbee house and away from the prying, inquiring eyes of the various agents, officers and news media now gathering on the front lawn. Individual reporters had broken through the police line at both ends of the street, finding their way through backyards and churchyards onto Bacon Avenue.

Normally a peaceful part of town, happenings on Bacon generated above average attention. The Kirbee house was one of the smaller ones on the street, not anywhere near as spacious as the mansions several blocks away on Prospect Hill. Still it was highly mediagenic. Tall, red brick and solid with its fanciful terracotta decorations, it was individual. New Haven did love a story about its eccentric inventor scientists, having been home to its fair share including Eli Whitney, founder of Whitney Arms, inventor of the assembly line for the manufacture of rifles and the cotton gin, and also Goodyear of rubber tire fame.

Anson obediently, but not happily, took the carrier into which Halloran had coaxed Cleome and placed it on the front seat of the car. Anson backed into the driveway to facilitate a quick exit. He had parked the car not too close to the garage, but far enough behind the house to shelter it from view of the growing crowd on the lawn. Cleome's supplies were hastily loaded into the trunk that was still khaki colored, not yet repainted.

Halloran himself opened the back door of the car for Em. "Sit in the middle of the car. Be ready to put your head down out of sight. Don't raise it until I say it's clear." Em looked askance at him. "Care to see yourself on the evening news?" he suggested. Em took one look at the expression on Halloran's face and climbed into the car, sliding over to the center of the seat. Halloran followed her in, seating himself closer to the window on the house side.

"My car?" Em thought to ask.

"We'll have it brought in to be checked."

"Don't you need the key?" Halloran just looked at her. "Oh, I guess not then. Are they going to hot wire it?"

"Too much TV. Our garage man would consider that crude. Get your head down. Here we go. Anson, take us out of here. Don't take any of the Press with you." Halloran brought his right hand to his forehead, shielding his face.

Em ducked her head down to her knees. She felt a hand resting on her shoulder. Turning her head to look up, she found Halloran looking down at her. "Stay down," he said softly.

Anson bided his time until Sergeant Gianelli cleared the driveway, then took his newly acquired wheels down the drive and out onto Bacon Avenue smoothly, without pause, and down towards the far end of the street. He pointed the car away from the large crowd behind a yellow tape line.

The car exiting the driveway passed the two DoD personnel who recognized its color and body style. The man in the Army uniform turned to the New Haven detective who was standing next to a taller red headed woman in an FBI vest. "Who the hell was that? It looked like a damned

General's staff car. You let it go!" the Army man accused Nilsson.

No ready reply came to mind so Nilsson simply said, "Wasn't it one of yours?"

The Army man laced his response with a string of expletives drawn from the vernacular of at least four wars.

"Why exactly are you two here? Care to explain that to me? Signed, in triplicate?" Nilsson barked back. "The Army has no jurisdiction here."

With enough antagonism on the lawn already, the woman in the Army uniform had the good sense to make a brief apology. She hastened her partner away to interview the more communicative, if less knowledgeable, Homeland Security representative.

Nilsson turned to the red haired FBI agent, Nancy Dombroski, standing by him, who said quietly, "I'll show you mine, if you'll show me yours." Nilsson's keen blue eyes brightened, his long mustache twitched in speculation. The afternoon was looking up.

"But only on paper." The woman, who was taller by a good couple of inches, accurately read the light in Nilsson's eyes.

"Drew, you surprise me, I didn't realize you have a sense of humor. With any luck we'll have a sketch soon, but you didn't hear that from me." Nilsson's mustache twitched again.

"Of course not, I never hear a word you say, Nils." She grinned, and thought, *I'd like to see the signature on that little piece of art. It must be Em they took out in the car.*

"You don't listen." It was Nilsson's perennial argument to Nancy.

"That would spoil the fun. We start communicating one agency to another and the earth would move."

On that note Nancy decided to take herself off, leaving Nilsson to contemplate the crime scene and Nancy's tall form as she made her way through the crowd. She might be quite tall, but he was feeling up to it. Nilsson twirled the end of his mustache with his fingers. He watched her stride away, his mind diverted to her until Gianelli came to let him know the canine unit was readying the dog to search the house and garage.

Halloran's hand slipped from Em's shoulder.

"I could use a…" Em sat up on the car seat beside him.

"Latte, I know." He filled in. "Stay back from the window, they're not tinted yet."

"A ladies' room, I was going to say. Though one of the almond horns from the Café would be nice, to help me concentrate on my sketch."

Em sat back against the leather car seat, close to the federal man. She was quiet, which was unlike her, and spoke not a word for blocks. When they passed the center of the city and were nearly to the office, Halloran became concerned.

"Alright?" he asked.

Em, so close their shoulders were touching, gave a long sigh. "I could have driven out with that car. It seems to me the keys were hanging in the kitchen yesterday when I fed Cleome. It was rigged to kill whoever started the car. Why? Is there something in the garage, another work area at the back there?"

"I'll have it photographed and searched."

"He's still out there, isn't he? He hasn't found what he wants." She could feel he was watching her carefully

"We'll check over your car and get you an escort home. Anson, you heard?"

"Number 2 pencils and a sketch pad," were Em's only words until they reached Halloran's office.

Gladys met Em as she came through the visitor's air lock and hastened her off to the nearest ladies' room, alternately known as a women's conference room. Gladys waited for Em inside, seating herself on the comfortable red Naugahyde chaise lounge she visited more and more often lately.

Her friend Bertha managed to find them as Em was washing up, splashing water on her face and all down the front of her tee shirt.

"Lady, we heard you been having more adventures. What's with the spidery accessories? You been crawling through some old haunted house, right!" Bertha took a damp paper towel to rub the cobwebs and dust off Em's back.

Em smiled and thanked her.

"There, that's better. You were looking pretty forlorn there. 'Round here if you don't almost get yourself shot or run off the road, you're not doing your job. Except me, I'm special, you know? They don't send me out too much, too much for me to do right here." Bertha beamed.

"It's not only that, he caught me sliding down the banister," Em moaned.

"Who did what?" Bertha exclaimed.

Gladys hooted, she'd heard some of this on Halloran's mic.

"Halloran, your boss, that's who," Em exclaimed with s sudden burst of energy.

"Tell us what happened, I gotta hear this right from the source." Bertha had been in the Armory that afternoon and received a highly edited version from Garvey.

As Em told them her story, her energy and good spirits returned. She described hearing the intruder, seeing him in the bedroom and mimed throwing her shoes at him and running for the stairs.

"Then I grabbed the newel post, swung around onto the railing and slid down the banister really really fast. Just as the guy is coming after me down the hall. You should have seen the look on his face, it was priceless. My buns hit the newel post at the bottom harder than I wanted because I couldn't slow myself down in time. You use your hands for brakes, you see." Em demonstrated the necessary handhold, gripping both sides of the railing.

"So I think this guy is chasing me. I sit straight up, and Halloran's standing right there, looking me straight in the eye. And he says to me, 'Second childhood?' I was so embarrassed I didn't know what to do. But still I was glad to see him, 'cause he wouldn't be there alone. Then he called the Hardy Boys, that's what we call Agents Vargas and his pal Rankel, and they go running up the stairs."

Out in the hallway, a discreet distance from the ladies' room door, Halloran stood with his arms folded across his chest. Anson stood next to him, awaiting instructions. A muffled woman's voice could be heard. Halloran heard his name, then raucous women's laughter and hooting from three distinct voices came from the ladies'.

Halloran turned to Anson. "She'll be fine now. Get her set up in the front conference room. Get her the latte and pastry or we'll never hear the end of it. The analysts can provide you with the art supplies."

Anson grimaced, going into Analysis required more hassle than he liked, perhaps he could call in his request and have them hand the stuff out through their security to him.

"Keep an eye on her. See if she needs anything else. As soon as the sketch is done, if it's a reasonable likeness, give it to Gladys. She'll do the distributions to the other agencies." Halloran paused and lowered his voice. "Keep Ms. Huber here until I'm done with the call to Washington. Check to make sure Leroy has cleaned her car and it's ready to go. Start your report, we'll have a transcript of the call made so that will help. Okay?"

Anson muttered an affirmative. "Yessir, one thing. What do I do with that cat?"

"Put Cleome's carrier in the conference room with Ms. Huber. Get her some tuna fish and water." Halloran spotted Schwartz coming down the hall towards them.

"Joel, you ready? Let's go call in, they'll have seen the news feed by now." Halloran and Joel Schwartz headed for the large conference room with the best view of the harbor and the flag in the corner to call Washington.

Still new to the job, Anson felt like a general factotum, driver and butler to a very eccentric establishment. Tuna and water for that terror of a Siamese cat, latte and pastry for an unexpectedly unpredictable older woman. He asked himself, *What the blazes will they have me do next?* and decided to call downstairs to the Café to share his grief with his friend José.

————◆————

Em took her seat in the conference room located close to Garvey's desk. It had not improved any since her last visit. She settled in, her eyes merry and her cheeks flushed with laughter. Laughter truly was the best medicine, and that story would be worth retelling at home. Em stopped to realize she had no one but herself to blame. One option she could have chosen was an uneventful retirement, collect checks at the end of the month and bask in inactivity, boredom and additional weight gain. Her income was not strong enough to allow travel or the luxury of season tickets to anything of interest or even more than a magazine or two. And, she had the girls to support as well.

"Damn I like it," she exclaimed softly. "Hopefully, my client will survive to pay his bill."

Anson hustled into the conference room with the cat carrier. The puzzled Siamese inside was voicing her concern, and she complained loudly when he set the carrier down on the floor with a thud. The screened window of the carrier was placed facing the wall, which did not help matters in the least. When Anson returned a few minutes later with tuna on a plate, water in a dish, latte and pastry on a tray, he found the cat carrier moved up on the table next to Em. The two guests were discussing their situation. Em was resting her head on her hands and looked the cat in the eye.

Balancing carefully, still unsteady without his wheelchair, Anson put the tray with the refreshments for woman and beast down on the table. He received a polite thank you, and to his surprise the cat said something that sounded like the very same thing. Anson pulled three sharpened Number 2 pencils out of his pocket and a sketch pad out from underneath the tray where he'd been carrying it. Even as a rookie federal agent, he was not about to volunteer to feed that cat.

"Ma'am, Mr. Halloran asks that you wait with us until he's off his conference call. We're checking your car and will provide an escort home for you and your friend there. Probably me. My desk is right outside, please call me if you need anything. I'll take your sketch when it's done. No rush."

Em opened the top of the cat carrier and briefly considered letting the cat out. Cleome was hunkered down and not looking like she wanted to leave the carrier any time soon, so Em placed the tuna and the water into the carrier.

"Once I get going on the sketch, it shouldn't take me too long. I need to sit and think, to visualize it all over again," she confided to the cat and incidentally to Anson. A noise that sounded like a deep throated purr came from the cat carrier. "A tuna wogg, I knew it!"

"Glad she likes something. The boss said to get her tuna," Anson remarked.

"Yes, Agent Anson, I expect they have been friends for awhile." She opened the sketch pad, took up one of the pencils and made as if to start sketching.

Anson smiled briefly, turned carefully and walked back to his desk, report writing on his mind. Civil engineers didn't necessarily excel at essays, but Anson hadn't been half bad at it in college. Now this skill, underrated in the past, would come into play more often than he'd imagined. Accuracy and the ability to describe events in sequence and surroundings and evidence in detail would be a plus.

And, anything was better than fluid dynamics, read in sewage.

As soon as Anson closed the door, Em put down the pencil and picked up the pastry.

"Well Cleome, we're all in one piece, and we're well fed. Now you will have to help me remember what I would rather forget."

Half a pastry later, Em picked up the pencil again. She began her sketch, trying for the general shape of the man's head. Her first effort was too long and narrow. She pulled the paper off the pad, crumpled the sheet and threw it at the waste basket in the corner. It bounced off the wall above the basket and dropped in. Her second sketch was closer but still not a success. The shape of the head was too square. Frustrated, she again crumpled up the sketch, tossed it over her shoulder at the waste basket and missed.

"Time to try another way. Time to think this through," she told Cleome who watched her sympathetically from the carrier. Em sat for a moment to call up her most vivid visual memory of the intruder in the bedroom. This did not produce an image she could draw, it was a blur of movement, only flashes of memory. Then, after staring at the blank wall in front of her, she decided to go through her memories like a video replay. The first sketch was quickly and fluently done. Looking down out of the attic window, she pictured the painter's pants, butt, legs and shoes disappearing into Kirbee's bedroom window. This produced a humorous sketch that showed the detail of the man's shoes, which were not work boots.

Once she started, the next sketch came easily. A view from the hallway through the bedroom door caught the man in the painter's pants as he rifled Kirbee's sock drawer. His comb over showed. Em even drew the objects on the bureau and sketched in the items on the floor.

Without stopping, Em sketched the man's full figure as he turned towards her, his mouth open in an exclamation.

This was the one vivid memory she had tried to reach before. She felt a rush when it finally back came to her. Taking this sketch, she used it to create another one, from the shoulders up as the man might look without speaking. Although it had taken her several tries to get there, she was reasonably satisfied with her efforts.

As Em prepared to pack it in, to go in search of Anson to give him the sketches she stopped to think. Another memory jogged lose by the series of sketches demanded her undivided attention. She stared at the third sketch, then she sat staring intently at the blank wall for all the world as if it was a movie screen. This time she engaged her brain for sound with her visual memory.

Em replayed the action in her mind from the thud of the ladder bumping against the wall of the house, tiny creaks from the attic stairs, then outside the bedroom door the louder creak from the floor board beneath her feet. In her mind she slowed the action down as if she were controlling a dream. The man in the painter's pants turned slowly towards her. He saw her, a look of surprise on his face, their eyes met for an instant and he said, "You!" Em heard his gruff baritone voice as if he was standing in the room with her. With a shock she realized he had not been about to say "You bitch!" or whatever other nasty thing he had in his mind as she first assumed. It was an exclamation of recognition. He knew who she was, he had recognized her.

Em's thoughts tumbled one after another.

"Anson!" she yelled.

Garvey sat up straight in his chair. He'd been reviewing Internet security logs for another of their particularly difficult cases. Garvey relayed the call to Anson who was already getting to his feet.

"Anson, I need you!" Em yelled again, startling the cat in her carrier.

"He's on his way, ma'am," Garvey called back. The men

exchanged concerned looks.

As soon as Anson set one foot in the door, Em accosted him. "Come here, look at these!" Em had her sketches lined up in order from right to left on the conference room table with the first one in front of her. "This is the way I first saw him. Clean pants, street shoes. Here he is again, totally clean painter's pants. Balding." She rushed. "Now look at this one. He said one word." She had written "You!" under the picture. "He recognized me, I'm sure of it now. He's probably the one who shot at us in the canoe. If he knows who I am, he knows about the girls, and he can find out where we live! He may try my house next!"

Anson was not happy with this conclusion either. The sketches were more than useable, they were very good — clean lines, details suggested, and the main images were carefully shaded to show size and shape.

"I'll need to call home. My cell phone doesn't work in here. He hasn't found what he's looking for."

"Come out to my desk, I'll get you an outside line." Anson gathered the sketches and made it back to his desk with surprising speed. Conscious of document security, he hastily stuffed his report paperwork into the self-locking desk drawer. He punched a code into the phone.

"Sit here please. This is a secure outside line. I'll take the sketches to Gladys and be right back."

Leaving Em under Garvey's watchful eye, Anson needed to chase down Gladys who was not at her desk. He checked the Armory, several conference rooms, even knocked on the ladies' room door. It took him longer than he hoped to locate her. She was paying a visit to the head of Analysis. When he found her, she was making her way through the security procedures to exit the Analysis office.

"They practically strip search you on the way in, and then they do it again on the way out. I swear Martin enjoys it. Both ways. What's wrong with you, Anson?" Gladys was amazed to see her new recruit up on his feet, moving into crisis mode.

Listening intently as she steamed down the hall to the Control Center, Gladys heard about Em's concerns for the safety of her family at home. In her mind, she ran down the locations of all her available field staff. She was holding the sketches when they rounded the corner to the front corridor where their desks were located. The chair in front of Anson's desk was now empty.

"Garvey, where is she?" Anson demanded loudly.

"Said to tell you and the boss she had to go home right away. No one was answering the wire line or either of their cell phones. The girls should be there. The security system is off, too."

Anson made a noise in his throat that sounded like a cross between a war cry and the growl of a very large member of the cat family. Hearing this, Cleome yowled from the conference room. He unlocked the drawer where he kept his badge and his new service weapon and strapped on his gun. "Call Leroy, tell him to get the boss's new car out and ready to roll," Anson directed this request to Garvey.

Gladys was at her workstation reviewing a map showing staff locations.

But Anson was not about waiting. Having the temperament of a fireman, he was brave, fast acting and not easy to stop once in action. With greater speed than he'd showed yet, he paced down the hall to the large conference room door, banged on it with his fist and yelled "Boss!"

Halloran and Schwartz were intent on presenting the details of the case to a gathered audience in three video equipped conference rooms across the country. The pounding on the door was clearly audible across the network and brought Halloran to his feet.

"Joel, you're on deck." Halloran grabbed his cane and made for the door.

"What?" Halloran took in the badge and the gun on Anson's belt, and the look on Anson's face.

"She's gone, sir. Said she realized the man knew who she is, and maybe the girls from the canoe, too. They should be home, but they're not answering and the security system is off."

"Get the car!" Halloran ordered.

"Done, sir," Anson barked back.

Garvey rescued Cleome from the conference room to stop the wailing and approached them carrying the cat carrier.

"Bring the cat," Halloran directed Garvey. "Gladys!"

"Recalling Vargas and Rankel, sir." Gladys was online and on guard.

"Good. Brief Joel."

Halloran race walked to the elevator with Garvey carrying Cleome, followed by Anson.

On the ground level garage, Leroy had the new staff car pointed towards the street, motor running and four doors open. Anson hopped around the car in haste, sliding behind the wheel. Halloran got into the front seat next to him. With only a moment to spare, Garvey tossed the cat carrier into the back seat and slammed the car door. Leroy slammed the fourth door and the car sped up the driveway by the Café.

"Fly low, Anson. Take the highway."

"She's got maybe ten minutes on us, sir. I can cut that down."

"I should have cuffed her to her chair," Halloran muttered.

"It wouldn't have done any good, sir, she'd have found a way to get out of it or take it with her."

33

BACKYARD INVASION

———•———

THE ADRENALIN RUSH HIT RIGHT after Em called into her home security system, the one her son Joshua engineered for her. The security system was off, the girls must be home. But neither answered the landline or their cell phones. They were never without their cell phones. Like underwear, cell phones had become a necessity for them. Em grabbed her bag and bolted to Garvey's desk. She demanded her knives back and threw them into her bag.

"Garvey, don't argue, I'm not under arrest. Give me my stuff. Tell Anson and Halloran I can't reach the girls at home. I've got to get there!"

"Ma'am, you shouldn't leave. Anson went to find Gladys to give her your sketches. He'll be right back."

"You don't understand, the security system is off. They are there alone. Garvey, let me out. Just tell them."

To do Garvey justice, he was alone on desk in the front corridor and had building security to maintain. But he could not hold her against her will. He was also not fully read into the developing situation, having come in to cover the evening second shift at 5:30 p.m.

Fortunately, Em still had her car key. The aging van was

parked facing out, ready to go. She piled in, threw down her bag, and was out the driveway.

She knew the town well and was on the highway before she drew a full breath. Rush hour was approaching. Everyone who could was speeding above the limit. The van was not fast enough to pass the eighteen wheeler in front of her, so Em tucked in behind it, drafting off the massive truck.

The road from the highway to the Spring House became a twisting two lane nightmare in the winter. She chose not to drive it often in the summer either. Tight turns limited visibility. Cars driven at speed tended to forge down the middle of the road. In spots there was no shoulder, no escape for a driver advancing from the opposite direction. The colonial era stone walls still lined sections of the road. Inherently cautious, she slowed her speed, which proved fortuitous because she spotted a dark car with New York license plates driven off the side of the road, half concealed by tall grass and bushes. If she had been going any faster, it was probable she would have missed it.

It was through this same patch of woodland that the miscreant at the Rent Party escaped to his car. This indicated to Em he approached the Spring House from the back through the woods. Making the last turn in the road, heading down the grade, Em pulled the car over to the opposite side of the road. She succeeded in parking close to the hillside, hiding it from view of the house and especially from the backyard.

Working quickly, hands shaking, Em pulled her cell phone, house keys and the Swiss Army knife out of her bag and tried to jam them in her jeans pockets. Since they all wouldn't fit any better now than they had earlier in the afternoon, she hastily pulled on a denim vest she found between the seats. Sticking the house keys and the cell phone in the vest pockets and the knife and car key into her jeans pocket, she was ready to go. Quietly closing the car door, she heard noise from the back of the house, but she was not sure and the sound did not repeat.

Em unlocked the front door and entered a silent house. Everything seemed undisturbed. She closed the door behind her, taking care to make as little noise as possible until she could find the girls. Checking the kitchen first, she walked down the hall to the living room wall where the security system panel was located. The system was disarmed, and then she found her first evidence of trouble. The security remote, they called it the Panic Button, lay in its usual spot on a small table beneath the panel. The girls should have taken it with them if they went out. She stuffed the remote into her vest pocket.

Checking the highest risk and most vulnerable location first, Em immediately crossed the living room to the side door that led out to the rock garden. The house door was open an inch or so, with only the screen door in place. This gave her the momentary hope the girls might have gone out, carelessly leaving the door open. She could have been angry with them, but now she was frightened.

At the doorway, Em stopped to listen. She opened the door cautiously. Sounds resolved themselves into voices that came from across the backyard. Em eased herself out the door, down the stone steps and across the patio to the corner of the house. Down in the middle of the yard the girls had dragged two heavy wooden Adirondack chairs into the sunlight. What she saw made her blood run cold in her veins.

A man whose face she couldn't yet see stood in front of the chairs. First he spoke to the girl in the farthest chair from Em who must be Sandy. As he moved towards the girl in the closest chair, she caught a glimpse of the face of the intruder from Kirbee's house. He was holding a gun awkwardly in his left hand. With a quick movement he reached out and struck Deanna across the face with his right hand.

Em gasped. She was armed only with a Swiss Army knife. Desperate for something to use as a weapon against the assailant, her eyes searched the rock garden. The specimen rocks and crystal formations were too large to be useful. Only the smaller rather dull and ugly metallic chunk held any promise. She flew over to the spot where the metallic rock sprouted out of the ground and tried to pull it free with all her strength. It resisted, surprisingly rooted into the earth. An exclamation from the man in the yard had her running back to the corner in time to see a spray of red blood from Deanna's mouth hit the man's shirt.

"You little bitch! Look what you've done!" Deanna had marked her attacker. The man raised his hand to hit Deanna again. Em was gathering her strength to mount her own attack when she heard a distinctive voice.

"Hey, what are you doing?" yelled Halloran in his deck-clearing voice. Without his cane, sans jacket as well, he was walking up the slope from around the side of the house.

Certainly the law had arrived, but Halloran appeared to be alone. There was no sight or sound of anyone else. All Em could think of was to call for backup and pressed the panic buttons on the security remote for Police and Ambulance. Immediately a tiny voice responded asking for her emergency. Em confirmed name and address, and then said the words she knew would bring the police flying.

"Home invasion, actually backyard invasion. My two girls are tied up to chairs in the backyard and being beaten by a white male early fifties, balding, 5'10" dark clothes. There is a federal officer on site who needs assistance. He doesn't appear to be armed. At least one of the girls is injured, and someone else will be very soon!" Em ended the call abruptly.

She ran back into the house with the remote device in her hand and raced down the cellar stairs towards her workbench. Climbing up onto it, she reached up to grab a long soft leather case. Jumping down, she stuck the landing with feet planted flat on the cellar floor. Working quickly, she opened the case and withdrew a bow and a quiver of arrows. She strung the bow with practiced hands. As an afterthought, she opened a small box and snatched up three tournament standard darts that she stuck in her vest pocket with the remote. She took an arrow out of the quiver and placed it with five remaining arrows over her shoulder. The cellar door leading out onto the lawn was close by the workbench. Em took a deep calming breath, unbolted the cellar door and slipped out, bow and arrow in hand.

The cellar door was screened from view of the backyard by an old stand of purple lilac bushes. Moving stealthily, Em could see Halloran had managed to lure the assailant away from the girls and down towards the bottom of the field, closer to her. The man's back was now towards her. He held his gun in his right hand, ready to use it. Halloran endeavored to convince him he was Kirbee's silent partner, and that he was the one who had the thumb drive with the specs for Version 5 of SunSprite, just not with him.

He's stalling. Good time to end this parley, she said to herself.

Loading the arrow onto the bow string, Em squared her stance and calculated for wind drift. The leaves of the trees were not moving. She gauged the pull needed to send the arrow straight to its target without ripping through it. The distance to her target was not great. She sighted her aim, took a deep steadying breath, held it, and let the feathers fly.

Halloran saw the arrow fly straight into the back of the man in front of him. It landed with a solid sound in his right shoulder. The assailant cried out in astonishment, there had been no gun shot. Whipping another arrow out of the quiver, over her shoulder and onto the bow string, Em reloaded her bow as quickly as she could. She stepped out from behind the lilac bushes to get a better angle for her next shot.

"Drop it!" she commanded.

The man with the arrow sticking in his back foolishly turned towards her. As soon as he presented a full frontal view, she let the next shot go. It struck him in the pec muscle at the top of his right arm. The man staggered and groaned.

"Drop it!" Em growled.

"You're a bad shot, bitch!" The man was still defiant.

"Try her!" Halloran stared at Em as she readied another arrow on her bow. "Keep talking jackass and you'll bleed to death!"

"You're done, bitch…" The man never finished. She used her third arrow to strike him in his thigh. As she did so, her peripheral vision caught Halloran's shift of balance. In one sweeping move he came up, pointing a small gun between the eyes of the assailant.

"Now drop it or I will shoot you. Federal officer. You are under arrest."

"Mother Fucker! You said you were unarmed," the man protested.

"I lied," was the reply.

Em reloaded her bow and was picking her next target.

"I've got this. Lower your bow."

That was not happening.

"Miranda, put the bow down now. I've got this." Halloran ordered her to stop. "He's no good to us dead."

"He hit my daughter. Just one more. In the foot, no one would notice," hissed Em. In the distance sirens could be heard approaching. "I called the cops and an ambulance. I said we'd need both. He's lucky I didn't call for a hearse. I told them someone was going to get hurt *very badly.*" She glared at the man she'd shot full of arrows.

A fleet car screeched to a halt on the cobblestone pavement. Car doors flung open.

"We're in the backyard," Halloran said into his collar.

Rankel and Vargas raced into the yard with Rankel in the lead. After rounding the corner he stopped so short Vargas careened into him.

"What the hell. It's a frickin' porcupine." Rankel took one look at Em with the bow and arrow in her hands and said, "Nice going, lady."

"My first moving target," she replied with pride.

Em turned towards them and let the arrow slide off the bowstring. A loaded bow, after all, could be a dangerous thing. Her next concern was for her daughter and Sandy. Up the yard, the two Adirondack chairs stood empty with streamers of duct tape hanging from their arms and front legs. Em looked back quickly at Halloran in alarm.

"Anson," he said. "I had Anson come around the other way, over the hill. He's taken them into the house."

Behind them a window was flung open. "We're here. We're safe, but Deanna's still bleeding," Sandy's voice exclaimed. Em was ready to put down her bow to run for the house.

"Anson!" Halloran barked.

"She's okay boss. A couple teeth went through her cheek. Maybe a mild concussion. Needs a doctor. I'm putting ice on it now to stop the bleeding. We'll be in the kitchen."

ANSON TO THE RESCUE

HALLORAN AND ANSON HAD COME off the Interstate not so very long after Em's van. They did indeed fly low, and if they had not been driving a car with government plates, the State Police car they passed would have given chase. Anson, unfamiliar with the twisting back road, nearly passed the black car that was pulled off to the side. However, Andy was now on their shared communications channel and gave them a description of the location along the road where he found traces of the getaway car during the Rent Party. It was at the head of the path through the woods. Down the road approaching the Spring House they spotted Em's van in an unusual place on the wrong side of the road. Anson pulled in behind it. Halloran headed for the front of the house. He directed Anson to go over the edge of the road through the undergrowth and the woods to reach the backyard.

Anson had doubts, but he decided to get through the underbrush and through the woods above the Spring House if he had to crawl all the way to do it. *Wouldn't be the first time*, he thought. With more stumbles than he cared to count, Anson made it up the incline. He discovered he could pull himself along using the tree branches around him. Using crutches and training in a racing wheelchair, he'd developed his considerable upper body strength still further. As he came closer to the backyard, his instincts kicked in. Crouching low among the trees above the rock garden, he was reconnoitering the lay of the land when he saw Em Huber run up the stone steps into the house. A position farther along the ridge brought him a good view of the lawn. He could see the girls taped into the heavy wooden chairs. Every muscle in his body tensed, it took an effort of will not to charge down the hill. It was a back-yard, not a battlefield.

Anson got himself into a concealed position as close as he could to the chairs while staying in back of them. Then, he watched patiently as Halloran negotiated the man away from Deanna and Sandy down towards the bottom of the yard. As soon as he judged the man to be far enough away, he made a stealthy approach, coming up behind the chairs. Army knife ready, he slit the duct tape binding Sandy's arms and legs. It was a stretch for him as he tried to stay out of sight behind her chair.

"Go quickly, make for the house," he whispered to Sandy, who pulled the duct tape off her mouth.

"Deanna," she said. "He hit her very hard!"

"I'll bring her. Go!" Seeing that Sandy made it to the shelter of the garden, Anson slit the duct tape holding Deanna's wrists and ankles. Creeping around to her, he murmured, "Deanna, it's Dave. Can you move?"

Deanna opened her eyes, took one look at Anson, lurched forward, turned her head away from him, and threw up a mouthful of blood onto the lawn. As she sat up, Anson, who was kneeling beside her, reached out. He held her face in hands almost the size of a lion's paws and looked earnestly into her eyes. "Deanna, look at me, straight."

Deanna looked at him. With a tear running from one eye, she nodded and rose from the chair. Next to her Anson hoisted himself up from his kneeling position on the ground using the chair for balance. She wrapped her arms around him. Together they turned to shuffle as fast as they could towards the rock garden and into the house. A man cried out. Down the yard he could see his boss react with surprise. What looked like an arrow stuck out of the other man's back. With no time to waste, Anson hurried Deanna into the garden and then into the house. Sandy locked the door behind them.

"Let's get her into the kitchen. We can put ice on the side of her face." Sandy supported Deanna on the other side.

"Have to spit," Deanna gurgled as she spoke and moved quickly to the kitchen sink.

"Looks like you could use some ice on that eye, too, Sandy," Anson remarked. He was limping on one leg, having slammed the knee down too hard in his quest to reach the backyard through the woods. Deanna sat in the middle of the kitchen while he washed his hands thoroughly to get the dirt and the blood off of them. In the refrigerator Anson found two bags of frozen peas. Quickly wrapping the bags of freshly frozen veggies in the mouse brown recycled paper towels Em favored, he gave one to Sandy who promptly held it to her face.

Still holding the cold peas to her eye, Sandy dug into a kitchen cabinet and pulled out a steel bowl. She handed it, without comment, to her friend Deanna. After Deanna gave one great spit, Anson encouraged her to open her mouth wide so he could assess her injury. Holding her face gently in his hands he moved her head so he could examine the gash inside. It was apparent to him that several teeth had been slammed into her cheek by the force of a blow. The gash appeared to be long enough and deep enough to need a few stitches.

The windows in the kitchen were open. They heard Em yelling and then Halloran. Suddenly more alert, Deanna came up out of the chair. "Mother!" she burbled. Anson and Sandy headed to the living room to get a better view with Deanna following, cold pack of peas held to her face and a bowl in her hand. They heard the sounds of a car stopping short in front of the house, car doors slamming and feet running by the house. They made it down to a window at the far end of the house overlooking the bottom of the yard. From the window they saw the backyard intruder with arrows sticking out of him, his hands up and Halloran's gun in his ribs.

"He got my mother really *pithed*," Deanna said and spat into her bowl.

"She was our camp archery instructor," Sandy chipped in. "Serves him right."

Anson unlocked the window, took a firm hand to it, and the bottom of the window flew up with a sharp rapport.

———◆———

LOCAL HISTORY LESSON

————————

G UNS DRAWN AND READY, VARGAS and Rankel advanced on the man now under arrest. Vargas pulled a pair of standard metal hand cuffs out of his back pocket. Rankel removed the gun from the man's right hand.

"How are we going to get cuffs on this guy without ripping out one of these arrows? You hunt with these, ma'am?" Vargas asked Em.

"Don't try it, you might rip through a vein. We can't have him bleeding out on the lawn here. We have lots of questions." Halloran was solicitous of his newly captured prisoner, who gripped his injured shoulder with his left hand. The man blanched, shaken, his color went to a grey pallor. Interrogation seemed to hold particular terrors for him.

Em returned the arrow she still held in her hand to the quiver and slipped it off her shoulder.

An ambulance and one police car roared up the road. Sirens wailing, a second police car came over the hill. Halloran walked to Em, who was staring daggers at the man who assaulted her daughters.

"You are Swiss, right?" he asked.

"Oh yes, they gave me my first bow with suction cup arrows when I was little and they kept on giving me better ones as I got older. I shot in college. People want me to be related to William Tell. I'm not that I know of, and I'm not good enough to shoot an apple off my daughter's head. He hit Deanna so hard she was bleeding." Em had pain and anger in her voice.

"She'll recover, maybe with some help. There are counselors for victims of violent crimes."

"My fault," Em choked. "I should have figured this out sooner."

"Don't do this to yourself. You figured it out fast enough. We were here in time. That's the important thing. I'll go talk to the police. Can you give a statement?"

Em nodded.

"Keep it brief. I'll be with you. Okay?"

"Please don't call me Miranda when anyone else can hear you."

"Not fond of Miranda Elice are you, M.E.?" Halloran smiled at her.

Em looked up at Halloran with a sorrowful stare. "They called me Miranda Panda when I was a kid. It's our distress word."

"Alright, I won't, I promise. Thank you for not damaging my suspect too badly. I'm going to explain it to the locals." Halloran sauntered off to collect his cane and jacket from the grass where he had thrown them on his way into the yard.

"Good," Em said to his departing back. She watched as Halloran intercepted two police officers heading towards them.

Officers Flaherty and Carmen De Galves regarded the field agents guarding the prisoner with suspicion. Their own detectives were engaged in a drug issue. With federal officers on scene, the detectives opted to wrap up their own case first. Both she and Flaherty were set on doing their best in the initial work of the investigation.

The paramedics advanced, hauling their stretcher along the side of the house across the most even ground, one a stocky man approaching six feet and another man, shorter, who acted as if in charge.

"What are we supposed to do with this guy?" the lead paramedic asked Vargas.

"He's in custody for..."

"We know that. I mean with the arrows sticking out of him at three different angles. We can't lie him down on the stretcher."

"He shouldn't walk with that one in his thigh," said the other paramedic in the "You dummy" tone.

"Come on back to the bus, we'll need more supplies. I'm going to call in for instructions." The lead paramedic obviously wanted more privacy to consult with the hospital doctors. The paramedics left the stretcher and headed back to the ambulance.

Seeing her opportunity, Em walked over to speak in a barely audible voice to her former target.

"You hit my daughter. People are sensitive about family in this town. Harming family, hurting the girls fits that category. People who do? Well, cement doesn't float, does it?"

The man began to rumble. Em gave him a swift kick. A stream of crude and unimaginative profanity came out of his mouth, making Em take a step backwards.

"Whadd'ya say to upset this nice man?" Rankel asked Em.

"Just gave him some helpful advice," said Em through clenched teeth.

"I'll bet," commented Rankel, who looked with satisfaction at their prisoner.

Officer Carmen De Galves approached the man suspected of assault and battery with determined strides. "Like to hit young women, do you? Judges here take issues with that. So do lots of other people. You are likely to find your hearing well attended." To the returning paramedics she snapped, "Where have you been, why aren't you ready to go?"

"Complicated case, needed more supplies," they answered. They were carrying their usual large bags but also pillows and rolled blankets. With deliberate speed they examined their recalcitrant patient, who continued swearing under his breath. Good patients got better care, and this man was obviously not one of those. He complained every time they tried to move or touch him.

Crime scenes were always tough work for paramedics.

They had to collect samples of the blood they found on his hands and spewed on his jacket or risk being reprimanded for damaging evidence. They finally cut off his jacket and bagged it for evidence. The arrows were taped in place so they would be less likely to shift in transit. When they tried to get the man's right arm into a sling they discovered his right side covered with bruises over the liver. He yelped so loudly as they tried to tape him up that everyone outside the house stopped talking. "That little bitch punched me," he bellowed.

"Good for her," commented Carmen De Galves to Flaherty. "I'm going to get a statement from the mother."

"Well, she cracked a rib or two for you," said the shorter paramedic.

The paramedics managed to get their patient onto the stretcher in a sitting position. A pillow was taped to his chest to protect the ribs from the weight of the right arm in the sling. Rolled blankets supported his back. Vargas contented himself with handcuffing the man's left wrist to the stretcher. He planned to escort the prisoner to the hospital in the ambulance and to stay with him until he was treated and in a secure situation. The paramedics made the less than smooth trip across the lawn with the stretcher. Their patient bellowed and complained at even the slightest bump. "My ribs, my ribs, be careful!"

"Big baby," Em remarked quietly to Officer De Galves.

"People who hurt others, who abuse others often are. Please tell me what happened here. We will need a brief statement from you now. We can get more later if we need it. Can we also see your daughters?"

Halloran walked up to stand beside Em, carrying his cane and jacket. "Officer De Galves, good to meet you. You might give Ms. Huber a few minutes. It's been a long day for her."

"So you've said." Carmen De Galves was not unsympathetic but business-like, in pre-promotion to detective mode.

Flaherty had been interviewing Andy Vargas, concerning their ongoing investigation.

"I have an agent with Deanna Huber and Allesandra Waitely. He says both could benefit from medical attention as soon as possible. Deanna Huber may have difficulty speaking right now due to her injuries. You will need photographs of their injuries and medical reports. We can provide those," Halloran stated.

Em gave a very brief, highly edited version of the events since she reached home. She made sure to tell the officer she witnessed the man strike her daughter while Deanna was taped to the lawn chair. She said she called the police first, and then found the man holding a gun on a federal agent. Halloran confirmed this and added that Em's proficient archery distracted his opponent long enough for him to go for his gun. This seemed to satisfy Office De Galves, who now needed to see Deanna and Sandy for herself.

"I should go into the house. I haven't seen the girls yet," Em argued.

"We'll all go. Officer De Galves, come with us. Ms. Huber, can you show the officer where you found the girls?"

"Rankel, get your camera. We'll need pictures. No art shots. We need to be able to tell which side is up this time. So will a jury," Halloran admonished his star photographer.

Rankel slumped off to the fleet car in front of the house, considering how he could best do both effective evidence capture shots and more arresting photos. The Adirondack chairs had distinct possibilities.

Em, Halloran and Officer De Galves walked around the house, through the backyard towards the wooden chairs that still retained duct tape. Em noticed blood stains on the arms of the chair where Deanna had been restrained. Her eyes teared up, and Halloran moved in to stand closer to her. With an effort, she calmed her racing thoughts to tell them where she had been standing and pointed to the corner of the house and the path into the rock garden. They followed her up the stone steps where she tried the door. Finding it locked, she reached into her pocket for the house keys.

Outside, Rankel took pictures of the lawn chairs from various angles, including the blood spots. With a quick, sure eye for composition he included some angles that his boss wouldn't recognize, for good measure. With a casual salute to Flaherty, who stood by the chairs eyeing him dubiously, Rankel followed the others towards the house. There, he joined the group as Em unlocked the door to the living room.

In the kitchen they found Anson holding the cold packet to Deanna's face. Sandy removed her pack of frozen peas, revealing a fast darkening and swelling eye. Extra Large plastic evidence gloves from Anson's pockets covered the girl's hands in hopes of preserving evidence of their defensive injuries.

Em and Deanna looked at each other and Em moved swiftly to hug her daughter and reached out an arm for Sandy. The three Spring House women hugged each other for what seemed like an age. When Em finally looked up from the family hug, she found Halloran's eyes on her. She looked back at him with tears, and he nodded to her.

"We should have them seen to by a doctor and have evidence collected as soon as possible, sir, ma'am." The look exchanged between his boss and Deanna's mother hadn't escaped Anson's notice. "Mild concussion and a torn cheek on Deanna. Black eye and bruising on Sandy. They said Sandy scratched him. Deanna landed a solid punch on that guy's ribs and gave him a nasty kick in the shin," he said with poorly concealed relish.

"Dave, Agent Anson, cut us loose." Deanna had a hard time forming her words.

"Would you like to see their hands before we go? Would

you have a marker or tape and a pen?" Anson asked Em. She went to a drawer in the kitchen to fish out an indelible black marker. Anson instructed Deanna and Sandy how to remove the disposable gloves without touching the inside. He then wrote their names and "left" or "right" on each glove.

"The perp was complaining about his ribs. I think I heard the paramedics say you cracked at least two of them. Good job ladies. Let's see the hands," Carmen De Galves agreed. Rankel was playing paparazzi, shooting pictures of Deanna's face, annoying the officer. When he crossed the kitchen to take pictures of Sandy's black eye, she pulled up her sleeves to reveal bruises that showed the prints of large hands on her arms. Em sucked in her breath at the sight, covering her mouth with her hand. Calmly, carefully, Officer De Galves examined their hands as Rankel took pictures for documentation. The girls were asked to put their gloves back on, correct hands, please.

Rankel continued to take pictures of the group until Halloran said, "Outside. Garden. Backyard. Side of the house. Get up the road to the car parked in the brush with the New York plates. Call Leroy for pickup."

This was the first Officer De Galves heard about the getaway car, and she used her radio to order an officer to accompany Rankel to find it. "I'm needed outside. The young ladies can go for medical treatment. We will need to get statements from them soon. They say there's a cat howling in a tan car up the road."

"Anson get the car, bring in the cat and her stuff," Halloran said. He was well pleased to leave Cleome at the Spring House.

34

SMITTY —
DOCTOR'S EVENING OUT

———◆———

A S SOON AS OFFICER CARMEN De Galves closed the living room door, Halloran continued his instructions to Anson.

"Contact Garvey, have him notify the Doc he's needed. We have three patients coming in. Has Gladys run through the procedure with you? So you understand what I'm talking about?"

Anson nodded in the affirmative.

Halloran turned to Em. "We're going to see that these two get the medical attention they need. We'll have evidence collected and get medical reports. You wouldn't want them to sit in the Emergency Room for hours would you? Neither would we. I've instructed Anson to arrange for our own doctor to see them in his office. He works with us on a regular basis and is up to speed with our procedures and paperwork. Name is Smithers."

"Dr. Smithers, I never heard of him." Em was dubious.

"Actually you have heard of him. His name is Dr. Roland Smithers Williamson, III. We call him Smitty. He specializes in trauma medicine. Patches up the staff when they need it. He says it's restful for him."

"Including you?" Em asked him quietly.

"Yes. Okay with you?"

That answer was good enough for Em. "I'll go with them," she said.

"No, best you stay here to answer questions so they don't have to do it. Officer De Galves went light. We can expect at least one detective to follow up. They will be fine with Anson, who should get his knee seen, too." He pointed to Anson's right knee. "That's an order Agent Anson. I want three reports."

Deanna looked up from under her bag of defrosting peas. She hadn't realized Anson was limping as he brought her into the house, but his boss Halloran had seen it.

"It will be fine, I bumped it," Anson replied. He took one look at Halloran' serious face and said, "Right. Three reports."

"I have to go change before we go. I got kind of damp." Sandy was embarrassed.

"He didn't touch you, did he?" Em said in a sharp voice.

"No, I just peed my pants," Sandy admitted. Deanna stifled a giggle. The effects of a successful chokehold were known to both of them. After seven seconds without air, the person in the hold loses consciousness and things let go on their own.

"We'll need those for evidence," said Halloran in an even tone of voice.

"I'll go get you clean clothes. You can change in the bathroom down here. Do we need Deanna's shirt, too?"

"All clothes would be best. The car Anson," Halloran directed.

Em returned with complete sets of clean clothes for both girls. While they were changing, she collected the bags of now almost defrosted peas and filled three plastic bags with ice. She handed one to Anson for his knee, who took it with some reluctance since he was on his way out to get the car.

While Em put the kettle on for tea, Halloran sat down at the kitchen table and talked into his collar. He was talking to Leroy who had been working late on the blue Mercedes. He gave Leroy directions and cautions about the road on the hill to the east of the Spring House where what turned out to be a rental car was partially hidden. Leroy and his assistant were ready to roll out their truck within a few minutes of the call.

Deanna and Sandy presented Em with plastic bags of clothing to be examined for evidence. Em looked into one of the bags. "Deanna where is your belt?"

"It's my favorite," her daughter protested.

"Go get it," her mother ordered, and the belt joined the rest of Deanna's clothing for the duration.

Anson brought the car down the hill and turned smartly onto the cobblestone pavement in front of the Spring House. The car was now equipped with hand controls and a few other adaptive devices, but not yet all. Anson could practice balancing the bag of ice on his sore knee. Em Huber was proven right, the ice did seem to help.

Deanna and Sandy came out of the Spring House together, Deanna with a pillow tucked under her arm. Anson opened the back doors of the car with the touch of a button. The doors didn't open very far yet. The mechanism was still in development. Leroy had more success getting the doors to snap closed. No one knew why. Anson closed the doors to the surprise of the girls. He welcomed them to his new staff car, promising them a speedy and comfortable ride. He pulled out onto the road smoothly and drove back up the hill heading down the twisting country road towards the highway.

"What kind of car is this?" asked Sandy.

"Mr. Halloran instructed me to equip a car so that anyone on the staff could drive it. I took that to mean especially both of us. When I thought about it, I realized we could both use more assistance than hand controlled brakes and gas. He injured his right leg. He uses a cane on that side, although he should use the cane on the left side. But he's also right handed, and that means he would have to take the cane out of his right hand to open the car doors." Anson had not yet realized Halloran was ambidextrous, a useful asset the older man concealed.

"The car windows operate with small motors already. The doors lock automatically with a touch switch. Why not open and close the doors with a button, too? Watch the button on the doors, by the way, they're not all working yet."

"We're gradually building in other things for security and usability. There are grab bars on all the doors, on the back of the seats in front of you and over the doors. If you look at the back seat between you, you will find that a section in the center pulls down to become an armrest. It has cup holders so that both passengers in the backseat can choose which side to put their beverage, door side or center. It also contains two flat shelves that swivel out for reading, writing or computing." Anson didn't mention what else could be contained in the console for emergencies.

Deanna pulled the center section of the backseat down, rested her arm on it, put her pillow behind her head and closed her eyes. She murmured, "Tell me when we get there," and promptly fell asleep.

It was a short drive. Anson was not especially rushed, so it took them only half the time Em usually required to go into the city. The doctor's office was a block or two from their own office. Anson knew the layout because his employment physical had been conducted there. He guided the car into the driveway, down and around to the back of the building to the sunken parking lot. It crossed Anson's mind to wonder why anyone would create a below ground level parking lot so close to the sea. There must be some reason, unless it was meant to be something other than a parking lot at some time.

Anson parked in one of the spots designated for handicapped use and hung the state issued handicapped parking pass on the mirror in the front window. He was not about to walk the girls too far that evening. Halloran and Anson were both entitled to the use of the handicapped spot and agreed to use it only when absolutely necessary. To them, others with more serious health or mobility issues might need the spots more than they did. Halloran had been known to threaten arrest to a young and able man accompanied by a young blonde woman, who parked his red convertible in a handicapped spot to access his favorite ATM. Being approached by armed federal officers did make an impression on the convertible driver.

Anson woke Deanna and helped Sandy out of the car. Sandy had been pulled about in the struggle with the intruder in the backyard. She ached across her shoulders and down her lower back. Deanna, the more physically active of the two girls, stood up, stretched and was ready to march off into the doctor's office after her cat nap in the car. A ramp led up towards the door of the office building. At the top Anson flipped open a metal cover to reveal a key pad. He typed a code on the keypad, and the metal door opened for them. Anson and the girls crowded into a small vestibule and the outside door closed behind them with a soft click. Anson pressed a button on the wall that Deanna and Sandy took to be a door bell, but wasn't. They felt the air change around them, they assumed it was air conditioning. A light flashed on a second key pad, Anson entered another code and the glass door on the inside slid open.

"Fancy security," said Deanna, a comment Anson chose to ignore. He led them down a white hallway where they were greeted by a man of middle age, moderate height and build in a white coat that seemed too long for him.

"Agent Anson, good to see you again. This must be Ms.

Huber and Ms. Waitely. I'm Dr. Williamson, you can call me Smitty. Everyone in your organization does."

"Smitty, sir, really?" asked Anson.

"Yes, my first name is Roland. I don't know what my parents had in mind for me. When my younger brother called me Rollie I had to beat the shit out of him to get him to stop."

The girls laughed. Smitty was so composed in his tone of voice they could not picture him raising his hand to anyone.

Smitty guided his patients into a large room that seemed to be a multifunction medical suite. A dental chair inhabited the corner by the door. A long flat table was in the center. A hospital bed was pushed in against the far wall. Two of the usual narrow examining tables, one with stirrups, were towards the center. The girls did not like the look of the one with stirrups. What suspiciously looked like a shower stall without curtains was evident in one far corner. Several chairs with various supports for arms and legs lined up against the inside wall. Two sinks were right up by the door. Cabinets and counters ran down the inner wall next to the sinks.

"Sorry, no nurse yet. Sal is still in the ER. Had a bad accident out on the highway and a couple gunshot wounds tonight. Of course there were the two guys who had a knife fight. Last time I passed by them they were handcuffed to stretchers next to each other talking about whether the woman they fought over was worth it anyway. Why didn't they do that before they got out the knives? The police were asking them the same thing."

"So you will have to help out. Anson, any evidence to collect off of you? No? Good. Go scrub up to your elbows, count to thirty while you're washing. Put gloves on. They're on the counter. Ladies, you can sit down on those two examining tables. Your choice which one. Anyone have any allergies to medication? No? Good!" Deanna was faster on her feet than Sandy and got to the examining table without the stirrups first.

With practiced hands the doctor put together two separate metal trays of implements, sterile supplies and evidence bags. He took a clipboard with evidence log sheets that stood ready on the counter and handed it to Anson. "You're going to label and list the evidence for me, Anson. Then we will both sign the sheet when we're done."

"Ms. Waitely, Sandy is it? I understand you scratched your assailant. We're going to do your hands first. Ms. Huber, Deanna, you look like you could use another cold pack, am I right?" Smitty walked to a small refrigerator to retrieve three pre-made ice packs filled with sterile crushed ice. He gave one to each of them. "We use many of these. Water the flowers out front with them later." He was determined to be cheerful.

After slipping off the oversized disposable gloves that covered Sandy's hands, he examined them thoroughly. Using an assault kit and a selection of specialized tools, most looking like various dental picks, the doctor removed the debris, blood and skin, from beneath Sandy's fingernails. Smitty clipped the tip of the nails as evidence, too. He bagged his samples and told Anson what to write on each small plastic envelope. Then the doctor painstakingly cleaned Sandy's hands.

"I'll have to snip this fingernail down further, it's ripped to the quick. There we go. Okay, let's take a look at the bruises." He rotated Sandy's wrists back and forth slowly. "Any pain? No? Good." Next Smitty took a swab and some sterile water and wiped it gently across Sandy's cheek bone under her darkening black eye. "You will have quite a shiner, Sandy." He examined her eyes and found no damage.

"Very good! Defensive wounds on hands and arms. Anything else I should be aware of? Are you sure?" He looked pointedly at Sandy. She voiced a firm negative. "Good. Do you know how to scrub up? Go scrub your arms all the way up as far as you can get. Go use the sink and the soap. Do your face, too. Then use the hand sanitizer liberally all the way up to your elbows. After that we'll see if we need to bandage anything for you. I'm sure if Sal were here you'd get the benefit of more personal service, and he'd enjoy doing it too." After washing up as directed, Sandy took up her ice pack and settled down for a rest.

"Anson, pack up the evidence bags. Put them in that container by the door to go to the lab." The doctor proceeded to strip off his gloves and to wash up again. "New pair of gloves and a wash for you too, Anson. Keep those gloves clean, my man. Don't touch your nose or your toes!"

Taking the second tray he had prepared over to Deanna, Smitty instructed her to remove the disposable gloves herself without touching the insides. Taking Deanna's hands in his own, he examined her palms and her fingers. "Defensive wounds but nothing under the fingernails. You punched him right? No scratches." Deanna noticed his hands were small but strong. To be thorough, he dug under her nails with his tools but found nothing. "Nice and clean, good girl!" He cleaned her hands and bandaged her knuckles. Smitty pulled up her sleeves and looked at her elbows. "Light bruising, no abrasions. Long sleeves have their uses."

Smitty looked at Deanna's eyes through an instrument, an ophthalmoscope, and used another, an otoscope, to look into her ears. "Mild concussion. You will need to rest and to take it easy for the next week or so. No more fist fights for you. Repeated concussions are bad. Good. The eyes themselves are fine, although both of you will look like you tangled with a very nasty man for awhile. Now, Deanna, open up, let's look inside here. Anson, what did you see right after the event?"

"Long gash inside her right cheek. Three or four teeth long." Anson looked at Deanna's face earnestly.

"It's still bleeding, isn't it? Alright, let's get you cleaned up to repair that laceration."

Deanna yelped.

"Oh, come on now, you took on a full grown man, gave him two cracked ribs, a bruised liver, a dent in his shin, and you're worried about a couple of little stitches that no one will ever see? Please." Smitty chuckled and fussed with the instruments on his tray then changed gloves yet again.

"I cracked his ribs?" Deanna asked with surprise in her voice.

"That's what we all heard in the ER. He was bellowing about it all the way into the hospital. The paramedics basically dropped him off and ran." Smitty talked as he cleaned Deanna's face, swabbing it first for evidence. "We're going to move you over to this adjustable chair over here."

Deanna moved reluctantly to the dentist chair. She was not a fan of visits to the dentist, having spent years in orthodontia of an extensive kind.

"Alright Anson, you are going to be scrub nurse."

The doctor prepared his tray with topical anesthetic, needles, suture material, syringes and small bottles. He opened a cabinet close to the dental chair to find a hunk of rubber sealed in a plastic bag, which he ripped open. He gave Deanna antiseptic mouth wash, told her to rinse and spit into a kidney-shaped plastic bowl. Smitty asked her to open her mouth and carefully placed the rubber bite block between the teeth on the left side of her mouth then told her to bite down.

"Comfortable? Good. Hold it there while I do the exam and the laceration repair. We'll numb your cheek so you will feel only pressure. Okay?"

Deanna gurgled in response.

"Good. Let's begin. I like this part. I have small hands, always regretted it until it comes to small spaces like this." Working quickly he numbed the area with topical anesthetic, and then a shot and he took four small stitches. "These will dissolve on their own. It may feel lumpy. That will go down. I'll give you some mouth wash to use twice a day, and you should use salt and warm water after every meal please. We should take a look at this in four or five days.

"I should give you the standard lecture, although you must know it by heart. Nice dental work by the way. Someone did some very nice work in there for you. My kids had terrible overbites. Maybe I should say terribly expensive overbites. Don't chew until the anesthetic wears off. Nothing hot to drink either. If you have pain, swelling, fever or nasty tasting discharge, call right away. Anson will give you the number."

Smitty stripped off his gloves to wash up again. Deanna noticed his white coat remained pristine throughout his work while she on the other hand managed to spatter on her sleeves.

"Anson, you're next. Sit up on that table over there," Smitty said, directing him to the long table in the middle of the room. "Roll up your pants!"

"But Doc…" Anson protested.

"I was told to make three reports. And we're going to do that." Smitty was firm. Recalcitrant, reluctant or downright ornery patients were nothing new to the trauma surgeon.

"They're here," Anson said in a low voice.

"Oh come on, we won't look if you don't want us to," said Sandy.

"You've already seen my tonsils for cripes sake," Deanna said in a muffled voice.

That did it for Anson. He climbed up to sit on the table without another word. "You walked in here on your own, so you're not badly injured, right?"

"Right, sir."

"Then roll up your pants above the knees before I do." Smitty was tempted to say, "That's an order," but helping transition Anson to civilian life as a federal agent was part of his brief from Halloran.

Anson dutifully rolled up his pants to show the swollen knee and his prostheses, lower legs and feet. One shin was shorter than the other, making it easier to injure one knee.

Sandy kept her promise not to look at Anson, but Deanna managed to sneak a look around the doctor as he examined first one of Anson's knees and then the other.

"Humph. Swelling from compression. Keep the ice on it, I'll get you a good knee brace for it." Smitty examined Anson's legs and feet. "No damage here. VA standard issue. Not bad but not the best for your current occupation. Now that you've had a qualifying injury in the line of duty, Halloran can sign for a more athletic pair of feet for you. Good job in the field by the way. I have a friend in Boston who can do a custom set for you."

"Extra strength analgesics for everyone. Tetanus shots for the ladies."

Deanna and Sandy moaned at the mention of shots, which were quickly done.

"Well, we're done. Feel better! Nice to meet you ladies, I'll see you again in a few days. You, too, Anson. They will need you to get in here."

"This place is like some sort of a fortress," Deanna remarked.

"I like to think of it more as a shelter. Very good. We're finished in time for me to make the curtain at the Yale Rep. We have season tickets." Smitty beamed at them.

35

TELLING THE TALE

———•———

S HORTLY AFTER ANSON SPED AWAY from the
Spring House with his passengers hanging on in the
back seat, Em sipped her mint tea in the kitchen. Halloran
made himself right at home at the kitchen table and was
talking with his office. He was typing into a handheld
device retrieved from the car before its flight into New
Haven. As usual he enjoined Anson not to exceed speed
limits, a thoroughly thankless task. Cleome explored the
house with apparent delight at the presence of several
flavors of mouse.

Em stepped to the refrigerator and pulled out dinner. A
casserole of mashed potatoes with fresh chives received a
sprinkling of paprika. The ceramic baking dish of lemon
pepper and rosemary chicken came out to warm up on
the counter. To Halloran's amusement, Em opened the two
melting bags of fresh peas and poured them into a pot with
some water and left them on the stove ready to cook.

"How long do you think it will take them to get back
from the doctor's office?" Em asked the man who she supposed was paying no attention to her.

"About two hours, maybe less," Halloran said without
looking up from his screen.

"They are going to be hungry when they get home. They left without so much as a granola bar. Will you and Anson stay for dinner? You can get their statements after that."

Halloran stopped for a moment. It was unusual. But then they would be providing security until Vargas and Rankel came back on duty later in the evening, and he said so with thanks.

Em was visibly tired and her energy fading. She reached up into the kitchen cabinet, got down the plates, added the silverware for five and placed the stack on the dining table at one end of the living room. She looked longingly at the couch. Halloran was typing away, and she let him know she was going to sit down to rest for a few minutes.

When half an hour passed without so much as a sound from the living room, Halloran went in search of Em. He only needed to look at the couch. She was fast asleep, feet on a hassock, wrapped in a lacy shawl, holding a square throw pillow in her arms as if she'd fallen asleep within a heartbeat of sitting down.

Okay, tough girl! Halloran thought, *I can heat up dinner. I'm good at that.* He went back to work at the kitchen table and in good time, put dinner in the oven. Halloran himself was getting peckish, and when he spotted the loaf of bread ready for slicing on the bread board, he gave in to temptation. He hacked himself a thick slice and went hunting in the refrigerator for butter. He found a small crock of fresh butter from Em's friends up the road and made free with it. On the refrigerator door he found a neat line up of bottles of locally made soda, and three bottles of Sam Adams. After he put dinner in the oven, one of the bottles of Sam Adams made its disappearance from the fridge.

Em awoke on the couch in exactly the position she had been in over an hour before. She woke to the smell of chicken in the oven and immediately assumed Deanna and Sandy were back from the doctor's office. Wrapped in her shawl, she wandered into the kitchen to find Halloran still at work on her kitchen table. "Where are the girls and Anson?" she asked as the house was very quiet. She spotted a beer bottle almost empty in front of her guest.

"Anson called. They're in the car on the way back now. I put dinner in the oven."

"And found the Sam Adams, it's my son's," she said in an amused voice.

"I owe him one then." Halloran looked up from his work.

"We owe you more than a beer, thank you. I should thank Anson, too."

"That would be appreciated. Rescuing young ladies in distress may be just what he needs, after his 'Dear John' letter. Your daughter got him out of that wheelchair, now he comes to work without it. He has a way to go yet, but he has a hell of a lot of potential. That's why I hired him. Drives too damned fast though."

"The tires squealing out front must be them then," remarked Em dryly.

———◆———

Five sat down to the supper Em made in the morning and Halloran put in the oven. Deanna's cheek was swollen and still numb, but she was close to famished. She sat gumming her peas and mashed potatoes. Lemon pepper rosemary chicken would have to wait for a little while until the anesthetic wore off.

"Now tell us how this happened," Em asked Deanna and Sandy as she passed the casserole of mashed potatoes to an appreciative Anson. He mounded potatoes on his plate. Home cooking was on his list of things he missed most about leaving Maine.

"Swamp Thing's fault. Can't talk." Deanna's speech was still garbled. "You tell it, Sandy."

Sandy looked up, one eye was darkening further and not

fully open. Bruises from rough handling dotted her arm in the pattern of large hands, they would be truly ugly by morning.

"Lucas, what does he have to do with this? Was he here?" There was an undertone of surprise and disapproval in Em's voice that the girls couldn't miss. "Sandy, tell us what happened, the guys here need to know."

With all eyes on her, Sandy set down her knife and fork, thus avoiding Deanna's tendency to wave cooking implements for emphasis.

"He called. I was in the living room. Deanna was in the kitchen raiding the refrigerator. The phone rang, she picks it up, and talks for a minute, and starts laughing."

Deanna chuckled derisively.

"She yells, 'Swamp Thing is on the phone for you. He says you're not answering your cell phone.'"

"I said, 'It's charging.' Deanna tells him that and then says he wants to know if I would like to go to the movies on Friday. She held the phone out in front of her and says really loud, 'I didn't know the *Creature from the Blue Lagoon* was playing.' She's impossible when she gets going." Deanna stifled a cough. "I told her to say that I would call him right back. Then she started to sing."

"Oh no, you didn't," groaned Em to Deanna who did her best to grin.

Sandy sang to the tune of the oldie "Wild Thing." "Swamp Thing, you make my heart wring, you make everything gooey. So I gave up and asked her if I could borrow her cell phone to call Luke. And, I walked out of the house without the Panic Button. I know I should have taken it with me, but I was mad at Dee."

"Why is this guy called Swamp Thing?" asked Anson, puzzled.

"He's the last guy who got my mother really mad. Came up out of the swamp down the hill all covered with mud." Deanna managed to get all of this said coherently.

"It's a long story," said Em to their two male guests.

Deanna shook her head, smiled and said, "All that mud!"

Em stifled an impish laugh. "It was pretty funny. So what happened next Sandy?"

"Well, I went outside to sit down and call *Lucas*." Sandy directed the last to Deanna, who snorted, a rather unlady-like noise.

"I finished my call with Lucas and was sitting in the lawn chair when a man grabbed me from behind. He wrenched the cell phone out of my hand and threw it into the garden. I tried self-defense moves but the chair got in the way. He got me in a choke hold from behind, I scratched his arm, but I panicked. I turned my head the wrong way and passed out. He was taping my legs to the chair when I came to, and when I tried to scream he slapped me and taped my mouth."

"Oh dear, I am so sorry!" Em's voice caught.

"Nuts, Mom," said Deanna. "I came out of the house then."

"He hid against the corner of the house where she couldn't see him and grabbed Dee as she came out of the garden into the yard."

"He swung a right at me!" Deanna demonstrated.

"But she ducked, she's good at that."

"I punched him in the ribs as hard as I could with my left and kicked him in the shin." Her left hand swung out over her plate, and Deanna paused for breath.

"He knocked her down and knocked the wind out of her. He slapped her once. I couldn't tell whether she was conscious or not, but she was only dazed. Then he hauled her into the chair and he taped her down too," Sandy continued.

"Did he do anything else? Did he touch either one of you?" There was a distinct female growl in Em's voice, and they could see fire in her eyes.

"No!" both girls said together.

"He kept asking Deanna questions. He said you had something he needed, and where was it? That he didn't want to have to search another house for it."

"What is it, Mom? What did he mean? Something from Professor Kirbee?" Deanna guessed.

"He did search Professor Kirbee's house in New Haven this afternoon." Em consciously left out the part about the incendiary devices and resolved to avoid the evening news on TV until the girls were in bed. She reckoned they had had enough of their own excitement for the day. "I don't have whatever it is he's looking for that I know of."

"Anyway, he threatened Dee, and when she told him he was an ugly stinking jackass of a man…"

Oh, where have I heard that before, thought Em.

"…he hit her again."

"That's when I spit blood all over him," pronounced Deanna.

To which Anson replied, "How far did it go?"

"Don't encourage her," Em said, sensing collusion between Anson and her daughter that included a contest with watermelon seeds.

"This is where I come in," Em took over. "I came out of the side door looking for the girls. From the corner of the house I saw him hit Deanna so hard. I was frantic. I tried to find a rock or anything I could use. I even tried to pull up our little hunk of the universe out there. But it wouldn't budge. There must be more of it underground."

"Mom, that's what meteorites do, they fall. Hard." Deanna's speech was becoming clearer. She looked with hungry eyes at the chicken pieces and made a quick jab at a plump chicken thigh impaling it with her fork.

"It wouldn't budge, so I ran back to the corner of the house. That's when I saw you." She indicated to Halloran. "Once I saw you, I knew you wouldn't have come alone, but I didn't see or hear anyone else."

This was a testament to Anson's capacity for stealth. He

was on the hill above her at the time.

"So, I decided to call the police for backup and an ambulance. When I found no one in the house, I remembered the bow and arrows in the cellar and you know the rest."

"What were the darts for?" asked Halloran, puzzled.

"I think of them as short range arrows," she replied. "Can I have my arrows back? They're very good, flew nice and straight."

"Mother!" exclaimed Deanna in shock.

"Well, maybe not," Em said sheepishly in response to the disapproving looks she received from around the table.

"Mom, question. If we screamed in the backyard would the security system have heard us?"

Halloran looked sharply at Em for an explanation.

"Uh, we'd have to ask Joshua. You see this system is sort of his experimental lab…" Em began.

"And we're the rats, too many mice already," chimed in Deanna.

"Some security systems listen for noises when they are active, some systems sense motion and some rely on broken contact between moving parts like windows and doors. Joshua's system does all of that and some more," Em explained

"Josh got a little creative with this one. He recorded our voices, laughing, talking, and singing, whatever. If we scream the system is programmed to analyze the sound and will call for help," Deanna emphasized the word scream, and delivered this ruefully.

"We were fooling around one time and we set it off," Sandy added.

"Fortunately, I could call to cancel it. They were having a shrieking contest."

"Say the secret word and win two hundred dollars." Deanna laughed.

Halloran was taking all this in. He knew the secret word already.

"Joshua is into acoustics, big time, comes from being a musician," Deanna ventured.

"What does he play?" asked Anson.

"Saax," Deanna attempted to reply while chewing her chicken.

"Yeah, that too." Sandy laughed.

"Josh always tinkered with things, as a kid he took all sorts of things apart. I guess that's how engineers start. It got out of hand when he was in high school. It got so bad we had to send him to MIT," said his mother with a grin.

"The old house was full of weird stuff of his. I wonder if he got it all out." Deanna happily bit into her second piece of chicken.

"I sure hope so, I keep waiting for a call from the new owner. 'My refrigerator is whistling Dixie. Can you make it stop?' Or something bizarre like that." Em shook her head.

"It wasn't Dixie, Mother, it was something else that it whistled when you opened it."

"On that note, I think it's time for dessert." Em got up from the table and headed into the kitchen. Dessert was fresh strawberries from the yard and fresh cream.

Fatigue set in, both physical and emotional. Long pauses and yawns invaded the conversation. Even strong tea and sweet dessert couldn't prolong the evening. The girls were badly in need of sleep to recuperate. Final questions were asked and the men prepared to leave. The night shift would be covered by Vargas and Rankel who would be checking in shortly. Vying to be the first to shower, Deanna and Sandy headed upstairs. The house was in lock down mode, so Em needed to tap in the security code to let the men leave without setting off the system. Anson paced directly to the car. Halloran lingered by the front door to speak to Em.

"We'll need a formal statement from you. Come into the office tomorrow, call first. You will probably have a detective with you for breakfast. I'm surprised we didn't see one this evening. Be sure to reset the system tonight. You need more than one remote unit. Each one of you should be carrying one. Keep all the outside lights on," Halloran admonished Em.

"It sets itself at dusk and does whatever else it needs." The presence of the federal government car probably served to ward off a visit from the local folks, but she didn't say it to Halloran.

"I'd like to talk to your son about that."

"I'll bet you would. Thank you again," she said softly.

"I owe him a beer." Halloran smiled at her in a way not often seen.

JOSHUA'S TOYS

EM STEPPED INTO THE LIVING room with a second cup of tea in hand and settled down on the couch, wrapped in her shawl and said aloud, "System electronic umbrella up!"

A digitized version of Joshua's voice issued from the panel mounted on the wall. "System confirming electronic jamming is activated."

"Mother! My cell phone isn't working!" came a howl from Deanna's bedroom.

"Go to sleep. I'm calling your brother," Em yelled back.

"System page Joshua Allen. Call on wireline. Miranda Elice."

"System paging sys admin Joshua Allen Huber," the panel replied at the sound of its mistress's voice.

Within a very few minutes the wire line phone rang. "Joshua, it's your mother," she said although the system would have identified her in its page.

"Hi, Mom. What's up?"

"We had a little trouble in the backyard this afternoon." Em took a deep breath and as succinctly as she could, she gave Joshua the blow by blow of the assault on Deanna and Sandy. "So they were wondering if the system could hear them scream in the backyard. I know in the past you said it was a problem with the rabbits. Also, it's been suggested that one panic button is not enough, that we should each have our own. The federal agent in charge of the case told me to ask you if you could enhance the system some now because of our issues here."

Joshua knew his mother well enough to know he had not yet heard the full story. He prompted, and he questioned, and cross-questioned until he felt a degree of confidence he understood the situation well enough. He could then devise some new bells and whistles, and maybe activate several programmed but dormant capabilities in his security system at the Spring House. Concerts on the property with a myriad of voices would have been too serious a challenge to take on without Beta testing. And then there were all those damned birds and animals. Halfway through the conversation they heard a sharp clicking on the line.

"Which federal agent, Mom?" Joshua asked although he had a sinking feeling he knew the answer to his own question.

"Man named Michael Halloran, why?"

"My boss knows him. One of his people named Agarwal called to check on me. It must be because of this case of yours."

"He met your Uncle Bob."

"Yeah, I think he knows a lot of people, and a lot of people know about him. Scuttlebutt is he told off an Under Secretary of Defense over the handling of prisoners. He went all the way back to the Trail of Tears and talked about how the Army had a history of mistreating people from other cultures that they did not understand. And then blaming individual soldiers for decisions made by others. "

"He's not short on backbone, that one. He has Eastern Band Cherokee people in his family. There are people who would have sent that video viral, if there was one." Em was duly impressed.

"Not known, Mom. Got a reprimand and a bunch of handshakes. He resigned from the Navy not too long after that. People heard he went off fishing — seems as if he took this job instead. Word is he gets along better now with the new administration in Washington. There are bars in Washington where he can't pay for a drink, and some places where he just plain can't go."

Em was lost in thought until Joshua recalled her.

"Mom, be careful. I have a few ideas. I'll call you tomorrow and probably send you some stuff. I can raise the level on the security system from here. Right now it's armed, Mom. Try to get some sleep."

———◆———

Back at the office in New Haven, Halloran and Anson greeted Garvey at his desk. He was drinking steaming coffee from a vastly oversized mug.

"I found it boss! Took most of the evening, but we've got the trail he left in the Internet log. We can move for a warrant now and seize the whole business. Import/Export, my ass!" said Garvey with satisfaction. "Smart bastard though."

"Good job. Knew you could do it. Been quiet? I need a residential or twenty-four hour business phone number for Joshua Huber, Em Huber's son, lives up around Boston. Right now."

Halloran sat at his desk, booted up his computer and looked through his email for a copy of Nancy's report. He found two copies of it, one from the source, and one from Nilsson attached to an email containing a copy of his report.

Garvey sent an email with two numbers for Joshua Huber. Halloran tried the first cell number and it rang out to voice mail. The second number was busy. It was late in the evening for a long call, so he decided to read the reports and wait a few minutes before trying again.

After several repeated tries, Halloran called the Operator in Joshua's Area Code. He explained who he was and asked the Operator to check the line. She tested the line and reported that it was active, that she heard garbled voice, not the sound of Internet use. Halloran asked if she could tell if the voices were male or female. The Operator replied with patience that customer communications were private, that her system only allowed her to hear garbled voice, but one might have been a woman. The Operator asked if he needed an Emergency Interrupt on the line to ask one person to cede the line for another incoming call. He decided not. She suggested giving the calling parties ten minutes to clear the line, and he agreed. Halloran decided to try Em's wire line number, and sure enough it was busy, too.

Halloran felt the need to stretch his legs and went in search of the source of the fresh coffee that smelled so good from Garvey's mug. Coffee cup in hand, he finally reached Joshua Huber, who was indeed still audibly at his computer. A rapid fire of key strokes met Halloran's ear from Joshua's end of the line.

"Joshua Huber? This is Michael Halloran. I owe you a beer. Did your mother call you?"

Joshua had picked up the phone without looking at the Caller ID, he'd expected to hear his mother's voice with some last complaint. "Yes, we just got off the line. It's okay about the beer. Did she give you this phone number?"

"No one has to give us phone numbers," Halloran replied. "Did she tell you what happened in detail, or did she give you the edited version?"

"She tried the edited version first. She is the 'don't worry the kids' type of mother. It took me awhile to get her to spill it, or most of it. I heard you wanted upgraded security,

I've done what I could. Tomorrow I'll try to get her three key fob remotes. I have to set the signal IDs. They're satellite connected so they will work anywhere there is satellite reception. It's not perfect, but it's the best I can come up with on short notice."

Halloran agreed that sounded like a good idea but asked about increased perimeter security for the Spring House.

"Well, here's the thing. She's against cameras in the house or outside. Worries about what might be seen and what might become of the digital images. Hacking into video feeds and stuff. Same thing for constant voice monitoring. She's a very private person, something to do with her old job. Overly cautious about stuff like that." Joshua understood his mother's limits, he didn't always agree with them.

"What about enhancing surveillance outside at night? They're out in the woods, there are no close neighbors. She doesn't have a dog and I understand she will be alone when Deanna and Sandra are away." Halloran was persistent.

"Here's another thing, too much noise at night. There are too many animals and those damned turkeys around. You could sneak a platoon in behind that flock of wild turkeys. They yak to each other constantly. They scratch the ground and flap those big wings. They can fly, did you know that? I didn't. It's a long slow take off. And there are fourteen of them around there. Plus the deer, the males fight, they all stomp around and the fawns are into everything. The raccoons raid the garbage. But the rabbits are the worst. When an owl, a coyote or a fox catches them they scream bloody murder. It sounds almost like a human scream. I'm better at fish."

"Can you think of something soon? Maybe something you haven't done before. Good challenge." Halloran was used to dealing with inventors, like Kirbee. Patience, encouragement and challenge, plus a deadline usually equaled results for him.

"I can't get down there to install anything myself, that's part of the problem. We've got these freakin' sharks along the coast. They don't usually come up this far north or in this close, and they're screwing up my stuff," Joshua came close to wailing.

Halloran commiserated. "Sorry about the sharks. What about your mother's friend, Tina? She seemed to think the system could use some added things, and she's right here."

"Yeah, that could work. She's into data center security stuff. I could send her things to install. She could maybe think of some things of her own to do, too."

"You could work on it together." Halloran believed collaboration could be a good thing if it didn't get out of hand.

"Now I need to find a way to get the key fobs down to mother. Can't exactly send them any old way," Joshua moaned.

To Halloran he sounded very much like one of his own sons.

"Do you have access to secure courier service?"

Josh had to admit he did.

"Then send me the bill. Here's my number if you or your mother need anything else. One other thing...."

———◆———

On towards two o'clock in the morning the country road, unlit by streetlights and overhung by trees, was in deep darkness. A fringe of clouds draped a quarter moon. Trees in full leaf rustled with stealthy and erratic breezes. The Spring House's joints creaked and issued occasional, unexpected pops as the house released the heat of the day into the quiet of the night. The fieldstone facing of the house cooled more slowly than the wooden timbers and they seemed to grate as they moved against the stone.

Still Em could not settle, she twisted the sheets around her. In their bedrooms, Deanna and Sandy slept the sleep of the weary and young. *Why can't I be like them?* The adrenalin of the day should be gone from her system, but she still tossed. Even the dullest technical reading failed to induce sleep. Likewise the formal poetry of the psalms in an old rare but battered prayer book did not soothe her. Attempts at meditation could not hold her mind in quiet. It replayed her near escape from the burglar, the shock of the scene in the backyard and most especially the sight and sound of arrows hitting flesh in a seemingly endless loop. It wasn't fear, but something else. Hyper alert to every sound, she lost patience. With nerves on edge and senses that refused to shut down, she threw the covers off. In the half consciousness between wakefulness and sleep, she sat up abruptly, swung her legs to the edge of the bed and had to let the dizziness pass. Her feet shuffled around the bedside rug to reach well-worn slippers.

Trying to rouse herself fully, she hoped to staunch the flow of memories, the constant review of high stress points. *What have I missed? Something's not right, my mind keeps going over and over it.* Em realized it was her intuition prompting her. Determined to give her mind a rest from half waking dreams, to give it a chance to surface what she believed to be a missing part of the pattern of events, tea was in order. To her eyes accustomed to darkness, the hallway appeared to glow with a pearl grey shadowless light. She easily passed the girls' rooms and heard Deanna's soft snoring accompanied by little cat snores from Ash, curled up on the bed at her feet. The staircase was in blackout with only the barest smudge of light at the base. She made it down with hands on the walls. The front hall was cool and she shivered a bit. The flagstone floor and the fieldstone walls in the oldest part of the house above the spring room never truly warmed. They were built to refrigerate ice.

Down in the kitchen, she turned on only the low light over the stove as she believed the bright ceiling light would hurt her eyes and make falling asleep more difficult. She filled the kettle with spring water and lit the gas. Purposeful little blue flames jumped to meet the bottom of the kettle. Rallying her flagging wits, Em reached to find a clean mug and chose tea from the cabinet by the stove. Celina's custom blend of chamomile and herbs was a guarantee of drowsiness and sleep. She took the packet out of the cabinet, paused and then replaced it. Instead, she chose cranberry tea, a New England favorite. She had thinking to do first. The kettle whistled, she brewed the tea to a deep ruby red and tried a sip. It was almost too hot to drink, so she held the mug carefully out in front of her with one hand and leaned against the counter waiting for it to cool.

In the still night she heard a heavy car come around the steep bend to the east and over the hill towards the house. It seemed to slow briefly. Her instincts flared. The car accelerated, burning rubber on the road. In front of the house came the sound of glass smashing on the cobblestone paving outside, followed by a loud rushing sound with force behind it. A sudden bright orange light lit up the kitchen. The mug of tea flew from Em's startled hand. Scalding tea showered her bare legs and spattered her fingers, burning them. She cried out. Split seconds later, strong white lights flooded the country road, and all around the house, a series of whoops and clangs and sirens sounded across the sleeping valley.

"Joshua!" Em exclaimed.

"Intruder alert! Intruder alert! Smoke detected. Fire alert! Protocol A1 initiating. Contacting Emergency Services and Sys Admin. Confirm status all residents. Repeat Protocol A1 in progress." The security panel in the living room barked and was suddenly awash in a rapid sequence of flashing lights. Upstairs in Deanna's bedroom, Ash howled in full throat. Cleome joined in chorus. The security system demanded confirmation repeatedly. Em was not about to wait for the volunteer firemen. She went down on her painfully tea-scorched knees in front of the sink to pull out her fire extinguisher from the cabinet. The extinguisher was meant for kitchen fires and not large.

Em shouted at the security panel and kept going. When she reached the front hall, Deanna and Sandy shocked from deep sleep, called out to her and she returned their calls. The square leaden glass window in the solid oak front door showed leaping flames. Gasoline smoke penetrated into the house. From the eye level window in the door, Em gauged the distance to the fire. She could feel its heat through the glass and was grateful for stone walls and the heavy door.

"Mom, what the hell? Are you alright? It scared the crap out of me." Deanna stumbled down the stairs and barged into her mother with Sandy right behind her.

"We've been served a cocktail, a Molotov cocktail."

"Huh, what?" Deanna gripped her mother's arm.

"Someone did a drive by and threw a fire bomb at the house."

Seeing the extinguisher in Em's hand, Sandy said, "You can't go out there, it's not safe! You're in pajamas and your bare feet."

"Like that's really going to stop her." Deanna spoke as her mother tried to free herself from her daughter's anxious hold.

"I can't let the house burn down either," Em argued in a terse voice. "Get my boots they're in the closet."

Down the hill from the Spring House in the white clapboard farmhouse, Mireille rocked a colicky baby boy in her bedroom, trying to quiet his lusty cries. Philippe paced next to her. The still night was broken by a medley of alarm sounds. He rushed to the window. They could see a blaze arcing in front of the Spring House. A black sedan barreled down the hill past the farmhouse, fleeing the scene. Briefly illuminated by their roadside lamppost, Philippe caught a picture of the speeding car on his phone.

"Your friend has serious enemies, *ma chere,*" he said. "Call 911. Stay here. I must go to help." The crying baby, suddenly silent, cast his eyes between one parent and another, and let out a moose-sized burp.

"*Mon Dieu*, finally!" Mireille replied. "*Vite! Vite!* Go, Philippe!"

ACKNOWLEDGEMENTS

One novel grew and grew into two, chapters moved, some were removed to be saved for another day. A hearty and much deserved thank you to my first readers of the two Spring House Mysteries, they read the works in pieces, some of them not in order, not even finally in the same book, and still they persevered. Each one added their insights, caught my inconsistencies, and raised questions for me. I hope they enjoyed the process as much as I did; Rachelle Cooper, Frederick Walters, and our trainer Jenni Keenan-Shettleworth, owner of Fighting Fitness Performance Centers, Orange, CT, for martial arts consulting. Most especially I owe a debt of gratitude to Barbara Whitcomb Walters, now deceased, who at 80 years old caught the smallest typos that snuck by the rest of us. She let me know that I needed to finish both books so that she could, too. The last chapters were returned to me with her notes after she passed. For her patience with a first-time author, and her guidance, thanks to the woman who never met a coma she couldn't delete, my editor Judy Roth. The errors are all mine. My three children Kate, Dan and Beth were endlessly supportive of me and my work.

I would also like to acknowledge the people in Cambridge for training in competitive intelligence, and my former colleagues in the telecom corporation CI group, Jackie, Ryan, Tom, Gloria, Ann, Jordan, Korling, Jon, Jim, Peter, Donna, Tony, Cynthia, Jan, Pam, Jerry, our friends in

Legal, and to Ed who knew who to ask for information.

Two books owe their existence to the contacts, mutual support, mentoring, and resources of the Connecticut Chapter, Romance Writers of America and Sisters in Crime Guppies. You all rock! Special shout out to Jane Haertel and Gail Chianese. If you have any thoughts of writing novels, join up, come swim with the Guppies.

For inspiration and comradery from corporate co-workers that grew into a sisterhood, Rachelle Cooper, Carole Vissicchio, Lisa Hess McLeod, Lorrie Young, Norma Simmons, Johnnie Mancini, and Karen Kimble.

BIOGRAPHICAL NOTE

K.M. Umbricht right out of college apprenticed at the largest independent academic bookstore between New York and Boston where she learned from Manager Theodore Wilentz that booksellers could be publishers, too. After a twenty year career in Information Technology research, she "took the offer" to leave the competitive intelligence group of the largest American telecommunications corporation. She founded Black Crow Press LLC with a nod to the memory of TW.

She lives on a glacial lake in woodsy Connecticut where red foxes casually patrol the shoreline looking for their favorite meal of Canada Goose, while coyotes slink off into the trees. Snapping turtles lay their eggs in the herb garden. Peepers, tiny little tree frogs, fill the spring evenings with their music. Bull frogs chorus at night under the windows. At midnight you can sometimes here a fisher cat scream. Sadly, she is cat-less after the passing of Shadow, the elegant, intelligent and highly vocal model for Ash in the stories and his younger fellow stray Patches. A daughter working for her PhD shares the place.